THE LAST OF HIS NAME

Book 2 of The Veseile Conspiracy

First paperback edition, December 2025

ISBN (paperback edition): 978-1-7384190-1-2

Published by M. L. L. Publishing

For mum. Thank you for everything.

An excerpt from 'Mythology of the Gods: Volume IV':

All knew that to call forth Mortus, God of Death and guardian of every soul in the underworld, was foolish. Eliza did not heed the danger, abandoning her fate to Death. Slicing lines into her wrists, blood flowed like rivulets until his presence neared.

"Mortus, hear me!" she cried to the god, lurking in the shadows waiting to claim her life. "I call you to strike a bargain."

No mortal could lay eyes upon the God of Death and live, so Eliza closed her eyes as she made her demand.

"I wish to trade with you my own soul for more time with my lost love. I would give up my Veseile lifespan for but a day with him, whose life you stole too soon."

Mortus spoke, every echo of loss, every dying cry and whimper sounding in his thunderous voice.

"You would abandon centuries of life for a fraction longer with a human whose flame was already extinguished?" he asked of her.

"I would."

Mortus, God of Death, cradled one of Eliza's blood soaked hands in his when he agreed. "I accept your bargain."

A pulse of magic flowed between them. When Eliza next awoke, her lover held her in a close embrace.

Like he had been when she'd lost him, his skin was delicate and lined with age. Lifting her hand to caress his face, Eliza found the same fragility in her own skin and knew that Mortus had drained all of her life but this one final day.

When the sun set again, Mortus returned to claim them.

1

LUELLE did not want to think of herself as a captive, despite the fact that she had not been allowed to leave her new room in the castle and her meals were delivered through a hatch in its modified door.

Prince Malcolm had not yet ordered her official arrest —as far as she was aware. She doubted her lodgings would be so comfortable if he had.

Sure, some might say he had forced her to return to the castle against her will, planning to punish her for stealing the Power from his dying human father and returning it to all Veseile, as well as freeing the unexpectedly violent God of Chaos, Vesanya, in the process. But, in truth, Luelle had nowhere else to go. If Malcolm had verbally offered her the option to go elsewhere, she would have chosen this same fate.

Probably.

On their arrival at the capital, Malcolm's stern spy master, a Meteile named Leena, had escorted Luelle to this room and the prince had disappeared in another direction, leaving her alone with her thoughts for company for days now.

Her room was simple, one of many identical guest chambers on the second floor of the castle, though it was in a wing Luelle had never visited when she had worked undercover as a servant. Weeks ago, she would have cleaned quarters like this, preparing them for whichever lords and ladies were visiting the capital to attend Prince Malcolm's coronation. The room contained a bed wide enough for two, a large wooden dresser, a square table with two matching wooden chairs, and two softer, cushioned seats beside the single window. From the window seats, Luelle could stare at a small corner of the castle gardens and imagine she was free to stroll through the courtyards like the many guards, nobles, and servants she witnessed each day.

Things could be worse. As they'd travelled from the Caeleste Peaks to Cerulya, the realisation had dawned on Luelle that she was most likely heading to her doom. During their journey back to the capital, soldiers kept Malcolm occupied, updating him on how the realm had fared in his absence and leaving him with no time to speak to her. In contrast, most of her journey was spent alone in a small carriage, trying not to dwell on the slaughter she'd witnessed after returning the Power to its source in the cavern.

She had also spent a long time trying not to think about the way Zeke and her old companions had spurned her when she'd seen them again after over half a decade apart.

Occasionally, the prince's spy master would intrude on her solitude to ask prying questions. The break from her thoughts was a welcome reprieve but never lasted long.

On arriving in Cerulya, Luelle had expected to go

straight to the castle's dungeons. She'd visited them once when working undercover, days after her first shift, to remind herself of where she might end up if she failed or was caught. Her current room was a far cry from those dingy, claustrophobic cells, but the presence of guards stationed outside her door confirmed that it was a cage, nonetheless.

The guards refused to speak to her. Meals were shoved through the floor-level hatch three times a day, though the door itself remained locked and shut. Every time a plate slid into her room, Luelle leapt towards the door and called through the wooden barrier, trying, in vain, to initiate conversation. She didn't expect to receive information about her fate or Malcolm's whereabouts but hoped the guards might at least indulge her with some idle gossip or small talk to stave off her boredom.

Her efforts were futile. Stony silence met her each time she called through the door, no matter what inane topics she broached. Servants were more likely to gossip but none entered her room. On her first day, Luelle had learned that no one would come in to clear away her old plate, and hoarding the crockery only meant she would receive no more food. She was permitted a spoon with any meals too messy to eat with her hands but never a knife or fork, even after requesting more appropriate cutlery.

It was fine. She didn't need to talk.

After two weeks of trekking across the kingdom and sleeping on the ground, followed by another week sleeping on a firm bench in a cramped carriage, the wide bed in the castle was a welcome luxury. Luelle slept through most of her first night and day in the room, waking only to eat and to use the small, attached bathing room.

Before her arrival, someone had removed the door from her bathing room, denying her any privacy if the guards chose to enter—not that she believed they would, any more. Her bathtub was barely large enough for her to sit in and was fed by freezing cold water. Fortunately, the privy was positioned at an angle that was not visible from her bedroom door, so she would get a brief warning with the sound of the door opening before anyone emerged to spy on her during that particular moment of vulnerability.

She spent hours slumbering on that first day, but it did not take long for the blessing of dreamless, uninterrupted sleep, fuelled by exhaustion, to cease. By her second full night back in the castle, Luelle's dreams were plagued with unwanted memories and her waking hours were filled with restless energy that people-watching from her window could not soothe.

She exercised in the small space between her bed and armchairs, working until her muscles were sore and she collapsed into a heap on the scratchy rug that covered her floor, barely able to stumble to the bath. It was an ideal method to while away some time but was not enough to quiet the unwanted thoughts swarming her mind like angry wasps in a disturbed nest.

Everything she wished to ignore lingered at the edges of her mind. If she gave any attention to one of the thoughts, they all swept forward, drowning her in panic.

The only family she had ever known had rejected her. Her ancestry was a lie. Growing up, Luelle had believed she had centuries to explore the world and forge a path for herself but, if Zeke was correct about her human heritage, she may die a natural death in only a few decades. She was trapped in Prince Malcolm's home, waiting for an unknown punishment, surrounded by people who hated her for the treason she committed. And, on top of it all, she could no longer trust her own judgement. Although she'd restored the Power to its source, returning it to its rightful owners with Veseile blood, she had not anticipated the severity of the consequences. Her actions had unleashed a terrifying, vicious deity onto the world, whose motives remained incomprehensible and unpredictable.

Visions of Vesanya's stone prison melting away and the havoc that followed ran through Luelle's mind the moment she closed her eyes each evening. Even daylight was not enough to chase those gory images away; whenever she let her thoughts wander, the violent memories returned to haunt her. Luelle saw her old companions and friends being flung through the air, bodies limp and soaring across the width of the cavern. She watched life drain from Veseile who had been youthful and healthy moments earlier, before they came into contact with the God of Chaos. When she wasn't reliving Vesanya's return and attack, she saw Zeke spitting accusations at her.

More often than she expected, she experienced panic-inducing memories of Zeke pressing his foot on Malcolm's throat, the prince's face darkening with blood as he was held in place, unable to breathe and powerless to defend himself.

Getting more than a few hours of sleep at night became impossible. Any time Luelle managed to fall into a doze, she would wake drenched in sweat, gasping for breath, throat raw as if she'd been screaming. Each time, she would scour her dark, empty room for enemies—for Zeke or Vesanya lurking in the shadows—but she was always alone. It took longer for her racing heartbeat to slow with each new nightmare.

The guards outside her room refused Luelle's requests for additional candles or more than one moonstone lamp, so she spent every second after sunset curled in a trembling ball atop her bed, staring into the shadows, flinching at any sound, and fighting for an easy breath.

Freeing Vesanya's Power and returning it to the Veseile had been her life's goal. For years, she'd planned and worked tirelessly to achieve it. She'd succeeded. Yet, somehow, she'd lost everything in the process—her family; her identity; her confidence; her home. Living without a goal to drive her was a new, aimless state that was as suffocating as it was daunting.

She needed to find a way to make herself useful again. When she was a child, Zeke had recognised her determination and resourcefulness. If she could demonstrate the same qualities to Malcolm or another influential noble, she stood a chance of surviving this imprisonment.

If she was useful, they wouldn't kill her.

She repeated the thought to herself until it was almost believable.

At the very least, a new purpose in life might drive off the nightmares that haunted her.

After the events in the cavern, the prince knew she was no real fighter; she would be of no value to him in that sense. Besides, the castle was overflowing with guards and soldiers who had trained to fight and kill for their entire lives; Luelle would never stand out against them. She could be cunning and calculating, but Malcolm had an entire council of advisers who must be equally competent at planning and strategising—more so than her because they were so much more familiar with high society and its unspoken rules.

A romantic involvement was off the table, no matter how frequently her mind might wander to memories of waking pressed against the prince toward the end of their travels or to her admiration of his savage skill when he'd fought a path to her in the cavern, skin speckled in blood and glistening with sweat, refusing to leave her behind.

His ferocity in battle had been so at odds with the gentle nature she'd glimpsed while they travelled together. She blamed her current loneliness for the traitorous fond memories about the colour of his eyes in the morning sunlight, of forearms flexing as he lit their fires, and the charming blush she had so often managed to elicit with the mildest implications and innuendos.

Even if their social standings were closer, Malcolm would not be manipulated into falling for the person who stole the Power from his dying father and unleashed it to all Veseile, putting the stability of his entire reign at risk.

The Power could be of use to her, though. In truth, it was her only option.

She had studied it for years. Despite her lack of practical training, Luelle knew more about it than the average Veseile, particularly after Malcolm had taught her the basics. Now that all Veseile could access the Power, society would change. The *world* would change. Malcolm might wish to train tutors to spread through the realm. On their route to the Caeleste Peaks, he had stated it was safer travelling with her when she knew how to control the Power. Learning to control it had reduced the risk of another explosive outburst, like the incident she'd experienced in Tolhurst. Leaving that same destructive potential in the hands of citizens with unknown motives would concern him.

Luelle could take advantage of that.

Trapped in this room, she was free from distractions beyond her troublesome thoughts. Malcolm had taught her the bare minimum; she could figure out the rest on her own. With nothing to do but practise, she could hone her skills and volunteer to teach others for the prince when she next saw him.

From her third day shut away, Luelle filled every waking minute with practice and meditation, stopping only to exercise or when she had another opportunity to try and speak with her guards.

At first, even using the Power to shift the pillows on her bed drained her to the point of needing rest, but after two days of pushing herself to her limits, she was able to lift and move them repeatedly before collapsing from the toll. Sweat drenched her each time but she did not lose consciousness as she had in Tolhurst.

Slowly, she learnt to ration her mental reserves. Malcolm had not explained how long it typically took for his ancestors to perfect their abilities, so she had nothing to measure her success against. Any pride she felt withered whenever she remembered how quickly the prince had mastered the Power to fight off Zeke's companions in the cavern.

Learning to tease away the smallest amounts of the Power for delicate tasks was as exhausting as moving larger items of furniture in her room, but within a few days, Luelle felt her improvement.

As her confidence and skill grew, so did her creativity.

She used the Power to eat her meals, slicing into the

food and lifting bite-sized pieces into her mouth from across the room. Through trial and error, she learnt how to freeze fresh water into cubes of ice for her drinks and how to heat her icy bath water until it was bearable and pleasant to soak in. She even managed to braid her hair without using her hands. When no one was around, she used the Power to pluck flowers from the gardens, drifting them into her room through her window and weaving them into her plaits.

As she'd hoped, the toll of constantly using the Power was enough that when she collapsed into her bed at the end of the day, she slept too deeply for nightmares to affect her. That alone made the strain worth the effort.

When she wasn't using the Power, exercising, or sleeping, she meditated, honing in on every sound that drifted through the window—birdsong, passing conversations, crunching footsteps. She isolated and identified the exact intonation and volume of the guards' voices outside her door in an attempt to identify their shift patterns. Every scent that wafted into her room presented a new challenge to analyse and her meals were spent trying to decipher the individual ingredients in her food. It was just enough to keep her thoughts from straying to Vesanya or anything else that had occurred in the cavern. And, if her plan worked and she could use her newfound skill with the Power to forge a new purpose in life, she might leave those dark memories behind altogether.

Of course, the prince may reject her offer of help. However, if that happened, Luelle would simply leave the castle. She'd escaped once before and was certain she could achieve it again, despite the larger number of obstacles she would experience. She regularly listed those obstacles to herself, striving to come up with solutions to each.

This time, she did not have free rein to memorise guard shift rotations or scout the castle for alternative escape routes in case something went wrong. On top of that, plenty of people in the castle now knew her face and regarded her as a threat, so escaping would require remaining hidden.

Not to mention she had nowhere to go.

Home had once meant Zeke, Freya, and Imbryl—her chosen family. None of them would take her in now and she wouldn't stay with them even if the offer existed, not after all three had been so quick to reject her and shut her out when she'd tried to explain herself. No, she would have to start afresh, without money or shelter. Summer had long given way to autumn, bringing colder temperatures and harsher weather. Soon, winter would arrive, making it harder to survive in handmade shelters and driving up the cost of inns. Fleeing a warm, free room without a sure destination was foolish.

Escaping would have to remain a last resort.

For now, she would channel all of her attention into becoming an asset to the prince so he couldn't afford to execute her. He was the only other person that might understand why she couldn't sleep through the night or why unexpected sounds made her flinch and double over, unable to catch her breath for minutes at a time. If he ever deigned to speak to her again, he might even be able to explain how she could move past the resentment she felt towards her human ancestry, if Zeke had been telling the truth. The prince had brought her back here without force. Either he had full confidence he could retrieve her if she fled, now that he had the Power in his control, or

he trusted her, at least a little.
She could work with that.

2

"You are doing it again."

Malcolm blinked, pulling his attention back to the present and away from visions of the cavern in which he'd watched a god emerge from solid stone.

Viv sighed. Across the room, Zasha and Edwyn were bickering, though Malcolm had long lost track of why. Beside them, their mother was settled in an armchair, her slight figure nestled among plump cushions. Her dark eyes followed her two youngest children, the ghost of a smile on her lips. Her long fingers, bedecked with rings, wrapped around a teacup.

Today was Malcolm's coronation.

He and his family had gathered in his dressing room under the pretence of preparing for the event. In reality, they sought some privacy from the influx of visitors present in their home.

"You cannot zone out today. The image you portray at the coronation will be one everyone remembers. Plenty of people will be searching for signs of weakness due to our mixed heritage. You cannot reveal any." Viv chided him for the second time this morning.

Malcolm mumbled an apology, turning his gaze back to the mirror he was seated before and attempting to fix the unruly curls framing his face.

Viv had dabbed a cream underneath his eyes earlier but the bruise-like shadows still seeped through, betraying his exhaustion. Since arriving home, he'd barely slept. Meetings and preparations for the coronation had filled his days, leaving no time for himself. He trudged through it all, shrouded by grief at the absence of his father. Fatigue was a physical weight upon his shoulders. Yet, no matter how tired he was when he fell into bed at night, sleep evaded him. He would lay awake, staring at the stars through his open windows, trying not to think of his father; of Zeke and the Eile in the cavern who had tried to kill him; of Vesanya, who had butchered his people without breaking a sweat. Trying not to think of Luelle.

His family—Viv in particular—had been unhappy with Malcolm's decision to keep Luelle alive, branding her a traitor despite the fact that there had been a sliver of truth underlying her actions. Instead of immediately executing her, Malcolm had locked Luelle in a guarded room within his suite. Whenever he woke from a nightmare or lay in bed unable to find rest, he had to resist the overwhelming urge to leave his bedchambers and check on her. He wasn't sure what he would say to her and had no answers for the endless questions she would surely ask, but it would be a comfort to see if she was plagued by the same horrors that haunted him.

"What were you thinking about this time?" Viv's voice interrupted his tangle of thoughts.

Malcolm scrubbed at his face with a hand, only to have it yanked away by his sister.

"Stop that! You shall ruin my hard work. Today requires you to look at least a shred regal. It's bad enough that you refuse to let anyone cut your hair. You look like a wild beast," she snapped.

He shrugged her away, scowling. "I shall consider it after the coronation. I've had no time since getting home."

"You have had plenty." Viv arched her brows, meeting his glare in the mirror. "What were you thinking about this time?" she repeated.

Malcolm swallowed, making an effort to relax his tense shoulders. "The cavern. Father. All of it."

She nibbled on her lower lip. "Are you certain you saw Vesanya?"

He nodded. "How could it have been anyone else? She was identical to the depictions and was trapped in solid stone. Only a god could survive such a fate or manipulate the Power to slaughter a room full of people and walk away without a scratch."

Viv's expression morphed into the same frustrated frown he'd seen in his own mirror so often since returning home.

"If you truly saw a god, why have we heard nothing about her fleeing from the cavern? A being that large and powerful should not be able to hide so easily."

Malcolm gritted his teeth. "I do not know. Besides, we have more pressing matters to concentrate on. I have soldiers searching for Vesanya or a trace of destruction that might suggest where she fled to. Leena's most recent reports suggested nothing out of the ordinary. If it was the god, she must now be lying low." He lowered his voice to avoid disturbing his mother and other siblings.

"For now, let us focus on maintaining stability. The changes to the Power are not going to make our challenges any easier."

Viv nodded, her expression returning to its usual cool, collected mask. "The training is going well enough."

On Malcolm's return, he had told his family everything about his journey in complete detail, before even giving himself time to bathe and change into clean clothes. They'd stayed locked in his parents' chambers for hours before emerging, decided on the story they would spin and how they must proceed.

Almost immediately, he and Viv had selected a small group of trusted Veseile guards for her to begin privately training in the Power. After the coronation, when his Thanes returned to their distant homes within the kingdom, Malcolm would send a portion of those newly trained Veseile with them, ready to teach other soldiers across the realm. Their training would be far from complete, but any amount of control was better than none. Soldiers trained in the Power would be a necessity to subdue any defiant Veseile once word spread that the Power was available to them.

There was still so much to learn. Malcolm and Viv had started small, testing the Power's limitations within their family. So far, all of them apart from Edwyn were able to use the Power. Devastation consumed Edwyn whenever he failed but Malcolm wouldn't give up on him.

Viv monitored the soldiers as she trained them, documenting everything to debrief Malcolm at the end of his busy days. Nothing yet appeared different about the Power, beyond the number of people who could use it, but Malcolm did not truly know what differences he should be looking for; the experience of using the Power was as new to him as it was any other Veseile.

He felt like a fraud. King Alaric had taught Malcolm plenty in theory but, without his father around to guide him, Malcolm had to rely on his memories and any documents in the royal library that described the Power. All he could do was work with his family, inventing and disproving various theories until their knowledge was as complete as it could be.

"Have you made a decision about the traitor?" Viv asked, eyes straying to the crystal relic that had once been used to pass the Power from monarch to heir. It lay on Malcolm's dressing table, atop a messy stack of parchments he had been sorting through before his family arrived, little more than a glorified paperweight.

Malcolm took a deep breath, preparing to rehash the argument he and his sister had been having since he'd returned home. "I cannot kill her, Viv. She knew what would happen to the Power when it was returned to that cavern. She could know more about the Gods. While Vesanya remains at large, I have to use every resource at my disposal to learn how to stop her from killing any more of my people."

"I understand that, Malcolm, but it does not change the fact that this woman committed treason." Viv glanced at their family across the room and lowered her voice. "You know that when we were pretending Father was still alive I had to tell the council that she had been part of an assassination attempt rather than a plot to steal the Power. That cannot go unpunished without revealing our lie."

Malcolm winced at the reminder of how his family had bought him time to find Luelle after she'd stolen his Power. If his return had been delayed much longer, his family may not have been able to continue fooling the council, pretending that King Alaric was still alive.

Almost all of the old king's advisers had been suspicious about the situation, particularly when Viv denied their entry into her father's chambers. However, none of them had proof to support their doubts or theories, and they were now preoccupied trying to gain Malcolm's favour to earn a spot on his royal council. He had replaced the majority of the old advisers with new, trusted choices when he returned—or emerged from his father's room, where they believed he'd been sequestered all along.

Viv continued.

"People in the castle gossip. The servants are always overhearing things. It was inevitable that the story would leak once we started using it. The public believe there was an attempt on Father's life and if we let it go unpunished, it could endanger *you*, especially when people begin to learn about the Power. It was a strength to you before, when only the monarch could wield it, but this situation is as new to us as the rest of the realm. You are more vulnerable than ever."

Malcolm cringed away from the truths his sister stated so matter-of-factly. However, each reason only seemed to justify his need to keep Luelle alive. They had so much to learn about the changes to the Power, which she could help with. Even if her knowledge was limited, Malcolm could use her to lure out her old companions and steal the information they'd collected over time, or at least to squash any lingering threat they still posed.

Viv must have seen his resolve strengthen. She lowered her voice further, barely a whisper.

"A public execution is expected for high treason, Malcolm."

Nausea swirled inside him at those words. Every decision since returning to Cerulya had been impossible. The fate of his reign and the stability of the realm as a whole depended on so many factors, yet they all seemed trivial after everything Malcolm had witnessed in the cavern. Saving his people from a fate like that superseded all else, but he couldn't protect anyone unless his rule was stable and he was able to learn the truth about the Gods.

"There must be a way to achieve it all," he mused aloud.

Viv's brows knitted together. "Pardon?"

"Oh." Malcolm shook his head, remembering his sister could not read his mind, no matter how often it felt that she could. "I mean, there must be a way to stabilise my reign and learn what we must about the Gods and the Power. I suppose you would be unhappy if I rigged a trial for Luelle's innocence."

She rolled her eyes. "We tell the world someone tried to murder our father, the king, and you think a trial and a slap on the wrist will solve things? People want blood. You will only look weak if you fail to provide that. You would invite further assassination attempts into our home, only this time you will be the one at risk and the criminals might be armed with the Power."

He huffed an angry breath through his nose. "Is there anyone else we can punish in her place? People in the castle knew her by a false identity, anyway. They expect Belle to be on trial, not Luelle."

Viv snorted. "Not unless you plan to dress up a

common criminal for the execution and continue hiding the real traitor down the hall forever."

Malcolm sat back and raised his eyebrows.

"That was a joke."

"We could make it work. If we fooled everyone about Father's death, this would be no problem." He talked faster so she couldn't immediately dismiss the idea.

Viv buried her face in her hands, hiding her despairing expression.

"It solves both of our problems, Viv. The public would be satisfied, but I could keep Luelle for questioning about the gods."

"If anyone saw her around the castle, they would realise your deception. Do you truly wish to risk further destabilisation if someone, a servant or anyone else in the castle, confronted you about it?"

Malcolm shrugged. "I think that would be unlikely. I could disguise her, anyway. I imagine she would be eager to play along if it means she gets to keep her head. Besides, Philip is aware of the situation and the need to keep other servants from recognising her."

Viv sighed. "We can discuss it further after the coronation."

"Fine, but it is our best option," Malcolm got the last word as he rose from his seat. He and Viv crossed the room to join the rest of their family. Their mother smiled up at them. Slowly, she was returning to her usual self, though she hadn't quite regained the weight she'd lost over the past few weeks and Malcolm regularly caught her staring into the distance, lost in her thoughts.

"You both look lovely," she murmured.

Malcolm collapsed onto the sofa beside his mother,

ignoring Viv's tutting as he crumpled his clothing. They needed to leave soon but he would relish these last few moments of peace before he publicly stepped into a role that would change his life forever.

Within the next few weeks, he would make an announcement that would spin his realm into even more chaos—publicising the changes to the Power. History may record him as the last monarch to have sole use of it, despite the fact he'd gained it at the same time as every other Veseile.

When they could no longer delay, Malcolm strode towards his fate with his family following close behind. His coronation, like that of every monarch before him, was to occur in the Great Temple, the largest of its kind in Cerulya and the rest of Arazia. Malcolm and his family rode in private carriages through the city, their pace slow on the cobbled streets as civilians fought to catch a glimpse of their future king, struggling against the soldiers holding them back. Leena and Theo lingered somewhere outside his carriage, on high alert for threats among the crowds.

Malcolm kept his eyes ahead when the carriage eventually rolled to a stop. Noise overwhelmed him as Theo opened the vehicle's door from the outside. People cried and shouted for Malcolm's attention as he stepped into the street. He swallowed. Taking a slow look around, he met as many stares as he could with a wide smile fixed upon his face. With a straight back, he ascended the many steps to the temple.

Inside, the Great Temple was only slightly less crowded than Cerulya's streets. Malcolm stopped as he stepped inside the doorway, gazing at the large, decadent room.

Sunlight shone through the circular stained glass window above him, painting the tiled floor in rainbow hues. Nobles lined every pew, pressed together at the shoulders to squeeze into the benches.

At the opposite end of the temple stood a choir. Their voices echoed from the tall, domed ceiling, the harmonies raising the hairs on Malcolm's arms. Statues of the six gods overlooked the choir. Each one stood atop a white plinth that lifted them to reach half the height of the room.

Malcolm's mouth dried as his eyes fell on the depiction of Vesanya. This statue was far larger than the one in the cavern had been, with noticeable differences, even from this distance. Whoever had carved this statue had failed to achieve the exact intricate details of the version he'd seen come to life. This statue wore no mask. Her hair fell in a simple, homogeneous wave, descending over one shoulder, and her clothing was painfully plain compared to that of the armoured deity that had emerged from stone half the realm away.

Despite the evidence that this depiction of the God of Chaos was man-made, Malcolm's throat tightened. His heart hammered an uneven beat against his chest. Around him, the room spun, its wide walls suddenly pressing in.

Everyone in the temple had turned to stare at him lingering in the doorway, but Malcolm could not tear his eyes from the statue. His feet may as well be nailed to the floor.

Sweat beaded on his brow.

All he could see was the God of Chaos as she moved gracefully through the cavern in the Caeleste Peaks, tearing strangers limb from limb or sucking the life from their bodies with a single touch, leaving withered corpses in her wake.

A hand on his arm jolted Malcolm from his frozen state of panic.

Managing to turn his head a fraction, he saw his mother standing beside him. Under normal circumstances, he would approach the altar alone, letting his family follow behind him to the first pew, where they would be seated, but his mother slipped her arm through his. Though she smiled, her eyes were knowing. Since returning home, Malcolm's family and closest friends had seen him descend into a state of hysteria all too frequently due to memories of Vesanya in the cavern.

His mother took a step forward, gently tugging Malcolm alongside her. He fixed his stare upon the priestess at the end of the aisle waiting to give a sermon and lay his crown atop his head. A ringing in his ears drowned out the choir. Malcolm's body was stiff but he pushed forward, forcing each stilted step.

He kept his eyes off the statues, even as he reached the end of the aisle. Underneath the collar of his tunic, his skin was clammy. He felt ready to retch feeling those stony eyes on him, but only the priestess was close enough to notice his pallor.

Malcolm barely heard her speech. Fortunately, he managed to kneel at the appropriate moment for his crown. When he turned to leave, exposing his back to the likeness of Vesanya, his skin crawled, but it was easier to stride away. Focusing on what must happen next allowed him to slow his steps to a regular pace, rather than fleeing the church in a panic.

Outside, soldiers continued to hold the crowd back,

ready for Malcolm to demonstrate the Power. The nobles remained behind him, inside the Great Temple until the demonstration was complete. They would have the opportunity to see their king use the Power more frequently; this demonstration was primarily for the benefit and enjoyment of the regular Cerulyan.

Malcolm and his newly chosen advisers, including Graman and Viv, had spent several meetings discussing what display Malcolm could put on for the masses. His father had called forth rain clouds, manipulating the weather to create rainbows above Cerulya's people. Malcolm could still remember his awe, watching a small sliver of sky from inside the Great Temple.

Throughout history, each monarch had created an astounding, visual display to mark their ascension to the throne. Malcolm had studied documented descriptions of every one.

Three generations ago, Queen Mildred had ordered soldiers to bring an abundance of prepared planters from the palace and willed thousands of colourful flowers to grow and bloom, allowing civilians to take any blossoms they could snatch at the end of the demonstration. Rumour suggested some of the flowers still growing throughout the city had been cultivated from those royal seeds.

Mildred's father, King Branden had engaged with the crowd, choosing several volunteers and propelling them into the air, lifting and spinning them into coordinated poses above the rest.

His father, King Alvin, earned a reputation for cruelty with his display. He had brought his wife and second son forth, unsheathed his dagger, and sliced each of their throats with shallow, bloody cuts. He had used his Power to heal them and wiped away the blood to reveal their freshly scarred skin. However, despite the remarkable feat, the crowd had been so lost in their horror that the feeling tainted public opinion of his entire reign.

Though he had no desire to be like King Alvin, Malcolm's demonstration of the Power must be equally impressive. It was vital to forging his first impression as a monarch.

Last-minute panic flooded him. Was it possible he and every other Veseile now shared a limited source that might restrict how much Power he could use? Their current tests hadn't suggested such, and in the cavern it had acted as he'd expected, but those memories could be tainted by the stress he'd been under.

For now, he had to trust his gut and his research.

A cool breeze tousled his hair at the top of the steps. His crown was an unfamiliar weight. Taking his time, Malcolm gazed over his people, silently reminding himself that he was safe from Vesanya here, that the depiction in the temple was only a statue.

When the cheers and applause faded, he took another breath and lifted his hands in front of him. Movement wasn't necessary when using the Power but the people crowding these streets wouldn't know that. They came expecting a show and Malcolm would gladly provide one if it meant not standing in their scrutiny with his arms held awkwardly at his sides.

He and his advisers had planned two parts to the demonstration. Over the past few days, he'd spent hours practising, albeit in a smaller setting and without an audience. At the castle, servants had removed petals from hundreds of flowers. Those handpicked petals were currently waiting for him inside several barrels, kept under guard in a nearby city garden. He envisioned where they were and stretched a thread of his Power across the city towards them, willing the petals to rise into the sky and fly to him as he reeled the thread back towards himself. Simultaneously, Malcolm sent more threads of Power to the city's nearest fountains, willing water from each of them to do the same.

The water arrived first. As it drifted in the sky above, Malcolm used his Power to manipulate it into various shapes. Ships of water sailed through the air, shifting and transforming into a flock of birds that swooped, diving low enough to splash against the fingers of any upraised hands. Laughter and cheers sounded. Minutes later, the petals appeared, a speck of colour in the sky. Malcolm shaped the water into a grove of trees and willed the petals to arrange themselves atop the liquid branches. He held them in the sky just long enough to hear the cries of appreciation from his crowd before whipping the water and petals back into a mass of dancing swirls. Once they were spread evenly over the now deafening crowd, he willed the water to patter down in thousands of gentle droplets, releasing his grip on the petals so they drifted down among the water.

People scrambled to grab the petals as they neared the ground, eager to claim one as proof of their attendance at the historic event.

Malcolm forced a smile onto his face and waved at the people around him, attempting to appreciate their awe. However, he couldn't shake the dread that had gripped him since laying eyes on the statue of Vesanya.

3

Isolation was boring.

Even using the Power was becoming tedious with only the same four walls and plain furniture to play with.

Luelle was using the Power to hurl peas from her lunch plate at a makeshift target drawn on her wall with gravy when the door swung open, crashing against the wall. Jolting at the sound, she lost control over the food. Peas rolled across the floor.

A tall guard with a heavy brow and deep-set eyes stepped into her room.

"Hands on your head!" he snapped.

Luelle froze, too shocked to move. This must be it. The prince had finally made a decision about her fate. Whoever was on the other side of the door was here to drag her to an execution. Was her control over the Power strong enough that she could make an escape?

The guard drew his sword. "Hands on your head!"

Two more guards entered the room behind him. White streaks in their hair indicated their Veseile heritage. From them, Luelle felt a pulsating pressure, as she had when

Malcolm had used the Power in the cavern. However, they did not use the Power to lash out at her. The only visible indication of the force was the shimmer of air between them. A barrier? Luelle examined it with a frown as she obeyed the first guard, standing from her seat at the table and placing her hands on her head.

"Turn around!" he barked.

She did as he commanded. Could she escape? Could she take on two Veseile guards and a regular soldier? More guards could be waiting in the hallway. Her stomach sank at the challenge. It was a futile thought. Patience had never been her strongest virtue but she forced herself to calm, to wait the situation out before attempting any rash action.

A soldier shoved her from behind until Luelle's front was pressed up against one of the walls. Hands were on her, roughly patting her down. Instinctively, she recoiled from them but was held in place. Fury burned through her at the injustice—they knew she had no weapon, they controlled everything she had access to.

"I really do not think all of this is necessary," an unfamiliar voice spoke from behind.

"We have our orders to ensure your safety, sir."

"Yes, well, I think that we have all heard that message. You may leave us."

"Sir, I do not think it is wise—"

"You will remain outside. I will call if I need any assistance."

Luelle continued to stare at the wall as the hands dropped away from her body and footsteps receded from her room. She did not turn around even when the door clicked shut. Instead, she concentrated on her breathing

—on fighting against the panic that had risen within her and controlling the burning Power that writhed underneath her skin, yearning for an outlet.

"You may turn around."

When her breathing was under control, Luelle turned to look at the stranger. A large Adeile with green-tinted skin stood in the middle of the room. Small wire spectacles were sliding on a slow but determined path down his short, flat nose. Pain spiked in Luelle's chest at the sight of the stranger's large frame, so reminiscent of Imbryl.

Neither one of them moved. If the Adeile was here to escort her to her punishment, why had he sent the guards away? Luelle's confusion grew as the stranger stepped further inside her room, turning aside from her as if he did not consider her a threat.

"Shall we, uh, take a seat?" He gestured to the table and chairs, gaze catching on the peas strewn across the floor. His voice was a deep grumble, tempered by the soft volume he chose.

Luelle shrugged, not taking her eyes off him for a moment. Adeile were known for their size and strength, and this one was no different, despite the frilly scholarly clothes that might restrict his movement. If he attempted to grab her, her strength would be useless against his. The Power was the only thing that would give her an advantage and the guards outside clearly knew how to use it, at least to an extent. They could hinder any attempt she made to escape.

The Adeile was oblivious to her inner debate. He stepped around the peas and pulled out a seat at the table. Wood creaked as he sat, dwarfing the chair.

With him seated, Luelle finally found the strength to

unfreeze her limbs. She approached the table, sitting opposite the stranger, tense with anticipation.

He shoved his glasses higher up his nose with one large finger and offered her a small smile.

"My name is Graman. I am an adviser to the king and was one of his tutors as he grew up." He folded his hands together atop the table between them.

Luelle held back a gasp.

"The coronation has happened?" she asked. Had time really passed so quickly in her captivity? Trapped in this room with such a broken sleep schedule, she'd lost track of the days. In her attempts to master the Power, she'd stopped paying attention to the world outside her room.

"Yes, it was an hour or so ago. I apologise for not coming to see you sooner, but I am sure you can imagine how hectic things have been since you all returned to the capital."

Luelle gaped at Graman, unsure what to say. Why was he visiting her? What response did he expect?

When she gave no reply, he continued. "I have begun reading through the documentation the king brought back from the cavern you led him to. Most of it duplicates texts found in our own libraries, but there are a few interesting opinion pieces about the origins of the Power."

"Zeke liked to write his thoughts down."

"Ah, so this Zeke was the author? Are you certain it was not another?"

Luelle shrugged again. "There's a possibility it was someone else, I suppose, but Zeke was the most passionate about the research. He was endlessly annotating documents and binding his own theories into books. Few of the others were literate enough to bother dedicating their time to it."

"I imagine Zeke and I would have some very interesting conversations, were it not for everything that happened!" Graman chuckled. His laughter cut off quickly when he noticed the frown on Luelle's face. He cleared his throat and changed course. "I am only a fraction of the way through the documents. Did you get a chance to look over any of the texts that were brought back?"

Luelle's frown remained in place. Was this a distraction technique? Was he lowering her guard so it was easier to escort her elsewhere or was this the real reason Malcolm had kept her alive this long?

"Only from a distance. I didn't examine the specifics, but I read most of the things Zeke gathered and wrote when I lived with him. I imagine his collection grew while I was away."

"Do you believe there is a chance any documents remain at the cavern? Only, there are a few gaps in the information, so far." Graman pushed his glasses up again.

"Well, I don't know how thorough the soldiers were or if they missed any of Zeke's favourite hiding spots. I wasn't searching alongside them."

"I thought that might be the case." Graman nodded, eager.

Luelle spoke up again before the Adeile could continue rambling about Zeke's book collection.

"What will happen to me now?"

Her blunt question seemed to take him by surprise. He shifted in his seat, fingers fidgeting.

"Unfortunately, it is not really my place to discuss that

with you, not without the king's permission or presence." He toyed with one of his silver cufflinks, shaped like a small quill. The other wrist revealed a miniature silver ink pot.

"And will Malcolm find the time to come and discuss that with me or is he planning to leave me alone in this room forever?" She couldn't help the edge to her tone.

Graman frowned a little at her use of Malcolm's name. "He has been very busy."

"I could help him," Luelle blurted. Malcolm must trust this Adeile to make him an adviser. If Graman could pass on Luelle's intention to help, the prince—the *king*—might decide not to kill her, or at least delay the decision until they could speak. "I've been practising with the Power."

Graman flinched, eyes flickering to the door where the guards awaited his call.

"Not that I would hurt anyone with it," she added. "I want to redeem myself. I'll help in any way I can if it means Vesanya can't harm anyone else." Her throat dried at the thought of the God but she ignored her discomfort.

"I am afraid it is not my decision to make. However, I will pass on the request when the king gets a moment's respite from his visitors."

Graman's tone was almost gentle but Luelle couldn't stop to analyse that before he spoke words that made her palms sweat and her heartbeat race.

"Vesanya is one of the reasons I came to speak with you."

"Has she attacked again?" her voice emerged as a whisper.

"No," Graman reassured her, quickly. "No, we actually have no idea where she is, but I believe there is a chance you can assist us in narrowing down the options. Since there was an element of truth to your beliefs about the Power, we cannot ignore the possibility that other beliefs we once rejected may be an accurate part of history, too."

Luelle nodded, her mind racing as she scrambled to plot a new path for herself. "If I was able to leave my room and view the texts, I could fill in any gaps I remember."

A small smile curled on Graman's lips. "Once again, I cannot offer such permissions, but I am sure the king would feel more inclined to consider that request if you would answer some of my questions."

She squared her shoulders and nodded, ready to face the uncomfortable memories this would no doubt cause. Graman was a more polite interrogator than she'd expected to receive. She would answer his questions if it meant avoiding the torture Malcolm had once threatened her with, when he'd first caught up with her on her journey to the Caeleste Peaks.

"How long did you live in the cavern?"

"A few years. I'm not sure exactly how long. We moved around a lot before then, so it all blurs together."

"And how much of the cavern's structure did you and your companions alter?"

"What do you mean?"

"Did you carve any new passages or engravings?" He pushed his glasses up.

"No, we did nothing like that. We used it as a place to rest and research more than anything. If Zeke hadn't decided to steal the Power from King Alaric, we probably wouldn't have stayed there much longer. It was very isolated."

"So, the statue, the star map, and the archway..." he trailed off.

"They were all there when we first arrived." Luelle nodded. "As was the crystal sphere and the plinth it rests on. One of my companions tried moving it once, but it never budged." She could still picture Imbryl with his shoulder wedged against the plinth, straining for hours to push it on its side, but collapsing with exhaustion and giving up without even shifting the stone.

"Interesting." Graman leaned forward. "And the statue never changed? You never got a sense that it was alive?"

Luelle swallowed. "I always had a strange feeling in the cavern, but I had no idea the statue was anything more than stone." She'd spent so much time sitting in the statue's presence, oblivious to the hateful being trapped within. Had Vesanya been aware of their presence? A chill ran down her spine at the thought.

"What were Zeke's theories about the statue?"

"I don't think he had any." She searched her memory for conversations with Zeke, Freya, and Imbryl, recalling their nights in the cavern with a pang of bitter longing. Had they always believed she was less than them? Had Zeke ever truly cared for her? She pushed the thoughts aside. "He believed the cavern was an old pilgrimage site. As far as I'm aware, he thought our Veseile ancestors carved the statue."

Graman nodded. "And who commanded Zeke's allegiance?"

Luelle frowned at the question. "No one. He worked for himself. He had contacts, but everyone treated him like a leader."

"You are certain?"

She narrowed her eyes at the Adeile. "What do you suspect?"

Graman ignored her question. "Where did Zeke predominantly obtain his resources?"

"Most of his research came from the more populated parts of the realm. He has friends everywhere. I visited most of Arazia with him over the years to retrieve something or speak to someone. His collection of documents contains something from every province. It's hard to be specific when we visited so many places. If I could see the documents you're referring to, I might be able to match them to specific locations."

Graman nodded, a frown forming. "I understand. Worry not, this is all useful information. There is no guarantee the locations would offer further answers, regardless. Perhaps you stumbled across the single truth in all of the documentation."

"That would certainly make things easier," Luelle muttered.

"Though, it would leave us with many unanswered questions. How did Vesanya become trapped in our world? Why only her and not the other Gods? Assuming they exist too, of course. Did the Power always belong to the Veseile, as you claim? If so, how did a human obtain it and how did the tradition of passing it from monarch to heir begin?"

Graman appeared to have forgotten Luelle's presence as he pondered aloud. She'd wondered the same questions since leaving the cavern but was no closer to finding the answers for any of them. Zeke's documents and musings had suggested theories to answer some, such as how the humans had stolen the Power in the first place, but they were only theories. Most of them contradicted one another, and some were so outlandish that even Luelle dismissed them without a second thought.

"Do you recall any documents concerning the star map in the cavern?" Graman asked, eventually realising he'd been talking to himself.

"No. When I was living there, we didn't even know we were walking on a map. Malcolm was the one who pointed it out to me. Zeke was more concerned with information that referenced the Power. I don't know if any of them figured it out while I was away, but when I lived there, we didn't look into it."

"Do you have any theories about it all?"

"Perhaps." Luelle's guard shot up. "But I want to know more about my own fate before I share everything with you." No matter how friendly this Adeile seemed, Malcolm would have one less reason to keep her alive if she shared everything she knew and believed. Graman clearly thought she could be a valuable resource, but he wouldn't return to her room if he left believing he walked away with every answer he needed.

Besides, despite her concerns and paranoia, she was enjoying the conversation. Life trapped in a room by herself was lonely—lonelier than life had been working in the castle, when she'd been free to roam the halls, to eavesdrop and pretend she was part of something.

Graman's lips curled into a small, tight smile, though Luelle didn't miss the frustration that flashed in his eyes. "I understand. Thank you for your help so far, we have covered good ground today. I must get going to help with the preparations for tonight's celebrations, but I will speak with the king and return with news when I can. Or with more questions."

Nerves fluttered in Luelle's stomach as Graman rose from the seat opposite her and strode to the door. He knocked a quick pattern. Locks slid on the other side. She would be unable to open that door from within if she ever attempted to escape.

Was she pushing her luck? Should she have told Graman what little was left to know? Should she make something up, just to keep the company?

Before she could decide, the door opened. Graman left without saying goodbye, locking Luelle in her room with only her thoughts once more.

4

HOURS after his coronation, Malcolm was still reeling from the fear that had gripped him at the sight of Vesanya's statue in the Great Temple. He hadn't had a second to rest since then. As soon as he'd entered his carriage to travel home, his family had insisted on talking to him—analysing the crowd's reactions and commenting on his performance, noting the things he should have done differently. He felt an overwhelming urge to flee the city, to find somewhere he could enjoy a quiet afternoon away from the meetings and celebrations due to fill the rest of his day.

Several times over the past week, Malcolm had found himself longing to return to the Godswood. Travelling with no possessions, with no concern beyond finding food and warm shelter each day, had been more exhilarating than he'd expected and remained more enticing than anything Cerulya had to offer. Life as a prince had been busy; life as a king was bound to be chaos.

Footmen whisked Malcolm away the moment he

stepped inside the castle, taking him to prepare and redress for an immediate meeting with the realm's four Thanes. Each Thane had been chosen either by Malcolm's father or Grandmother. With their titles came the responsibility of lands to care for, either until their death or until their position was revoked by the reigning monarch, a decision that was only made possible when at least half of the elected mayors from towns in the Thane's territory petitioned the crown. In return, the Thane dealt with local taxes, upheld the law, and maintained the welfare of every citizen living on their land. Now he was king, Malcolm would meet with them twice a year to discuss general matters, as his father once had, though he would likely speak with them individually much more frequently.

Malcolm entered the familiar board room, where his Thanes awaited him. They rushed to stand when he stepped inside. Despite exchanging brief greetings before the coronation, this was his first official meeting with his Thanes as their king, their first official meeting without his father's guidance. The room felt empty with only five seats at the table. Someone—perhaps Philip—had removed his father's chair before Malcolm's arrival, but he keenly felt its absence.

Wilted flowers sagged in a blue vase in the corner of the room, their petals browning slightly at the edges. The castle was full of similar displays. Servants had plundered the castle gardens upon the announcement of King Alaric's death, plucking armfuls of the bright blossoms to honour the old king in every room of his home. At first, people had admired the colourful displays with tear-filled eyes; Malcolm had been the only one unable to look at them.

Now, when others had lost interest, he couldn't tear his eyes away from the limp, withering bouquets and their silent reminder of his father's lost life.

He ached to smash each and every vase.

He had never been one for fits of rage in his youth, but grief had turned him into something volatile.

When Malcolm took his seat, more servants poured into the room, bringing wine, freshly-pressed juices, ale, and boards of food. He invited his Thanes to sit. Servants stepped forth to present each one with a small box containing a newly forged signet ring. The gift was a tradition, a token of trust and acceptance from the monarch to their Thanes. Engraved on the ring was a depiction of his coronation's Power demonstration—a small tree with small blue gems decorating the branches to depict the watery blossoms—carved in advance of the event by Cerulya's best silversmith. He wore a matching ring on his right hand.

Each Thane accepted the gift with a formal thanks. Malcolm's heart sank. Before now, the Thanes had always been friendly and jovial towards him. With his new title came a change in their interactions, a shift in the power dynamics between them. He was no longer a peer, a friend; he was their ruler.

After what felt like an age, the servants finished laying the refreshments and left the room. Guards stood in the hall outside to ensure no one disturbed the meeting. Malcolm took a sip from his wine, silent permission for the Thanes to tuck into the feast before them. Two of them, Adira and Wren, did so with enthusiasm.

Adira was a Dileile. The Dileile race were descended from Dilectya, the God of Love and Invention. Like most of her kind, Adira was shorter than average, smaller even than most adult humans, but she was scrappy, endlessly brave, and muscular enough that Malcolm never wished to find himself in a physical brawl against her. She retained the Camthryn Peaks, where most of Arazia's ores and precious minerals were mined, and everything north of the mountain range, as far east as the coast beyond the Iron City.

The Iron City was almost as much of a melting pot as Cerulya, although it contained a significantly larger Dileile presence, despite the majority that dwelled in the mining communities deep in the Camthryn Peaks. Malcolm had visited it once in his childhood. He'd been fascinated by the veils that the mountain-dwelling Dileile wore when they ventured into the bright world above ground. Since she lived permanently in the Iron City, Adira kept her eyes bare and uncovered.

Beside her, Wren lounged in his seat, his casual posture suggesting much more comfort in the firm chairs than Malcolm felt. Wren was the oldest in the room by almost a century, though a stranger might not have predicted such. He retained the Midlands, living in the Godswood in a Meteile settlement significantly larger than the one Malcolm had visited with Luelle.

Wren's hair, patterned with alternating shades of brown like a feather, flopped over his forehead as he tilted his head to examine the burgundy wine swirling in his glass. His green eyes reminded Malcolm of Anwyn and Pansy.

"I believe we should start this meeting with a toast." Wren raised his glass, the liquid sloshing inside. "To our new king."

Malcolm raised his cup with the others, nodding to each Thane with a small smile as they wished him a long, prosperous reign. To Malcolm's left sat Edyth, a Colleile and Thane of the Southlands. To his right sat Isme, an Adeile and Thane of the Eastlands. Their glasses clinked against his.

"Do you feel different now you have the title, Your Majesty?" Wren asked from across the table, cheeks rounding with the hint of a smile.

Malcolm shook his head. "I imagine it will sink in soon enough. And, please, call me Malcolm. We do not need to maintain such formality in a private setting such as this." He tried to keep his tone light and pressed on with their agenda, reluctant to waste too much time here when he had so many other social obligations to fulfill today. "There are two things I wish to inform you all about before opening up the discussion to more routine matters."

They each nodded at him.

Malcolm took a deep breath. "Firstly, I trust that you have all been informed about the circumstances surrounding my father's death."

"The assassination." Edyth confirmed, her round, brown eyes boring into Malcolm's. "I admit, I was shocked to hear of it." She swept her dark hair over her shoulder, full lips downturning into a frown.

The other three Thanes murmured a solemn agreement.

Malcolm gave a short nod. "We apprehended the assailant and are currently holding her under guard in the castle. I hope to schedule her execution as soon as possible, likely next week. Of course, I extend the offer for you all to remain here in the interim if you wish to attend." He met each of their eyes, praying they could not hear the lies in his voice.

"I am sure I speak for all of us when I say we would be honoured," Adira said. Her ruddy complexion had already deepened further from the few sips of wine she'd taken.

Malcolm kept a neutral expression as the other Thanes agreed, willing his racing heart to slow. He wouldn't execute Luelle, not when she might be vital in his quest to get rid of Vesanya, but Viv was correct that the public's bloodlust must be satiated. In the few spare moments he had, Malcolm continued to piece together a plan to deal with the entire situation.

"The second thing," he continued, "relates to the Power."

Adira and Isme straightened in their seats. Edyth raised her brows. Even Wren settled his goblet on the table, leaning forward where he lounged.

"As you know, for millennia, humans have reigned and the Power has been contained by a single wielder, the monarch. However, since my father passed the Power to me, my family and I have noticed an unexpected consequence. I am the first king of mixed blood in documented history so my scholars and advisers believe the change may result from my Veseile heritage. In short, it appears that other Veseile now have access to the Power."

"What?" Wren asked, glancing at Adira, whose mouth hung open in shock.

"All Veseile?" Edyth's voice cracked on the words.

"Possibly, though we are still testing the theory in private." Malcolm gave a curt nod.

Stunned silence filled the room. Edyth was the first to break it.

"What are we going to do about this?"

"This will change life as we know it," Isme exclaimed, eyes wide. "The danger is unfathomable!"

"Isme is right," Adira said, leaning forward. "We must detain the Veseile if there is any truth to this. Think of the violence they could commit. They'll slaughter innocent people with such a weapon at their disposal!" her voice rose as she spoke.

Malcolm opened his mouth to reply, to regain control of his meeting, but Wren beat him to the draw.

"Would it even be possible to detain so many? How did nobody predict that this might happen?" he demanded, brow furrowed.

Isme rose, her seat screeching across the stone floor. Her glass of wine tipped on its side, red wine spilling across the table and flooding a nearby platter of fruit. "We must warn the nobility in our land immediately!"

"Enough! Sit down," Malcolm demanded, voice loud enough to startle each of the Thanes. They turned to him, wide-eyed. He cleared his throat and attempted to moderate his tone, to temper his panic. "Please. Isme be seated. We must not let panic spur us into rash action. This matter must be handled delicately to avoid widespread chaos."

Tension remained, thick in the air. But, slowly, Isme returned to her seat. Her blue-tinted skin was paler than usual. She swallowed. "How is this possible?"

"We do not know, but my advisers are researching all available documented history for a clue." Malcolm took a deep breath, curling his hands into fists beneath the table to avoid running them through his hair. "Some Veseile extremists believe that the Power once belonged solely to their race, rather than humans. I do not agree and will not allow this rumour to prosper. However, we do not yet know the extent of Veseile that can use the Power, and we must start considering whether there is any truth to the more trustworthy beliefs and myths we once dismissed."

"And how to contain any threat that the Veseile population may now pose." Edyth's frown deepened. "How did you discover this?"

"My siblings have shown the same abilities as myself," Malcolm voiced the lie he'd been preparing. "I have been evaluating them in private and am working closely with my advisers to extend these investigations to other Veseile. I am also training a small group of Veseile soldiers to send back to your lands with you. They will be able to assist with keeping peace and training further soldiers with the Power to provide a new level of protection. I am drafting laws regarding the Power's use, which will be distributed when I make the announcement after the execution. Until then, we must continue learning about the changes so we are better equipped to contain any threats that arise. We must not presume all Veseile pose such a risk. The Power can be a tool for good as much as it can be used for harm."

"What containment methods are you considering?" Adira asked, panic still evident in her tone. "Would physical restraints work?"

Malcolm shook his head. "Not for anyone adept with the Power. They could easily break free and, regardless, physical restriction would not stop them from using the Power against their guards or anyone else nearby."

Initially, he had wondered if Veseile soldiers would be enough to contain any threats; it was wishful thinking. Even if he could train them fast enough, there were not enough Veseile soldiers to maintain a constant, firm-handed presence across the realm.

He'd considered imprisonment for any potential deviants, as Adira had suggested, but a prison was not guaranteed to hold a criminal with the Power nor to stop them from wreaking havoc.

His final idea had come to him when he'd been lying awake in bed one night, reminiscing about his short time at the Meteile camp with Luelle and wondering if he could find an excuse to return. In the room Anwyn had given them, he had read a journal documenting some of the produce exported from the Godswood to the rest of the kingdom. One product he had recognised was shadowbell, a flower whose seeds were frequently ground into a powder and brewed into a tonic that could relieve pain and induce sleep. Given a large enough dose, it could render a person unconscious for hours. A medical text Graman had sourced even theorised that a blade or arrow coated in the thick fluid could administer a small dose directly into the blood.

"Wren, I believe the shadowbell flower could be our solution, if we can significantly increase production and exports. We could sedate any Veseile that cause trouble to avoid them using the Power to escape imprisonment. It is only a temporary solution, but would offer a method to de-escalate violent situations."

"If we can farm enough." Caution filled Wren's tone. "It will take time to grow and distribute the amount we would need to subdue an entire race. We already lose a lot of land throughout the Godswood to farm the flowers."

"Hopefully, we shall not need enough to subdue the entire Veseile race." Malcolm raised an eyebrow. "And while I accept your concerns, I cannot see another solution that would work so well. It is the safest method I have found to neutralise any threats. I am open to other suggestions, but mass production of the flower must be a priority until we find a better solution," he instructed. "With Meteile guidance, we can grow crops in each province so we all have immediate access and less risk of running out for long periods. I need you to prepare a report on the flower's ideal growth conditions."

Wren tilted his head in acknowledgement. "I will begin as soon as we finish here."

"Would the sedative properties work in any form other than a liquid?" Malcolm asked.

Wren pursed his lips. "I believe so. We would need to test it. The tonic is more palatable than a powder, though, easier to swallow."

"Only for willing consumers," Adira said, following Malcolm's line of thought.

"I see your point." Wren frowned.

"If it has the same properties when inhaled, we could attempt to create some sort of long range weapon. Of course, a fine powder puts our soldiers at equal risk, since anyone nearby could inhale it, but a projectile weapon would lower that risk," Adira suggested, fingers tapping a beat on the table as she considered how such a weapon might work.

"We can run tests this week, while you are in the capital. Perhaps we can create some prototypes." Malcolm suggested to Adira and Wren, who each nodded.

"And what about the long term?" Edyth asked. "Of course, short-term detainment is important, but we must acknowledge that an entire race obtaining sudden access to the Power could be detrimental. It could easily lead to a civil war."

Malcolm nodded. "I share the concern. However, to understand the true long-term consequences, I must continue learning the extent of the change we face."

"How long would we be able to detain people under sedation?" Wren asked, his brow furrowed. "If we are not planning to wake them to feed them, killing them from the start would be a simpler solution."

"I will not permit killing them," Malcolm said, voice firm. "There will be a natural transition period. We cannot expect people not to make mistakes during it. The Power is a volatile skill tied to emotion. I will not consider death as a punishment until my people have had a realistic opportunity to learn how to control themselves."

"What about mind-altering drugs?" Edyth suggested. "There are plenty of those produced in the Godswood and beyond. Without the sedation element, you would be able to keep people alive and the influence of the drugs may affect their ability to use the Power."

"It is something we should test," Malcolm agreed. "Although I would be wary of any mind alterations. It may only make people less predictable without altering their ability to use the Power."

The Thanes grumbled with agreement.

"Is there any way to remove the Power from a person?" Edyth asked.

Caution flooded Malcolm. Instinctively, his defences rose; why would Edyth need to know that? He had to admit, it would be an ideal solution if any Veseile did indeed use the Power for nefarious purposes. But, it would highlight a significant vulnerability in himself.

Forcing himself to relax, he considered it. He hadn't

read of any such ability but it had never been a point of study when the Power had only belonged to the realm's ruler. Now, it could become a necessity to ensure people's safety.

"I do not know. I will look into it," Malcolm promised.

Isme rubbed her eyes with a finger and thumb. "Is there a chance that people will learn about it before you make the announcement?"

"Unfortunately, yes. As I said, the Power is closely tied to emotion. Some Veseile may lose control of it if they experience strong bursts of emotion."

"Even if it is not discovered before you make an announcement, news will spread like flames after a drought the moment you do," Wren grumbled.

Malcolm nodded, hoping his despair didn't show. The more he considered the future, the less he could see an outcome that did not result in chaos across the realm. How could he protect his people without enforcing tyrannical rule? Was it possible to be both a strong and caring leader?

Beyond that, any problems caused by changes to the Power paled in comparison to the potential harm Vesanya could cause if she emerged from her hiding place with the same malicious intent Malcolm had witnessed in the cavern.

He'd considered telling his Thanes about the god but had quickly decided against it. News of changes to the Power was shocking enough; he needed their attention on that. Besides, he had no real evidence of Vesanya's presence and the threat she may pose until his scouts located her again.

"I say we push this problem back until tomorrow's

meetings." Adira slung her head back, emptying her goblet and immediately reaching to refill it. "We all need time to allow this information to sink in. The best ideas take time to brew and we came here to celebrate. I intend to do exactly that until we can put off these problems no longer."

Wren shrugged and nodded, holding his empty glass out to her with a wink.

"I suppose if we stay until the execution, we have plenty of time to plan for any eventuality." Isme's brow furrowed. "I would like to visit the libraries here before we discuss further."

Malcolm did not object when Edyth grabbed the nearest jug of wine and refilled his glass to the brim.

5

Luelle's brief visit from Graman made her isolation all the more intense. In the hours after he left, she recounted every detail of their conversation a hundred times over, dwelling on the smallest details, like his expressive face and careful choice of wording. At some point, she lost confidence over which memories were accurate and which were tricks of her own mind, attempts to make her situation seem a little less dire.

When the overthinking became too much, she practised with the Power, following it up with a long, luxurious bath, scrubbing every inch of her body and hair clean, and reheating the bath water with the Power whenever it chilled. When she emerged from her bathing room, the sky was dim and a fresh plate of food awaited her on the floor inside her door. She fetched a plain tunic and pair of leggings from her wardrobe, dressing quickly to stave off the chill.

Luelle kept her curtains open and unshuttered her moonstone lamp to brighten the room before she ate. Muted music drifted from somewhere deep in the castle as Cerulya honoured its new king; jaunty tunes on string instruments. No doubt the nobility would be dancing in pairs to it, twirling around the castle's great hall, connected by only their hands until they consumed enough alcohol to abandon their sensibilities.

Regular people, further in the city, would have started celebrating as soon as the ceremony finished, but the nobles had clearly required time to preen and primp before their debauchery began.

Among her overwhelming sense of resentment, Luelle recognised the bitter sting of jealousy. Of course, not everyone in the city would be celebrating; crime and poverty continued quietly no matter what else was happening. However, alone in her room, it felt as if she was the only individual in the entire realm excluded from Malcolm's party. Plans for this day had been underway long before Luelle had started working in Cerulya, intent on stealing Alaric's Power. Though the old king had been in better health six years ago, everyone knew his life would not extend much longer; he was human, after all. Despite believing she would be far from the capital when the coronation occurred, it had been impossible to avoid getting caught up in the excitement surrounding it.

When stars blinked to life, Luelle tried to sleep through the noise, but laying in bed listening to strangers having such a nice time only increased her agitation.

How different might her life be if she'd never met Zeke? Would she be celebrating this day with friends, or a family? Would she have loved ones who wouldn't abandon her after learning she was only half-Veseile, knowing they risked loving her for only a few decades before they had to continue life without her?

Throwing back her bedsheets, she clambered out of

bed, unable to continue lying alone with her thoughts. She needed a distraction.

Malcolm, or whoever was making decisions about her fate, wouldn't even let her out of the room to decipher Zeke's materials, despite knowing she was the best person for that task. She considered practising with the Power again, but the thought soured her mood. The Power was the reason she was trapped here. If she'd never stolen it from Alaric, if she'd never cared that it had been in the hands of the wrong people, she would be free. The Veseile race would be in the same position they'd been in for thousands of years, Malcolm would have sole access to the Power, and Vesanya would still be contained in the cavern, nothing more than a harmless statue.

Had it all been a mistake?

Luelle hauled one of her armchairs closer to the window and curled up on it, bringing her knees to her chest and wrapping her arms around them. A perfect crescent moon hung in the cloudless sky. Stars speckled the broad expanse of darkness, too many to count. Unintentionally, Luelle's thoughts strayed to Malcolm, who had spent every night of their travels together gazing at the constellations.

People would be vying for his attention tonight. He wouldn't get a moment alone. After all, the celebrations were to honour him. Was he enjoying it?

Did he really intend to leave her shut in here forever?

Watching the moon travel across the sky, Luelle let her mind drift, listening to the occasional muffled melodies and distant voices change in volume as doors and windows opened and closed elsewhere in the castle. Her room contained no clock. She only had her internal body rhythms to tell the time, and those were a much less reliable indicator than they'd been when she'd worked in the castle. Now, her sleeping pattern was dictated by the presence of nightmares. Without her previous responsibilities, she regularly stayed awake through the night to avoid dreams and worked herself to exhaustion during the day, getting rest in short doses whenever she managed to drain herself of energy by practising with the Power.

Despite her erratic body clock, the sky revealed the late hour, though that didn't mean the festivities were nearing their end. History books described coronation celebrations that extended for days at a time as nobles gorged themselves on food, wine, drugs, and other physical pleasures. Could Malcolm risk letting it continue for so long, knowing that Vesanya was somewhere in the realm? She could attack again at any point.

On the other hand, could he afford to cut it short, ending centuries of tradition and letting the world know something was wrong this early in his reign?

Staring up at the stars, Luelle pretended she was back on the road. Memories of her short trip with the prince were her happiest in a long time, even if he had been surly and uncooperative for most of their journey. Before that, her most precious memories involved travelling with Zeke, Freya, and Imbryl, but those recollections were tainted by everything that had happened during their reunion in the cavern.

While working in the castle before King Alaric's death, Luelle had yearned to be back with her friends. Now, even if she was able to escape the capital alive, she could never live alongside them again. She would never trust them, never believe they were willing to accept and support her the way she had once supported them.

Tears slipped down her cheeks.

A knock sounded at the door.

Luelle lifted her head, swiping at the moisture that had dripped to her chin. Was Graman back with more questions at this time of night? Or was he bringing her some documents to look through? Hopefully the guards would be less rough this time. She made no move from her seat beyond craning her head to see the door; she did not need to make it easier for the guards to manhandle her.

When the door opened, no guards entered. The figure that stumbled in was smaller than Graman, mostly obscured by the gloom in the room. Luelle jerked with surprise when she recognised her guest.

Malcolm closed the door behind him without meeting her stare. He wore a dark green, silk tunic, embellished with delicate golden embroidery and tiny jewels that glimmered when they caught the faint light of her lamp— more decadent than any outfit she'd seen him in. His crown contained matching gemstones, the largest central stone shaped to fit the six-pointed star that represented the gods. The crown perched off-centre atop curls that were somehow wilder than they'd been when travelling with no combs or valets.

When Malcolm finally lifted his eyes to meet Luelle's stare, he seemed unable to focus on where she was sitting. He leaned back against the door and gazed around the plain room. Unfocused eyes passed over her messy bedsheets and the empty plate on her table. As he moved his head, she noticed more gemstones glinting in his ears, threaded through his earlobes on thin pieces of gold.

Should she stand for him? Was that was he was waiting for, now he was the king? Had he come to gloat over his captive, finally revealing the sick punishment he'd planned for her?

Anger flushed through Luelle at the thought.

She unfolded her legs and moved to stand, simply to avoid the psychological disadvantage of remaining seated if this came to an argument.

Malcolm held out a hand to stop her.

"No, please," he said. "People have been standing and bowing and staring all day. I need a break from it."

Fresh annoyance blossomed in Luelle's chest. She'd been trapped in this room for days on end and he was complaining about people being overly-polite to him?

"So sorry, *Your Majesty*. Your life is so full of troubles," she muttered, letting sarcasm shine through her tone as she collapsed back into her chair. She turned her back to him, facing the window. As much as she'd been wishing to return to her travels with Malcolm, only fury burned in her now, seeing him decked in finery.

Behind her, uneven footfalls sounded as he plodded across the room. She expected him to sit in the other armchair or at the table, as Graman had earlier in the day, but when Luelle turned around, Malcolm was slumped in a heap on the floor beside her bed, leaning his head back against the side of the mattress behind her chair so he could look out the window over her shoulder.

Now he was closer, the overwhelming scent of wine washed over her. Luelle frowned, angling her chair back so she could look at him without craning her neck.

"You're drunk."

"Well, it is my coronation." Bitterness drenched the words. He raised his eyebrows and waved a hand at the crown, but Luelle got the feeling his scorn was not aimed at her.

"It went that badly?"

He scrubbed at his face with his hands, letting his arms flop back to his sides with a thud against the floor before he replied.

"No. It was fine, I suppose. I froze up in the Great Temple, but got through it and performed the required demonstration to the public. They seemed happy enough with me. The nobles have barely stopped talking about it, asking me to perform more tricks for them, as if I am the court jester, not their king." He gesticulated wildly as he spoke.

"Why are you here, then? Shouldn't you be off enjoying the attention?"

Malcolm pulled a face. "I told you, I needed a break from it."

Luelle gritted her teeth. "I imagine there are better places for that than this room you've locked me in. Or did you actually come here to gloat? To talk about how incredible life is for you now?"

"What? Of course not." He frowned, redoubling his efforts to look at Luelle.

She scoffed, turning around to glare at the stars. Deep down, she knew she should use this opportunity to win Malcolm over, to prove her worth as she'd initially intended when she next saw him, but would it really change anything? In his inebriated state, he likely wouldn't remember anything she said to him by tomorrow morning.

What had her life come to? She'd never felt so glum. Lifelong friends had abandoned her in an instant; why did she think she'd find a home here working for Malcolm, someone who barely knew her? Even if he decided to use her, she would be constantly watching her back in case anyone in the castle recognised her face.

"Are you angry at me?"

The disbelief in his tone made Luelle whip around to face him again.

"I am angry at everyone!" she snapped at him. "I've been stuck in this room since we arrived back in the capital. No one will speak to me. I don't know what's happening in the world—if Vesanya is hurting more people, if my friends are still alive, or if news about the Power is spreading. I have no privacy from the guards standing outside my room, who are at liberty enter whenever they please, whether I am bathing or sleeping. Not to mention that you've started sending your advisers to question me and I just have to accept that? Did he tell you how your guards manhandled me on his visit? I'd say it's only natural for me to be angry, Prince."

"Not any more." Malcolm pointed at the crown again.

She rolled her eyes.

"Must I remind you that you committed treason when you stole from my father? Did you truly expect a normal life when you returned here in my charge?"

She made no attempt to respond.

"You should be grateful I don't listen to my sister's wishes regarding your fate," he muttered, sounding as surly as he had on the first days they'd spent travelling together on their way to the Caeleste Peaks.

He was still frowning at Luelle from the floor when she

turned back around.

"What does she want to do to me?"

"A public execution."

Luelle's mouth dried. Malcolm's expression was blank as he observed her reaction. She pulled her knees back to her chest, resting her chin atop them.

"Why aren't you listening to her?" she forced herself to ask.

He took a deep breath and averted his eyes to the night sky. "It's complicated. None of them truly understand or believe what we witnessed in that cavern and the public are unaware of so much. My lies have returned to haunt me."

"What lies?"

"The lies woven to disguise what truly happened during our trip." He waved a hand around vaguely. "Everyone but a select few trusted individuals currently believes you were involved in an assassination plot against my father."

Luelle bit her tongue to stop a sharp retort and silently thanked the alcohol for lowering Malcolm's inhibitions enough to tell her all of this. She let him ramble.

"Your death would appease the majority and would strengthen my appearance as a decisive king, but you were right about the Power. What else might you know? I cannot deny your value as a source of information and I must discover the truth about the gods and the Power if I'm to maintain control," he stumbled over his words as he spoke.

"So what will happen to me?"

"The execution must go ahead but you will not be here when it does."

That did nothing to slow her heart rate.

"You plan to stage my death?"

He nodded. Tension lined his jaw even in his inebriation, suggesting it wasn't as simple as he implied.

"Are you going to kill someone innocent?"

"Not innocent," he corrected her. "There are criminals already awaiting execution that look like you, from a distance at least." He gestured at her face. "But, there is no need for you to know the details of the plan." He scrunched his eyes shut, as if trying to clear his thoughts.

"And, let me guess, I will be waiting in this room, ready for you to use whenever you need me?" she tried to disguise the disgust in her voice. If that was his plan, she'd find a way to escape. Her control over the Power improved every day; she'd manage to leave the capital if she needed to.

"No. I am sending you back to the cavern."

She flinched. That was worse.

"Guarded, of course, so you cannot escape. Graman will take you to retrieve anything we left behind, search for clues about Vesanya, and so on."

"You realise Graman and I will not live to bring anything back if Vesanya is still there. You may as well kill me here instead of using a decoy." She hated the tremble in her voice at the thought of the God she'd witnessed.

"Vesanya is no longer there." He shrugged. His crown slid further off-balance. "I have soldiers searching for her and posted in the cavern to prevent anyone from entering without my permission. I shall know the moment she tries to return there, if she tries at all. I will also give the guards accompanying you strict instructions so they know what to do if you encounter Vesanya."

"I doubt any guards would be able to protect me if she appears."

"No...but they can provide a distraction. And bring you back here safely so you can keep helping me."

Though he was offering a version of the future Luelle had proposed for herself to Graman, the desire to challenge him reared its head.

"And what if I refuse to help you?"

His lips curled into a small, wry smirk. "Were you not pleading with Graman to help me only hours ago?"

Heat flooded her face. "I did not plead."

Malcolm laughed—a deep, loud sound, accompanied by a smile that transformed his entire face and made Luelle's stomach tighten. How drunk was he? She'd never made him laugh before.

"If you refuse to help, my sister will be pleased to carry out your public execution," he said, mirth still sparkling in his eyes, "but I would rather have you at my side. I need all the help I can get." He closed his eyes, snorting a small self-deprecating laugh and slumping into a less upright position, bracing his hands on the floor to steady himself.

"You really open up after a few drinks, huh?"

Malcolm smiled again, but kept his eyes closed. She took the opportunity to study his face. Bruise-like shadows rested below his eyes—evidence he got as little sleep as her. Although his hair was unkempt, he'd taken the time to shave away the stubble that had grown on their travels, exposing his sharp jawline.

"I would be able to help you more if you told me the problems you're dealing with," she pried when the silence between them pressed on her.

"I will when you prove I can trust you."

"I didn't lie to you once when we were travelling together."

He opened his eyes. "True, but you did steal from my dying father, punch me in the face, lead me to a near-death encounter, and free a trapped god intent on killing everyone she sees."

Luelle looked away. Guilt about all of that had worn her down over the past week; she didn't need the reminder.

"What do you expect me to do in the cavern?"

"Find out the truth for me," he whispered.

How different would his answer be if he was sober? Did he truly think she would find any answers there or was it simply a ploy to get her out of his hair for a while?

He continued. "You were right about the Power. You must have other theories or evidence about Vesanya. Maybe a way for me to get rid of her or trap her again before she hurts anyone else. And, you said the Power was once common. I wish to know more about what things were like back then. How did people manage it and stop anyone from using it for…nefarious purposes?" Malcolm's brow creased. "Graman will be there to guide you. I spoke about it with him briefly, earlier today."

Luelle nodded once. "When would I leave?"

"Tomorrow night," he said. "You will report your findings to me on your return in two weeks. Only to me. You cannot discuss this with anyone else, bar Graman. You'll travel on horseback, so it should take less time than when we were travelling together."

"And what then? After I return."

He shrugged. "That depends on what you learn, I suppose. I must find a way to deal with Vesanya, so I hope you discover a way to achieve that."

"Why are you so confident that I won't simply escape?" She frowned. "Even if you send soldiers to accompany me, I have a better grip on the Power now. I could use that against them and leave you to deal with all of this alone."

"I do not believe you would. Where would you go? Back to your old friends?" He watched her expression sour. A smug smile played on his lips. "I thought not. You can make a living for yourself here if you help me. You would have to live in hiding if you tried to escape. I can have all of the soldiers in the realm searching for you in an instant."

"I could leave the realm."

"I would like to see you try." Challenge laced Malcolm's tone, his confidence inflated with alcohol. "I have connections everywhere. Besides, I found you once before, I can do it again."

"We are no longer linked by the Power."

"I would find a way."

She didn't respond.

He filled the silence.

"So, you've used the Power since our return?"

She nodded. Taking a deep breath, she focused on the warmth in her chest. She willed a thread of her Power to grip his crown and reeled it slowly towards herself, placing the surprisingly heavy headpiece atop her own head.

Malcolm's eyes widened as the crown left his head, but he made no move to snatch it back. His cheeks rounded with a suppressed smile as Luelle tilted her head to show off her new accessory. He shoved himself back upright, the movement clumsy.

"Not bad," he murmured. "Still a thief, through and through."

Forgetting her anger towards him for a second, she smiled. "I'm sure it looks better on me."

He returned the smile. The weight of the crown lessened as he used the Power to lift if off her head and back onto his. The movement was more dramatic than she'd expected, the crown flying higher and faster than necessary, almost crashing into Malcolm's head as it whizzed closer to him. He scrunched his eyes and brow with concentration as he tried to focus.

As he used the Power, Luelle felt a faint pull, reminiscent of what she used to sense when Alaric was nearby and the sole wielder. Accompanying that pressure came a familiar presence, a breath of brisk air and woody musk, a forest moments after rainfall—Malcolm's aura ghosting against her. She suppressed a shiver.

He was oblivious to it.

"Perhaps you can protect the guards, rather than the other way around, if you encounter anything hostile," he suggested.

Something told her he was not only referring to Vesanya.

"I doubt we'll find anyone there, especially if you have people stationed outside."

"It could be beneficial if you did find someone. You were away from your friends for a while. They might have new information about Vesanya or the Power that they could pass on to you."

"They are no longer my friends. Are you instructing me to seek them out?"

"Do you not wish to see them again?"

Luelle swallowed. "Not particularly. Maybe you didn't notice, but they weren't very welcoming to me during our reunion."

"I suppose I was a little busy having my throat stepped on," Malcolm joked, once again oblivious to the way her eyes flicked to his neck, though the markings from Zeke's foot were long gone. "Your old friends would not pose a threat to you, since you can now use the Power more proficiently. You will be guarded, too. I doubt they would attack you."

"I thought the same last time."

"That's in the past. I need you to do this. I must learn more about Vesanya and if you want to stay alive, this is your only option."

Luelle sighed. "I know. I understand I have no choice, but that doesn't mean I'm thrilled at the thought of returning."

"It is only for two weeks and most of that will be spent travelling. I want a full report of everything you notice out there, even if it seems unimportant. We are clearly missing something."

"Fine."

For several minutes, they sat in silence, watching the stars. The anxiety that had plagued Luelle since returning to Cerulya faded in Malcolm's presence, her breathing slowing to match his.

Her eyes jerked back over to him when a snore escaped his lips. He was so slumped that he seemed on the verge of falling completely to the ground. Luelle frowned at him, eyes flickering to the door of her room. The guards beyond would likely believe she'd hurt the king if Malcolm stayed for much longer. They did not even trust her with privacy bathing; they would not trust her if they discovered the king asleep on her floor.

She coughed, loudly.

Malcolm startled, jerking awake and upright. For a second, pressure flared against Luelle as he seized control of the Power. It faded as his unfocused eyes took in the room, recognising where he was.

"I should get going," he mumbled.

"You have a party to get back to."

Malcolm wrinkled his nose. "They will not miss me down there. I think I need some sleep. Someone will come to collect you tomorrow. You'll leave after nightfall. If you have any other questions while you are away, speak to Graman." Faltering, he pushed himself to his feet, leaning heavily on the bed and stumbling as he crossed the room. "I will see you in two weeks."

Luelle watched him knock on the door and leave without saying anything else, unsure whether to be pleased she was getting what she wanted or unhappy that she was, yet again, working under someone else's control.

At least it was better than the alternative punishment.

6

A persistent, dull ache plagued Malcolm's head the morning after his coronation.

Celebrations had stretched into the night, longer than he'd expected, giving him scant opportunities to take a break, whether that was to snatch a bite of the food being ferried around the guests on silver platters, drink something that didn't contain alcohol, or recuperate after an unwanted conversation.

Malcolm could not understand how the castle was housing so many people. His home was packed with strangers, all of them nobles he knew little about eager to pull him aside for a few words. He suffered through every experience. Endless congratulations interspersed the numerous requests for help with some trivial matter now he was king and several thinly veiled attempts at seduction. Whenever he escaped one conversation, hoping to find friends or family, he was promptly caught and trapped by another stranger.

As the festivities strayed into the early hours of the morning, Malcolm had devised his escape plan. He'd intended to speak with Luelle about sending her back to the cavern earlier in the day, but Wren had insisted on starting the celebrations early. No nobles knew where she was being kept, so they wouldn't know where to look for him if he succeeded in sneaking out of his own party. Not even his own rooms or private facilities like his observatory felt safe with so many people intent on monopolising his time.

Taking the first opportunity that presented itself, Malcolm slipped away from the celebrations and rushed to Luelle's room, alternating between hiding behind corners until strangers passed and sprinting down empty halls to put space between himself and the masses. On his arrival, he'd instructed the guards standing outside Luelle's accommodation not to let anyone interrupt. They'd objected to him entering without a guard present but he had dismissed that suggestion quickly.

Visiting her after drinking so much had been a foolish idea but she needed to learn about his plans at some point. After leaving, he vaguely remembered instructing the guards to knock if they wished to enter Luelle's room. Her complaints about their rough treatment of her had lingered in his mind throughout their conversation. It was a small gesture he could make that might endear her to working with him, and he didn't like the thought of them walking in on her in a vulnerable position, no matter how much that concern would make his sister scoff.

By the time he made it to his own bedroom, Malcolm was drained. He managed several hours of uninterrupted sleep—or, rather, alcohol-induced unconsciousness—before Theo arrived to rouse him.

Today's schedule was set to be equally busy, although the morning was bound to be quieter as the nobles slept off their headaches. Their absence for the next few hours was the main benefit of last night's celebrations.

Malcolm donned simple robes that had been laid out earlier by a servant and exited his dressing room, walking to his chamber's greeting room where Viv and Theo awaited him. Leena was already off elsewhere in the castle, finalising preparations to accompany Graman and Luelle to the cavern.

"Ready?" Viv asked, seeing her brother enter. She lounged on a low, upholstered divan, basking in the early morning sunlight that shone through the window. Theo stood by the bookshelf, covering a wide yawn with his fist.

Malcolm nodded.

"Are you certain this is what you want?" She straightened.

"Yes, Viv, you can stop asking."

She exchanged a concerned glance with Theo, filling Malcolm with suspicion that they'd been discussing him while he dressed. All three of them stayed still, waiting for someone to break the silence.

"It is clear you both wish to say something, so get on with it," Malcolm snapped.

"We only wonder if this is the best course of action." Viv took charge of the confrontation, folding her hands gracefully in her lap. "Do you truly intend to fake the traitor's death so you can send her on a glorified game of hide and seek?"

"I am not sending her on a glorified game of hide and seek," Malcolm scoffed. "She is the only person who knows those caves well enough to find everything that might remain hidden within. I can send soldiers through again, but they could easily miss something and it will take considerably longer. It would also mean more people will learn what I am searching for, which I must avoid."

"True, but I trust our soldiers and scholars considerably more than your traitor. She has already stolen from us once before, she may do so again. Particularly since she would be away from your influence. What if she finds information and destroys it rather than bringing it back to us? Or takes it for herself and reunites with her friends? The very friends that tried to kill you, might I add."

"She would not do that. She is afraid of seeing her old companions again."

"You do not know that."

"Yes I do, she told me such last night."

It was lucky Viv was already seated, for Malcolm feared his sister would have stumbled and fallen in shock if she had been standing.

"You saw her last night?" Her voice rose an octave. "Is that where you disappeared to? I thought you had retired to bed! Why would you do such a thing? Did you seek her out to—" she cut off with a strangled noise, her hand rising to rest against her forehead.

"Of course not," Malcolm snapped at her, heat rising in his face at her implication. "Someone needed to tell her what was happening and since it is my plan, it made sense for me to do so. I needed a break from all of the attention, anyway."

Fury replaced Viv's initial shock. Her dark brows drew together, mouth pinching into a frown identical to their mother's most disapproving expression. Malcolm battled not to cower under it.

"Regardless, you cannot trust her after a single

conversation, especially after the amount you drank last night. I am surprised you are even able to remember what she said."

"I do not trust her, but I know this is her only option." Malcolm crossed the room and perched on the arm of a nearby sofa, since this discussion was clearly going to be long and heated. "Her companions rejected her after learning about her human heritage. We have sketches of her face drawn up ready to spread through the realm if she tries to flee. Besides, she was the one requesting to help us when she spoke to Graman. She knows, as well as I do, the problems we might face when Vesanya resurfaces."

"I still do not think that excuses lying to the public about her fate."

"You were the one who suggested this!" Malcolm threw his arms up in exasperation.

"In jest! It was never a serious suggestion," she shouted back. "Theo, tell him how ridiculous he is being."

Theo's pale eyes widened as both siblings turned their attention to him. His throat bobbed. Throughout their childhood, Theo had played the role of mediator, since Leena was more adept at avoiding Malcolm when he and Viv were squabbling.

"It is not my place to contradict my king."

Malcolm rolled his eyes, scoffing. "Shut up Theo, just give me your opinion."

"I do think it is a risk to trust the thief with this," he admitted. "She committed treason against your family."

Malcolm ran a hand through his hair. "I need to keep her alive. She can help us, I know it. When we were travelling together, she always spoke about doing what was best for Arazia. I do not believe she would act against that now, not after what we witnessed. She had plenty of opportunities to harm me and never attempted it. She kept me alive, rather than leaving me to fend for myself."

The conversation paused as Viv and Theo considered Malcolm's point. In the absence of their voices, quiet noises from the open window seeped into the room: distant screeching seabirds, a bell ringing somewhere in the city, almost silent echoes of hooves and wheels over cobblestones.

"Despite all of that, are you really willing to kill someone else in her name?" Theo asked, bringing Malcolm back to the argument.

Malcolm swallowed. "I am not sentencing an innocent person. We are only considering criminals who would face execution at a later date due to the severity of their crimes. It is best for the realm. If one unlawful death can prevent other innocent lives from being lost, I shall bear the weight of that."

Viv shook her head and sighed, but neither she nor Theo made any further objection, sensing that Malcolm's opinion would not change.

"Leena has prepared some candidates that look similar enough to the thief." Theo straightened when he stood. "They have been transferred to the palace dungeons, so we can inspect them whenever you are ready."

Malcolm nodded. Briefly, he had wondered whether he could simply choose a random prisoner and refashion their face with the Power to create a closer similarity to Luelle's appearance. However, none of his research suggested that the Power had ever been used for such a thing, and he had no desire to start experimenting on living subjects now. Instead, he would play it safe and choose someone with a naturally similar appearance.

Despite the strength of his resolve, doubts lingered at the edges of his mind. Would he be able to go ahead with this plan when he looked these women in the face? Even if they were criminals facing lifelong punishments or death, was it really his place to end one of their lives prematurely?

Pushing the uncomfortable thoughts aside, he stood and gestured for Theo to lead the way.

Side by side, the three of them strode through the quiet castle halls.

The dungeons were underneath the castle, on the far side of the building from the crypts. The descent was equally unsettling. Malcolm's last trip to the castle's lowest levels had been to witness his father's burial. Sweat broke out on his nape at the memory. He clenched his fists and pushed on, hoping Viv and Theo did not notice how his steps faltered.

At the bottom of the descent, they emerged into a long, musty hallway. Cells lined either side, each one a far cry from the room Luelle was staying in. Moonstone sconces hung above each door, illuminating the small viewing slot that allowed them to examine the criminal lurking within. All viewing slots were currently closed.

Silence hung, heavy and pressing. The guards who would usually patrol these halls waited upstairs at Theo's orders, in an attempt to protect Malcolm's plans from general knowledge.

"How many did Leena select?" His voice bounced off the walls.

"Three." Theo's expression was grim. "The first three doors on the left."

Malcolm nodded. It took several more breaths before he found the motivation to step up to the first door. Theo and Viv stayed where they were, watching and awaiting his decision, if he could follow through with it.

"Who is in this one?" Malcolm asked.

"Does it matter?" Viv challenged him.

"I wish to know."

Theo pulled a small, folded sheet of parchment from a pocket at his chest.

"This one is a human named Sofia."

"What was her crime?"

"Kidnapping and trafficking human children."

His stomach twisted at the offences. Was his face as pale as Theo's and Viv's had become? Or were their peaky hues simply a consequence of the moonstone lighting down here?

He straightened his shoulders and slid the viewing slot open.

Inside, the cells were as bleak as the hallway. A single moonstone orb lit the room from the tall ceiling, bathing the cell in dim blue. On the floor lay an empty wooden plate and a bucket that Malcolm did not examine too closely. Beside the bucket was a thin mattress on which a woman was curled.

She raised her head at the sound of the slot opening and met Malcolm's eyes. Dirt coated her skin and knotted her hair, but it did not disguise the fact that she did not have the unpigmented streak that would typically identify a Veseile or some people with Veseile heritage, like himself and Luelle. From the exposed skin Malcolm could see, the first prisoner was far slimmer than Luelle, bones jutting out at her clavicle. Her eyes were rounder and her lips thinner, but no one else knew Luelle well enough to note those details, especially from a distance.

He closed the slot and moved on, keen to get this over with.

"This one is another Veseile, called Penny. Arrested for serial murder." Theo anticipated Malcolm's questions.

The woman inside was scratching her broken nails into the far wall. She twisted to look at the door as the slot opened. Clumps of hair surrounded her on the floor, presumably torn from the several bald patches atop her scalp. Abandoning the wall, the prisoner spun and scrambled across the floor, racing towards Malcolm.

He slammed the slot shut, leaping backwards as he heard her collide with the door. His heart raced. Theo and Viv's stares were heavy on his back as he moved to the final door.

"And this one?" He cleared his throat when his voice emerged gruffer than expected. Moaning cries echoed from the cell he'd left behind.

"Half-human, half-Veseile. Named Willa. Arrested for multiple thefts, including orchestrating a robbery that left three civilians dead and several injured."

Malcolm opened the viewing slot and looked inside, every inch of his body tense with apprehension. The criminal sat on her mattress with her hands folded in her lap. The ends of her greasy hair brushed against her collarbones. It was a close match in colour to Luelle's, with the same white streak that marked her Veseile heritage. Her cheekbones were more pronounced and her eyebrows thicker, but, like the other prisoners, she was similar enough from afar to fool any crowds that witnessed the execution.

Malcolm closed the viewing slot. "Let us return to my chambers. We are less likely to be overheard."

None of them spoke on the walk upstairs to Malcolm's suite. Tension radiated from Theo and Viv at his sides. As soon as Malcolm closed his drawing room door behind them, his sister spoke up.

"Well? Which one do you choose?"

"I thought we might discuss it first."

"What is there to discuss?" Viv crossed her arms and jutted out her hip as she glared at him. "You are the one who wants this. You can choose which of them deserves to die in the traitor's place."

"They are all due to be executed eventually..." Theo spoke up in Malcolm's defence but quieted as Viv turned her glare on him.

"You must stop referring to Luelle as a traitor, otherwise all of this will be pointless." Malcolm frowned.

Viv's glare evolved into a scowl.

Malcolm ignored it and continued. "If all of them face execution, I think the only factor to consider is appearance. Whoever we choose must look similar enough to Luelle that no one notices the differences. The first and last were the closest matches, but we would have to fix the first inmate's hair if we chose her. Luelle has the Veseile streak."

"Even then, the differences are recognisable if anyone takes a closer look." Theo wandered across the room to an armchair and sat down.

Malcolm followed, hearing Viv move behind them. "Only if someone knows her well. Philip reports that

Luelle was not well-liked when she worked here. And she has been away for several weeks, now. I would be surprised if the people that knew her noticed the small differences. Besides, we can keep people at a distance before the execution and I can burn the body to prevent anyone from getting a proper look afterwards." He flopped onto a sofa, Viv sitting with more grace on the cushions beside him.

"What if anyone on your father's old council calls for an official trial?" Theo asked.

"That is partly why I made Viv my Chief Justiciar when choosing my new council," Malcolm explained. "Father made us all study the law so she knows it as well as anyone else in the palace, but it also means she can ensure we avoid a trial altogether."

"I can overrule council requests, whether they come from current or previous members." Viv nodded. "Ideally, though, we would need a witness to confirm the criminal's identity."

"What about Theo?" Malcolm suggested.

"I think we would be better off using Clarisse or Benjamin."

He frowned at Viv. Of course, he now knew Luelle hadn't been working with his father's old guards, that she'd deceived them as much as anyone else in the castle, but Malcolm had struggled to forgive them for letting her into his father's room on the night of his death. Neither Clarisse nor Benjamin had received an official pardon for their actions. Both were under house arrest in the city, awaiting news of their fate from Malcolm's council.

"You could make a deal with them," Viv suggested. "They agree to publicly confirm the traitor's identity at the execution and you grant them an honourable discharge and a peaceful retirement. They would not retain their previous positions in the castle, but it is still more than they might expect, and likely more than enough to secure their continued loyalty."

He knew it was a sensible suggestion but something inside Malcolm still cringed away from the bargain.

"I need time to consider."

"You must decide by this evening. If we are to make an agreement with them, it must happen soon. The execution should go ahead within days if you hope to avoid making the city's crowds too restless. The tourists will not leave until they have seen it."

"Fine, I will have an answer for you by this afternoon."

"Pick the criminal by then, too. We can gather the council and plan a date."

Malcolm nodded.

"When is the real traitor leaving?"

He glared at his sister.

"Sorry." She rolled her eyes, correcting herself. "When is Luelle leaving?"

"This evening. Leena is taking her after sunset. They will travel with Graman and a handful of soldiers."

"Will a handful be enough?" Viv's gaze flickered between Malcolm and Theo.

"Leena is one of our best fighters, not to mention likely the sharpest mind in the castle," Theo confirmed. "She is more than capable of keeping Luelle in line."

"She is not Veseile, though."

"I am sending Leena with a reserve of shadowbell essence. If Luelle becomes a threat at any point, Leena can neutralise her and bring her back unconscious,"

Malcolm said. Yesterday's schedule had been too busy for him to work on a new method of ingesting shadowbell, but Leena could improvise. In a worst case scenario, a blow to the head would knock Luelle out just as easily.

"I think Mei should go, too."

Malcolm raised his eyebrows at Viv. Mei was a member of his sister's personal guard and one of her closest friends. "Why?"

"She is Veseile. She can access the Power."

He frowned at her. "Have you been teaching her? She was not on the list of soldiers we agreed upon for initial training." A thread of suspicion wormed its way into his mind. Although they were family, Viv was his only true rival to the throne. Deep down, he had always wondered if she was better-suited for it, but that did not change the fact that he was the king. Was she training soldiers in secret in case she ever decided to make a play for the crown?

No, she would not tell Malcolm about the soldiers if that was the case. He shrugged off the toxic thought, putting it down to the lingering effects of last night's alcohol and the lack of sleep he had been getting recently.

"No." Viv returned his frown. "Not formally, but I had a suspicion since you revealed that all Veseile might be able to access it. She used to meditate with me, growing up, so I made her try to use it. Besides, even with shadowbell essence, we should send a Veseile that can use the Power with Leena. If the thief is the only person with it at her disposal, Leena, Graman, and the other soldiers will be at a disadvantage, particularly if Leena cannot get close enough to use weapons. Mei can help to keep the traitor in check."

"Stop calling her a traitor!" Malcolm snapped, pushing himself upright to better scowl at his sister.

"Mei is a good fighter, too, even without the Power." Theo chimed in before another argument could ensue, nodding his respect to Viv. "Her brother also works in the guard. He is a skilled scout and tracker."

"Fine." Malcolm rubbed at his temples but did not manage to scrub away the ache lingering there. "Bring Mei and her brother to me after this so we can brief them. I shall find Leena and we can update her on the new additions."

"I will fetch them now." Viv stood and brushed off her skirts. "Choose your criminal and think about Clarisse and Benjamin," she instructed.

Theo exited with Viv, leaving Malcolm alone to brood over his problems. He ignored them all for now, thinking instead about his father and holding the amulet pendant around his neck, which he had not removed since returning to Cerulya.

7

SLEEP eluded Luelle, even after Malcolm left her room on the night of the coronation. Music from the celebrations continued until the sun rose. She spent most of the night and the following morning contemplating their conversation.

He was offering her the opportunity to be valuable, which was what she wanted, but it all felt too easy. Should she have pushed for something more? Working for him would be signing herself away to a life of paranoia. Unless she found a way to even the stakes between them, Malcolm could always hold the threat of punishment and execution over her head.

She practised using the Power until she collapsed into her bed, sweaty and exhausted. When she next awoke, it was to the sound of rummaging.

Luelle bolted upright, bleary eyed, heart hammering. Instinctively, she seized control of the Power inside her chest, readying to strike.

"Good, you are awake."

Luelle managed to release her grip on the Power

moments before flinging the stranger through her window. Chest heaving, she took deep, steadying breaths until the burning heat beneath her skin settled. She knew the slender, dark-skinned Colleile tugging clothes out of her wardrobe and tossing them into a pile on the bed atop Luelle's feet.

"I remember you." She clawed through her memory for the Colleile's name.

The stranger turned and raised an eyebrow.

"Leela?"

"Leena." Annoyance laced her tone.

"Oh, sorry. What are you doing in my room?" Luelle sat up, throwing back her covers.

"Packing. We leave tonight."

"You're coming to the cavern?" She tried not to let her disappointment show.

Leena had made her distaste for Luelle very clear, from the first time she'd threatened her in the Great Forest to almost slicing her neck open on the Caeleste Peaks and ignoring Luelle for most of the journey back to Cerulya.

"Someone needs to keep you in check." Leena exposed the elongated canines that betrayed her Colleile heritage with a smile that felt more threatening than friendly.

"I thought we were leaving at nightfall."

"We are."

"It won't take all afternoon to pack for me." Luelle gestured to the clothes on the bed. "I don't own anything else."

"Technically, you do not own these, either." Leena placed a hand on her hip. "As far as I am aware, your lodgings and everything within them are a current loan from the king."

Luelle scowled. Leena turned away and continued talking before she could think of a witty response.

"I am not simply here to help you pack. A large part of Malcolm's plan relies on you not being recognised, so I am here to help with that." She ambled to Luelle's bathing room.

When she didn't reemerge, Luelle sighed and got out of bed to follow her. A foul smell greeted her in the doorway. Recoiling, Luelle covered her nose before pressing on. Inside the bathing room, Leena was stirring something in a small wooden bowl.

"What is that?"

"Dye. As I said, we cannot risk anyone recognising you as we leave. We need to cover your Veseile streak."

"What's it made of?" Luelle stepped closer and peered inside the bowl, finding a red-brown sludge with suspicious clumps distributed throughout.

"Flowers, plants. All natural stuff."

"Natural stuff?"

"Primarily pig kidney and liver."

Luelle's eyes widened. Clamping her hand tighter over her nose, she fought the urge to retch. "I am not putting that in my hair."

Leena levelled her with a stern glare. "You will put it on today and once a week from here on out or I will do it for you. It will continue until we return and Malcolm decides whether it is safe for you to expose your regular hair. I will also be cutting your hair, though I will allow you to keep more than me." She ran a hand over her near-bald scalp and grinned.

Luelle failed to see the humour in the situation.

"The execution is due in a few days. It remains an

option for you if you will not comply with my instructions." Leena shrugged when Luelle did not reply.

Luelle took a deep, calming breath, feeling her scowl return. "Malcolm has already threatened me. You do not need to continue it."

Leena's stirring stalled. "Do not call him Malcolm. He is your king, not some casual friend or back alley drinking companion."

Luelle briefly considered how dire the fallout might be if she used the Power to dump the malodorous dye on Leena's head.

"*His Majesty*," she laced her voice with sarcasm, "has already thoroughly threatened me. I get the message. I'll dye my hair, but can I do it with a colour that doesn't require internal organs?"

"This is easiest. You already have a hint of red. It will look the most natural and will require less paste to blend." Leena returned to stirring.

Luelle tilted her head back, suppressing a groan of frustration. She didn't continue pushing her luck. If she was to travel with Leena, she should probably try to lessen the hostility between them. Otherwise, it would be a long two weeks.

"Fine. Where shall I sit?"

Leena's brow furrowed. "I will not be putting it on you unless I have to. I do not want it on my hands. Start with your unpigmented hair and work any remaining dye into the rest. Wash it off your skin as soon as possible, but leave it in your hair until I return. I have other things to see to before we leave. It should give the dye enough time to work. Oh, and keep it off your bed sheets and clothes." She deposited the bowl in Luelle's hands and strode past her to exit the bathing room.

"Wait." Luelle followed her out, bowl in hand. "I have questions about this trip. Malc—I mean, the king left before I could ask everything last night."

Leena turned back and sighed. "What questions?"

"Who else is coming?"

"Graman and some soldiers."

"Alright. I don't know if the king told you but I have to be back here in two weeks. How long will it take to travel to the cavern and back?"

"Of course he told me. Ensuring you return is part of the reason I will be coming." Leena glowered at her. "We will travel in a carriage for the majority of the journey, picking up fresh horses at designated stops. You do not need to know the specific route we will take. However, I estimate it will take around five days to reach the cavern and the same on the return journey, giving us approximately four days to gather what Graman seeks at the site."

"Alright."

"Anything else?" Sarcasm laced her tone, turning the innocent offer for information into something more scornful.

"How different are you going to make me look?"

Leena ran an appraising eye over Luelle. "As different as the king needs you to be. Enough that anyone who might accidentally glimpse you as we leave the castle will not realise who you are. I doubt anyone will see us leave but we cannot take the risk. When I am not here, or unless the king says otherwise, you will stay in this room."

Luelle bit back her objections, knowing she would only

face further threats. The question that emerged from her mouth shocked her as much as it surprised Leena.

"Why do you hate me?"

Leena frowned. "Is that a trick question?"

Luelle shook her head.

Leena stared at her for a heartbeat before listing the reasons. "You have stolen from and harmed one of my closest friends and my king. You forced his family to live a lie in their own home to cover his tracks while he retrieved what you stole. You denied him a peaceful handover of power and made him question his moral code. You threatened the stability of the entire realm, risking our future peace and putting thousands of lives in mortal danger. Do you truly expect me to like you after that?"

"I never harmed him," Luelle replied, lamely, hoping Leena didn't know about the punch she'd landed on Malcolm's face, "and he wasn't the king at that point."

"But he was still my friend, and you risked the well-being of every person in this realm with your careless scheme. You did not consider the real implications of such a change."

The words were a sharp knife in Luelle's heart. She understood what it was to care so much for a friend that their grievances became her own. For most of her life, she'd believed her friends held that same passionate loyalty toward her. Now, she was aware of the lie she'd been living. Her friends did not care for her in the same way Malcolm's cared for him. Jealousy, hot and bitter, flushed through her.

Leena continued.

"That time was one of the toughest periods in the

king's life, one in which he had to juggle the grief of losing his father and the joy of his new title. Yet, thanks to you, he spent it traipsing across the country, unsure if he would even survive to wear his crown."

Luelle pondered Leena's fury as she wondered if the weeks after his father's death could ever have been a joyous period in Malcolm's life. Had she truly snatched that from him, or was Leena in denial?

"Malcolm insists you are to help us," Leena said, regaining her composure. "I will tolerate you in his court for his sake, but your soul would have to belong to Mortus before I could trust you."

Luelle said nothing.

"Is that everything?" Leena demanded again, her sarcasm replaced with curt anger.

She nodded and watched her new nursemaid leave the room.

When she was alone again, Luelle glared at the bowl of red dye, directing her own fury and frustration towards the paste. If she threw it out of her window, Leena would only return with more or shave her head.

She sighed and returned to her bathing room. At least the dye offered an opportunity to try something new with the Power—applying it to her hair without staining her hands in the process.

8

LEENA and Viv arranged Malcolm's meeting with Benjamin and Clarisse, deciding to host it at Leena's family home, a manor in the city's outskirts, to reduce the risk of anyone in the still-crowded castle overhearing Malcolm's proposition.

Malcolm savoured the tea that Adom, Leena's father, had prepared for him, overlooking the vibrant garden from his seat in the sunroom. Beyond the flowers, he had a clear view of the Kendra River winding through the city, snaking a path to the sparkling sea. Sweet, citrus flavours suffused his taste buds with each sip of tea, calming his racing thoughts. Viv and Theo sat in the room with him, speaking with Adom and Osei, Leena's mother. Elsewhere in their home, Clarisse and Benjamin awaited, guarded by Theo's soldiers to ensure they remained in the room without attempting anything suspicious.

Malcolm's knee bounced as he predicted the many different ways the upcoming conversation might play out. Clarisse and Benjamin could reject his request. They

the burning fire it had been before his journey with Luelle. None of the problems that had once concerned him seemed as important as the threat of Vesanya and the chaos that would erupt when people learned about the changes to the Power. Instead, Malcolm felt a stab of pity and a sense of overwhelming sorrow when he looked at Clarisse and Benjamin. Memories of his father emerged at the sight of them, memories of his childhood growing up under the watchful eyes of the two guards who now sat before him. Clarisse had always turned a blind eye to the mischief Malcolm, Leena, and Theo got into, while Benjamin had kept a watchful gaze over Malcolm's interactions with other noble children, sneaking him sweet treats from the kitchens to soften the hardships of the alienation he experienced. He had never imagined they would end up in this situation.

"Clarisse, Benjamin. I trust you have both been well," he started, his voice emerging quieter than he'd intended.

They nodded but stayed silent, letting their king finish whatever he had to say before replying.

"I come to you today to propose a deal of sorts." He forced himself to make eye contact, to push away the negativity lingering around him like fog. How would his father handle this conversation? "Both of you dedicated your lives to serving my father, my entire family. I grew up knowing you, trusting you."

They shuffled in their seats at his words, gazes dropping from his once again, guilt washing over their expressions.

"I imagine you have heard about the truth of the incident that night in the castle. That the servant who deceived you was involved in an assassination attempt against my father," he reinforced the false story that was circulating. "That night disturbed the trust between you and I, but I am trying to find ways to rebuild the bridges that were burned. I am here today seeking your assistance in carrying out justice for my father. The events surrounding that night are complex and not appropriate to discuss here, but life as we know it will soon change, as a result. The servant who tricked us on the eve of my return from Stodor is heavily involved in these changes. Unfortunately, her continued cooperation is vital for the overall good of the realm. Executing her could have devastating consequences, which I cannot allow to happen, but I am aware the public must observe justice for their previous king."

Clarisse and Benjamin looked up. Confusion and curiosity shone in their furrowed brows and twitching fingers.

"I will carry out an execution in the upcoming week. The public will believe the criminal is the traitor who was involved in the assassination attempt against my father. In reality, the traitor will be under my power, working toward the continued stability of the realm and the safety of my people. She will spend the rest of her life serving me and my reign. However, the execution must go ahead."

Briefly, Malcolm wondered how Luelle would react to those words. He could almost see the scorn on her face at the thought of serving him for the rest of their lives. Unlike everyone else in his life, he couldn't imagine her changing her attitude to him now he was king. His lips twitched with an inappropriate smile; he shoved thoughts of her out of his mind with a frown.

He took a deep breath, exchanging a glance with Viv, who nodded.

"During the execution, we will need people to confirm the identity of the criminal," she said. "People who witnessed her on the night of the attempted crime."

"I propose that both of you fill that role. In return, I will extend the offer of a peaceful retirement," Malcolm said. "You will receive an allowance to support you and your families until the end of your lives and an honourable discharge, living where Theo sees best fit to place you."

Eyes widened across the table. Silence descended. Malcolm waited, letting the guards process the offer. Several times, one of them would open their mouth only to close it abruptly. Nerves churned in his stomach.

"You may ask questions," he permitted.

Clarisse was the first to speak.

"Your Majesty, thank you for trusting us with this," she started, her voice slow and hesitating. She faltered, glancing to Benjamin.

"Continue, Clarisse," Malcolm instructed. "I will forgive any insolence, you may be frank."

Her throat shifted as she swallowed. "I only wish to ask if Your Majesty is certain it is wise to keep this criminal alive when she was involved in an assassination plot against King Alaric—Mortus protect his soul."

Malcolm tilted his head, conceding the point.

"I understand your concern, particularly given her history, but I assure you I have the situation under control. I intend to keep my enemies close. My plans for her will eliminate the risk of a repeat incident."

"What exactly would be required of us, Your Majesty?" Benjamin asked.

Viv spoke up. "I will be leading the execution process.

I will work with you on the days leading up to the event to ensure everything runs smoothly. All you must do is verbally confirm that the criminal at the execution is who I say she is. Confirm she is the servant who entered our father's chambers that evening."

Benjamin's face paled but he nodded. "And would we be condemning an innocent person, Your Highness?" he asked Viv.

"No," Malcolm interjected. "The replacement will be another criminal facing capital punishment. Their death would merely be brought forward. The public should not realise the difference. Neither should anyone from the castle, if Belle was as isolated as Philip claimed." He made sure to use Luelle's false name, hoping the emphasis he placed on it was not noticeable.

"She kept to herself, Your Majesty. I believe you would have no problems with that," Clarisse said.

"Your Majesty, will there be a court martial regarding our involvement in that night?" Benjamin asked.

Malcolm shook his head. He had considered it, but after learning Luelle had acted alone, he understood he was simply lashing out. Clarisse and Benjamin had been manipulated, just as he had. Malcolm's father had been a trusting man—perhaps too trusting, believing he owed people his faith and confidence until they gave him a reason to rescind it. After seeing the harm such an attitude could cause, Malcolm was more inclined to withhold his trust and respect until people earned it, as Luelle was in the process of doing. If she continued helping him, as she claimed she would, perhaps she could have a place in his kingdom and his life.

His eyes widened at the unbidden thought of them

living in harmony alongside one another. He did not want Luelle to be part of his life. He was only keeping her alive to protect his people. He cleared his throat and spoke to distract himself.

"Neither Viv nor I believe it is necessary. The criminal confessed privately to acting alone, without the assistance of anyone else in the castle," he said.

"I am honoured that you trust that claim, Your Majesty." Benjamin's brow furrowed. "Although, if you can forgive my impertinence, while Clarisse and I were not working with her, there are hundreds of others who could have been vulnerable to her manipulations during the course of her employment."

"That is something we have considered." Malcolm nodded. "We will be tightening security measures within the castle and taking steps to prevent another incident. I will not share the details, but we have ways to identify anyone who was working with her," he lied through his teeth. His tenuous trust in Luelle's word was the only proof he had that she'd worked alone, but Benjamin and Clarisse did not appear to suspect it.

Benjamin's fingers twitched and spoke again, glancing at Clarisse. "Your Majesty, I do not wish to speak for Clarisse, but," he paused, "of course I wish to assist you in any way possible. My guilt over that night has haunted me ever since—" his voice broke, gaze dropping to the table as he collected himself. "I would gladly speak for you at the execution you have planned and put my faith in you that it is the best thing for the realm. I am humbled that you would see fit to allow us our freedom and an honourable retirement. Although you may have forgiven us for our part in that night, I am certain there are many who have not."

"You were manipulated just as the rest of us were." Malcolm frowned.

"Even so, Your Majesty. I believe that our presence in the city could lead to disruptions, which would threaten the stability of your rule in Cerulya and jeopardize the peace of the retirement you intend for us."

"In which case, Benjamin, I feel it may present an excellent opportunity to discover the many sights of Arazia beyond Cerulya's gates. Theo, will you be able to take steps to ensure the safety of Clarisse and Benjamin far from the castle?"

Theo stepped forward. "Of course, Your Majesty." He turned to Clarisse and Benjamin. "We can set up lodgings for you in another city of His Majesty's choice and send your regular allowance to this new address. Anyone who attempts to find you for ill purposes or to interfere with His Majesty's decision would face appropriate consequences. I can enforce measures to protect you both if you believe you would become targets."

"Thank you, Theo." Malcolm turned back to Benjamin and Clarisse. "Of course, your families would also be permitted to accompany you wherever you would retire and I would fund the cost of your move. I feel it is unnecessary to inform you how your future may look if you decline this offer but, regardless, I will give you the rest of the day to make your decision," he said.

The two older guards looked at one another, a silent conversation passing with a short glance. When they turned back to face Malcolm and Viv, they nodded.

"We accept, Your Majesty. We will do all we can to atone for our part in the attempt against King Alaric's life," Clarisse said.

"As I said, I have already forgiven you both for that." He swallowed, glancing at Viv, knowing what must come next. "I cannot stress the importance of your roles enough in keeping this deception private. You will be implicit in this plot, so revealing it would only invite your own swift demise."

They each nodded, faces sombre.

Malcolm took a deep breath and returned the gesture. "Good. Theo will remain here today to discuss the finer details of your retirement. Then, you will return to the castle and meet with Princess Vivyenne to discuss your role in the upcoming execution. You may speak of this to no one but myself, Princess Vivyenne, and Theodas. I do not need to remind you of the consequences if you do."

Malcolm stood from the table once he finished talking. Chair legs scooted across the floor as Clarisse and Benjamin rushed to stand for his exit. He nodded a farewell to the two guards and turned, hearing Viv follow him from the room and leaving Theo behind to finalise their plans.

9

Travelling to the Caeleste Peaks as a prisoner turned out to be considerably more pleasant than it had been as a free woman. Instead of walking until her feet blistered each day, constantly alert for threats, Luelle lounged in one of the two comfortable carriages, fit with padded seats and windows to gaze out at the passing scenery. Warm, cosy rooms in inns replaced the beds of leaves and moss she'd slept on weeks earlier. Each evening brought hot, nourishing food—richly spiced stews or freshly baked rolls stuffed with thick slices of cheese and smoked meats. Measly handfuls of nuts and berries were a distant memory.

Even her company was less surly. During the day, Graman shared her carriage. Though he rarely initiated conversation, it was easy enough to prompt him into sharing his knowledge of the passing sights. His rambling chatter was a pleasant contrast to the silence Luelle had endured in the castle. She listened with rapt attention, soaking in every story the large Adeile spun.

Envy of Malcolm's childhood blossomed anew as

Graman bestowed tales of history, agriculture, architecture, and more. Receiving a formal education had been impossible for Luelle. Schools were costly and required staying in one place for years at a time, which was a luxury she had not had. Zeke had taught her to read and write, but his efforts to continue her schooling focused on practical skills. It fostered in her an aching hunger for knowledge that she'd never quite been able to satisfy, even after devouring every piece of written work she could find. History and philosophy were subjects Zeke had only cared about in relation to his goals and his pursuit of power, so she took advantage of Graman's enthusiasm for teaching and debate as they travelled.

As Malcolm had promised, a party of guards escorted Luelle, riding outside the carriage on horseback; alongside Leena, there were four day guards, two armed drivers, and two additional soldiers who slept in the supply wagon during the day and kept watch over them all at night to prevent any attempt at escape. Part of her was flattered that Malcolm thought so many soldiers were necessary to keep her from fleeing; another part of her was certain she could use the Power to slip away from them if she truly wished to.

Whenever they stopped for a break or to rest for the night, Graman joined the soldiers' ranks with ease, leaving Luelle with no company. She was not permitted to stray out of sight, even to relieve her bladder, which she had to do in the company of Leena or another female soldier. She watched and listened to the soldiers' conversations as surreptitiously as she could manage, observing the personalities and opinions of the people she was travelling with and collecting snippets of information about their backgrounds.

Leena and Graman were familiar enough but Luelle did not recognise the other eight guards. She rarely saw the two who slept through the day and guarded the wagons at night, and never for long when she did catch a glimpse of them. The drivers were both human and often busied themselves with the horses and tack. The day soldiers were the chattiest of the lot. Two were human. Although their personalities were stark opposites of one another, both treated Luelle with open suspicion bordering on aggression. The younger was a man named Rob, with rosy cheeks and a tendency to fill every quiet second with conversation, radiating energy wherever he walked. The other was an older woman named Pat, quiet and brooding, hair shot through with grey and shoulders ever-tense, as if she persistently anticipated trouble.

The final two guards captured Luelle's interest the most. They shared enough traits that Luelle was certain they must be relatives. Tao often disappeared ahead of the party as they rose and began their travels each morning. He returned to meet them wherever they stopped for lunch to deliver Leena a report from his scouting. Mei was the final guard. Like the human day guards, she spent her time on horseback, keeping close to the carriage as they travelled.

Both Mei and Tao had a streak of white through their dark hair, indicating Veseile heritage. They must have access to the Power, whether they knew it yet or not. Both shared the same high cheekbones and sharp jaw, although the left side of Mei's face was disfigured by a smattering of scars, cutting from her eyebrow down, pulling at the corner of one eye. None of the other soldiers acknowledged it.

More curious than the mysterious injury was the

obscene amount of time Mei spent blatantly staring at Luelle. Luelle met her unblinking gaze the first few times, receiving a small, knowing smile in return—not that she could decipher what that meant. After the first day, Luelle stopped bothering to meet Mei's stare, keeping her eyes fixed on her food and the strangers who walked past their camps or surrounded them at each inn.

On their third day travelling together, Luelle was jolted from a doze by a large hand on her shoulder. As she jerked awake, she unconsciously gripped the Power in her chest. It flared as she readied to use it, blinking her vision clear.

"We have arrived at tonight's lodgings," Graman said to her, oblivious to the danger he'd almost faced by waking his sleeping companion.

Memories of the destruction she'd caused at Tolhurst, weeks ago, flashed in her mind: dust hanging in the air, choking her with each breath; remnants of the nearest buildings lying in pieces around her; a sharp ringing in her ears. That violent potential could've snatched Graman's very life away before Luelle had the chance to think twice.

She swallowed, attempting to smother the warmth in her chest.

Outside the carriage's open door, Luelle found Mei's familiar scarred stare, her eyes such a rich brown they were almost red in the setting sun. Mei's hand rested on her sword's hilt, mouth set into a harsh line. Her posture relaxed as Luelle released her grip on the Power. Did she know? Had Malcolm already begun telling all of his soldiers about the change? Why would Mei rely on a physical weapon, if so? Even the Veseile guards who had barged into Luelle's room, back at the castle, had relied on their swords, only using the Power to create a barrier between themselves and Luelle.

Luelle, like Graman, was unarmed. Did Malcolm still not understand how hard she had been working to gain control of the Power? He had seen her lift his crown, but that was nothing compared to the full extent of her abilities. Physical weapons were worthless to her, as they should be to Mei and the other Veseile soldiers if they were truly knowledgeable about their new skills.

They were the weapon.

Luelle shook the thoughts away. She followed Graman from the carriage and into the inn they were staying at tonight, leaving Mei to trail them, as usual. Mei grew tense at every inn, muscles stiff as she regarded the crowds, warning anyone from getting too close with a vicious glower.

Leena awaited them inside the building's entryway. Warmth flooded Luelle as she stepped inside, a pleasant contrast to the chill outside. Conversation and the scent of food and ale drifted from further down the hallway. A passing glance revealed Tao, already seated in the inn's dining room with a stern expression. Luelle did not get a chance to investigate the source of the delicious smells before Leena spoke and pressed a bag of supplies into her arms.

"Follow me."

With a final lingering look down the hallway, Luelle complied, swinging the bag over her shoulder. Leena led her upstairs to the small room she would sleep alone in. As far as Luelle was aware, from her limited perspective, Mei and Leena shared a room while Tao and Graman took a third. Rob and Pat left each inn after they ate in the evenings and were always ready and waiting with the carriages in the morning, leaving Luelle to suspect they simply slept in the carriages or stables to watch over the vehicles.

Like the lodgings in each previous inn, Luelle's room was simple, containing a narrow bed and worn, scratched furniture that was always bolted to the floor. In the first inn, Luelle had tested the windows, only to find the shutters were also bolted closed. She hadn't bothered trying in subsequent inns, realising Tao's early arrival must necessitate such changes to hinder any escape attempts. Her door never had a handle from the inside, forcing her to knock for assistance if she needed anything. Each night, she would hear the quiet murmuring of the night soldiers, who woke in time to guard her as the others slept.

Luelle wandered into the room and threw her bag on the bed. She'd learnt from the first night that Leena expected her to attempt an escape if she didn't show immediate signs of settling into her new, temporary prison. She perched on the bed, smoothing her hand over the covers, wriggling to test the solidity of the lumps in the mattress.

Leena was staring at the bed, a wrinkle in her nose. "I cannot wait to return to the palace. This is the last inn we will stay at until our journey home and even this is not worth the coin I paid for it."

"It's better than sleeping on the floor."

A smile toyed at the corners of Leena's pursed mouth, threatening to break the tense atmosphere. She turned her gaze out the window, overlooking the hills beyond the road.

"I can hardly believe Malcolm slept in such conditions for almost two weeks."

"He made his distaste of the situation well known at every opportunity."

Leena snorted. "I can imagine. What did you eat? He and I have had little time to discuss the details of your journey."

Luelle shrugged, surprised to find herself in conversation with someone she believed to hate her. "Whatever I could find while foraging. I fished when I could but it didn't always yield."

Leena opened her mouth to reply, but closed it again.

"What?"

"I am surprised you went to so much effort to keep the king alive. The gods know you did not care to make the same effort for the previous one."

"That's not fair." Luelle frowned. She had cared for Alaric until the final moment. "King Malcolm insisted on following me. It was the least I could do."

"Even so."

"Is this your way of saying thank you?"

Leena's gaze hardened. "No. I hardly think you deserve thanks for serving your king and taking a break from committing treason."

"He was only the crown prince at that point."

The corners of Leena's lips twitched, though Luelle couldn't tell if it due to was anger or humour.

"Besides, his help foraging resulted in disaster, so it was best left to me." She left the vague phrasing hanging, hoping curiosity might spur Leena into more conversation.

"Disaster?"

"Did he not tell you he accidentally ate hallucinogenic mushrooms after attempting to forage while I was asleep?" Luelle grinned at the memory.

Leena's eyes widened. "He did not."

"He did. Ask him about it when we return. He spent most of the morning speaking with insects."

A loud, abrupt laugh burst from Leena. Her hand rose to cover her smile. "I cannot believe it." She shook her head. "I understand now how even this inn seems luxurious compared to your last journey, I suppose."

Luelle smiled. "Bathing in rivers was the real killer. I will never be ungrateful for a heated bath."

"Speaking of baths, I will fetch a guard so you can freshen up before we eat," Leena said, gesturing to the small attached bathing room. Like her one in the castle, it had no door.

"I will wait until after, if that's alright."

Leena nodded, but lingered.

"We will likely arrive at the Peaks tomorrow. What should we expect when we do?" she asked, all traces of humour and good nature fading as the conversation became as serious as usual.

Luelle's brow furrowed. "I don't know. Zeke fled as we did when Vesanya appeared, and Mal—the king said there was no sight of her or Zeke and his crew."

Leena eyed her.

"You don't trust me," Luelle said.

Leena straightened. "I do not hate you, as you accused me of in Cerulya, but I cannot say I like you, either. The king believes you may be able to help us and appears to tolerate you, so I will not be hostile to you, for his sake. However, trust is a quality that must be earned and you have not yet given me reason to trust you."

"I haven't tried to escape on this journey," Luelle pointed out. "And, as you have said, I made an effort to protect Malcolm when I travelled with him."

Leena placed a hand on her hip, jutting her weight to the side as she contemplated that, choosing to ignore Luelle's use of Malcolm's name instead of his title. "True, but we are returning to the last known location of your friends. Logic would suggest this is what you have been hoping and waiting for."

"I hardly think I am able to call them friends any more."

Leena's expression softened. "Malcolm told me about what happened when they revealed your heritage."

Luelle's guard shot up, her voice hardening. "That information was not his to tell."

"While you are his captive, it is. Until the day he chooses to free you or clear your charges, you have no secrets."

Luelle scowled. "I am working with you all, offering everything I have to help Malcolm maintain peace in the realm. How am I supposed to earn your trust if you will never see me as more than a prisoner, despite everything I am doing for Arazia?"

Leena shrugged. "You want me to take the word of a traitor that they will not betray us again? I told you in Cerulya you will belong to Mortus before I can fully trust your word."

"I feared as much."

A small smirk curved Leena's lip and she turned away, briskly leaving the room.

Despite her words, fresh determination bloomed within

Luelle as her guards escorted her downstairs into the inn's busy dining hall.

10

A sheen of sweat coated Malcolm's forehead as he steeled himself outside the wooden door to the castle's mortuary. Corpses awaited him inside, carried back from the Caeleste Peaks. On his arrival home, he'd ordered the bodies sent straight here for the coroner to examine and discover precisely what had happened to the poor souls. Perhaps that understanding would give him an advantage when he eventually had to deal with Vesanya.

Although that was enough to make his skin crawl, it was not the main reason for Malcolm's trepidation. More distressing was the fact that this was the same room in which his father's body had lain and been prepared for burial shortly after Malcolm's return to the capital.

He had visited his father's body only once. The body he'd observed lying on the coroner's table had contained nothing of his father. All that had remained was a frail, empty shell of a human, skin dull and wrinkled, the scent of death a nauseating perfume that lingered underneath the pungent herbs that the coroner burned.

During that visit, Malcolm had observed the coroner

working from across the room. Despite feeling as though he stood in place for hours, he had left after only a few minutes, as unsatisfied as he'd been when he had entered the mortuary.

His father could not give him answers any more.

Malcolm would never know if his father might have approved the choices he'd made to retrieve the Power, whether he had done the right thing by following Luelle to the end of her journey rather than forcing her back to the castle to torture or kill her in the hopes of retrieving his stolen birthright. Now he could only live with the consequences of that decision and continue trying to do the right thing for his people.

Despite that conviction, doubt invaded every corner of his mind, staining each thought. Was he right to allow Luelle to live, killing another person in her place? No matter how awful the crimes of the other prisoners in the castle dungeons, did any of them deserve to die in the name of someone else's misdeeds, in the name of a lie, even if they were destined for the gallows at a later date?

Leena, Graman, and Luelle had left the castle two nights ago. Malcolm felt their absence every few hours, thoughts returning to one or the others of the trio and how they might fare on their trip.

Meeting with Clarisse and Benjamin, as well as accepting the attention of any advisers or nobles that sought him out, had kept Malcolm distracted enough to avoid his misery during the day. Even when his schedule lulled, his mother and siblings filled his time, sharing private grief for King Alaric and enjoying respite from the visitors that lingered in the castle.

However, Malcolm had no company through the quiet,

torturous nights. Every time the moon rose, he lay awake in his room, overthinking the decisions he had made that day, pouring over the ways the upcoming consequences of his actions could play out and the alternative decisions that may have been better for this realm.

When he did manage to rest, Vesanya haunted his dreams, even though she hadn't shown her face since that destructive afternoon in the cavern.

What if she never did?

The entire point of keeping Luelle alive was to increase his chances of learning the truth about the gods and prepare a defence against any threat they might pose. But, what if Vesanya never appeared again?

Luelle had committed treason, stolen from his father whilst he lay on his deathbed, led Malcolm into danger, and given an entire race free reign of the Power, even if the majority of them remained oblivious to it. Once the changes to the Power became public knowledge, the risk of civil war increased, as well as violent acts by Veseile extremists, particularly against humans. Luelle's actions could lead to the destruction of Arazia. Justice called for her punishment, for her death, but if keeping her alive could help Malcolm prevent further loss at the hands of Vesanya, he was duty-bound to guard Luelle's life with his own.

The dilemma was a vicious cycle that had led him here, to where he stood outside the closed door of the mortuary, stiff with fear of the memories he would face inside: his father's body, lying pale and still on one of those tables and Vesanya sucking the life from his people while he cowered and fled instead of fighting for them.

His discomfort was necessary.

Seeing the corpses and learning anything the coroners had discovered would provide a visceral reminder of the threat Vesanya posed and offer reassurance that Malcolm was doing the right thing. Besides, it was more productive than restlessly tossing and turning in bed, as he'd been doing for hours before giving up and forcing himself here.

Steeling himself with a deep breath, he lifted his fist and knocked on the door. The metal handle was cool in his clammy hand. The door's hinges squeaked as he nudged it open, shoulders aching with tension.

Cool air washed over Malcolm as he stepped inside, bathing him in a musty, acrid scent underlined by something uncomfortably and unexpectedly sweet that would likely haunt his memories for days. He closed the door behind him.

Several tables lined the back of the room, each topped with a covered body. In the centre of the room stood another long table hosting an uncovered corpse. Looming over it was a human dressed in dark clothing and a black apron. Umber hair, shot through with grey, was pulled back into a tight knot at the man's nape. He looked up. His frown vanished when he recognised who stood in his doorway. Stepping back from the body atop the table with a sharp examination tool in each hand, he swept into a bow.

"Please, Frederick, there is no need for such formalities in this setting." Malcolm waved a hand, too weary to mask his discomfort. This visit was hard enough without the constant reminder of his importance. He kept his gaze on the coroner, avoiding the withered body on the table where his father had once lain. Sweat prickled his back.

Frederick straightened, adjusting his apron as he did.

Malcolm did not wish to learn the origins of the stains that decorated the leather.

"Forgive me, Your Majesty. I was not expecting visitors so late at night."

Malcolm offered a stiff smile. "I apologise. I could not find sleep. I was hoping to see if you had made any progress with the bodies I sent here last week."

Frederick gestured to the table. "Well, this is one of them. Of course, it is harder to examine bodies that have been dead for as long as these, but I must admit they have been quite fascinating." His bushy brows furrowed.

Malcolm closed the gap between himself and the table with several rigid steps, trying to shake off his anxiety as he moved.

The corpse was as withered as Malcolm remembered, skin leathery and tight against the skeleton beneath. Its mouth stretched open in an eternal scream of terror. A long incision ran down the centre of the body's torso, skin peeled back on either side to reveal the shrivelled organs within.

"How long would you say they have been dead?" Malcolm asked.

"From the state of the corpse, I would estimate years. However, if that was accurate, I would expect their stomach contents to look very different." Frederick glanced up from the body. "The organs are as dehydrated as I would expect, in line with the rest of the body, but I have found incredibly intact stomach contents. Take this one, for example." He gestured to the body between them. "His stomach contained undigested chunks of meat and fibres from vegetables that had not yet broken down, all appearing as fresh as if this man had eaten them a few hours before his death. Since removing them, they've decayed at a rate I would expect, but I cannot fathom what has preserved them so well, given the state of the rest of the body."

"What about the cause of death?" Malcolm pressed. Despite seeing the Eile in front of him die firsthand, he still had no idea what Vesanya had done to them. Their deaths were like no mortal end he had ever witnessed, even after watching his father use the Power to kill.

Frederick's frown deepened.

"It is hard to differentiate what damage is from decomposition and what may have been the cause of death. Some of the bodies have broken bones, but there are no consistent injuries or damages other than the state of decomposition. The corpses are very dehydrated, but I do not see how that is possible if they were simply found in a cave, as you said." Frederick cleared his throat, eyes widening as he realised the implication of his words. Hastily, he continued. "Not that I am doubting your word, Your Majesty. All I mean is that, usually, bodies would only end up in this state if they were left in very dry conditions, or perhaps retrieved from swamps or ice. Whichever of the three, the conditions must be extreme, not mild or damp, as is the atmosphere in most caves. I have observed bodies from the Northern Wastes similar to these, but even then, their stomach contents were nowhere near this well preserved. If I did not know better, Your Majesty, I might claim it was unnatural."

Bile rose in Malcolm's throat as memories of Vesanya's attack threatened to overwhelm him. He pushed them away, as he always did. Three deep breaths later, his panic was under control.

"How long would it take a body to reach this state?"

Frederick pursed his lips. "It depends on the environment and the process, but I would estimate at least a few months."

Or a few seconds at the hands of a God.

"Can I provide any other information that might help you learn more about their deaths?" Malcolm's voice rasped as he spoke. He cleared his throat.

Frederick shook his head. "Our facilities here are better than most, Your Majesty. Given time, I assure you I will learn more. My assistants help during the day, though I have been working overtime to sate my own curiosity."

"And from your findings so far, the deaths appear natural?"

Frederick shrugged. "I believe there was some form of struggle based on the pattern of damage, but the mummification makes it harder to provide a more accurate picture of their cause of death."

Malcolm nodded. "Thank you, Frederick. Please let me know as soon as you have any other findings or if you think of anything that might aid your research. Consider it a matter of urgency. Do not hesitate to contact me if there are any changes."

Frederick dipped into another bow as Malcolm left the stifling room.

Outside, the air in the hallway felt thin and overly warm. When the door clicked shut behind him, Malcolm leaned against it, taking a moment to catch his breath.

Seeing the corpse again had pushed away any doubt that he was doing the right thing. Anything that could cause such extensive harm to his people was a threat he could not ignore. Even if Vesanya was lying low now, she could return at any point. He had to learn how to get rid of her, even if he condemned his own soul in the process by lying to the people he was sworn to protect and perverting justice for his father.

Growing up, his father had emphasised the importance of Arazia's people; they must always come first. Malcolm would prioritise them over his guilt now.

11

LUELLE, Graman, and their squad of guards arrived at the base of the Caeleste Peaks late on their fourth day of travelling. Brisk temperatures accompanied the night's darkness, even under the shelter of the trees at the mountain's base. Wrapped in blankets, not even permitted to share her small tent for warmth, Luelle yearned for a campfire and a hot meal. No inns existed this close to the mountains. Regular patrons would never stray this far from the main roads further south.

Unlike her last journey, Luelle was exempt from watch duty throughout the night. She was no longer the protector, but the one under surveillance, guarded constantly. She would have basked in the luxury of having no responsibilities if she was able to get any rest, but with every passing second, her chest grew tighter. Laying on her thin bedroll, she closed her eyes and willed her body to relax. Sleep continued to evade her. Forced to pass the night awake, she picked at the skin around her fingernails, trying not to think about the mountains looming outside.

Pale sunlight filtered through the tent's fabric walls as morning crept around. Luelle felt no better rested than she'd been the previous evening. After an early breakfast of seeded bread, fruit, and hard cheese, their party split into two, leaving behind the wagon drivers and the night guardsmen; they remained at the base of the valley to maintain the small camp and mind the carriages, which were too wide and bulky for most of the mountain paths. To Luelle's dismay, Leena also chose to leave behind the horses, committing them to a long hike.

Their route to the cavern was not the same as the one Luelle and Malcolm had trekked a few weeks earlier, since they were approaching the mountain range from a more southerly angle. They walked the valley, finding a makeshift rope ferry system Malcolm's soldiers had constructed to cross the water until a proper bridge could be erected.

Leena and Mei exchanged pleasantries with the guards on duty. Despite feigning disinterest, Luelle listened intently in case they mentioned Vesanya. None of them did, too interested in discussing more mundane topics, like the festivities following the coronation.

On the other side of the Caeleste River, they followed a path carving a steep zigzag into the side of the mountain, rather than the shallow incline Luelle had led Malcolm up. After only half an hour of walking, Luelle's chest heaved and her thighs burned. Even her hours training in her room over the past two weeks was not enough to prepare her for the exertion of this steep march. Beads of sweat rolled down her temples, sticking her hair to the sides of her head as if she'd been caught in a rainstorm. Her shirt clung to her back, too warm despite the cooler temperatures as they ascended.

Bitterly, Luelle recognised there may be some truth to Zeke's accusation; her fatigue and struggle could be a sign of her humanity, a failing that none of her Eile companions suffered from. Each of them showed better resilience against the climb. Even Graman fared better. His muscular build, typical of the Adeile race, gave him strength and stamina despite his leisurely occupation as a scholar and tutor. Luelle's mood soured with the observation.

Only when they stopped for lunch, giving Luelle the chance to catch her breath, did she recall the dangers awaiting them at the end of their journey. She nibbled at a stick of dried meat, unable to stomach anything more.

Tao, as always, chose not to rest and eat with them. Instead, he took a small parcel of food and disappeared in the direction they'd been walking. Sharing his impatience to scout ahead, Leena soon packed up their food and ushered the small party onward.

Eventually, the odd unusually-shaped tree or boulder tugged at Luelle's memory, though she was too distracted by anxiety and paranoia to pay much attention to the familiar path she walked.

Ahead, as the sun was dipping in the sky, unfamiliar soldiers came into view, wearing the same uniforms as those escorting Luelle and Graman. They gathered in small clusters at the entrance to the cavern, milling in the remaining light, speaking in low voices. Tao stood among them. Smiles lit the soldiers' faces as they laughed and joked, oblivious to the danger of their location. One waved to Mei when they noticed the new group approaching.

Luelle's legs stopped working.

She fell behind Leena and Graman as her companions continued, walking faster with enthusiasm now their destination was in clear sight. Mei stepped around Luelle from behind, turning to frown at her and staying close enough to grab her.

Gloom awaited them in the tunnel ahead. Screams echoed in Luelle's memory. She could still feel Imbryl's iron grip around her waist, hear Malcolm's shout of pain as Freya stabbed his forearm and his choking breaths as Zeke rested his weight on the prince's throat.

Sweat slicked Luelle's palms anew. Blood rushed in her ears. She couldn't tear her gaze away from the entrance, let alone will her static limbs to carry her far away. Around her, the trees and mountains disappeared. All she could see was the tunnel leading to her demise, to the source of her nightmares.

"What are you doing?"

A voice, thick with suspicion, broke through the ringing in Luelle's ears. She opened her mouth to reply to Leena but no sound emerged.

A different voice sounded. "Go ahead. I can deal with her. We will meet you down there soon."

Luelle couldn't comprehend the murmured words until a scarred face blocked her line of sight to the tunnel.

"Slow your breathing," Mei instructed, her voice deep and quiet. "Do it with me."

Luelle fought to copy Mei's long, slow breaths, concentrating on the details of the guard's face to distract herself from the fear suffocating her: Mei's lips pursed as she exhaled; dark lashes framed her eyes; the round apples of her cheeks were stained rosy pink from their climb.

As she attempted to slow Luelle's breathing, Mei adjusted their positions, rotating them until Luelle's back was to the cavern's entrance. Though she knew it was still there, turning away from the tunnel lessened Luelle's shaking to a tremble and eased the nausea rolling in her gut.

"Was it was that bad down there?" Mei's stare roamed Luelle's face.

She stayed quiet. How much information had Malcolm entrusted to Mei? Did all of his Veseile guards and soldiers already know the truth?

As if she could read Luelle's mind, Mei answered.

"Princess Vivyenne explained some of the details of your recent past with me so I would be aware of the dangers to expect when accompanying you all here." She lowered her voice, glancing behind Luelle to where the other guards remained. "I know what you and the king claim to have seen down there."

Luelle managed a nod. "You don't believe it, though."

Mei shrugged, expression carefully neutral. "I have heard many soldiers make incomprehensible claims to cope with traumatic events. Though, I will admit it was intriguing to watch the king's reaction to Vesanya's statue in the Great Temple during his coronation."

Flinching at the mention of the God's name, Luelle latched onto Mei's other words for a distraction.

"His reaction?" She averted her eyes to the wide, open sky, following the flitting shapes of a flock of birds creating dark ribbons fluttering against distant clouds.

"It was similar to yours, I suppose. Though, he had to recover quickly with half of the capital watching his every move." Mei's unscarred eyebrow quirked.

Reassurance fluttered in Luelle's chest, hearing that Malcolm must be equally affected by the horrors they witnessed. Somehow, she felt stronger, knowing he shared the burden.

"I'm not sure if I can go back inside the cavern." The admission emerged as a whisper.

"Today will be the hardest, but if you do not conquer your fear, it will control you forever. I know how difficult it can be but it is possible to overcome it. For years, I was unable to step inside taverns."

"Why not?" Luelle choked the words out.

"My father was a slave to drink. My mother ran away when I was young, left my brother and I in his care. We eventually left him too, to train as soldiers, but not before he did this to me." Mei gestured to the scars on her face. "My drillmaster learned of my past when she heard I never accompanied my fellow cadets to inns or taverns when we were given time off from training. She was the one who forced me to face the fear tied into those memories. It is still hard going into an inn. It has been hard on this journey. I will never completely undo the damage, but every time I enter a tavern, I regain some more control over the memories."

Luelle took a deep breath, considering the way Mei's entire demeanour would change as they entered each inn on their journey. If she hadn't been observing her guards so closely, she might never have picked up on the reaction. Mei's response to her fear was subtle, even if only due to time's influence. In contrast, Luelle had frozen and fallen to pieces simply at the sight of the cavern's entrance. How could she ever conquer that?

"When did you last practise using the Power?" Mei

asked, interrupting Luelle's thoughts.

Luelle jolted with shock, prompting a cat-like grin to spread on Mei's face.

"Did I not say Princess Viv filled me in?"

"Can you…" Luelle trailed off. Malcolm must know more about how extensive the Power now was, but Luelle remained in the dark about it, as she did with most things these days.

Mei glanced over Luelle's shoulder again. Did that caution mean only some guards knew? Satisfied they were not being observed, Mei used the Power to pluck a small daisy from the ground. It drifted upwards into her awaiting palm. As she had when Malcolm used the Power in front of her a few evenings ago, Luelle felt a pulse of pressure, only this time it was accompanied by a brush of warmth, tinted with floral notes, sunlight over a field of flowers in the height of summer.

"I have been a member of Princess Vivyenne's personal guard for almost two decades and a soldier in the castle for long before that. When she was a girl, the princess talked me into meditating with her when she felt too foolish to do so alone. She is the one who revealed our new gift to me after King Alaric's death. Neither she nor King Malcolm want word spreading until they are ready to announce the change, but they informed me you are aware and able to use it."

Luelle nodded.

"So, when did you last practise?"

"The day we left the castle."

"I shall speak with Leena and arrange for you and I to spend time each day meditating and practising in private whilst we are here. It is an extra weapon in our arsenal in case we run into anything hostile."

"I thought you didn't believe what Malcolm and I saw?" Luelle eyed her.

Mei's smile returned. "I like to keep an open mind. Besides, I do not believe whatever you encountered is the only hostile thing in these mountains."

Luelle swallowed, memories of her friends and the troll she and Malcolm had fought merging in her mind. Did Mei know the true reason she and Malcolm had been here? Did she trust Luelle more than Leena did?

"Are you ready to try again?"

Looking up, Luelle met Mei's expectant stare. Envisioning herself walking into the darkness inside the Peaks made her throat dry.

"No matter what you face inside, you are better equipped to defeat it than you were the first time," Mei murmured. "You have the Power in your control and there are countless guards to alert us in time to make an escape. The king issued orders for us to retreat and observe if we think we are in danger at any point, especially by threats that do not appear to be of this world. He wants all of us, including you, back to the capital safely."

Luelle doubted all of the guards and soldiers in the realm would be of any use in a fight against Vesanya, let alone the few who were here, but she didn't voice the opinion. She was only here and alive because she was still useful to Malcolm. If she could not go back inside the cavern to retrieve any further information stashed within, he may very well change his mind and host a second execution.

Taking a deep, shaking breath, she followed Mei to the

tunnel's entrance. She tried to concentrate on the world around her to avoid her memories—the metallic scent of the mail vests the soldiers wore, the chill breeze against her neck, her shoes pinching her heels. Her fists were curled so tight her nails bit tiny crescents into her palms. Stepping into the darkness, she faltered, but Mei slid her hand around Luelle's arm and urged her forward.

Pale blue light from the moonstone veins in the walls guided them deeper. Luelle blanked out for the majority of their trek, emerging into the cavern at the end of the descent. Sweat coated her back and her breathing remained shallow, but she managed to stay upright when Mei released her arm.

Inside, the cavern teemed with people. Soldiers flocked around the stone plinth and gathered at both tunnels leading from the main space. A few smaller groups sat on the floor close to the water, eating and drinking together as they rested. Gone were the corpses that had littered the floor on Luelle's last visit, though dark stains remained splashed across the stone, a reminder of the blood spilled, waiting to be found when anyone looked closely enough.

On the far side of the cavern, the stone archway stood lonely in the centre of the island, no longer accompanied by the tall statue of Vesanya.

Jerky steps carried Luelle after Mei, across the cavern to where Graman and Leena waited. They stood beside the stone plinth and the round crystal sphere atop it. Inside the crystal, the Power that Luelle had returned writhed and pulsated, glowing far brighter than the moonstone ore stretching above them in the high, arched ceiling.

"Realistically, we have four days at most to achieve

everything you wish here before we must leave, if we are to return by the agreed-upon date," Leena was saying to Graman.

He nodded, pursing his lips around his upward-protruding tusks. "That should be plenty of time. I do not plan to complete any of my analysis here. I only hope to find records to bring home and document anything we cannot physically carry back with us. Today, since our journey has been long, I think we will be best served starting to transcribe the floor's map onto parchment to compare to star charts in the capital. I sent supplies ahead before we left. Are they already here?" He peered at a nearby soldier, who nodded.

"One other thing." Mei joined the conversation, tugging at Leena's arm and pulling her close enough that no one would overhear her quiet request. "I believe Luelle will be more useful if she and I set aside time each morning to practise using the Power."

Leena's brow furrowed.

"I will find somewhere discreet for us to do so. It will help build on her sense of control and her ability to defend herself if anything happens and the rest of us are not around to assist. It will reduce her anxiety and paranoia, which will save us time in the long run if she is to work in a location that causes so much stress."

Leena exchanged a look with Graman, but nodded. "Fine. One hour each morning and then she is Graman's to instruct. I object to the suggestion she would ever be alone and in need of defending herself, but I cannot deny reducing her anxiety will benefit us."

Mei tilted her head in acknowledgement.

"I will return with your supplies in a moment," Leena

said to Graman and strode away from their group.

"Will you require any help recording this map?" Mei turned to the scholar beside her. "I would rather not be roped into guard duty here, when all it appears to require is standing around."

Graman smiled, pushing his wire spectacles up his nose. "The more help, the better."

12

TROUBLED dreams haunted Malcolm the night before the trial and execution. The upcoming day played through his mind in a hundred ways; sometimes it was Luelle who died, though often it was someone completely innocent, and several times his own life was taken. Vesanya was usually the one who struck the killing blow, before turning her violence on the awaiting crowd.

Screams echoed in Malcolm's pounding head when morning arrived.

Despite some brief resistance from Philip, Malcolm dismissed his footmen, unable to deal with people fussing over him when he was still shaking off his lingering nightmares. He was dressing himself when one of his guards announced the arrival of Theo and Viv.

"You look terrible," his sister declared when they were all shut inside Malcolm's dressing room. She lounged on one of the settees as he finished buttoning his black tunic.

Malcolm glared at her, offering the same look to Theo when he noticed his friend failing to hide a smirk. Theo cleared his throat and hid his face with a hand under the pretence of fixing his floppy, golden curls.

"It may come as a surprise, but there is more to being a king than looking good." Sarcasm drenched Malcolm's tone. "Is everything in place?"

Theo nodded. "Clarisse and Benjamin await us at the Great Temple. They have both been settling in fine. Their staying here is only temporary, as you know. There was one scuffle, which was quelled quickly and the trouble-makers reprimanded, but the majority of other guards have accepted their retirement without question. More importantly, I do not believe anyone will doubt their testimony."

"And they know what they must say during the ceremony?"

"Of course. I spent hours preparing them," Viv said.

Since the Great Temple was in a paved clearing in the centre of the city, there was plenty of room on the surrounding streets for the public to witness the event. Most executions occurred at the public gallows, but the first case of treason in centuries required a grander stage. It would take place atop the large balcony at the back of the Great Temple, high enough that no one in the crowd would be able to distinguish the details of the criminal's face, reducing the risk of unveiling the deception at play. Few attendees would know the criminal's identity and fewer still would recognise she was not who Malcolm claimed. Still, he could not take the risk.

Leafleters and criers had advertised the event for days, drumming up excitement. A short, public trial would precede the execution. The entire thing should be over well before midday. Carrying out the trial in public was not strictly necessary but Malcolm's advisers had strongly advocated for it. Executions for treason were rare and a trial offered the perfect opportunity to secure support among the general population.

"Is she prepared?" Malcolm asked.

Viv frowned. "Who? The criminal?"

He nodded, unable to voice the words. Yes, she was a criminal but she was a person too. She was one of Malcolm's civilians. Guilt and sorrow overwhelmed him whenever he thought of the woman he was sentencing to an early grave today.

"She is ready," Theo confirmed.

They had settled on Willa, the final woman Malcolm had observed in the castle cells. She remained ignorant of the plot she was involved in. The other prisoners had been returned to their usual cells to continue awaiting justice for their crimes.

"We have supplied her with new clothes but it will work in our favour that she remains unwashed. Tidying her up would only make it easier for people to recognise her, even from a distance. Her case was popular enough that some may still know her face from the posters," Theo said.

"Agreed." Malcolm swallowed his discomfort. "And you are certain it is best to let her represent herself?" he asked Viv, who had arranged the brief trial's proceedings.

She nodded. "She will deny the charges, of course, but that is what everyone will expect, even if the crimes were hers. It is why Clarisse and Benjamin will be present as witnesses. It will be fine. The people wish to see an execution. They will not look closely at the details as long as they remain entertained."

Malcolm turned back to his mirror to place his crown atop his head. Certainty filled Viv's tone but it did little to ease his worming paranoia that something would go wrong today.

An hour later, they began their journey to the Great Temple, travelling in a procession of carriages.

Nothing good ever seemed to arrive for Malcolm at the end of this journey. His father's funeral, the weight of the crown atop his head, and now this attempt at deceit.

Crowds were already gathered on the streets surrounding the holy building. Children had clambered onto nearby buildings, perching on roofs and rafters to get a better view of the balcony on which the trial would take place. Adults on the ground jostled for the best position, straining against the soldiers holding them back in a broad curve around the temple. Some families had brought picnics wrapped in linen to make a day of the event. Many were already joking and laughing with one another as they shared home-brewed bottles of wine and mead.

Malcolm shared his carriage with Viv, Theo, and his mother, who had agreed with him that Zasha and Edwyn should remain safely at home today. Heavy silence hung between them on the journey.

When they arrived, Theo was the first to exit into a corridor of heavily-armed guards. Awaiting Malcolm beyond them was a squad of his royal guard. More soldiers stood to attention nearby, ready to escort the other royals.

Malcolm emerged from the carriage before his mother and sister, ignoring the cheers and shouts that erupted at the sight of him. Today was not a day for casual interactions with his people, for the depiction of a friendly, relaxed ruler. Today, he was a man who must dole out justice no matter the cost, a resolute king who was willing to take another's life in front of the gods. He could show no weakness. Striding up the Great Temple's steps, flanked by four soldiers, he kept his head held high.

Nearing the large doors at the top of the ascent, Malcolm's heart began to race. He'd spent days stewing in the knowledge that he must face Vesanya's statue again. No harm had come to him during his coronation and the same would be true now, especially since he would spend barely any time in the statue's presence today.

A young human priestess met him at the door and indicated for the king to follow her with a small tilt of her head. Rosy hues flushed her cheeks as she briefly met his eyes and quickly averted her gaze. Rather than looking at the statues of the gods as they passed, Malcolm kept his stare fixed on the back of the priestesses's head. Her braid was exposed, snaking out from underneath her fabric headdress, reminiscent of the practical pattern Luelle usually wore her hair in.

The priestess led Malcolm and his guards up a spiralling flight of stairs. Their boots thudded against the marble flooring, armour clanking with every step. Smoky incense filled Malcolm's every breath, growing stronger as they climbed.

Eventually, they emerged into a spacious room, bereft of furniture beyond a simple wooden table with eight chairs. Adorning the ceiling was a mosaic of Cerulya. Sunlight bathed the pale floors from a wall entirely made of glass, interrupted only by regular stone columns and a single set of intricately carved doors that led to the balcony overlooking the city.

Malcolm waited for Theo and his family to catch them up, his guards automatically spreading to stand beside each doorway, leaving Theo to take his place at Malcolm's side as a personal guard for the event.

"Is there anything you need from us before you start, Your Majesty?" the priestess asked, hands folded neatly in front of her waist. Colour still flushed her cheeks, though perhaps only from their climb.

"No, thank you. You have all been kind enough, allowing us to carry out justice here before the gods." He offered her a smile, hoping it would hide his nervous guilt. Would he face punishment in the Underworld for lying in a holy place or for the gross miscarriage of justice he was about to commit?

"Please let me know if you change your mind. I will retrieve the High Priestess for you." She dipped into a shallow curtsy and left the room, steps so smooth she appeared to glide.

"Are you ready?" Malcolm asked Viv.

Her eyes flicked between him and the balcony doors. Though she nodded, tension lined her brow.

"Clarisse, Benjamin, and the prisoner await us in the adjoining room." Theo gestured to a door on the far wall. "I shall bring the accused through when the trial starts."

"We will begin when the High Priestess arrives."

On the balcony, another priest was preaching to the awaiting crowds. His muffled voice leaked through the windows to Malcolm and the others, hailing the brilliance of the gods.

The High Priestess ascended the stairs to greet them long before the priest on the balcony finished. She wore the same pale robes as the other priests and priestesses, distinguished only by the golden threading on the fabric. Covered mostly by her headdress, her white hair was bound at the nape of her neck. She curtsied to Malcolm and his family, age preventing her from dipping too low.

"Your Majesty, Your Highnesses."

"High Priestess." Malcolm dipped his head in response.

"Please, as always, I must ask that you call me Jude." She smiled, the delicate creases around her eyes deepening.

"Jude," he amended with a small smile of his own. "Thank you again for allowing us to host the trial here and for agreeing to represent my father in the matter. Princess Vivyenne assures me your integrity is second to none in the kingdom." Oily shame slithered down his spine watching the High Priestess's eyes light up at the compliment, knowing he made her a partner in his deception.

"You are too kind, Princess." Jude beamed at Vivyenne. She lowered her voice, expression growing serious. "I am honoured to represent King Alaric. The gods will watch over us to ensure truth prevails and justice is served."

For once, Malcolm hoped not.

Viv's responding smile was calmer than he felt. Was her heart hammering like his underneath her poised exterior?

Smattering applause sounded outside, signalling the end of the sermon.

Malcolm took a deep breath, his mouth drying. How must Willa feel about her imminent demise? He shook off the thought. Dwelling on that only elicited the urge to call off the entire ordeal. Theo had informed the criminal of her upcoming trial, though she was not aware of the new charges she would face. Kept in isolation as she had been, she had likely not even known she had a new king until days ago.

None of them could predict Willa's reaction to the new charges that would be announced. Viv remained optimistic that no action could convince the bloodthirsty crowd of her innocence, but doubts had crawled into Malcolm's mind and set up permanent residence.

The priest from the balcony entered the room, leaving the doors open behind him and bowing to Malcolm and his family. Like most of the other priests and priestesses, the man was human.

Jude led the way outside. Sunlight glared off the temple. Noise erupted as the High Priestess emerged, a choir of excited murmuring.

Malcolm and Viv lingered near the back of the balcony, waiting for their guards to situate themselves around the edge to overlook the crowd and anticipate any violence before it reached the royals. Malcolm pushed a thread of the Power toward Jude, willing her voice to amplify over the city below as she welcomed the crowds, gave thanks to the gods and to Malcolm, and introduced Viv as the Chief Justiciar and chair of the trial.

Viv and Malcolm exchanged a glance and a nod. She strode to the edge of the balcony to speak, amplifying her voice using her own Power, though none but him and their mother knew. An undeniable impression of his sister reached him as she used the Power, the scent of rain and the crackle of static, a sense of apprehension moments before a storm.

"Good people, I stand before you as Chief Justiciar to learn the truth in this trial of treason. Following the death of His Majesty King Alaric, the realm's judiciary and I have reviewed the evidence into allegations of grand treason. We meet here today to host a summary before you, the people of the realm, King Malcolm of Arazia, and the gods, with whose authority he reigns." She swept her arm across the crowd and toward the sky. "Today, His Majesty King Malcolm, second of his name, will pronounce a verdict and justice will be served, either by exoneration or execution."

Excitement stirred below.

"The High Priestess will represent King Alaric and summarise evidence against the accused. The accused, Belle Amery, will represent herself." Viv used the fake name Luelle had supplied when working at the castle. Soft cheers and jeers sounded for the High Priestess and the accused, in turn. "The charges levied are as follows: one charge of fraudulent representation, one charge of high treason, and one charge of assault resulting in death."

Malcolm's stomach was a knot of anxiety as Viv moved away from the edge of the balcony. To the side of him, the doors opened. Clarisse and Benjamin emerged dressed in royal armour but unarmed for the event. Each of them stepped to him and bowed before retreating to the opposite side of the balcony, waiting to be called upon.

With them in place, more soldiers escorted Willa onto the balcony. Although her wrists were bound behind her back, leaving her unable to resist her fate, the soldiers flanking her kept their hands clasped tight around her upper arms, hauling her forward. Simple grey clothing hung from her slender body, overly slim from weeks of the under-nourishing food given to those awaiting execution. Beneath her collar, dust and grime stained her skin, remnants of her cell. Limp hair hung in knotted clumps around her face, matted at the back of her scalp and falling into her line of sight as she hunched over her own chest.

Now she was here, the absurdity of the plan struck Malcolm. People would easily see through his deception. Willa's hair didn't even have the same copper sheen as Luelle's in sunlight—it was simply a dull brown. The only feature they truly shared was the lock of unpigmented hair marking Veseile heritage.

Jeers erupted as Willa was led forward. Her shoulders curved further inward in response to the sound. Malcolm stayed poised and ready to contain any violence she attempted with the Power, but she gave no impression of even realising the change she and other Veseile had undergone.

Jude moved to the front of the crowd after a nod from Malcolm confirmed he would amplify her voice again.

"People of Arazia!" She raised her palms to she sky, quieting their shouts. "King Alaric ruled our realm for thirty-four years, caring for his people and strengthening our borders against any who might oppose us. He was devout, and the Gods rewarded him for his faith with a strong lineage and a peaceful reign. However, despite everything he offered his people, individuals hid among you, lurking in wait to act against the throne and, by extension, the gods themselves. The woman standing before you today, already hanging her head in shame, is one such person." The High Priestess sneered over her shoulder as shouts of agreement and disgust rose in response to her words.

With long, slow steps, Jude paced the width of the

balcony, seeming to look at every person gathered below.

"This criminal," she spat the words, "acted against the will of the gods and threatened the stability, security, and harmony of our realm. In doing so, she has threatened each and every one of you, the people our king is gods-sworn to protect. When she committed treason against our king, she committed an act of violence against each and every person in Arazia, Eile and human alike." Sharp jabs of her index finger emphasised her point.

At Jude's words, Willa's head rose from where it hung. Malcolm watched closely as her brow furrowed. She stared at the High Priestess, who continued her verbal tirade. Blood rushed in Malcolm's ears, drowning out the words. Would he need to intervene? What if Viv was incorrect and the people sided with Willa?

The High Priestess abruptly spun toward the bound woman, who flinched at the movement.

"What say you in your defence? Will you deny, in front of the gods and the people you have betrayed that you committed treason against King Alaric on his deathbed? That you plotted to murder him before his soul could peacefully leave this realm and journey to the Underworld? That you cruelly deprived his family, including our current king, their final opportunity to bid him a peaceful farewell as he passed? That you risked the loss of the Power, a gift from the God of Chaos herself and the key to a millennia of peace on the continent?"

Willa faltered at the High Priestess's approach but her composure seemed to return as she spoke.

"I deny it," she said. Malcolm willed her voice a fraction louder for the benefit of the crowd, though he kept the volume lower than Jude's, using less of his

Power. People might grow suspicious if he didn't let them hear the accused at all but, this way, he could cut her off before she reveal her true name and the nature of her real crimes.

Viv glanced at him, offering an almost indiscernible nod.

"I never committed treason," Willa objected. Her eyes darted from the High Priestess to the stern faces of the others on the balcony. "I didn't—I never tried to murder the king." Her face scrunched with confusion.

"Lies!" Jude exclaimed, turning back to the crowd to give them the show they desired.

Malcolm cut off the shred of the Power that had amplified Willa's voice, silencing her continued objections to all beyond the guards nearest her. Even to them, her voice was drowned out by Jude's speech.

He recited the true nature of Willa's crimes in his mind. She was a thief, and her robberies had caused the injury and death of innocents. It became a silent mantra. He was only bringing her death forward in time. She had always been doomed to execution. It was a consequence of her own actions. She deserved this. She *deserved* this.

"She continues to refute the truth before the king and the gods!" Jude looked at Willa. "Do you deny that you are a criminal?"

"No, but I—"

"Yet, you still try to fool us into believing your innocence?"

"I never said—"

"Good people," the High Priestess continued, striding to the edge of the balcony, "she cannot get her story straight. What's more, our evidence against her is indisputable. With me today are witnesses who can confirm, here and now, they saw this woman entering King Alaric's chambers intent to murder him on the evening the treasonous act was committed."

Clarisse and Benjamin straightened where they stood as the High Priestess turned to them.

"You have already sworn the truth of your testimonies in front of the gods, correct?"

Malcolm's heart was a painful hammering in his chest. Fresh sweat broke out on his brow, but neither guard faltered. They answered in unison, without so much as glancing at anyone beyond the High Priestess.

"Yes, High Priestess."

"You have testified to guarding King Alaric's chambers on the night of the crime. Please confirm for us again, in the presence of the people of Arazia and the gods, who know the truths in the hearts of men, and King Malcolm, to whom you have sworn undying fidelity, Benjamin Tanner, son of Lars and Sibelle Tanner, did you witness this woman, disguised as a servant, entering the king's chambers?"

Malcolm felt as if he would be sick over the balcony's stone floor.

"Yes, High Priestess," Benjamin said once more.

"And do you confirm she did not leave the room via the doors at which you were stationed?"

Again, he declared it so.

Jude turned to Clarisse. "Clarisse Fletcher, daughter of Kai and Anette Fletcher, I ask you the same."

After each question, Clarisse agreed, repeating Benjamin's answers.

"In fact," Jude returned to the edge of the balcony to

address her audience, ignoring the increasingly distressed, stammering objections from Willa, audible only to her, "our witnesses' testimony confirms the criminal had disappeared from the room by the time King Alaric's family had returned, scurrying out of a window and scaling the castle walls down a rope in an attempt to escape without being caught. Does that sound like the actions of an innocent person?"

Shouts arose from the crowd, punctuated by shaking fists and expressions harbouring a blend of outrage and excitement at the prospect of a looming execution.

Malcolm ground his teeth together. *She deserved it, she deserved it.*

"Our king was betrayed by this criminal and she can offer no evidence to the contrary. She resorts to mewling pleas and lies directly to your faces. She continues to dishonour King Malcolm, whose very father she murdered in cold blood. She has already admitted she is a criminal, and these are crimes beyond the capacity of anyone but those accustomed to the grossest lies and deceit. Can any witnesses attest to your innocence?" She spun to Willa.

Willa dragged her dumbfounded stare from Clarisse and Benjamin to the High Priestess.

"Well?" Jude arched her eyebrows.

Willa closed her mouth. Hopeless resignation flitted across her face as she gazed at the crowds below, crying out for her demise.

"No." The words were a whisper, yet still boomed over the crowd, amplified by Viv's Power.

"And do you have an alibi for the night in question?"

A tear dribbled down Willa's dirty cheek as she

murmured the same response.

Malcolm's throat dried. All this talk of lying and deception chilled him to his bones. What punishment would await him for this plot?

The High Priestess lowered her voice, though it still reached every corner of the restless crowd.

"Chief Justiciar, you and your court have worked tirelessly over the past week to investigate this case from every angle. I believe we have all heard enough. I leave the matter in your capable hands." She dipped a small curtsy in front of Viv and stepped aside, giving the princess plenty of room to stand before the crowd.

The fabric of Viv's black skirts whispered against the marble, drowned out by the unintelligible blur of noise from the crowd.

"After a week of deliberation, myself and the royal court offered the accused one final chance to prove her innocence in front of the gods, the king, and the people. She has failed to offer us any new evidence of this."

The crowd's volume increased.

"I hereby declare Belle Amery guilty on all counts. If the gods disagree, may they intervene directly now, and if not, may justice commence." Viv raised her arms as she spoke, her voice almost lost in the roar of noise, even amplified as it was by the Power.

Malcolm gritted his teeth. Viv knew as well as he that Vesanya was present in their realm, fully able to intervene if she so chose. Such a declaration was traditional, and in cases such as this, it was tradition, not Malcolm, that reigned, but did Viv relish it? She had made her distaste clear when Malcolm had planned this deception, all to save Luelle's life and use her further. Did Viv hope the gods truly would intervene and punish him for making her complicit in such a horrific act?

Willa shouted again, doubling down on her protests of innocence against the charges but it was futile; her voice was a raindrop falling against the roar of a waterfall. The crowd demanded blood.

Viv raised her hand, calling for quiet among the thunderous audience.

"You all came here today to see justice served, and the gods have revealed the truth. For the crime of high treason, fraud, and murder, I sentence the traitor to death. In line with the laws of Arazia, she will face an immediate execution at the hand of King Malcolm."

The crowd grew frenzied. Below, guards and soldiers renewed their efforts to maintain order.

Willa's protests dissolved into babbling, incomprehensible prayers. Her shoulders curved again as she shrank in on herself.

Malcolm stepped forward. Over the balcony's edge, his people stared up to him with awe and apprehension. His chest tightened as his gaze swept over them. Some of the children were as young as his brother Edwyn.

All would watch as he murdered one of his citizens.

He steeled himself, settling his shoulders and raising his chin. If one person's death could keep every other individual here safe, it was worth it. None of his people deserved the fate Vesanya would bestow upon them, and he could make Willa's death quick, even if a spectacle was necessary.

Easing a tendril of his Power towards Willa, he willed her to slide towards him, dragging her across the balcony. She struggled against the force but could not see the invisible thread gripping her waist and tugging her forward, let alone stop it. She continued to show no awareness of her own Power, but Malcolm remained tense. Severe emotion could cause her to lash out with it at any point. He couldn't let things get that far, not when it would reveal his secret to the public before he was ready.

Malcolm willed her into the air, holding Willa above the edge of the balcony for all the crowd to see. Frenzied vocalisations sounded in response.

Before the trial, he and his closest advisers had agreed upon a death by fire. It was dramatic enough to sate the bloodlust of Cerulya's citizens, but Malcolm did not intend for Willa's actual death to be so prolonged. Being suspended in front of a crowd calling out for her death was torturous enough.

Even from afar, he could see her chest heaving as she hyperventilated as she hung, suspended in the air.

Unfamiliar pressure rose from her direction. He drew a sharp breath. It had to be now.

He flung his arm towards Willa. Flames danced close around his sleeve and burst from his palm in her direction. An instant before the fire engulfed Willa, Malcolm gripped her with another thread of his Power, snapping her neck as she disappeared from view.

The pressure that had been growing stopped the moment her life ended.

Bitter smoke with a coppery undertone filled Malcolm's senses as Willa's hair and clothes caught. As her skin burned and the fat beneath it melted, Malcolm moved Willa further from the balcony, positioning her high above the cobbled stone ground behind the temple. His soldiers had kept the space free from the crowds of onlookers. There, Willa's body would fall, landing in front of the audience. He let the flames burn until she was charred beyond recognition. When he was certain no one would unveil his deception from her corpse, Malcolm closed his fist, extinguishing the fire and releasing his hold on the body.

She plummeted, hitting the ground with a wet thud.

Striding forward, Malcolm forced himself to watch Willa fall.

Below, the soldiers stepped aside, letting the crowds rush towards the body, eager to snatch away any tokens that survived the scorching.

13

RECORDING the star map etched into the floor of the cavern was a painstaking job that swallowed the evening of their arrival.

Luelle's back ached by the time Graman grumbled with halfhearted satisfaction at their progress and agreed to let his helpers retreat to their bedrolls, tucked away in a darker corner of the large cavern. Mei fell asleep almost immediately, after reminding Luelle they would meditate together first thing the next day.

Sleep did not reach Luelle so easily, despite the physical and mental exhaustion weighing her down. Laying with her back to the wall, she listened to Mei's soft snores and Graman's scribblings as he worked long into the night, not that it was possible to tell the time so deep underground. Her eyes ached from staring around the large barren space, but Luelle couldn't rest knowing Vesanya could return to slaughter them at any moment.

Though, would she? After being trapped in this cavern for so long, would the Goddess have any desire to return here?

Trying to decipher Vesanya's motives was as exhausting as drawing the map to Graman's meticulous standards. Luelle descended into a light doze several times through the night. Each time, she jerked awake, heart hammering, skin sticky with sweat.

When Mei and a few other soldiers laying nearby grew more restless, Luelle stopped trying to fall back to sleep. When Mei eventually woke, Luelle also rose, hoping their meditation might allow her mind more rest than sleep had offered.

"Can we do this somewhere away from the main cavern?" Luelle murmured to Mei once they had taken the time to wash and redress for the day.

Mei nodded. Her thick hair was sleek and freshly oiled, reflecting the moonstone light from above.

"We need somewhere more private than this, anyway. For now, Leena and Graman are the only others that know about our abilities," Mei whispered, examining the cavern.

Brief confusion flickered in Luelle. Did Tao not yet know of the Power, despite being Mei's brother and accompanying them on this trip? Or was this a tactic by Mei to keep Luelle at a disadvantage? Of course, there was a chance that Tao might not have the Power at all; Luelle had not yet observed enough Veseile using it to understand exactly how far it had spread.

Mei continued speaking, interrupting Luelle's inner debate. "You know this place better than me. Where would you suggest we go?"

Considering venturing further into the tunnels filled Luelle with equal levels of enthusiasm as staying in the main cavern itself, though she would be forced to search them when Graman awoke, regardless of her desire to stay away. Returning to the tunnels for the first time with fewer people around to witness her panic might be better.

"There are a few places down here that we can try."

"Lead on." Mei nodded, resting her hand on the short sword at her waist.

Gritting her teeth, Luelle strode toward the tunnels, ignoring the guards standing on either side. Dread and familiarity washed over her as they walked. Uncomfortable memories of her old friends surfaced, begging for attention. Here, in these caves and tunnels, she'd laughed and joked with Zeke, Freya, and Imbryl, sharing their deepest desires and fears, forging a bond she'd thought nothing would break.

That bond had been more fragile than she'd realised.

The tunnels at the back of the cavern continued deep into the mountain, leading to several smaller caves and eventually to another exit, lower in the valley. Soldiers patrolled the tunnel, but none bothered guarding the smaller, shallow caves on either side of the main walkway. Luelle led Mei into the third alcove on the left, a small space that she'd once used as her own chambers.

Anxiety and comfort battled in Luelle as they settled into the space. Different furs lined the floor. Unfamiliar items were strewn within: water skins; stacked papers with messy, scribbled handwriting; piles of folded clothing several sizes too large for her; a cluttered stack of carved flint daggers and mismatched pieces of armour. A stranger must have claimed this space while Luelle was living in Cerulya. Zeke's numbers had grown so much that it may have belonged to several people in her absence.

Mei cocked an eyebrow. "Cosy, I suppose."

Luelle didn't bother commenting. "Is it private enough?"

"It will do." Mei looked around, hands on her hips. "Let us begin."

She followed Mei's lead, sitting cross-legged on the firm ground a few feet away from the soldier.

Mei closed her eyes, straightening her spine and resting her hands palm-up on her knees. She inhaled long and slow through her nose, breathing out through lips pursed in a perfect circle. Luelle copied her pose, mimicked the breathing technique, and tried to clear her mind.

She practised isolating every sense, as Malcolm had instructed her on their first journey together, the first time she'd succeeded at intentionally using the Power. Somewhere distant, moisture dripped onto stone. Quiet conversations bounced off the walls, echoes of words spoken far away. Each inhalation was musty, offset by the faint floral soap she'd used that morning and the rich rosemary hair oils Mei had chosen. A rogue itch on Luelle's arm called for her attention but she dismissed it, moving onto the next sensation. Turning her observations inward, she focused on how cold each breath felt in her nose, on the twinge of discomfort in her left shoulder blade, and the Power coiled, warm, in her chest.

Luelle wasn't sure at which point she fell asleep. She woke, slumped over, to Mei shaking her shoulder. Amusement glittered in the soldier's dark eyes.

"How am I supposed to concentrate on clearing my mind with your snoring rumbling in my ear?"

Luelle blinked, disoriented.

"Sorry," she mumbled, rubbing her eyes with the heels

of her hands.

Mei dismissed the apology with a wave of her hand. "I imagine we are nearing the end of our time, anyway." She rolled her shoulders. "We should try to incorporate the Power into our daily routines. Although, we will need a more private space away from the others when we use it. Even here, we are exposed. Meditating is one thing, but I imagine questions would arise if someone witnessed us flinging things around with only our minds."

Luelle said nothing, unsure if she was even supposed to be practising as she was. Malcolm hadn't instructed her against it when he'd visited her room in Cerulya, but he had been heavily under alcohol's influence. How much could she trust anything he'd said then? When she arrived back in the capital, he might act entirely differently.

As if on cue to signal the end of their time together, footsteps neared. Leena peeked around the narrow archway into the space where Luelle and Mei were seated.

"Morning," Mei drawled.

"How goes your meditation?"

"A little too well for some of us…"

Luelle glared at Mei's wide grin. To her astonishment, Leena huffed a laugh rather than chastising her.

"We should begin with our duties. Graman has a busy day planned for us. Bring those papers into the main cavern for him to start sorting through." Leena pointed at the small stack beside Luelle. "He can start looking through them while the three of us return and search these smaller rooms. I have sketched a quick map of the tunnel systems. Luelle, can you look over them and adjust anything I have noted incorrectly?"

Luelle nodded, hoping her face disguised the surprise she felt at being included.

"Good. Come on then, Graman awaits us." Leena disappeared as fast as she appeared.

Mei pushed herself to standing. "You must be full of energy after napping, so you can carry the papers."

Luelle sighed. Shuffling closer, she stacked the sheets into a more orderly pile and stood.

"Are you fully Veseile?" she asked as she and Mei ambled back towards the main cavern.

Mei nodded.

"Why did Princess Vivyenne tell you about the Power?" Luelle kept her voice low, even though the nearest passing soldiers were immersed in their own conversation.

"She and the king believed it was necessary and trust me to keep the information private."

"How many other soldiers know?"

Mei eyed Luelle, but answered after a brief, silent deliberation. "I believe Princess Vivyenne and King Malcolm have been training a small selection of soldiers in case of any hostility when the announcement happens, or in case any Veseile discover the abilities before then and need to be taught restraint."

Luelle nodded. Uncontrolled, the Power could deal extraordinary damage. Her experience in Tolhurst was enough to demonstrate how destructive it could be, particularly when linked to emotion and when the wielder had no real ability to manage it. Malcolm had said as much on their travels together, that it was safer to be in the company of one dangerously skilled with the Power than one dangerously unskilled. His belief in that was strong enough that he had chosen to teach Luelle the basics of the Power in the foothills of the mountain, despite having no Power of his own to defend himself with if she'd chosen to turn it on him.

"Is the princess only planning to teach soldiers?" If appealing to Malcolm did not work, Luelle may be able to convince Princess Vivyenne she was an asset.

"That is not information I can share." A knowing look spread over Mei's scarred face.

They entered the main cavern. Luelle's eyes automatically flicked to the stony island but it remained as still and empty as it had been last night, with no evidence of the statue that had once occupied it.

Graman beckoned them over. He sat near the plinth and glowing crystal orb. When they reached him, Luelle deposited the papers she'd brought at his side. Graman patted the firm, uneven ground, encouraging them to sit and help him sort through the current documents he'd gathered.

Minutes later, Leena and some unfamiliar guards approached, carrying food and freshly brewed tea for them all.

Luelle ate in silence, listening to the others converse and making some changes to Leena's map, marking the main areas she wished to search. Zeke had always kept his things close, only lending them to her with reluctance after months of begging to read the books he hoarded. If they were anywhere, they would be near Zeke's chosen living space. Luelle only had to hope he hadn't moved his lodgings after she'd left for the capital.

After finishing their breakfast, Leena, Mei, and Luelle returned to the tunnels, exploring each room on either side of the main corridor through the mountain.

Sheets of paper and worn books were scattered throughout the small cave system, strewn across the floor or gathered in unruly piles. The paper held personal musings from unknown authors, scribbles about their daily workings, sketches, and drafts of letters. They gathered everything, no matter how unimportant each newly found item seemed. Graman fretted as he flipped through the pages of every new document, wondering aloud if he would find the information he sought.

With Leena and Mei at her side, Luelle searched every crack and nook in the rock she could remember, recovering a few rolls of parchment and slender diaries that would have otherwise remained hidden. Several times through the day, they stopped to eat or organise the documents they'd found, but they continued working until Luelle's entire body ached anew.

When they emerged at the other end of the tunnel system, the sun was dipping below the peaks on the far side of the valley. They stayed outside, wandering away from the soldiers guarding the entrance and resting while gazing over the valley floor. Although Luelle had managed some form of control over her anxiety after a day working tirelessly in the tunnels, being outside lifted a weight from her shoulders. A cool breeze caressed her face, brushing strands of dyed hair from her clammy temples.

"What is our plan for tomorrow, now we have picked those tunnels clean?" Mei asked, stretching her legs in front of her.

"Do you believe we could have missed anything?" Leena asked, eyes flitting to Luelle.

"I doubt it. Unless Zeke got a lot better at hiding his things when I was away."

"Good. I imagine Graman will want help sorting through everything we found today."

The thought of staying inside the cavern for another few days made Luelle's chest tighten. She was speaking again before she had time to think through the words.

"We could explore the surrounding land to see if there are any other places Zeke stashed his belongings before fleeing, especially for anything Graman suspects we might be missing."

Leena's eyes narrowed. "Hoping to find your old friends?"

"No," Luelle said, quickly. "No, definitely not. But, the more we can find while we're here, the less frequently we will need to return. We'll have plenty of time to sort through it when we return to the capital. Malcolm actually—"

"The king," Leena corrected.

Luelle resisted the urge to roll her eyes. "The king actually said it could be useful if I ran into my old friends, in case I could learn any information they gathered while I was absent, anything that might not be written down."

Leena silently mused over the suggestion.

"It would be nice to spend some time outside of those tunnels," Mei added.

"Fine. It makes sense. We arrived later than I anticipated, so we probably have two more days before we need to head back down the mountain. It is logical to spend our time searching for anything else that might be around," Leena agreed. "I will assign some of the soldiers to work with Graman and start transporting our findings to the carriage in the valley. The three of us can search the surrounding area after you've meditated in the morning. We can spend one day looking down here and the final day searching the land surrounding the cavern's upper entrance. After that, we will head home."

"Great." Mei grinned. "I already look forward to having a real bed again."

Leena snorted. "You've gone soft after all those years guarding the princess."

Luelle smiled along with their teasing, letting herself pretend she wasn't truly an outsider for a while.

14

THE castle and the surrounding city were alive with exhilaration in the days following the execution, ensuring Malcolm was not allowed to forget his sins for a moment.

Nobles whispered to one another as they ate in his dining halls, their eyes flickering to him as they gossiped. Servants acted with increased caution when attending their king, eyes wide with awe or fear when he addressed them. Did they fear he might use the Power to punish or murder them if they displeased him, as he'd used it against Willa in Luelle's place?

Malcolm was certain he'd heard a stable boy refer to him as the *incendiary king* as he'd passed two conversing in the courtyard, perhaps a term the boy had heard from some bard in a tavern. Shame had burned through Malcolm. He'd scuttled away, seeking the respite of his chambers to overcome his stifling panic in private.

He got little sleep during those days, the discomfort chasing him into his bed at night.

The only upside of the time following the execution was the comparative quiet in the castle. Most of the nobles, including Malcolm's four Thanes, vacated the capital, returning to their homes elsewhere in the realm. With each Thane, he sent a squad of newly trained Veseile soldiers to protect and educate. The Thanes also had strict instructions to announce the changes to the Power on the same day Malcolm planned to in Cerulya.

Ideally, the announcement would have happened when Leena and Graman were back in the capital but they were not due to return for another week. The announcement had become a necessity. Without the distraction of the coronation or a public trial for high treason, the risk grew that Veseile civilians would learn they possessed the Power. Maintaining peace was vital.

The concerns plagued Malcolm as dawn's light spilled through his window. After failing to fall back to sleep through the night, he'd unshuttered his windows, staring at the constellations outside in an attempt to remember that the universe was more vast than the problems he currently faced.

Before his servants arrived to rouse him, Malcolm prepared a list of the most pressing matters he faced and instructed a guard outside his door to call his council for an urgent meeting.

Unable to face the wait in his own chambers, Malcolm dressed himself and arrived at the drawing room early, finding his Seneschal, Philip, overseeing the arrangement of breakfast and refreshments for the small meeting. Cured meats, ripe fruits, soft cheeses, and newly baked, sliced bread were artfully arranged across the long, wide table, interspersed with pitchers of freshly pressed juices and seasonal flowers. Philip looked up as Malcolm entered. His frown disappeared, replaced with a calm, businesslike expression.

"Your Majesty." He approached and dipped into a low bow. "Everything is according to schedule. Do you desire cupbearers for the duration of the meeting?"

Malcolm shook his head. "No, thank you, Philip. They can serve themselves. This meeting must remain as private as possible."

Philip bowed his head in acknowledgement. "Of course, sire. I will ensure the servants leave as soon as they finish setting up."

"Actually, Philip, I hoped to catch you before you finished to ask if you might sit in on this meeting. Your insight and experience would be useful for some of the matters I wish to discuss."

Philip's brows twitched upward but he regained composure quickly. "Anything you wish, Your Majesty."

Viv was the first to arrive, accompanied by Theo, as the last of the servants were leaving. Shortly behind, the other councillors trickled in—his mother, who remained Councillor of State after his father's death; the Royal Treasurer, a tall Adeile named Sinead; the court chaplain, a human priest named Roan; and the Councillor of Internal Affairs, a human named Jinny. Graman, being Malcolm's Royal Secretary and an avid historian, would be frustrated to miss the meeting, but Malcolm knew his adviser would understand the need for it to go ahead without him.

Last to arrive was the Field Master General, a Colleile named Omar, and Admiral of the Royal Navy, a Veseile named Nadja. The final two councillors entered the room together, deep in a discussion about tactics. They put their conversation on hold to bow to their king and seat themselves, eyeing the spread laid out before them all.

As he did every time he'd met with his advisers over the past few weeks, Malcolm felt his father's absence physically—an ache in his chest that stole his breath when he gave it his full attention. Grief was a constant distraction, pulling him away from his duties. Today was no different. Ten people were seated around the table, but the room still felt empty without his father.

Malcolm swallowed the ache and cleared his throat.

"Thank you all for coming at such short notice. Please help yourself to the food Philip has arranged. I do not know how long this meeting will take." He gestured to the feast, though he had little appetite himself; every mouthful of food had tasted of ash since Willa's execution. "There are several things I wish to discuss with you today. I have addressed these issues individually with many of you, but a full council meeting and discussion is long overdue."

He looked around the table, ensuring everyone was paying attention before he continued, waiting for people to plate up any food they wished. In his own place, atop his plate, was a stack of documents he'd brought for the meeting.

"As some of you are already aware, there have been some changes to the Power since I inherited it from my father. I have been testing the extent of these changes in private and it seems that individuals with Veseile heritage are able to use the Power."

"Every Veseile?" Philip asked, eyes widening.

"Not necessarily. Our current theories suggest a person must have certain traits to access the Power. Most notably, the unpigmented streak of hair seen in Veseile and some half-bloods." His thoughts flashed to his youngest sibling, Edwyn, and his uniform black hair—to the despair plain on his brother's face each time he was unable to use the Power as the rest of their family could. "Although, our testing remains in the earliest stages. For now, we must assume anyone with Veseile heritage has the potential to use it. We have not yet observed the same abilities in individuals from other Eile races, nor in pure-blooded humans." Malcolm looked at the Admiral of his Royal Navy, seated almost exactly across the table from him. "Nadja, if our current theory is correct, you will be able to use the Power."

She blinked. Her hand strayed to the streak of white at her forehead, pulled back into a tight braid with the rest of her hair.

"That could be useful during campaigns." Her eyebrows raised a fraction. She glanced at Omar, unable to hide her eagerness to continue their earlier discussion.

"It will undoubtedly have benefits across the realm, but will entail inevitable problems," Malcolm continued. "We are all aware of the history of tension between certain human and Veseile groups. When extremist Veseile factions learn of their new abilities, we will likely witness a large uptick in violent attacks and civilian casualties. Violence toward innocent Veseile may also increase due to fear of their new abilities and retribution for these attacks. At worst, this could conceivably result in civil war."

Concern dawned around the table, present in downturned lips and furrowed brows.

Malcolm took a deep breath and continued. "Therefore, we must get the situation under control immediately. I have begun drafting laws to publicise imminently and have already taken some steps to reduce the risk of widespread chaos and panic. I intend to announce the changes to the Power here and through my Thanes." He shuffled the papers in front of him and pulled out a sheet for each councillor with the drafted laws. "Please take a look."

The laws were simple, forbidding any use of the Power to harm another person or to aid in an act already deemed illegal. As soon as possible, Veseile were also to be bound, by law, to attend mandatory training facilities where they would learn to control the Power so none could commit harm with the excuse that it happened outside of their own intentions.

Silence fell over the room for a while as the councillors read and processed Malcolm's intended announcement. He toyed with the hem of his tunic until they were finished.

"Is training wise?" Jinny was the first to speak, frowning at the parchment in front of her. "Would it not give unsavoury Veseile more ammunition to cause harm?"

"They have access to the Power, regardless of whether they are trained or not. It is tied to the natural world and to the emotion of its wielder. A strong spike in emotion could lead to an uncontrolled burst of the Power, which may harm people. Control is imperative. I will not change my mind about this law."

Jinny conceded the point with a nod, lips pressed into a tight line.

"When do you plan to publicise these?" Viv asked.

"As soon as possible," Malcolm said. "The longer I delay, the more likely it becomes that someone will discover their new access to the Power, or that word leaks from the few who already know about it. I intend for us to finalise the laws today, and I will make the announcement tomorrow. We will control the narrative this way."

"How will we protect innocent civilians against any who would defy your laws?" Nadja refilled her glass, brow tight with tension.

"Omar has been working with my family and I to train Veseile soldiers over the past couple of weeks. Each Thane returned to their lands with a squad of trained Veseile. More remained here to continue studying and practising the Power. When their training is complete, I will dispatch some to the distant parts of the realm to share their knowledge. Hopefully, by that point, we will also be closer to establishing a form of wider teaching for civilians. On top of that, I have instructed Wren to take immediate action to cultivate large quantities of shadowbell. Of course, the flower's essence is currently primarily medicinal, but its sleep-inducing qualities will offer a method to temporarily incapacitate any violent Veseile who attempt to use the Power for wicked purposes."

"Are you certain of Wren's loyalty, Your Majesty?" Omar asked. "Or any of the Thanes, for that matter."

"Betrayal is always a risk when a new monarch inherits the throne," Jinny agreed. "If alliances are going to change, it is the most unstable time and therefore the best opportunity for it. This news will only increase instability, which the Thanes may take advantage of. Wren may not follow through with your request."

"I am aware of this," Malcolm said.

Leena had spies positioned in each of the Thanes' households and governing buildings, but there was no guarantee they would catch and report every hint of rebellion. His advisers' opinions on the matter were valuable, even if the entire topic felt minor compared to the other problems needing Malcolm's attention.

"Wren stands to gain from my order," he continued. "The Meteile in the Godswood are as vulnerable to an abuse of the Power as the rest of the realm, and his people will receive generous compensation for the additional crops they must grow and provide."

"Wren has never given any cause for concern in the past," Malcolm's mother spoke up.

"Nor has Isme, although she is the newest to the role," Jinny nodded at Vonya. "Neither of them have ever shown desire to extend their influence."

"And what about Edyth and Adira?" Malcolm asked.

"If any of the Thanes were to challenge your rule, it would be Edyth or Adira," Jinny said.

Sinead, the treasurer, joined the debate. "Adira is at an advantage living in the north. She has the best means to challenge you, if anyone would. The northerners' wealth is extensive and the Veseile population up there is small. If she chose to, she could ignore your orders and halt exports of resources mined in the Camthryn Peaks. Without her, we could be bankrupt before winter."

"But, she is isolated up there," Omar countered. "And, for all of the resources we receive, we send just as many back. The northern lands are not arable and her people would starve long before we ran out of money. Adira would need to collaborate with at least one other Thane, or an external power, to ensure her people continued to receive food if she made an enemy of the capital. Given that Wren and Isme's land separate her from Edyth and your fleet controls the western seaboard, Adira is in a very weak position to challenge you."

"She has also been instrumental in drafting early designs of tools to control any Veseile criminals who would use the Power as a weapon, which I have available to show you all when we move to that portion of the agenda. Under her instruction, Dileile smiths in the castle are creating a prototype for us to test," Malcolm said. "I am satisfied we can control Adira, so long as she has no cause to get behind. That brings us to Edyth. I know my father was always the most concerned about her loyalty." He looked across the table to his mother, searching for confirmation.

She nodded. "He certainly believed she had the most ambition compared to the other Thanes. When she was younger, she was allegedly involved in an independence campaign. Of course, she denies it, but there is rarely smoke without fire."

"She would be my biggest concern," Omar agreed.

"But, we cannot accuse her of anything at this point. We have no evidence she will move against you or that she even wishes to," Vonya continued. "She has just witnessed the execution. If she had any plans, that may have deterred her. You certainly made a spectacle of the criminal's death." She hid her expression of distaste with a sip of her drink.

Malcolm took a deep breath, biting back the reminder of how important that spectacle had been.

Viv echoed his thoughts aloud. "The execution was a necessary evil, Mother. Malcolm is the king, show some respect."

Vonya frowned at her eldest daughter, but gave a

stilted nod and turned to face Malcolm.

"I apologise. I meant no offence."

He shrugged off the apology and moved on, attempting to remedy the awkwardness that had settled over the room. "We should send a subtle reminder to Edyth of where the strength in this kingdom lies. Omar, what if we move a portion of our soldiers closer to the border with the Southlands? They can continue their training drills in a new environment, even use the Caeleste River."

A small, calculating smile curved Omar's lips. "I shall arrange it as soon as we finish here, Your Majesty."

"Excellent. And Viv, dispatch half of the current Power users to train there, too. Make sure they have some impressive and visible drills to practise." That was one item checked off Malcolm's mental list. "We can monitor the situation from there, but at least we will then have soldiers in place if Edyth does make a move." He turned to face Jinny. "If any of the Thanes were to move against the crown, they would not do so without public opinion, the nobility, or another Thane supporting them. I wish to create a plan to secure the loyalty of each of these groups. Doing so may be a challenge, given the changes I am about to announce, but it is vital."

Jinny nodded, her coiling curls brushing against heavily freckled cheeks. "Of course, Your Majesty. We can devise a publicity campaign. Balls and hunts to secure the nobility, charitable acts to sway the general public." She swirled her glass as she thought aloud. "We can create an overall picture of stability, prosperity, and safety."

"And what of your safety?" Theo asked. "The changes to the Power will expand the type of threat you may face when in public." He leaned forward to more easily meet

Malcolm's gaze from a few seats away. Since Malcolm's ascension to the throne, and perhaps in part due to Leena's absence, Theo's protective streak had grown.

Malcolm shrugged. "I cannot hide away after the announcement, I would appear weak. It would invite attacks, both on me and the citizens I am sworn to protect. Of course, guards will accompany me in public, with at least two trained in the Power, as you and I have previously agreed. Besides, need I remind you that I can defend myself, Theo?"

Theo's mouth quirked, as if his response might be different outside of this meeting.

"We must prioritise humans and Veseile in this campaign." Malcolm turned back to Jinny. "Tensions could spin out of control when the truth about the Power emerges. Arazia's human population must know I remain their protector, despite my Veseile heritage, and I will not tolerate harm to them. However, the Veseile must know that I will not discriminate against them because of a few extremists. They are my people as much as the humans."

"Perhaps," Viv spoke up, "we could consider waiving the charges against some imprisoned Veseile and human political criminals, to demonstrate our commitment to peace and our desire to limit further bloodshed."

Hesitant silence dawned on the table.

"Of course, I do not refer to the most violent individuals. Only those with minor charges. And not all of them, but a few," she amended.

"Prepare some profiles for me to look over, for any you think might be appropriate. We cannot release anyone who may still believe in such... a violent ideology. I will not take action that increases the risk of a civil war, but it is certainly something we can consider," Malcolm said. "Philip, I need you to work with Jinny and my mother as we plan this campaign to ensure our needs are met, particularly for any events we host in the castle."

Philip nodded, expression as serious as ever. "Yes, Your Majesty."

"Your Majesty," Roan, the court chaplain, interjected, "will your marriage form a part of this campaign?"

Malcolm stiffened as if he'd just leapt back into the freezing depths of the Ophidian Channel. He shuffled in his seat, clearing his throat to try and disguise his evident shock.

"I hardly think a marriage so soon after my coronation and the treason trial is necessary. I have years to make that decision. It it not something to rush into."

"On the contrary, Your Majesty. The people yearn for the announcement when a new monarch inherits the throne. It is a decision that can only strengthen your reign, particularly when you begin producing heirs. What's more, Thane Adira has an unwed sister and Thane Edyth a daughter. They are suitably noble and could secure the chosen Thane's allegiance, putting that concern to rest. Their Eile blood would also ensure you and your chosen partner could grow old together."

Discomfort flooded Malcolm at the thought. He barely felt more than a child himself. He'd only worn his father's crown for a few weeks. Besides, how could he consider having children until his rule was stable? Procreating just to produce heirs felt irresponsible, and certainly was not something he desired at this point in time. With his Eile heritage, time was not the same damning pressure it had been for his father.

What's more, he had no desire to marry someone he had never met, as Roan proposed. Of course, marriage was a royal obligation, but most noble women Malcolm had met treated him more like a king than a normal person. He would much rather marry someone who challenged him and held him responsible for his actions, someone like Luelle—

Malcolm managed to stop himself from physically recoiling from that thought. Heat rose to his cheeks, but he shoved the notion away and continued, hoping to move away from this entire topic as quickly as possible.

"That is not a current priority. The publicity campaign must show my people I have their interests and well-being at heart. Choosing a spouse would alienate a portion of my people, particularly among humans and Veseile. I cannot risk that at this point."

Of course, the option did remain to marry someone from another Eile race, as Roan proposed with Adira's and Edyth's relatives, but history had shown that children were only born among Eile of the same type, or between an Eile and a human. Malcolm's human heritage offered a slim chance for him to produce offspring with any Eile race, though it was much more likely to occur with a Veseile or, of course, a human. He could not imagine the council being satisfied with anything but the best opportunity for future heirs and breathed an internal sigh of relief that Roan's proposals would therefore surely be shot down, even if he pushed for them.

Roan frowned. He didn't persist with the conversation, though Malcolm had no doubt their discussion would continue at some point in the future.

"Back to the matter at hand." Malcolm shuffled through the papers he'd brought to the meeting, plucking a sketch from the pile and passing it to Viv at his left. "Please pass this around and take a look. It contains Adira's first drafts of a method to weaponise shadowbell essence in case we face violence after the announcement." He changed the subject in the hopes everyone would forget about his need to marry for a while longer.

15

LUELLE woke with a start to Mei shaking her shoulder. After a brief moment of panicked disorientation, she grounded herself in the cavern. She changed into fresh clothes, splashed her face with water from the pool spanning half the floorspace, and rose to follow Mei. The scarred Veseile beckoned Luelle to the cavern's main entrance, leading to the paths higher in the mountain.

Side by side, they marched upwards until Luelle's thighs burned and dawn's pale light spilled through the tunnels. A new shift of soldiers guarded the entrance. Mei nodded a greeting as they passed, requesting that they share her direction of travel with Leena when she arrived in search of them.

Pushing through overgrown bushes and ducking under low branches, they walked parallel to the path until they found a shallow hollow, set back in the shelter of some large rocks. Anyone walking the path in their direction would easily notice them, but it offered some shelter from the wind that turned the morning chill icy.

In silence, they settled on the floor, legs crossed, arms

almost touching in the lack of space the hollow offered. Peace was easier to achieve in the open air than it had been in the cavern and the tunnels. Luelle's breathing was calm and steady. A gentle breeze caressed her cheek, reminding her she wasn't trapped inside the mountain.

She reached out with her senses, feeling and listening for the tiniest details. A stray hair brushed against her forehead. Her back ached from her stony bed, but she ignored the distraction of that discomfort. Birdsong fluted to her in its many forms—harsh distant squawks, purring coos, and delicate song-like melodies. Far below, the Caeleste River rushed past, nothing more than a whisper of sound, fed by a hundred waterfalls. Closer to her, a laugh sounded, carried on the wind from the soldiers stationed beside the cavern's entrance. Sounds were the easiest to distinguish.

Luelle took a deep breath. The herby aroma of Mei's soaps and hair oils overpowered most other scents, though it was more pleasant to breathe in than the animal waste and occasional carcasses common in the wilderness on the mountain.

With every new connection she made to the world around her, the Power heated in Luelle's chest. If someone were to slice her open, throat to navel, she was certain they would see the Power as a physical, glowing ball of tendrils, encasing her heart.

Mei shifted beside her, breaking Luelle free from her observations.

"I see you managed to stay awake this time."

Luelle opened her eyes to glare at Mei, but couldn't prevent a smile from curving her lips. "I managed it yesterday, too." Yesterday's search had been unsuccessful.

The land lower on the mountain had yielded no new evidence of Luelle's old friends living nearby, but spending the day outside had been a welcome change.

Mei grinned, the soft skin around her scars creasing. "True enough. We should practise using the Power this morning. The other soldiers cannot see us here."

Uncertainty pooled in Luelle's gut. Could this be a trap? Mei was friendlier than any other soldier she'd encountered, despite knowing more of the truth about Luelle. Was it all an attempt to lull her into a false sense of security? Everything Malcolm and Leena had said about an execution whilst she was out of the city could be a lie. Mei might be manipulating her, pretending to be a friend so she could take Luelle's life more easily when Malcolm decided she was no longer useful. If Luelle hadn't been able to trust lifelong friends to protect her, how could she trust anyone?

Mei continued talking, oblivious to Luelle's inner turmoil.

"We can keep it simple, avoid any action that might attract attention. We need to maintain enough energy for the day's search, too." She twisted a plain golden ring on her thumb as she spoke, staring out over the valley.

"We could practise precision," Luelle suggested, abandoning her paranoia as well as she could, "or make a game of it." She stood and strolled several steps further from the path, to where the ground was less hard-packed. Grabbing a nearby stone, around the same size as her palm with a few jutting edges, she drew a makeshift target in the ground, layering several circles inside one another.

One of Mei's eyebrows was arched as Luelle walked

back, gathering small pebbles and stones as she returned.

"We can take it in turns to propel these stones towards the target, only using the Power. Closest to the centre wins. It's close enough that it shouldn't exhaust us, but may improve our aim and ability to ration our strength," Luelle said.

Despite her growing control, the desire to improve and continue learning about the Power gnawed at her, day and night. Malcolm still knew so much more about it than her and was likely discovering plenty about the changes to the Power in her absence. Did strength and ability vary among Veseile? Could someone with very distant Veseile heritage access it? She itched to know every answer.

Mei smiled as Luelle sat beside her again, dumping her collection of stones in a small pile between them.

"I like it. Do you wish to go first?"

"You can."

Mei grinned, unable to disguise her enthusiasm. Straightening her back, she stared at the pile of pebbles, her cheerful expression smoothing into one of intense concentration.

A small, round stone rose from the pile, lifting slowly into the air until it hovered at their eye level. Steady, faint pressure pulsed from Mei as she used the Power to hold the stone in place. As it had when Mei had last used the Power in front of Luelle, a sensation of flowers in a summer field brushed against her. A stronger pulse pushed against Luelle as Mei launched the stone toward the makeshift target.

The stone soared in a neat arc, overshooting the rings drawn in the dirt and clattering onto the dusty path beyond. Mei cursed.

"Your turn," she said, still frowning at the spot the stone had vanished.

Locked away in her room at the castle, Luelle had entertained herself with precision games endlessly, using her food or items from the garden below her window as ammunition rather than pebbles. Before long, she'd learnt she did not need to look at the objects she wished to control; she knew the pebbles were on the ground beside her and could extend the Power like a sixth sense to feel and manoeuvre them, even with her eyes tightly closed. Keeping her gaze trained on the target in the dirt, she took deep, steady breaths and attempted to judge the distance. She would only need a thread of the Power, a drop compared to the wave that had burst from her in Tolhurst. That had been enough force to level buildings; this was so little she could barely feel the effect on her energy levels.

The pebble soared through the air, landing in the second ring from the centre of the target. A warm flush of pride washed over Luelle.

"Impressive." Mei raised her eyebrows. "Somebody's been putting in the hours."

"I haven't had much else to do at the castle," Luelle admitted.

"Well, the practice has paid off. Show me how you did that."

Luelle shifted where she was sitting, getting comfortable and musing over how she could describe something so instinctive. How would Malcolm explain it?

"Think of the Power as an extension of yourself, rather than something new or foreign within you. It's part of you, as a Veseile. When you're meditating, you should focus on how it feels within you, on how to strengthen your natural connection and the instinctive hold you have on it. In the castle, I would practise using it with my eyes closed. It offers you a whole new way to see and interact with the world."

Mei nodded, her hand straying absentmindedly to her chest.

"Try throwing one of the pebbles but keep your eyes closed. Don't worry about hitting the target," Luelle suggested.

Mei closed her eyes and took a slow, deep breath. For a few minutes, nothing moved, but soon, Luelle felt the familiar pressure and floral aura as Mei managed to lift one of the pebbles. The Power pulsed as Mei threw the stone.

"That's it!" Luelle grinned. The pebble had travelled further than Mei's first attempt, but she had proven her instinctive ability. Her confidence would only grow. With more practice rationing her force, she could be as accurate as Luelle.

Mei beamed, opening her eyes and scanning the distant ground for the stone.

Taking turns, they continued throwing stones until Leena found them, their pile almost depleted. Leena carried two small bundles of food and had three flasks clipped to her belt alongside her usual daggers, all swaying like an unusual, uneven skirt. She handed out the small meal, explaining the day's aims while they ate.

"I have spoken with some of the soldiers stationed here. Some of them have also been exploring the mountains, hunting in their free time and exercising when they are off duty. I believe we will have better luck exploring the higher paths. They said if we continue in this direction," Leena gestured away from the cavern's entrance, "we will find another manmade path leading upwards."

Luelle didn't give too much thought to what, or who, might have made that path.

They ate their breakfast and set off, following the steep incline Leena had indicated.

Thorny bushes and overgrown plants encroached on the trail, growing wilder as they walked further. Large stones sought to trip them every step. A sheen of sweat that wouldn't wipe away coated Luelle's forehead. Her shirt clung to her back. Her shoes pinched her toes and heels. At one point, their path crossed underneath a waterfall. Moving in single file, they edged over the damp rocks, cringing away from the spray of water.

The first cave they found was long and narrow, forbidding them from exploring side by side. Luelle led the way, lighting the cave with a small sphere of fire forged by the Power. Sustaining the flames presented a new challenge to ration her energy. No smoke emanated from the sphere. Above, the crack in the rock extended high, hiding all manner of unknown things in gloomy shadows. Luelle kept her fireball low, unwilling for the light to disturb anything watching them from up there. After a minute of squeezing further in, the passage became too narrow for any of them to progress further.

"I don't think anyone could live in here," Luelle said, ignoring the way the small space made her heart race. Her voice bounced off the walls. She turned in place, shoulders scraping the rock at either side.

Mei's eyes glinted in the firelight as Luelle turned, her

sphere of flames moving with her.

"Let's turn back and move on," Leena ordered.

Luelle sent her fireball ahead, gliding it closer to Leena, who led their journey back into daylight. Walking at the back of the trio was far more terrifying than leading the way had been, particularly knowing the cave stretched deeper than they'd been able to travel. Luelle's skin crawled as they emerged into sunlight.

The rest of the morning offered nothing more promising. Although they found several other shallow hollows in the mountainside, all were empty beyond a few traces of animal dung or carcasses. When the sun was directly above them, the path ended at a wide waterfall cascading down steep rock, allowing no stable route forward. Pausing in a small clearing beside the water, the three of them rested, standing in a line to admire the powerful torrent and relish the cool spray in the air.

"Let's stop here to eat lunch," Leena said, glancing at the sun's position. "We can search the other direction for an hour or two when we are finished, but if we find nothing else, we must concede defeat. I do not want us walking around up here after the sun sets."

She crouched, starting to unpack the small backpack she'd brought along. Luelle opened her mouth, turning to offer some help.

Her question was drowned out as several Veseile emerged from the nearest trees and ran towards them, battle cries pouring from their lips.

Pressure pulsed in Luelle's chest as one of the Veseile used the Power to shove her and Leena off their feet.

Mei had the sense to shield herself. Though she was

driven back, she retained her footing.

Leena used the momentum of her fall to roll backward. She sprung to her feet, drawing her weapons in a fluid motion.

Luelle did not react so quickly. Her head bounced hard off the ground as she landed. Giddiness swept over her, her throat thickening with nausea. Dimly, she sensed pulses of the Power moving to and fro between Mei and the unfamiliar group of Veseile.

Metal clashed as Mei and Leena fought their attackers. Air froze in Luelle's lungs, fear choking her and locking her limbs in place. Memories of the cavern flashed in her vision, paralysing her.

Cries of pain began peppering the grunts of exertion and crunches of weapons striking.

Behind Luelle, the waterfall roared.

They were trapped. They would have to fight their way out.

Panic flooded her. Her hands trembled. Wrenching her eyes open, Luelle watched the fight, swallowing the urge to retch as the world spun slightly on its axis.

Mei and Leena had been split by their opponents. Mei fought against two enemies, while Leena was being pushed back by another three, driven away from Mei and Luelle.

The Power pulsed. Letting instinct guide her, Luelle threw up a shield in front of herself and felt a burst of force punch against it. Movement caught her eye. In the treeline, another two Veseile were standing back from the fight, concentrating deeply.

They were the ones wielding the Power.

Mei cried out as one of the Veseile slammed the hilt of

his weapon into her cheekbone. She stumbled backwards, towards Luelle. Blood welled in the wound.

The sound of Mei's pain broke Luelle from her frozen state.

Seizing the Power, she reached for Mei, yanking her closer. As soon as Mei was away from the strangers' weapons, Luelle used the Power to grab at Leena. A tendril wrapped around Leena's waist, tugging her up and over the heads of her assailants, like the stones she'd practised with that morning. Leena screamed in surprise, her startled expression mirroring that of the Veseile she had been fighting.

Luelle deposited Leena atop Mei.

Without hesitating, Luelle willed the five Veseile her companions had been fighting into the air.

A sudden desperate tug fought her. The airborne Veseile shifted in the air. Luelle's gaze flickered to the two Veseile who had been hiding in the trees. Sweat poured down their temples. They each held out their arms toward the five floating Veseile. Pressure pulsed again as the Power-users sought to drag their friends back to the ground.

In response, Luelle funnelled as much of her Power into the battle as she could manage, flinging the airborne Veseile toward the valley.

Five flailing bodies soared through the air.

Following shortly after, the two Power-users skidded past, clawing desperately at the dirt. Confusion and terror mingled on their faces, but they did not release their connection with the Power anchoring them to their doomed friends.

Luelle lay, frozen, staring at the horrified expressions of

the Veseile flying overhead. Screams sounded as they plummeted over the edge of the cliff, fading as their bodies descended far into the valley.

Before she could look around to confirm Mei and Leena were unharmed or check for other enemies, black spots obscured Luelle's vision and she sank into unconsciousness.

16

CHAOS reigned in the castle after Malcolm announced the changes to the Power.

Few changes had been made to his suggested laws during the council meeting, other than a financial incentive for Veseile to begin new careers as peace-keepers throughout the realm. Increasing the number of loyal Veseile soldiers would only strengthen Malcolm's ability to keep the majority of his people safe from the few Veseile who might cause trouble with their newfound abilities. He only hoped he would be able to trust anyone who volunteered for the role—and to afford them in the long term.

Leafleters and town criers spread the news throughout the city after his speech to the nobility, ensuring the awareness would spread beyond the walls of his home. He feared panic and confusion would spread with it. Today and the following few weeks would be the worst of it. Veseile would experiment, discovering the extent of their Power. It would result in injury and death across the realm, despite the steps Malcolm had taken to prevent such an outcome.

Spread throughout the capital were the majority of the trained Veseile soldiers who had not accompanied Malcolm's Thanes back to their land or been sent East with Omar. The remaining Veseile soldiers were under orders to travel to other cities and towns in the Westlands under Malcolm's direct control, to ensure peace.

This would be a new experience for everyone involved. All Malcolm could do now was observe how it played out —wait and see if he'd made the correct decisions or if he would need to abruptly change course to keep his people safe, even if he was only protecting them from themselves.

When he had opened the floor after making his announcement, the lords and ladies present had asked as many questions as he had expected. Malcolm had answered them all as well as he could, reinforcing the story that must spread—his mixed heritage was the cause of the changes. People could not learn that Veseile extremists had been preaching the truth all along. Zeke was still running free, likely lurking and spreading poison. He'd revealed his hand in the cavern; he desired to boost his own reputation, to step up and lead the Veseile people in isolation from the rest of Arazia's population. His belief of Veseile superiority put all of the humans in the realm at risk of harm, not to mention any Eile who chose to defy Zeke. Malcolm would not let Zeke's goals come to fruition, even if that meant killing Zeke himself.

In fact, he relished the idea.

Malcolm ended the announcement as soon as he felt he had addressed the nobility's key questions. He was aware they wished to ask more but there was no point exposing himself to questions he could not answer. Instead, he left them to reel in their shock, retreating to his chambers, where his family awaited him. Theo walked two paces behind him, unwilling to leave him alone for even a second now the changes to the Power were public knowledge.

Malcolm's family looked up as he entered the drawing room in his suite. They lounged across the sofas, seated around a box on a low table.

"How did it go?" his mother asked.

Malcolm pulled a face as he walked further into the room, sitting on the final settee, left empty at the head of the table for him.

"As well as we all expected." He sighed. "They had plenty of questions. There is nothing to do now but see how the rest of the realm reacts and hope our soldiers have enough control over their abilities to suppress any violence that occurs."

"The soldiers have been working hard," Viv said. "I have faith that they will succeed."

"There will be injuries, perhaps even death, despite the preparations you have made," their mother cautioned them. "However, through that, you must think of the potential devastation that could have occurred had you not taken the action you have. We can only learn from these events. We did not have long to prepare and I believe you have both made the best choices that were available." She hesitated, but continued, in a quieter tone. "Your father would be proud."

Malcolm's stomach twisted, tears abruptly burning in his eyes. He hated speaking of his father as much as he relished it. Every reminder of that loss brought him pain, but he couldn't bear the thought of ignoring those memories.

Silence fell over the room as each one of them faced their own inner turmoil at the knowledge that their family would never again be whole. Malcolm swallowed, taking deep, slow breaths until the grief was at bay, as far away as it ever was from him. Even Theo grew subdued, expression solemn as he stood at his post beside the door.

After several heavy moments, Viv cleared her throat, blinking away the moisture in her eyes and laying a hand atop the box that awaited their attention on the table. Malcolm focused on it, relieved for the distraction.

"This arrived from the smith working on Adira's prototypes. Philip sent them to your chambers along with some small pouches of powdered shadowbell, ready for us to begin experimenting whenever we need to." Viv removed the lid as she spoke.

Malcolm leaned forward for a better look inside the box. Four delicate spheres of glass were nestled amongst nests of straw to protect them from damage. He reached in, plucking the nearest sphere for closer examination. It lay in Malcolm's palm, only slightly larger than the marbles he had played with as a child. Holding it up to the light revealed just how fragile the glass was, blown thin enough to crush in his fist with the slightest pressure. The sphere was hollow, with a tiny hole at the top.

They were eerily reminiscent of the crystal relic that had once transferred the Power from monarch to heir.

Malcolm beckoned Theo over and held out the sphere so he could take a look. Zasha and Edwyn crowded around, shoving one another to get the best view inside the box without jostling their mother.

"These are weapons?" Edwyn scrunched his nose.

"They look more like ornaments. How can glass balls hurt anyone?"

Malcolm gestured for his brother to take one. "We do not necessarily want to hurt people with these, only to stop them from hurting others. Each one has a tiny hole at the top." He picked up another sphere and rotated it, showing Zasha. Edwyn rotated the one in his own grip. "We will use a funnel to pour shadowbell powder through that hole and seal the sphere with wax. Then, our soldiers will use the Power to push the spheres towards anyone who uses the Power to commit crimes and will burst the glass when it is close enough. If it goes as we hope, the target will breathe in the powder and lose consciousness so our soldiers can safely take them away."

"Will the glass shards not hurt them?" Zasha frowned, holding out her hand and taking the sphere from Malcolm.

"I suppose some injury will be inevitable but it should not be fatal." Malcolm conceded with a nod.

"And neutralising the threat is our priority." Viv added.

"Yes, we would only use this against people who broke the law."

Zasha's eyes sparkled as she looked up from examining the sphere and met Malcolm's eyes.

"Can we try them?"

The corners of Viv's lips pinched as she frowned, but Malcolm's curved into a smile.

"I don't think that is sensible," Viv said. "These are weapons, after all."

"We need to test the prototypes at some point." Malcolm pointed out. "Why put it off?"

"Yes, but we should test them with soldiers, not

children."

"I am not a child!" Zasha scowled.

"Theo is with us, he counts. Besides, we must all learn how to wield these weapons as well as our soldiers. I want all of us to know how to protect ourselves in case we are ever in a situation where it is necessary," Malcolm said.

"Mother, surely you do not agree with this." Viv frowned at their mother.

"Oh, leave Mother out of this." Zasha rolled her eyes. "Come on, Viv, let us have some fun, for once. Besides, Malcolm is the king, not Mother."

Viv's lips flattened into a line. "Fine, but do not blame me when this all goes terribly."

"Have you been practising using the Power?" Malcolm asked Zasha.

She nodded eagerly. "My control is better now. This will be easy."

Malcolm turned to Theo. "The great hall is the longest room but will still be busy after today's announcement, I fear. The library may be better. We will need guards on every door to ensure nobody enters as we are testing this."

Theo nodded. "I will arrange it, Your Majesty. I will send a page to let you know when it is done."

Dutifully they waited. Malcolm leapt to his feet when a timid knock sounded at the door. He dismissed the short boy delivering Theo's message, collected the box from the table and carried it, lid reattached to stop any passing servants from viewing the contents as they walked the corridors leading to the library. Fortunately, nobody interrupted their journey trying to speak with him. Soon enough, they were closed inside the library with four prototype weapons to test.

The library stored and displayed the kingdom's wealth as much as its knowledge. Jewels and art lined the walls and shelves alongside endless books and scrolls. Servants kept the room prepared for visitors even when there were no upcoming events. Mahogany wood stretched beneath their feet. Grand bunches of flowers adorned tables throughout the room, nestled beneath golden sconces for candlelight. Overlooking half of the large room was a balcony that hugged the walls, accessed by a central set of stairs with deep red carpeting. Above it all, the ceiling was painted, portraying beautiful landscapes and tales of gods and mortals so intricate that Malcolm could admire it until his neck ached, despite living alongside the artwork for his entire life. From that ceiling hung several moonstone chandeliers, bathing the room in a pale glow at all hours.

Malcolm stood with his siblings, mother, and Theo at one end of the long room, placing the box on the floor in front of them, musing on the best way to test the weapons without damaging any of the surrounding treasures.

"I want to see how easily we can shatter the spheres and how far the debris will fly, but we must also test whether the same process will work when the sphere is full of the powdered shadowbell," he said. "There is enough for us to attempt once each." He looked at his siblings. "I will shatter the first. Viv, please shield everyone behind me to ensure no one gets hurt if the glass flies further than expected."

She nodded, ushering their younger siblings behind Malcolm, to where their mother and Theo were standing.

Shielding was one of the first skills they had chosen to teach their Veseile soldiers. It had quickly become apparent that an individual could not use the Power through a shield. To test their prototype, Malcolm would have to stand beyond Viv's barrier of protection, vulnerable to the glass. Instead, he chose to shield the books and artwork around the far part of the room, where the explosion of glass could cause the most significant damage.

He crouched and plucked one of the delicate spheres from the box. Taking a deep breath, he allowed himself seconds to ground himself in the familiar space. Distant conversations and footsteps sounded from the halls beyond the closed library doors; each breath brought him the scent of the flowers decorating the room and the perfumes his family wore; against his skin, the brush of his clothing was soft and warm.

He held the sphere out on a flat palm. Using a small thread of the Power, he lifted the prototype until it floated several feet above them. Even without the glass in his hands, Malcolm could sense its delicacy as he handled it. He willed it further into the room, stretching his will until the sphere was at the far end of the library, still within the boundaries of his own shield and invisible to anyone who hadn't been following it's trajectory as it grew smaller and more distant from them.

He willed it to burst.

The sphere shattered. Tiny glass shards flew in all directions, ricocheting off the shield Malcolm had set behind it and scattering across the floor. Malcolm's shield had not extended far enough to protect everything. He winced as minute pieces of glass sliced through nearby petals and book spines. Graman would not be happy when he returned.

Regardless, the test had gone well, particularly for a first attempt.

"Perhaps a little less force," Malcolm said. He turned, finding Zasha bouncing on the balls of her feet, eager to try for herself. He beckoned her forward and stood at her side as she made her attempt with an empty sphere, ready to shield her with his Power the moment she shattered the glass.

She sent the next sphere across the hall. As she used the Power, Malcolm could feel his youngest sister's presence, the sense of her personality washing over him —berries and honey, the bubbly joy of laughter. Zasha used a larger amount of her Power than Malcolm had. He threw a shield in front of them the moment she released her Power. The shards of glass did not quite reach them, but flew further than his own explosion had.

"We will need to teach the soldiers precision," Viv observed from behind them, still shielding the rest of them. "Fighting will heighten their emotion, make it easier to use too much of their Power. A larger explosion will increase the risk of harming civilians or disperse the powder too widely to affect the intended target."

Malcolm nodded, squeezing his arm around Zasha's shoulders in a brief congratulatory hug. He turned to Edwyn.

"Would you like to try?"

Edwyn's expression was the stark opposite of the thrill on Zasha's. His eyes were wide and apprehensive, mouth downturned, chin tucked down. Still, Edwyn had not managed to yield the Power. Malcolm stepped up to him and knelt, placing his hand on Edwyn's shoulder and lowering his voice, speaking only to him despite the others standing close by, listening in.

"You do not need to if you do not wish it, but I believe you can do this."

"What if I cannot? What if I never can?" Edwyn whispered.

"You are younger than the rest of us. I've trained for over three times the length of your entire life to use the Power. Be kinder to yourself. You will get there, I know it."

A small wrinkle appeared between Edwyn's brows but he straightened his shoulders and walked to the box. Malcolm followed him, keeping his hand on his brother's shoulder to offer any strength he might pass along. Silently, he prayed today might be the day his brother overcame whatever blocked his access to the Power. Edwyn selected a glass sphere and straightened, holding it in front of him and glaring at it.

"Ground yourself. Think about your connection to the world around you. Use it to shape your will," Malcolm murmured.

Every tick of the large clock further in the library mocked Edwyn's delay. Minutes passed and Malcolm did not feel the pressure of his younger brother manipulating the Power. When Edwyn inhaled sharply, his bottom lip quivering, Malcolm knelt again.

"We can keep trying if you wish, or we can take a break and try again another day."

"Another day." Tears welled in Edwyn's eyes, voice quiet.

Malcolm's heart wrenched for his brother, but he nodded and smiled, disguising the disappointment he felt on Edwyn's behalf. Edwyn held out the sphere to Malcolm. He did not take it.

"You keep this one. We will keep practising together and, when you are ready, you can burst this just as Zash and I have."

Edwyn swallowed and nodded, fingers curling around the glass possessively.

As they'd been speaking, Viv had filled the final sphere with shadowbell powder using the small funnel Philip had provided with the flower's essence.

Malcolm stepped back, shielding his family as Viv took her turn. As he had, she sent the sphere far into the hall, balancing it so the unsealed hole remained pointing up. She shattered it with a small, controlled explosion. As glass shards flew, the powder burst from its cage, floating in a hazy cloud in the air.

A grin spread on Malcolm's face. "It works just as Adira suggested it would."

"Do we know if the powder works the same way as the shadowbell tonic?" Viv asked, turning to Malcolm, who dropped the shield between them.

"Not yet, but we can test it now."

In unison, he and Viv turned to Theo.

"You jest," he said, voice flat.

Malcolm's lips twitched, cheeks aching with the challenge of suppressing his smile.

"Someone has to test this part." Viv shrugged, not bothering to hide her own feline grin.

Theo shot Malcolm a look promising payback on the training ground. He ground his jaw and strode towards the powder, still gently floating towards the carpet. Particles swirled around Theo, unsettled as his movement stirred the air.

When he stood in the centre of the grey cloud, he turned back to Malcolm and his family. Through the haze, Malcolm saw his friend open his mouth, inhaling to say something, The words never escaped. As if in slow motion, Theo stumbled and fell into a heap on the floor.

Malcolm and Viv laughed. That sight would be worth whatever revenge Theo attempted. If only Leena had been here to witness it. Behind them, Zasha giggled. Glancing back, Malcolm even found a small smile on Edwyn's face.

"Can you shift the dust so we can collect him?" Viv asked.

Malcolm reached out with the Power, finding the task more challenging than he'd initially expected it might be. The cloud was not a single item to be manipulated. At his coronation, the petals he'd pulled through the city had been large enough they held together in a large group. This powder was too fine for that. If Malcolm was to move it, he would have to use the Power to nudge each individual particle.

The movement of air shifted some particles alongside the ones under Malcolm's control, but the effort still caused sweat to break out on his brow. New doubts about the efficacy of this weapon rose in his mind, but he pushed them aside for a later time. Eventually, he managed to shift the majority of the cloud away from Theo, letting it settle on the floor. He and Viv approached Theo's slumbering body.

"We will need to find a more efficient way of doing that," Viv said, frowning. "If we could easily manipulate the dust, we would be able to incapacitate any criminals who flee from the explosion without inhaling the essence."

Malcolm nodded, breathing hard. "We will continue testing it. At least we know the spheres work. I will speak with the smith and pen a letter to the Thanes, but for now, I should probably move Theo somewhere comfortable."

Viv snorted and left her brother to deal with that undignified task alone.

17

Luelle sat inside the cavern, at the edge of the still water in the very early hours of the morning. Moonstone light reflected in the pool's surface, making the entire lake glow blue.

She'd awoken on their return to the cavern yesterday afternoon, having been carried back by Mei and Leena. Unfamiliar soldiers had looked over Luelle for injuries, but aside from a bash to the head and a mild concussion, she was unharmed.

Mei had informed her they'd encountered no other foes when travelling back. Leena had demanded answers. Had the Veseile belonged to Zeke? Why hadn't Luelle acted sooner? Why hadn't she kept one of the attackers alive for questioning? Luelle hadn't been able to answer any of the questions, so she ignored most of them. Leena had eventually left her alone to get some rest, muttering to herself about thieves and rudeness.

When the day shift of soldiers awoke later, they would help Leena and Mei prepare for their departure.

Like them, Luelle should have taken the opportunity to

sleep but she could not find peace in this cavern. Anxiety plagued her, a parasite crawling under her skin.

Before arriving here, she had believed encountering Vesanya or her old friends would be the worst outcome she might expect. She'd been wrong. Coming back here and encountering some of Zeke's stray Veseile had been terrifying, but Luelle had protected herself against harm. Vesanya's absence was far worse. It filled her mind with endless contemplations about the god's potential whereabouts. Was she far from here? Did she plan to return and wreak havoc? Was she actually nearby, lurking in the shadows and preparing to kill Luelle if she dropped her guard?

She wandered to where Mei slept and shook her shoulder gently.

"Can I go back outside? I need to meditate or use the Power," she blurted, keeping her voice as low as she was able to prevent any nearby soldiers from overhearing. "I cannot sleep."

Mei looked at her, startled out of her slumber. She blinked several times. "Not unaccompanied. I will come with you. We will have to stay close, in case Leena or anyone else needs us."

"You don't need to. You can get some sleep."

Mei shook her head. A slight frown appeared in her brow. "You should not be alone, especially after yesterday. I will take a few minutes to get ready. Do not go outside without me. We will go where we meditated yesterday."

The fist gripping Luelle's heart loosened. Leaving the cavern would help, even if she could not stray far.

She found herself nodding, silently surprised that Mei trusted her to be out in the darkness at all. If she was to run away, to escape Malcolm's grip, this was the perfect opportunity for it.

Though, she still had no desire to run. She had nowhere to go. Forging a new life in Cerulya remained her best option for a future, even if it required living under Malcolm's command for a while longer.

This was an opportunity to prove her trustworthiness to Leena, to all of them. She could not let it go to waste.

When Mei was dressed and had gathered a few supplies, they crossed the cavern and ascended the long, stony tunnel to the open world. Luelle relished the bite of cold air at the top. The soldiers narrowed their eyes at her until they noticed Mei following behind. They offered friendly, if brief, greetings. Above, the sky was still dark.

Trudging the same route they'd walked yesterday, Luelle quickly found the space where they'd been meditating, set back from the path. The target that she'd scraped into the dirt remained, though certain parts were blurred and scuffed, likely from animals living in the undergrowth. Mei planted a torch in the ground and lit it with the Power, looking back toward the cavern to ensure the soldiers there would be able to see the light marking their position. The flames made the shadows around them flicker, creating the illusion of movement in the trees behind them.

Luelle turned her back to the forest, ignoring the false motion, and began to meditate.

A faint wind tousled her hair, which she had left unbound after their return to the cavern. Closing her eyes to eliminate distractions, Luelle concentrated on the scents around her—earthy soil, sweet flowers, woody bark. She could hear the soldiers murmuring to one another. Distant birds chirped early-morning songs, wind rustled the bushes, and some small animal broke a nearby twig as it skittered through the undergrowth. As time passed, her body relaxed. Breathing stopped being a battle.

Something small bounced off her back.

Luelle's eyes snapped open. She spun, scouring the ground for what hit her. Her heart raced. Stones and pebbles littered the dirt, but she did not know which had already been there from their target practice yesterday.

Her actions stirred Mei, who had been deep in meditation beside her.

Another pebble soared between them, flying inches from Luelle's face.

Both of them turned to the direction it had come from, scrambling to their feet.

Coarse shrubbery blocked Luelle's view. Icy fear rolled down her spine. She knew they could retreat and call a guard squad to investigate, potentially wasting their time if this was the work of an animal or if Luelle was imagining things—after all, she'd felt the paranoia of impending danger from the time they'd reached these mountains—or she could try and take a closer look by herself. She had defended herself and others against danger yesterday. She could do so again if she needed to.

Besides, it was unlikely that a risen goddess was trying to catch her attention by throwing stones.

She glanced over at Mei, who nodded firmly. Pressure pulsed against Luelle as Mei shielded herself with the Power.

Swallowing, Luelle took a step in the direction the pebble had come from. Thorns prickled her palms as she pushed through the bushes, forging a path. Several steps later, she emerged into another clearing and stopped short, face to face with a hulking Adeile.

Luelle stumbled backwards into the grove she'd been meditating in. The Adeile followed her. Mei was no longer in the clearing, leaving Luelle to face the stranger alone. Her stomach dropped.

As he emerged into the torchlight, she recognised him —Imbryl.

Dirt stained his torn clothing. Scratches and pale scars marred the exposed patches of his skin. His eyes were wide, lips pressed tight together, as if he was unsure what reaction to expect from Luelle.

"What are you doing here?" Luelle whispered. The Power in her chest was cold, dormant, her grip on it lost when she'd recognised her old friend. She would not be able to cause his death as easily as she'd managed it on the strangers that had attacked yesterday.

Behind Imbryl, a smaller figure stepped into the clearing, completing their old trio. Freya's dark, coarse hair bound in a thick braid, tight against her head. Deep shadows lay underneath her deep-set eyes, but if she'd suffered any serious injuries when Malcolm had flung her across the cavern, weeks ago, they weren't visible now.

"Freya." Luelle's voice did not gain strength. Emotion eddied inside her—distrust, sorrow, longing. In front of her stood her oldest, dearest friends; the very people whose betrayal had cut her so deeply.

They were alone.

She turned to scan for Mei, trying to keep Imbryl and Freya in her peripheral vision, but could not see the soldier beyond the glaring flame of the torch. The sensation of her Power remained, low and steady; since neither Imbryl nor Freya had Veseile heritage, they would not be aware of it. Was Mei lingering nearby, out of sight, to observe what Luelle would do? Luelle frowned. Imbryl spoke again before she could consider what she should do about the situation she'd found herself in.

"We've been waiting to get you alone," his voice was low. He glanced down the path in the direction of the soldiers at the cavern's entrance. He seemed unaware Luelle had been guarded only moments ago.

Alarm flared within her. She scanned the foliage behind Imbryl and Freya. They appeared alone but Zeke and his cronies would not be far, likely hiding nearby to recapture her and finish the violence Vesanya had interrupted in the cavern. If she could reach the torch and extinguish the light, Malcolm's soldiers would likely come to investigate.

She tried to draw on her Power but the conflicting emotions swirling within her made it impossible. Fear undershot it all, making her hands tremble. She curled them into fists and took a small step backwards, towards the torch.

Imbryl held up a large hand to stop her retreat, but did not attempt to close the distance Luelle had put between them.

"We're not going to hurt you."

"No, you're not," Luelle spat, fists tightening. Anger rose within her, hot and blinding. It unfroze her chest, breathing her grasp on the Power back to life; it instantly blazed within her, yearning to shape her will into reality. "I'm not so unprepared this time. Try to lay a finger on me and I'll break your hand."

Imbryl and Freya exchanged a glance. Luelle couldn't

see past the red haze lining her vision to interpret it.

"Where is he?" she snapped.

"Who?" Freya asked, her voice carefully neutral. Her hands were loose at her sides, away from the weapons strapped to her waist.

"Zeke."

Imbryl's chest rose as he took a deep breath. He glanced around them, as Luelle had moments earlier. "We think he fled to the Razors."

The Razors were a mountain range to the east, larger and less hospitable than the Caeleste Peaks. When living with Zeke, Luelle had travelled through the Razors once, but they had not stayed longer than necessary and Zeke had never expressed a desire to return.

"And I'm to believe he left you here? Did he order you to wait for my return?"

"No." Imbryl's face creased with frustration. "We don't have long. Just let us explain."

Luelle glared at her former friends, gritting her teeth to stop more angry words from spilling out. Malcolm had instructed her to find them before she'd left the capital. She could hear them out and flee or call for help before they tried to recapture her—she was stronger than them now. Besides, Mei remained nearby, revealed by the steady pulse of her Power, giving Luelle a secret, hidden ally.

"We aren't working with Zeke any more," Freya said.

Luelle blinked but didn't drop her guard. They were lying.

"Not after—" Freya swallowed. "Not after he turned against you like that. One of our own. We're sorry for being a part of what happened in the cavern. We've regretted it ever since."

"If that's true, why didn't you do anything to stop it? You disarmed Malcolm, Freya. Imbryl, you were the one who restrained me. Why have you stayed here if not to follow Zeke's orders again?" Luelle asked. Their apology meant nothing. Hearing the empty words only reminded her of the pain she'd suffered through since their hateful rejection of her.

Freya breathed a dry laugh. "We have nowhere else to go. We assumed the prince might hold a grudge." She ignored Luelle's former question. Hurt stabbed at Luelle.

"The king," she corrected Freya abruptly, suddenly understanding the smug satisfaction Leena must feel every time she did the same. "You can hardly blame him. You tried to kill him."

"Zeke tried," Imbryl objected.

Luelle scoffed. "Like I said, Freya was the one who stabbed him. Besides, we all know Zeke wouldn't have managed it without help. When has he ever gotten his hands dirty without implicating someone else to lay the blame on if things go wrong?" She'd had plenty of time to reevaluate her opinion of Zeke over the past few weeks, pouring over old memories and seeing his actions in a new light, rather than instinctively idolising him as she always had.

Since he'd picked her off the street in Vidamere, Luelle had viewed Zeke as her saviour. Now, she saw it for the lie it had always been. He hadn't truly wanted to help her, he'd simply seen someone easy to manipulate and had taken advantage of that. Why else would he leave behind every other child who needed help in her old city? He'd always been selective about who he recruited. It had never been random or from the goodness of his heart.

Imbryl opened his mouth to object, again, but Freya cut him off.

"You're right. And we don't blame the prin—the king for his anger towards us, but that's the honest reason why we're still here. You know us well enough to know I'm not lying."

"I thought I did," Luelle murmured.

Freya flinched away from the words as if they'd been a physical blow.

Luelle swallowed, trying to refocus on her burning anger to subdue her hurt. Angry, she could be decisive and use the Power. Upset, overwhelmed, or confused, she could do neither. She took a breath, looking for a way to organise her thoughts and twist the conversation to her advantage. "Do you know where Vesanya went?"

Freya shook her head. "We're living with some others who defected from Zeke after that evening in the cavern, but we've been laying low. We aren't stupid enough to try and follow her after seeing her slaughter so many."

"What happened to the bodies?" Imbryl asked.

"They're in Cerulya."

"Will they be buried?" Freya's brow furrowed. "They deserve that much."

"Do they?"

Freya averted her eyes. Luelle took a deep breath and changed course, hoping Mei was listening.

"Where are you staying?"

Another glance between them. They said nothing, both as untrusting as Luelle, despite their apologies. She couldn't blame them for that, but her heart ached to see how different their relationship now was.

"Why have you been waiting to get me alone?"

"We wanted to apologise. To make sure you're alright," Imbryl said.

It took every ounce of Luelle's self control to stop herself from lashing out at them with the Power. If fury's grip on her had been any weaker, she might have laughed in Imbryl's face to hear those words. Neither of her former friends looked dishonest but their words were a lie. Of course she wasn't alright. They only wished to speak to her to ease their own guilt.

"Was Zeke lying?" Luelle bit the words out. "About my parents."

Silence hung between them, thick with tension.

"Was he?" Luelle snapped, the slight rise in the volume of her voice making her old friends flinch.

Imbryl shook his head, reluctantly. "We went back to Vidamere with him a couple of years after you left. He took us to the orphanage where he'd found you and they showed him paperwork that confirmed it. It was old, poor quality, but it was your name and description."

Luelle averted her eyes, blinking away the tears pricking them. Part of her had been clinging to the hope that Zeke's accusation had been a vicious lie, that she remained Veseile, as she'd always believed. She'd spent so much of her life wary of humans, hating them for stealing from the Veseile, yet she was as much one of them as she was Veseile. A hollow space settled in her chest.

In the distance, a laugh sounded as the soldiers continued to converse.

"We can't stay here." Freya's eyes flicked in the direction of the noise and back to Luelle. She hesitated.

"You could come with us."

A lump rose in Luelle's throat. Cautious hope lit her former friends' faces. For a few long seconds, she yearned to accept the offer. The desire died as quickly as it came when she recalled the feeling of Imbryl's arms imprisoning her so Zeke could carry out his plans, the sound of Malcolm choking underneath Zeke's foot as Freya held his sword far out of reach, the way neither of them had defended her when Zeke accused her of betraying them.

"No," she said. "I can't trust you." She missed them, more than she could explain, but even if she managed to see past their betrayal, she did not want to live a life in hiding, always fearing the wrath of Vesanya or Malcolm's.

Disappointment flashed on Freya's face.

"Do you know what documents Zeke took from the cavern before he fled?" Luelle asked, desperate to learn some information that might prove her worth to Malcolm so she could live a freer life than her old friends.

Imbryl shook his head. "His theories were getting wilder towards the end. He was convinced a doorway to the realm of the gods would open in the cavern when you returned the Power but he was wrong."

"Lu, you—"

"Don't call me that," Luelle snapped in response to the old nickname. "You don't get to call me that any more."

Freya gritted her teeth. "You shouldn't keep looking into it. Zeke is dangerous and we've all seen what Vesanya is capable of. You're free of it all now. Live a happier life."

Luelle wasn't sure she would ever be free of it. Vesanya's destruction haunted her. She could not rest knowing the god was still roaming Arazia.

"Zeke was obsessive about the gods by the end," Freya continued when Luelle said nothing. "He found—" she cut herself off, looking at Imbryl.

"What did he find?" Luelle pressed, trying to decipher their silent conversation.

"More myths and stories. He called them theories," Imbryl muttered, cautious. "Theories about obtaining the level of Power that only the gods have. Sharing it with the Veseile race wasn't enough for him. We tried to convince him he was being ridiculous, but his mind was set on it. If he risked returning for anything when Vesanya attacked, it would be his theories," he spat the last word.

"The Power of a god? How would that be possible?" Luelle shivered at the thought of Zeke with Vesanya's destructive potential.

Footsteps crunched along the path, faint but getting closer. All three of them looked towards the sound.

"We have to go," Freya said to Imbryl.

"You're sure you can't come with us?" he implored Luelle, a final time.

She swallowed and shook her head. "I need to learn more. I can't let Zeke hurt more people."

Freya stepped forward, hand raised, reaching out. She paused when she saw Luelle tense. Her hand settled back at her side, hurt flashing across her face.

"Stay safe," she said from afar, instead. She turned and disappeared into the trees, her tread quiet and nimble.

Imbryl hesitated before following. "If you change your mind, come back here. We'll find you. I'm—", he swallowed, "I'm sorry for what I did, Lu."

Her throat constricted.

"Goodbye Imbryl. Watch out for yourself, it's what you're good at," she said, unable to stop the jibe in a last attempt to wound him. Even if the blow struck true, the damage would be nothing in comparison to the hurt they'd caused her.

Luelle turned to see a patrol round the corner, the details of their uniforms hazy in the darkness. When she looked back to the bushes, Imbryl was gone. Something glinted in the grass where he'd disappeared.

Finally, Mei emerged into the clearing from a hidden spot in the bushes. She crossed the space and stepped into the shadows where Luelle's former friends had disappeared, monitoring the direction of their retreat. She stood several paces in front of whatever Imbryl had dropped, oblivious to it.

Luelle approached it. While Mei was distracted, she crouched to examine the object.

Malcolm's dagger, the one Luelle had stabbed into Imbryl's thigh, lay in the grass, the blade wrapped haphazardly in a thin rag. Luelle snatched it up and tucked it in her waistband before Mei turned back to face her, covering the handle with her shirt and praying nobody would notice the bulge of it.

18

A flurry of thoughts distracted Malcolm from his journey through the wide castle halls on the way to his mother's suite.

Since the first weapon prototypes had arrived, he had not been able to tear his mind away from ways to improve the design. So far, none of his soldiers had required the weapons to control unruly Veseile.

In the city, a few skirmishes had broken out. A couple of buildings suffered structural damage, including a bakery that had caught fire. Each time, Malcolm's Veseile soldiers had been first on the scene, suppressing any violence by force and rebuilding the damage. The bakery's flames had only spread to two neighbouring buildings before being extinguished.

Even the castle had not been immune. Furniture in one of the guest rooms was reduced to rubble; the castle guard had found a Veseile noble unclothed and unconscious among the shredded material that had once been bedding. Malcolm hadn't given too much thought to which strong emotion may have contributed to that outburst.

Nevertheless, the weapons would likely be necessary at some point. In an ideal world, Malcolm would have longer to test them, but time was not a luxury afforded to him. Their brief tests in the library were proof the weapons would work and the shadowbell powder would incapacitate any violent Veseile. Theo had woken hours later, groggy and grumbling but overall unharmed.

Would it work against a god?

Though days remained before Luelle, Graman, and Leena were due to return, Malcolm found his thoughts straying to their trip to the cavern more frequently. Had they seen a glimpse of Vesanya? Or found anything that might help him learn how to banish the god altogether? If not, perhaps they'd encountered Zeke, who had orchestrated the plan to steal Malcolm's Power and had thrown his realm into chaos.

He hoped, for Luelle's sake, that they hadn't run into Zeke. In the cavern, Zeke had revealed Luelle's half-human parentage and had reviled her for it. Malcolm had experienced enough of that throughout his life to know the internal battles she must be fighting, the self-hatred that could come from such rejection due to something she couldn't change—something that should not matter at all.

Lost in his thoughts, he walked straight into an oncoming figure in the hallway.

"I apologise! Are you alright?" he blurted, catching the stranger's elbow and helping her straighten up. The guards trailing him stepped forward to intervene but Malcolm waved them away.

"The fault is mine, please forgive me, Your Majesty,"

the woman exclaimed, adjusting the dark coils of hair that strayed into her face and dipping into a curtsy. Like him, a streak of white permeated the darker strands at her brow.

"There is nothing to forgive. I was not paying attention to my path," he insisted.

She beamed at him, dimples rising in her cheeks. "Well, let us put the matter behind us. You do not recognise me, do you?" Her eyes sparkled, reminiscent of Luelle's whenever she had caused mischief or teased him while they'd travelled together.

Malcolm scoured his memories, scrambling for a spark of familiarity. Would it be better to pretend or would this stranger see through his lie? She spoke again before he could decide.

"Talia. We met briefly at the tournament in Stodor. My parents are Lord and Lady Barlowe."

"Talia, of course!" Malcolm smiled, the polite mask he always wore in front of the nobility slipping into place. In truth, he had met so many people at that tournament and hadn't paid attention to a single one. His thoughts had been occupied by his father's deteriorating health and impending death. He knew the Barlowes, distantly, as he knew most minor noble families. They were a Veseile family who owned a small island off the south of Arazia.

Talia dipped into another short curtsy, fluffing the skirt of her lavender gown. Like most other young nobles, she was dressed in finery, with jewels glinting in her earlobes and around her neck.

"I had hoped to speak with you before now but have not wished to interrupt. You have been so busy since the coronation."

Malcolm breathed a laugh that he hoped sounded less awkward than it felt. "Yes, it has been hectic."

Talia lowered her voice, large eyes widening further.

"And I imagine the changes to the Power are only contributing to that? I must admit, it came as a shock to learn I might be able to wield it."

Malcolm nodded, the movement stiff. "With time, all Veseile will receive more guidance. These first few weeks will be the most chaotic but I am sure we will not remember life without it soon enough."

"Perhaps you can teach me some tricks." She smiled at him, gazing up from beneath dark lashes. "One to one."

He forced a smile in return. Teaching soldiers was his priority and Talia looked far from a fighter, but he did not voice that opinion. He cleared his throat. "I apologise but I am afraid I cannot linger. I am on my way to a meeting."

Talia straightened, smile faltering slightly.

"Of course, Your Majesty. I hope to see you around again soon." She curtsied and stepped aside, letting Malcolm continue in the direction he'd been walking before they had collided.

He made it at least ten steps before he was accosted again, this time by Roan, his court chaplain. The priest's brown hair was slicked back with oils, his robes pressed to remove even the suggestion of a crease.

"Your Majesty, I see you have found the time to reacquaint yourself with Lady Barlowe," he exclaimed, stepping in front of Malcolm and drawing him to another standstill. Once again, Malcolm had to wave his guards away, irritation growing with each passing moment. When was the last time he'd been able to walk through his home uninterrupted by someone he had no desire to speak with? Had his father always had this problem?

Malcolm took a deep breath, gritting his teeth. "I was under the impression most of the nobles had returned to their own residences by now," he said.

Roan shrugged, eyes no longer meeting Malcolm's.

"I may have suggested that a few remain for slightly longer," he admitted.

Anger flared in Malcolm. Life was difficult enough right now without having to host guests in his home.

"That is not a decision you should make without consulting me."

Buds of pink arose in Roan's cheeks.

"I had hoped it might benefit your upcoming publicity campaign."

"Regardless, you should have asked me first."

Roan dipped his head. "You are right, as always, Your Majesty. However, their presence does offer an opportunity for you. I know we did not discuss your upcoming marriage for long at the most recent council meeting but the High Priestess and I are certain the holy union will benefit your reign. Now the chaos surrounding your coronation has died down, you have the opportunity to get to know some of the eligible, noble ladies available to you."

Malcolm frowned at the chaplain. "I already told you at the council meeting, this is not a decision to be rushed. Chaos remains due to the changes with the Power. I do not have time to court anyone. You are well aware that making a decision on marriage this early in my reign risks alienating either the humans or the Veseile entirely, which I must avoid now more than ever. You have overstepped." His voice was quiet but icy cold. "How many did you invite to stay? How long must I entertain your foolish ambitions to create a public spectacle?"

Roan shifted where he stood, staring steadfast at the floor.

"Forget it, I do not have time for this today. I am late." Malcolm cut the priest off when he opened his mouth. "We will continue this conversation another day. That should give you plenty of time to prepare your excuses."

Without waiting for a response, Malcolm stepped around Roan and strode away, his expression thunderous enough to ward off any further encounters until he reached his mother's suite.

He found her seated in an armchair in her drawing room, angled to watch the distant city and sea from her bay window as she sipped from a delicate teacup. Her head turned towards the door as Malcolm entered. She placed her cup on the small circular table in front of her as he closed the door behind him and leaned against it, shutting out everyone else in the castle.

"What troubles you?"

Malcolm scrubbed his face with his hands. He needed a good night's sleep. All of his problems would be easier to cope with if he could get more than a few hours of restless slumber at any point.

"Nothing. I am simply sick of people interfering with my private life."

"Is anything private in a king's life?" His mother cocked an eyebrow. A wry smile curved her lips as she gestured for him to take the seat beside hers.

"Some things should remain private and personal." Malcolm crossed the room and slumped as well as he could manage in the uncomfortably upright seat, ignoring the reproachful look his mother gave him.

"Zasha and Edwyn are coming to join us after their lesson. I believe Vivyenne will also call in when she is finished with the soldiers she is currently teaching." His mother stood and smoothed her skirts. "Let me send for some refreshments. Have you eaten yet today?"

He shook his head.

She frowned at him and moved to the door, making her requests to the guards outside so they could send for a servant. Malcolm had mostly managed to smother his annoyance by the time his mother returned and was seated across from him again.

"Who was interfering this time?"

"Roan. He took it upon himself to extend invitations to several eligible nobles in the hopes I will take a fancy to one and wed them." He scoffed.

His mother picked up her teacup again. "Well, it is not a subject you can avoid forever."

"That does not mean I must rush into the decision. I have years to make it."

She opened her mouth to reply and closed it again, looking away.

"Just say it," Malcolm said.

She took a deep breath. "Losing your father was the hardest thing I have experienced but it pales in comparison to the thought of losing you and your siblings before Mortus claims my own soul. You are part human, Malcolm. We have no way of knowing how long you or any of your siblings will live." She swallowed. "Why do you think it is so rare for an Eile to take a human as their spouse? It is not just because they might lose the person they love whilst they still have centuries of their own life ahead. They could also live through generations of their family dying before they make their own trip to the Underworld."

Malcolm averted his eyes to the floor, searching for a way around the hard truth.

"Although Roan is approaching the topic in a clumsy manner, marriage is something you must consider, even if it is uncomfortable. If your lifespan is comparable to Ric's —" her voice softened on her old nickname for Malcolm's father, "you might only have a couple of decades to produce heirs and teach them to rule, as your father did for you."

Malcolm tilted his head back, resting it against the cushioned seat. Talking about his father was doing nothing to improve his mood. Sorrow returned, as stifling as ever, clogging his throat until he could not breathe. Tears pricked his eyes. Guilt ravaged him stronger than before, not just for his failings yesterday, but for his insensitivity. Somehow, he had never considered that his mother might have to witness her children's deaths long before she reunited with his father in the Underworld.

"You are correct. You do not need to rush the decision, not with everything else going on, but it would not hurt to keep a future marriage in mind. You could incorporate it into your publicity campaign," she suggested. "Throw a ball for the nobles. It will give them something to be excited about and you an opportunity to get to know some potential matches in a more natural way."

"I have no time to plan a ball," Malcolm said as the door opened. Zasha and Edwyn entered ahead of a queue of servants carrying covered trays of drinks and food for them to pick at.

"We're having a ball?" Zasha gasped, rushing over to them with Edwyn on her heels.

"No," Malcolm said. From the corner of his eyes, he saw his mother smile and shrug.

"Oh, Malcolm, *please!*" Zasha clasped her hands together. Behind her, Edwyn twirled in circles, holding his arms out to dance with an invisible partner, narrowly dodging the servants attempting to lay out a feast for the royal family. Malcolm's mood lifted slightly at the sight of some joy on his youngest brother's face—the first in a while. Perhaps a ball would be a good opportunity for them all to relax.

"You will not need to plan anything," his mother said. "Philip and I will take care of the arrangements. And Zasha, of course," she added, seeing her youngest daughter open her mouth to object. "All you must do is attend and speak with the nobility. Strengthen your relationships with them."

Malcolm suppressed a groan, not wanting the servants to overhear his blatant lack of enthusiasm.

"Fine," he said. "But you will run the final guest list by me before sending out invitations. There are some people I wish to invite."

19

On the journey back to Cerulya, Luelle did not tell any of her travelling companions about her interaction with Imbryl and Freya. Malcolm had instructed that she was to report only to him, so she would do exactly that. She did not know if Mei would reveal it to Leena, since Luelle had not abandoned them and Mei had failed to capture either of Luelle's old companions.

On the fourth day of their journey, the capital came into view. Wisps of chimney smoke revealed the city before they crested a hill to see the sprawling mass on the horizon, still several hours' journey away. They took a break at the side of the road, letting their horses graze on the grass and eating the last of their rations—hard cheese, fried meat, and stale, herby bread purchased from the inn they'd stayed at last night. They washed it all down with water collected from springs and a bottle of spiced wine, also from the inn.

Whilst they ate, Graman poured over the latest document in his stack, perched on a tree stump. Luelle had tried reading with him in the carriage but it had only resulted in a churning stomach, so she waited until they were stationary to offer more help, all the while pondering the brief interaction she'd had with Imbryl and Freya and the scant information they'd given her.

Was it possible to obtain the Power belonging to another being, let alone a god? In the cavern, the Eile had been playthings to Vesanya, as threatening as a cloud of one-winged flies. Vesanya's existence in this realm proved there was truth to the myths so many people dismissed, and Zeke's theories about the Power belonging to the Veseile were clearly true. Was he also correct about the cavern holding a doorway to the gods' realm? If he was right that a person could obtain a god's Power, did he know how to do it? Stealing from Vesanya was a laughable idea. Even Zeke was not clever enough to trick a god into giving up her Power and he would never risk his life by getting close enough to physically take it from her.

Though, someone had managed to trap her in that cavern for years, so what if it wasn't such an outlandish theory? Could the gods be more vulnerable than myth suggested?

"What are you reading now?" Mei asked Graman, leaning against the side of the carriage behind him.

Graman looked up a moment later, as if hearing the question on a delay.

"This one is a collection of myths about each of the gods. I have not seen an author noted anywhere, but each one is handwritten." He frowned, flicking through the pages. Beside him lay some of the sketches he'd made of the cavern while Luelle, Mei, and Leena had been searching for more documents.

"When I travelled with Zeke, he wrote a lot of the documents himself, recording stories told by people we encountered as we moved around the realm," Luelle said, glancing at Zeke's familiar, scrawling handwriting filling the sheets of parchment.

A deep line dissected the space between Graman's heavy brows. "Perhaps one of our first tasks should be to try and organise our sources. However, that begs the question: what method of categorisation is best? Topic? God? Our own intention? Would you remember the date of any documents collected or written whilst you were in their company? Even vaguely," Graman asked Luelle. "It could help us track how Zeke's theories developed over time."

"Maybe." Luelle nibbled on the edge of her bread. "I was with them for a long time. I can't guarantee the dates would be entirely accurate. Zeke would collect things without explaining his reasoning to anyone else. The only reason I used to read so much of it was because there was nothing else to read. Zeke was the only one who really kept track of it all because of his desire to return the P—" she stopped mid-sentence, glancing at the other guards who had reunited with them at the base of the Caeleste Peaks. Like their journey out, the guards who watched over them at night were currently sleeping in the second carriage.

Graman nodded, understanding flashing in his eyes.

"We will discuss it further when we reach the castle. For now, I am trying to find any documents that might explain some of the features of the cavern, such as the archway or the star map," he said, turning his gaze to the sketch of the stone archway.

After a brief hesitation, Luelle spoke. "Zeke believed

the arch was a doorway to the realm of the gods." She did not need to tell him when she'd learned that fact, not until Malcolm heard.

Graman's brow furrowed. "Interesting theory. I have certainly seen descriptions of doorways to other realms in some myths. Some of those suggested archways."

"Would you like help looking through the documents for information about it?"

Graman nodded, distracted again having already turned his attention back to the papers in his lap.

Luelle finished her final bite of food and got to her feet, brushing crumbs from her lap. Mei moved to sit on the ground beside Graman as Luelle approached the carriage door.

Slender books, scrolls, and loose sheets of parchment were stacked on the floor and one of the seats inside the carriage. Malcolm's soldiers had brought most of the documents back to Cerulya weeks ago, but Luelle, Mei, and Leena had found a considerable amount hidden in various crevices within the cavern's tunnel systems. Most of it would probably be of no use, just aimless scribblings from bored Eile who lived with Zeke, but Graman seemed to have faith that their journey had been worthwhile.

She clambered inside the carriage, settling in one of the free seats and grabbing the first book she saw. Its cover was plain brown, thin leather marred from years of careless handling. She ran her fingers over those bumps and grooves, the marks of life. Who had this once belonged to? Flicking through the pages revealed unfamiliar handwriting, looping and swirling as if it was eager to touch every inch of space on the page.

Anxiety sought to distract her from the words she read. Every inch of ground they'd put between themselves and the cavern had eased Luelle's breathing, but visiting the Caeleste Peaks and finding some answers had only raised more questions and problems she should be concerned with.

Zeke's whereabouts were unknown. If she trusted the word of Freya and Imbryl, he was somewhere in the Razors, seeking to consolidate his strength. His numbers were depleted following the events in the cavern—many of his followers had died there and some, according to her old friends, had deserted Zeke. However, a lack of support had never deterred him from achieving his goals. On the contrary, Luelle was certain it would make him more determined, more dangerous. Even if he could not find a way to obtain a god's level of influence and strength, he now had the Power in his possession. He would not let such a weapon waste away.

Beyond that, Vesanya was still presumably in the world somewhere, already in possession of the unfathomably destructive levels of Power Zeke sought, and willing to use it for harm. Which one of them was a bigger threat at this point?

Luelle read the sentence at the top of the open page in her book for the third time, unable to force the words to stick in her mind.

Mei's face appeared in the carriage doorway, blocking the light. Luelle squinted as her eyes adjusted to the sudden shadow. Mei eyed the book in Luelle's lap, smirking at the stack of documents awaiting her.

"I do not envy you this task. Do you regret offering to help yet?"

Luelle breathed a humourless laugh. "Yes. I don't think it's going to be an easy job. I can barely decipher the handwriting and reading while the carriage is moving makes me feel sick."

"Give it up, then. We are leaving soon. Leena wants us to reach the city by nightfall. You can read more when we arrive."

Luelle sighed. She'd barely spent any time helping Graman and the little help she had offered had been poor. He might not want her assistance when they arrived back in the castle. She set the book aside.

Mei's eyes were bright today, her entire disposition lighting up as they came closer to Cerulya. As she had on the journey out, she had closed in on herself whenever they'd stopped at an inn, growing silent and tense in the food halls and taverns. At each one, she appeared to try and keep tabs on every individual who had indulged in too much ale. Now those stays were behind them, Mei had shed the unfriendly persona like an item of clothing.

The others reflected her obvious eagerness to be home, chatting and laughing with more joy and vigour today than they had at any other stage of their travels. Luelle was the only one who was not looking forward to the end of their journey. She would give her report to Malcolm and then what? What would happen to her if he decided she was of no further use?

Knowledge of the execution Malcolm had carried out in her absence followed her like a shadow. None of her current companions had witnessed it. She would not find out if Malcolm's plans to deceive the capital had succeeded until they returned. If people hadn't believed she was the one being killed, she might be walking back to her own death.

Footsteps crunched behind Mei. Leena approached the carriage. Any injuries she'd sustained during the fight with the Veseile on the mountainside had healed quickly. By now, she was back to her usual self, as happy as the others to have her home in sight.

"I need to speak to Luelle."

Mei nodded, glancing at Luelle before leaving the two of them alone, wandering back to Graman and the other soldiers to find some entertainment.

"When we get back to the castle, there are some things you must remember," Leena said, when Mei was out of earshot.

Luelle swallowed, waiting to hear if Leena would confirm her condemnation.

"In your absence, people believe you were tried and executed. However, there are still plenty in the castle who could recognise your face."

"What will happen if someone does?"

"That is not an option." Leena's tone left no room for discussion. "I will escort you to your room on our return and you will spend the evening re-dying your hair. The king will come and speak to you tomorrow with further instruction, but until his arrival you will stay put."

Luelle swallowed her objections. So, she was returning to a prison.

"How long will I have to live in that room?" she asked, quietly.

Leena shrugged, a shred of sympathy flashing in her eyes. "It's not my decision to make. If it offers any consolation, it is for your own safety as much as it is to protect Malcolm."

"I know."

"I also want to thank you," Leena said, voice quiet but firm. "You showed bravery when the Veseile attacked us. I appreciate your aid. You could easily have left us to die and fled into the hills. I apologise for my anger that you did not leave any alive."

Luelle tried not to think about the people she'd killed, about the terror twisting their faces as they'd flown through the air and the screams echoing as they'd plummeted into the valley. Those sounds and sights had given her nightmares new material to chase her from sleep.

"I meant it when I said I would prove that I wanted to help."

"I also know you had an opportunity to flee when Mei allowed you to meditate outside of the cavern on the day of our departure, but that you did not take it."

So Mei and Leena had spoken about it. Luelle shrugged, uncomfortable at the memories of that day. How much did Leena know? Whatever she and Mei had discussed, it was not enough for Leena to dismiss Luelle as a lost cause.

That opinion might have changed had Leena known about Malcolm's dagger, which was still tucked in Luelle's waistband beneath her shirt. The handle dug into her stomach. Keeping it hidden from Graman and her guards had been a challenge, but no one had questioned her about it, so Luelle assumed her efforts were successful.

"I will bring you a cloak to wear when we arrive in the city so we can pass through the castle with your face hidden. Let me know if you need anything else. We should be home in a few hours." With that, Leena left, calling orders to the others to pack up their temporary camp.

Gloominess settled over Luelle at the thought of returning to her room but she gritted her teeth against it. This was only the first part of her plan. In order to find a place for herself in the world, she needed to secure her freedom and eliminate Vesanya. Only then could she know peace.

Tomorrow, she would report to Malcolm, giving him the information she'd secured in return for her freedom. His dagger was proof that Luelle had met with her friends, as he'd asked, and that the information was true.

If he didn't agree to her bargain, he'd struggle to stop her when she chose to leave.

20

MALCOLM paced his bedroom, agitation seeping from every pore. Since his conversation with Roan, every small inconvenience irritated him. Poor sleep worsened his short temper. Nightmares chased him from rest multiple times each night, growing with severity as time went on. Three nights now, he'd woken with Willa's sobs ringing in his ears.

In the hopes of preventing the dreams, he stayed awake as long as he could each evening, training in physical weaponry with Theo and in the Power with Viv until they insisted they were too fatigued to continue. He worked every spare second he got to try and exhaust himself, reading correspondence from his Thanes and local nobility who asked various requests of their king. When that inevitably failed to bring him dreamless sleep, he scuttled to the castle kitchens and smuggled bottles of wine, whisky, and mead into his suite, drinking himself to oblivion.

No matter how Malcolm tried to fix the problem, his nights remained restless, leaving him sluggish and sickly, a living corpse. Aching headaches and queasiness from all the alcohol he'd consumed didn't help, either. He regularly caught glances of concern from Theo and his mother, but Malcolm ignored them. Unless one of them confronted him about it, he had no desire to speak of the slow destruction he was dealing to his body.

This morning, he'd brought a stack of books from his personal library to his chambers and poured over myths about the gods for hours in the hopes that he might be a little more prepared for whatever information Graman and Leena would bring him. They were due to return either today or tomorrow, as long as their journey was on schedule. Receiving a report from them was a priority over everything else in his day. However, instead of being able to focus on that, Malcolm dwelled on the conversation he would have with Luelle.

She was vital to his quest to find out more about Vesanya and the other gods. Growing up in Zeke's care meant she was more familiar with his theories than anyone else. He'd been right about the Power—what else did he know?

On top of that, Luelle was the only other person who might truly understand why he could not sleep.

A knock sounded at his door. Malcolm called out permission to enter.

His sister and Theo entered the room, signalling the start of his afternoon's meetings. Viv had suggested a full council meeting for this update, but Malcolm's patience was running too thin to be around anyone other than his family and most trusted friends.

"Are you getting *any* sleep?" Viv asked, sweeping past Malcolm and settling on one of his sofas. She stretched over the entire thing, but not before yanking his low table closer to better reach the untouched selection of savoury bites, cakes, biscuits, and drinks Philip had laid out for Malcolm's lunch.

"I have no time to sleep," Malcolm grumbled. He rose from his desk and stretched out his aching back. Theo waited for him to cross the room, following him to the seats opposite Viv. Malcolm poured glasses of wine for all three of them, filling his own glass slightly higher than theirs. He ignored the eyebrow Viv raised.

"Is there a reason you cancelled the council meeting today?" She plucked a strawberry from the table, examining it for imperfections before taking a bite.

Malcolm took a long sip from his glass. "I only need an update, this does not require the full council. We would have Omar here too, ideally, but he's travelling with the soldiers that we're stationing closer toward the Southlands border. Besides, the council meetings always stray into irrelevant topics when there are too many people there." Like the issue of marriage, which Malcolm hadn't expected to consider for at least another few years.

"Omar's latest report actually arrived this morning," Theo said. "Things are going well. They've had no problematic communications from Edyth, and Omar sent a letter informing her of their training, so she's aware of their proximity."

"Good." Malcolm nodded. "Leena is due back either today or tomorrow. When she returns, we must update her and Graman about everything they missed. She has people in each Thane's inner circle and I need her to reach out to them with instructions to begin feeding back relevant information. I wish to know how each Thane plans to deal with issues related to the Power and whether their action differs from the intentions they communicate to me."

Theo nodded.

Malcolm turned to Viv. "How is training going?" The first wave of Veseile soldiers were continuing their training, building on the basics they'd learnt before Malcolm had announced the changes to the Power. Since then, Viv had recruited a second wave of Veseile soldiers and started their training. Two groups, at different stages of control, now worked under her command.

"Good. Everything is happening according to plan. I have drafted a third wave, too, which will start when Mei returns. She and her brother will be part of that group, as we discussed before they left."

"Do you have a list of names for the third wave? I wish to look over it."

Viv waved a hand in Theo's direction. "He has it. Most of the choices were his recommendations."

Theo pulled a small sheet of folded paper from his pocket and passed it to Malcolm. Placing his wine glass on the table, Malcolm scanned the names until his gaze caught on one that stood out from the rest.

"Arthyr? The barkeep from Tolhurst?" He shot a quizzical glance towards Theo.

Theo nodded, a blush staining his fair cheeks. "Since he knew the truth about you leaving the castle to follow Luelle, I thought it best to keep a close eye on him. I have been training him in weaponry in my spare time, and he has been sworn to silence about your whereabouts when we pursued you and Luelle. He is a quick learner and is eager to help where he can. He could be an asset."

Though he did not quite understand the decision,

Malcolm shrugged. "I trust your judgement."

"On the topic of unusual students, I think we should allow Zasha and Edwyn to train in the next wave," Viv said.

Malcolm's stare flicked from Theo to his sister. "Have you both forgotten we're meant to be training soldiers? Training for civilians is another matter entirely and is not a priority yet."

"It will be good for them." Viv grabbed a lemon cake. They have expressed a desire to train with others. We both know how isolating it can be attempting it alone. I have wondered if it might help Edwyn get past whatever is blocking his ability."

Malcolm sighed, rubbing his brow. "I suppose it might. I will consider it. When do you hope to start training the third wave?"

Viv pursed her lips. "It depends when Mei returns. I had hoped she would be here by now." She frowned.

Malcolm resisted the urge to smile. His sister and her guard were as close as he was with Leena, so he could hardly judge her impatience.

She continued. "I planned to examine my schedule this afternoon to fit the third wave around the other training sessions. I will train them in the undercroft in the west wing, as I have with the first and second waves because it is private and quiet. Although, now the public are aware of the Power, we can move to a more visible training ground, if you would prefer."

Malcolm shrugged. "As long as you do not blow up the castle, I am happy for it to continue there. How often will you train them?"

"As often as possible. Initially every day, or every

couple of days, as long as my schedule permits it. Once they have a basic understanding, they can train without me present, as the first and second waves did, but I will continue to assign someone with more experience to lead the sessions I cannot attend. We need as many soldiers as quickly as possible, correct?"

Malcolm nodded. "Correct. Fine, Zasha and Edwyn can join this wave on the condition that Luelle also attends."

Viv choked on the wine she was sipping, spluttering. "The *traitor*?" she exclaimed, eyes wide.

"I told you to stop calling her a traitor."

"No, Malcolm. Absolutely not. She betrayed our family and our kingdom!"

"She can use the Power as well as anyone else you have been training. And she was practising before she left to help Graman. She is well-prepared to continue."

"That doesn't matter! I have accepted her existence in my home, but this is a ridiculous idea. If anyone recognises her, they will realise we rigged the trial," Viv hissed, sitting straight on her sofa.

"No one will recognise her. We will take precautions when she is travelling around the castle. Philip can keep any servants who worked with her in other wings."

"It is not worth the risk!"

"What would you have me do, lock her up in her room until I need more information from her?" Malcolm frowned.

"Of course not! A jail cell would be my preferred option."

Malcolm gritted his teeth. "She is an asset to us, Viv. She knows more about the gods than any of us. She is the only other person who witnessed what Vesanya is capable of." Frustration bloomed in him. Why did no one else believe that finding a way to eliminate Vesanya eclipsed any other issues they faced? Luelle could help him do that, so he needed to keep her alive, even if she had stolen from his father and family. Her theft hadn't been in vain—it had uncovered the truth of a conspiracy he, and almost everyone else in the realm, had dismissed. Although, he was still not sure whether that was a good thing or not.

"I do not think it is sensible." Viv set her jaw, stubborn. "Do you think it is safe letting her train alongside our siblings?"

"If she tries anything, she will be surrounded by soldiers who would neutralise the threat. I will not change my mind about it. We must take advantage of every resource at our disposal." Malcolm's voice rose as his anger mounted. "Am I not your king?"

Silence fell between the two siblings, though they continued to glare at one another. Viv's jaw worked as she contemplated her next words. When she spoke, her voice was quiet.

"And what if she betrays you, too? As she did our father."

The words washed over him like a wave of icy water. Was he wrong to trust Luelle? What if Viv was right to assume the worst of her?

"We will take precautions against that, too." Malcolm ran a hand through his hair, leaning back where he sat. "We are building stores of shadowbell. We have a lot to learn about the Power, but the more we learn, the more we are able to use it in our own defence."

"If that is your decision." Viv leaned back against the cushions behind her, mirroring his position. "Keep your enemies close, I suppose."

Malcolm opened his mouth to point out, yet again, that their biggest enemy was Vesanya, but closed it, knowing it would be in vain. Luelle would have to work hard to prove her worth to everyone, but he'd witnessed her stubborn determination when he'd followed her across his realm. If anyone could do it, she could.

21

LEENA escorted Luelle to her room as soon as their small party arrived back at the castle.

Within minutes of being left alone, the walls pressed in on her. Luelle sat in one of her armchairs, breathing thick air, fingers twitching until she could no longer stand staring out the window at others enjoying their freedom.

Luelle tried to relax in her bath and unshuttered her moonstone lamp to stave off the shadows as soon as darkness fell. She tucked herself into bed but the covers were stifling. Unable to sleep with such a weight pressing on her, she spent most of the night pacing the room's perimeter.

Rest continued to evade her the following day. She re-dyed her hair with the malodorous mixture Leena dropped off and wiled away her time meditating and practising with the Power. Like before, Luelle's meals arrival at regular intervals, indicating the passing hours. She picked at the food, more nauseous than hungry, eating slowly and savouring each bite to distract herself from thinking about the importance of her upcoming conversation with the king, the need to prove she was a worthy asset.

By the time the sun was setting, Luelle was in bed, lying on her side to watch the skies darkening through the window. She closed her eyes and reached out with her Power, tested the limits of the unique perspective it offered of the rest of the world.

Willing her sixth sense outward, she reached beyond the walls of her room, seeking an insight into life in the wider castle. A feeling of being stretched overcame her, exhausting in a way no other previous use of the Power had been. She reeled herself back in, breathing heavily. Dark spots blotted her vision.

Closing her eyes, she breathed deeply took a moment to recover. When her dizziness receded, she tried again. Rather than casting the Power like a net, she moved in a single direction. Guards stood on either side of her door, vibrations of life coursing through them.

Sweat beaded on Luelle's temples from the exertion of the new technique. She stretched further, feeling her way down the hallway in one direction. As she concentrated on extending her presence further away, her impression of the world around her physical body grew fainter. Using the Power, she could visualise the space beyond her physical experience in pulsating vibrations and varying shades of light. She felt the shapes of a passing servant and a tall vase of flowers against the wall. They were a bright contrast to the grey, dead stone and planks of wood around them.

Marvelling over the new technique, she pulled back towards her body. Another figure had joined the guards at her door.

A knock sounded.

Luelle opened her eyes, her Power returning to her at speed. She shoved herself to sit upright, dizziness and a slight headache blooming. A crack of light spilled in from the hall as the newcomer eased her door open, not awaiting an invitation.

Malcolm slid inside, shutting the door behind him. He stayed there, leaning against the wood.

Luelle's pulse raced at the sight of him. His presence felt more familiar than anyone else in the castle. It was a comfort to see him, even if she knew, deep down, he must resent her for the chaos she'd brought into his life.

"I apologise if I woke you." His expression held a strange look, shadowed in the dim light of her room. "I would have called on you earlier but I have been stuck in meetings all day."

Luelle shrugged. "It's fine." She shuffled off the bed and walked to the cushioned chairs beside her window. She didn't look up to see if the king followed—his quiet footsteps behind her were confirmation.

"How are you?" he asked, when they were seated. His gaze poured over her face, searching for the answers he sought. Frequently, he glanced at her hair. Dark shadows underlined his eyes, clear even in the cold glow of the moonstone lamps and the rising moon. The contours of his face were a fraction sharper than they'd been when Luelle had last seen him.

She frowned. "What do you mean?"

Amusement ghosted Malcolm's expression, lips twitching with a smile. "I thought it was quite a straightforward question."

"Not one with a straightforward answer." She was

feeling too much to answer that question: residual fear and exhaustion from her time spent in the cavern; anxiety that she'd made the wrong decision by rejecting Freya and Imbryl's offer to run away with them and sadness that she and her former friends now walked very different paths in life; wariness of how much Mei had told Leena about that meeting and how much Malcolm might already know of it; determination to forge a better life for herself on her own terms.

"I did not expect you to look so different without the Veseile streak in your hair."

"I've only dyed it." She found herself smiling. "Maybe you've forgotten my face after a couple of weeks of absence."

Malcolm snorted. "Not likely."

Luelle frowned. He didn't pause to explain the comment.

"How did everything go?"

She took a deep breath, running over the main points she'd hoped to relay in this conversation, trying to prioritise whatever might make Malcolm wish to continue working with her. "Well enough. I believe we found everything Zeke left behind."

"And was there any trace of…" he trailed off, eyes glued to hers.

She didn't need him to finish his sentence to know he spoke of Vesanya. Luelle shook her head.

"Nothing."

He frowned but did not question her word.

"Leena said you struggled going back, initially."

Heat rose in Luelle's face. Had he really needed to hear of that weakness? Before she could defend herself, he spoke again.

"I understand." His eyes dropped from hers. The words poured from his mouth quickly, as if they would fester inside him if he did not get them out. "I cannot close my eyes without seeing her face. I spent most of the last two weeks waiting to receive a letter from someone who stumbled across your bodies—to hear she had been waiting for you and sucked your life away as she did to those others." His throat bobbed.

That explained the shadows under his eyes.

"I have nightmares about her too," she admitted in a whisper.

Malcolm looked up. "You do?" He leaned back into his seat, slumping against the backrest. "No one else here even believes we saw her. They all get this look on their faces when I mention it, like I am telling a story and they are bored of it."

"For their sakes, I hope they are able to continue believing that lie," Luelle muttered.

A wry smile curled Malcolm's lips.

"I ran into some old friends."

"Leena told me. She mentioned the Veseile who attacked you. Do you think they were Zeke's?"

"I don't actually mean them. But I imagine they did follow him once."

Malcolm's expression was carefully neutral. "Yes, I also heard you met with an Adeile and Colleile."

Luelle frowned again. So Leena had heard enough of that meeting from Mei to inform Malcolm.

"Their names are Freya and Imbryl. They approached me. The Colleile who took your sword and the Adeile I stabbed," she added, seeing the blank expression on

Malcolm's face when she said her friends' names.

"Did they attack you again?"

"Didn't Leena tell you what happened?" she challenged him.

"Yes, but I am interested to hear about it from your perspective."

"They didn't attack me, they just surprised me. It sounded like they were keeping tabs on the soldiers and the cavern from afar." She stood and walked to her bedside table, returning with Malcolm's dagger, the blade no longer wrapped. She held it out to him. "Imbryl returned this."

Malcolm took his dagger and rubbed his thumb along its handle. A line creased his brows. He twisted and tilted the dagger, recognising it. "Why?" He frowned at her.

Luelle shrugged. "They apologised for what happened in the cavern. I think it was an extension of that."

Malcolm lay the small blade on the table between them as Luelle sat back down. "Thank you for returning it. I presume Leena failed to tell me of this because she did not know."

Luelle shrugged, relishing her own smugness at keeping a successful secret from his spy master. "Why didn't the soldiers intervene when my old friends approached?"

"Leena was under instructions from me to observe what you would do if faced with the decision to leave with them. I assumed they might make such an offer." He gazed at her, seeing the confirmation written on her expression. "She must have passed those instructions onto the other soldiers you travelled with. As soon as Mei reported the details of your conversation, Leena sent soldiers to search for your friends."

"Did she find them?" Luelle's heart skipped a beat, though she was not certain what answer she hoped for.

Malcolm shook his head. "No and I do not care to waste the resources employing a thorough search of the mountains for them. Did they tell you anything useful?"

"They claimed they're no longer working with Zeke." She took a deep breath. "They believe he fled to the Razors. Apparently, he formed some crazy beliefs while I was away, theorising a way to harness the Power levels of the gods. They said he thought the archway in the cavern was a doorway between the realm of the gods and our world."

Malcolm's frown deepened. "I would say that is impossible but stranger things have happened over the past month."

"The problem remains that Zeke managed to take some of his possessions before leaving the cavern, so he has probably taken everything that would give us an insight into those theories."

"Graman said as much when I spoke to him earlier." Malcolm's gaze drifted to the windows, lifting to the stars that were beginning to flicker to life. Longing twinged within Luelle, a wish to return to the days they'd spent travelling together, when life had felt more full of opportunity.

"I can help him look through the texts," she offered.

Malcolm nodded. It was not an agreement, but indicated he would consider her request.

"Will I be allowed to leave this room?"

He glanced at her. "Things will be complicated if anyone recognises you."

"Isn't that what all of these precautions are for?" She

gestured to the auburn strands of hair framing her face.

"Well, yes. I have taken steps to minimise the risk but it is not entirely gone. If any of the servants recognise you, they will know I staged your trial and execution."

Luelle tried to swallow her frustration, but it remained, threatening to choke her. What had been the point in murdering someone in her place if she was not now able to move around freely?

"Did people believe it was me?"

He nodded once, unable to meet her eyes. His jaw was tight with tension.

"Has anyone asked questions?" she pressed.

"No. They all carried on as if it had not happened."

"Then no one will be expecting to see me. Please Malcolm, I'm going crazy in this room all day and night."

"It is comfier than a jail cell, is it not?" his voice took a slight edge.

"I thought we agreed I can help you," she challenged him again, heart hammering. "Nobody else believes Vesanya is truly a threat. You said so yourself. If I'm going to help you learn the truth about the gods, I need to be able to leave this room. I'm no use to anyone in here."

Malcolm stared at her. His chest rose as he breathed deeply. Eventually, he nodded. "I will arrange for you to study the documents you brought back with Graman. You can use my personal library or perhaps the observatory. In the meantime though, I need you to stay out of sight. I will arrange to have some books brought in here or some other things to pass the time. What do you enjoy?"

"Books are fine." She didn't truly know what else she enjoyed. She'd never had the time or means to attempt hobbies like the nobles endlessly carried out, embroidering intricate scenes or tinkering on their tinny harpsichords.

"There is another thing. I want you to start training with my sister and a group of Veseile to harness the Power defensively. You will need to leave this room for that."

Luelle's eyes widened, heartbeat picking up its pace again.

"Why? I already know how to use it."

"You can only learn so much by yourself and I do not have the time to spare to teach you. As I have already told you, it is safer to learn how to wield it. There may come a time where you need to defend yourself and others simultaneously. It will benefit you to learn how to work in a team."

Luelle bit back a retort.

"What? You've never held back on me before, why start now?" Malcolm raised his eyebrows, challenge written over his face.

"You're being very contradictory." She accepted the invitation, scowling at him. "One moment you deny me any freedom because you claim I must hide away and the next you order me to train alongside strangers."

"The soldiers you will train with are loyal to the crown and I doubt they will recognise your face from your time working here, since few of them worked with my father." Malcolm shrugged. "You would also continue your actions to alter your appearance and would go by your real name, this time. If you are truly concerned, you could wear a veil. You are too large to pass as Dileile, so an eye veil might draw attention, but a full veil is not an uncommon practice among nobility who are in mourning.

People would not question it if you were to offer that as an explanation."

Luelle had no desire to agree to it. If these soldiers found out the truth about who she was and what she'd done, they would turn on her, just as her old friends had when they learnt her Veseile heritage was corrupted with human blood. Only this time, she would face her death. Even if that did not happen, Luelle wasn't sure she could handle getting attached to others only to risk losing them, as she had her former friends. Malcolm was currently her closest attachment and theirs was only a bond of convenience—Luelle's only route to a real life in which every decision was her own and not dictated by someone else's aspirations. Training with these soldiers could help her get closer to that life, but could she do it without forming any sort of relationships with anyone? That did not sound like the sort of team Malcolm envisioned.

"This is important," he said, interrupting her thoughts. "You changed the world when you stole the Power and returned it to the cavern. These are the consequences of your actions. You must have known it would not be a smooth transition to the peaceful days Zeke told you about, when Veseile had the Power before."

Luelle averted her eyes to the table between them. Was it so naive of her to believe it might have been that easy? That people would want to use the Power for good rather than chaos?

"How often would this training be?"

"Most days. And when you are not training, you can assist Graman with his research."

At least it would get her out of this room.

"Fine."

Malcolm relaxed in his seat. "Would you like me to send veils here?"

She shook her head. "If you think no one will recognise me, I would rather go without."

He nodded. Quiet fell between them, interrupted only by the distant sounds of life elsewhere in the castle grounds.

"It was strange going back there." The words slipped out before Luelle could think them through. Malcolm wouldn't care about how she felt returning to the cavern. He wouldn't understand that part of the reason the journey had felt so unusual was because it hadn't been at his side, bickering whenever they weren't fighting to keep the other alive.

Though, once again, he seemed able to hear her unspoken thoughts.

His lips curled into a small smile. "I would have preferred travelling through the Godswood again than dealing with the petty issues and nonsense I encounter here most days."

"The food is better here though, I suppose."

He shrugged. "You made quite a good craybug."

She barked a laugh.

Maybe making a life for herself in the capital was not such a far-fetched dream. If Malcolm learned to trust her, being a soldier in his fight against Vesanya might be her best option. And, when that threat was eliminated, she could transition into a lifestyle better-suited to her, like teaching other Veseile their history or how to perfect their abilities with the Power.

She cradled the idea, tucking it into a deep corner of her mind to come back to. First, she had to continue proving her value.

22

MALCOLM stifled a yawn on his way to the castle observatory. Last night's conversation with Luelle had strayed so easily from her report to something more casual, he hadn't noticed the night slipping away from them. By the time he'd stumbled back to his own rooms, he'd quickly fallen into an exhausted sleep, unplagued by nightmares for the first time in days. When Malcolm woke, he sent Theo to escort Luelle to the observatory, where Graman was likely to already be working.

The observatory was close to Malcolm's private rooms, within his wing. Regardless of its proximity, he still strode quickly through the halls to ensure he gave no one the chance to accost him with conversation. He ordered his guards to wait outside and closed the door behind him, glancing around the familiar room that felt more like home than anywhere else in the castle.

High ceilings arched above his head, painted a shade of blue so dark it was almost black. A celestial chart decorated the background, displaying the night sky at all hours. As always, Malcolm's gaze was drawn to the mechanical, golden orrery taking up the majority of the room's floorspace, mapping out their known solar system. In the centre sat a large sphere depicting their sun. Surrounding it on slender metal arms that rotated automatically were the solar system's eight planets, each one with its moons circling it on smaller arms. The entire orrery stood at over twice Malcolm's height. Servants kept the room free of clutter, ensuring nothing was in the path of the planets as they made their slow rotations around the sun.

Either side of the orrery, beyond the space the planets required, were rows upon rows of bookshelves and chests, filled with rolled scrolls containing star charts or sketches and leather-bound books, spines worn and wrinkled with use. Beyond it all, a wall of glass gave view to a slice of the horizon, a sliver of the city snaking in front of the expansive sea. The sky was clear and blue.

Graman and Luelle were nowhere to be seen. They would be through one of the two doorways on either side of the room—the right leading to the tower that housed the telescope and cartography room and the left leading to the castle's smallest library. Guests were forbidden from entering the observatory without the monarch's express permission, due to the delicate machinery the rooms housed, so Malcolm was safe enough from intrusion here.

He strolled to the door on the left. As predicted, Graman and Luelle were inside, seated at the large square table in the center of the library. Messy piles of scrolls, books, and parchment surrounded them, spilling from the table to the floor.

Luelle looked up as he entered, though Graman's eyes remained glued to the words in front of him. She smiled.

It was only a small curve of her lips, but her eyes shone brighter than they'd been yesterday, when he had called in on her. Beams of sunlight descended from the room's tall windows, highlighting the copper in her hair, pervading even as Leena's dye tried to obscure it. He returned her smile without thinking and approached the table.

"Good morning."

Graman looked up at the sound of Malcolm's voice, blinking as if emerging from a dream. Teetering on the corner of the table was a tray containing three glasses and a jug of freshly squeezed orange juice. Malcolm's mouth watered at the sharp scent as he inhaled. He poured them each a glass, passing one to Luelle and placing Graman's in a patch of space between documents. He took the free seat opposite Luelle, where there was another patch of tabletop free for his own glass to sit.

"Are you sorting through these at random?" Malcolm asked, eyeing the precarious towers surrounding them. How had they managed to find so much stashed away in the cavern and tunnels? Though plenty of this was brought back from their initial return, there was enough to fill an entire carriage.

Graman pushed his wire spectacles further up his nose, leaning back and taking a sip of his juice.

"For now, Your Majesty, we are trying to organise them into a general timeline to track how Zeke's theories about the gods developed."

"These piles," Luelle gestured to the towers closest to Graman, "are ones I know Zeke collected when I was with him. I'm trying to locate ones I'm unfamiliar with, so we have an indicator of what he studied in the five years I was away. Oh, and those are ones without any relevance." She waved a hand over her shoulder.

Malcolm leaned to peer around her, finding a messy stack of papers and journals on the floor, their haphazard placement suggesting they'd been handled with significantly less care than the other documents.

"No relevance?"

"Mm, diaries, sketches, snippets of poetry and the like," Graman mumbled.

"Huh. Have you found much that you believe Zeke collected more recently?"

Luelle nodded. "The ones on the floor to my right. Graman's starting by reading through the ones I'm already familiar with. When he's caught up, we'll use them to identify the differences between these sources and traditional belief."

"How have you managed to organise so much already?" Malcolm was astonished by the number of documents already categorised, although they were still significantly outweighed by the amount left to sort through.

Luelle shrugged. "I'm quite familiar with a lot of these, so it doesn't take long to consider when they might've been collected. I'm not reading them properly, just enough to know whether they're new or whether I've seen them previously."

"Right." Malcolm frowned. "How can I help?"

Graman had already been sucked back into the sheet he was reading. Luelle glanced at the large scholar before pursing her lips.

"The same as Graman, I suppose. Familiarise yourself with the documentation in that pile, those are the ones I've already read."

Malcolm scrubbed a hand over his face and dragged a book from Graman's pile towards him. He read the first few lines but distractions sought him—an itch on the back of his neck, a buzzing insect floating past his ear, a tickle in his throat, the bouncing of Luelle's knee not far from his underneath the table. He returned to the start of the page several times in an attempt to retain the information he was staring at. The lines blurred.

Somewhere in a deep corner of his mind, a voice reminded him they could put in all this work only to read false sources. Zeke had been correct about all Veseile having potential access to the Power, but that didn't mean any of his other theories were correct. This could all be a waste of time. What if they were better served tracking Vesanya and trying to predict her intentions, rather than remaining stuck in the past?

He rubbed the bridge of his nose and sighed. Looking up, he found Luelle scowling at him, any earlier trace of friendliness vanished.

"What?" he asked, suddenly self conscious.

"I can't concentrate with your huffing!"

Malcolm frowned. "Perhaps if you spent less time listening to my huffing and more paying attention to the words in front of you, you would have more success."

"I am paying attention! This wasn't a problem before you arrived."

Malcolm crossed his arms. "This is my home, I can go where I please."

Graman took a deep breath, taking off his glasses and rubbing his eyes with a thumb and forefinger. "You are both as noisy as one another."

Malcolm exchanged a guilty glance with Luelle, though

he could have sworn her cheeks rounded with a suppressed grin.

"Perhaps we should discuss our overall aims with this work, rather than leaping into the sources blindly," Graman suggested.

Malcolm nodded, pushing away the book he'd chosen. "Are you sure there was no trace of Vesanya in the cavern when you returned?"

"Not since the bodies were removed," Luelle muttered.

Graman put his glasses back on. "There were signs of fighting further into the tunnels—markings and trails of what must have been blood from injuries that had occurred in the main cavern—but no other noticeable signs of destruction, damage, or conflict."

"Could a god leave any other type of imprints? Is there something we might be missing?" Malcolm asked.

"That is something we can search for in these documents." Graman snatched a blank piece of parchment and a quill and inkpot previously obstructed by the papers on the table to begin writing a list. "Our current knowledge of the gods is so little, but these texts might inform us of such possibilities."

"That will all take time," Malcolm said. "Even if we find something, we would then need to return to the cavern and follow up our research searching for a trace of Vesanya. We also have no guarantee of the credibility of these sources. Zeke was correct about the Power but the rest of this information might be speculation." His tone grew more frustrated as he spoke.

"What alternative is there?" Luelle challenged him.

"I gather a scouting party and search the realm for her."

Across from him, Luelle's face paled.

"I don't think that's sensible."

"I must consider any course that could save time. I need to stay ahead of Vesanya to minimise the destruction if she intends to attack anyone else."

"But, we don't know how to stop her if she does, or whether it's even possible to kill a god. You'd be sending people to their deaths if you sent them after her. You'd risk your own life if you accompanied them."

Malcolm drew in a deep breath, running a hand through his hair. She was right, but he did not want to voice that. "Alright, then I could send more soldiers to assist the current scouts and track her from a distance. If we can anticipate the direction she chooses to travel, we can evacuate populated areas before she arrives."

"Do your current scouts know her location?" Graman asked.

Malcolm shook his head. A small number of soldiers across the realm were ordered to observe for unusual activity and report back to him or Omar. So far, none had seen evidence of the god. The changes to the Power and the potential violence that entailed was a bigger priority for most of them.

As far as Malcolm knew, Vesanya had disappeared without a trace. If it weren't for Luelle's account to prove they'd witnessed the same event, he might think he'd hallucinated the entire afternoon in the cavern.

Graman's voice softened. "You cannot lead the charge into danger this time, Your Majesty. Arazia needs its king; your people need protection. This is a time of significant change. You must remember, Vesanya is not the only threat you face."

Malcolm swallowed. Graman should not be voicing

this in front of Luelle, even if it was the truth.

"Until then, research will benefit us. We must learn how and why Vesanya was in the cavern, if it is possible to kill a god, and if not, whether we can trap her in stone as someone else clearly managed to." Graman jotted each item on his list. "If we achieve that, we will be prepared to deal with the threat when your soldiers locate her, especially if she attempts to commit harm."

"You're right. I just wish there was a quicker solution. All of this sitting around makes me feel we are achieving nothing."

Graman smiled, lips curling around his tusks. "On the contrary, Malcolm."

Malcolm did not miss the way his adviser addressed him informally in a further attempt at reassurance.

"You were always a dedicated student growing up and learning should stop simply because you have aged. The wisest rulers continued their education throughout their reigns. How can a leader do what is best for their people if they remain ignorant or static? Life does not freeze simply because a new head wears the crown."

Malcolm smiled. Of course Graman could squeeze a lesson into this conversation. He had a point. Growing up, Malcolm had enjoyed his lessons, not just for the excuse to get away from people he disliked in the castle, but simply for the love of learning. Feeling slightly more motivated, he pulled the book back towards him and read until his stomach was growling and the words blurred on the pages. A glance towards the clock on the wall told him hours had passed, leaving him with scant time to dress and prepare for his first public appearance in the city since the execution—attending a service of worship in the Great Temple.

His hands grew clammy at the thought of being shut in that temple with the statue of Vesanya once again, but there was no escaping this. He could not avoid depictions of the gods forever; people would talk.

Malcolm stood, his chair scraping the floor. He stretched his cramped back.

"I must go, I did not realise the time. How long are you both staying here?"

Graman took a sip of his drink, reluctantly glancing at the clock. "Not much longer. Though, I admit I am loath to keep leaving this task. This morning's progress has proven it will take a while to work through all of this information."

Malcolm nodded, glum. "Do you need me to arrange a guard to escort you back to your room?" he asked Luelle.

"Graman said he would, when we finish here."

"Fine. I believe my sister wishes training to start soon. She will arrange your collection."

Luelle's lips tightened with a frown. She did not need to voice whatever unhappy retort she bit back, it was plain on her face. Malcolm suppressed a smile. Travelling together, she had once remarked how easy it was to wind him up; he was learning the same was true of her, and was coming to understand why she had enjoyed provoking him so much.

He turned, leaving Luelle and Graman with reluctance so he could publicly demonstrate his commitment to worship gods he no longer truly had faith in.

23

Lunch awaited Luelle in her room when she returned; creamy soup and a thick slice of bread slathered with a layer of herbed butter.

Another hour had passed after Malcolm left before she and Graman tore themselves away from the research. She'd been anxious about leaving Zeke's documents unattended in the observatory's small library, where anyone might stumble across them and ruin their careful work. Graman had been quick to reassure her that few people had a key to the observatory and none were allowed to use it without Malcolm's express permission, but doubts continued to crawl beneath Luelle's skin. Sensing her unease, Graman had instructed a pair of nearby guards to block the door from anyone beside himself and King Malcolm.

Alone in her room again, Luelle ate with speed, famished after hours of distraction. The food was cold, a slight skin forming on the top of the soup from the time it had spent untouched in her absence. She devoured it as if it was sent directly from Meto, the God of Harvest and

Fertility. She would never be ungrateful for the regular, nourishing meals she received while safely within the castle walls.

A knock sounded on her door the moment she put her spoon down, still chewing the last bite of her bread.

A guard stuck his head around the door after Luelle called permission to enter. She froze, bracing for another forceful show of detaining her, as she'd experienced on Graman's first visit. However, the guard did not step into the room. Instead, he raised a hand and gestured for her to follow.

"Where are we going?" Luelle asked, standing from the table and straightening her clothing. Malcolm had mentioned her training might start soon. Was this the collection he had spoken of? She objected to having an escort everywhere but could hardly refuse it when it eased Malcolm's concerns about letting her out of her room.

The guard did not answer.

Luelle sighed and followed him, regardless. She kept her head down in the hallways, letting her loose hair fall forward to shield her face from passersby. She needn't have worried; nobles did not spare her a second glance due to her plain clothing and the floods of servants rushing around were too preoccupied with their work to care about yet another castle guest being escorted through the halls.

Luelle's guard walked ahead of her. A glance behind confirmed a second guard trailed her, following close to ensure she did not flee or get lost. Their destination was in a different wing, another part of the castle Luelle had spent little time in before. Doubt grew inside her as they neared the suites belonging to the princesses and youngest prince. Princess Vivyenne was conducting the training, but Luelle had not expected her to do so in her private chambers.

The guard brought her to a double-set of doors, with shining silver handles and intricately carved wood. He knocked and waited for permission from within before pushing the doors open. When a faint voice called an affirmation to enter, he held the door open, nodding for Luelle to continue alone.

Luelle squared her shoulders and stepped forward, trying not to flinch as the door clicked shut behind her.

Princess Vivyenne awaited her in a surprisingly small, immaculately clean drawing room. Oak shelves lined the walls, displaying colourful book spines, delicate glass ornaments, and a plethora of other trinkets. Oil paintings of the sea hung on the wall space between the shelves.

The princess sat in one of two cushioned armchairs on the far side of the room, spine straight, hands folded in her lap. Slightly behind her and to the side stood Mei, dressed in the same dark uniform as the rest of the castle's guard, more formal than the clothing she'd worn when they had travelled to the cavern.

Relief and tension warred in Luelle, seeing Mei and the princess together. Princess Vivyenne's steel gaze locked on Luelle the moment the door opened.

"Come. Sit." Her voice rang out, clear and strong, instructing Luelle like she was one of the castle dogs. She bristled at the command but did as instructed, feeling the princess's stare on her with every step she took across the room.

She settled in the second armchair, wishing she had

eaten slower so her food wasn't sat so heavily in her stomach.

Princess Vivyenne took several silent moments to appraise her guest, dark eyes lingering on the details of Luelle's appearance—how her clothing was creased from sitting with her knees up against her chest all morning and how a tuft of her hair was still kinking in a strange direction from sleeping on her arm.

Luelle struggled not to squirm under that gaze. Mei smirked, out of the princess's line of sight.

"So, you are the traitor my brother has worked so hard to protect," Vivyenne said. Her tone was light and conversational, a stark contrast to the words.

Luelle was not sure how to respond.

"There is no need for shyness." Princess Vivyenne arched her neatly-shaped brows. "You are well acquainted with my brother and were with my father. Do you not wish to get to know me, too? Or do you feel the women of my family may be harder to manipulate?"

Luelle frowned. "I never—" She swallowed, biting back the denial and starting again. "I was under the impression you were calling me here because you wished me to begin training."

"The training will start tomorrow. And let us make no mistake, my brother is the one who wishes you to train. My suggestions for your fate were very different."

Luelle's stomach dropped. Before Malcolm had sent her back to the cavern, he'd mentioned that his family desired her death; the princess's hostility should not sting as much as it did.

"I will not disobey my brother's command to include you in the training. However, I thought it prudent for us to have a conversation beforehand."

A small bubble of hope ballooned in Luelle's chest, only to pop with the next words the princess spoke.

"I want to make it very clear, whilst you may have the king's trust, you do not have mine. You committed treason against my family, threatened Malcolm's reign, and endangered his life." Her eyes were cold and never left Luelle's face for a moment.

Luelle averted her own stare to her lap. Her cheeks burned, the shame made worse knowing Mei witnessed the entire conversation. Did she feel the same way? She had been friendly enough when Luelle had travelled with her to and from the cavern. Perhaps seeing Luelle speaking with Freya and Imbryl had soured any kindness Mei felt toward her.

"Has my brother told you what my family and I had to do whilst you were gallivanting through the realm with our Power?" the princess asked.

Luelle stifled the retort that the Power did not solely belong to her family, but to everyone with Veseile heritage —a truth that was only unveiled thanks to Luelle.

The princess took a deep breath, smoothing her skirts and clenching her fists in her lap. Any trace of emotion drained from her voice. "You left quite a mess for us to clean up, so there was no hiding that something had happened. However, we could not risk our enemies knowing Malcolm pursued you, vulnerable to attack. To hide the truth from the rest of the world, my family and I had to live in my father's chambers alongside his corpse, burying him in salt in his own bathtub to contain the stench of his rotting flesh." A muscle in her jaw pulsed as she briefly gritted her teeth. "As far as the rest of the castle knew, our father was alive and Malcolm was in those rooms with us, waiting to receive the Power. However, in reality, I did not know if my brother had managed to catch up with you, or if he was even alive."

Luelle stared at the princess, eyes wide, her lunch churning in her stomach. Her gaze flickered to Mei, who offered a brief nod to confirm the story. Why hadn't Malcolm told her that before she'd agreed to train under Vivyenne's jurisdiction? It was no wonder the princess hated her.

"I...I'm sorry," her voice emerged as a whisper.

Princess Vivyenne's hard stare returned to Luelle. "Yes, I should think so." She straightened, squaring her shoulders. "Regardless, I am not one to dwell on the past. Your actions have spurred some interesting consequences and I am eager to make the best of the situation. Tell me about your current skills with the Power. Mei has informed me a little of what you managed together on your travels but I wish to hear it from you."

Luelle glanced at Mei again, wondering how much the princess knew of their time together. Had Mei only accompanied them on the trip to find out more information to convey to the princess? Did Malcolm know how much information his sister sought behind his back?

"Malc—King Malcolm," she faltered over the title, "showed me how to use the Power when we were travelling together, but I didn't succeed much beyond moving a stone. Since returning to the capital, I've been meditating and practising, but there's only so much I can do in my room. I don't really know the limitations of it."

The princess nodded. "I doubt anyone does. Including

my brother and I, at this point. Our father taught us both, in case anything were to happen to Malcolm and I had to step into his role. However, even when the Power was only present in the monarch, records suggest each ruler had different strengths and weaknesses. I expect the same is true now but only time will tell. Do you favour any particular techniques?"

"Anything involving precision, I suppose. I've learned to ration my strength when moving larger items, but I enjoy honing my accuracy with projectiles."

"Yes, Mei told me of your game throwing stones."

Luelle's cheeks heated at how foolish it sounded. The urge to impress the princess flared within her, to brag about using the Power to visualise events in the castle beyond her room. She could describe the feeling of stretching her awareness out and using the Power as a new sense, not to physically see the world, but to sense her surroundings from the life pulsing within them. However, she hesitated before the words could slip out. Should Malcolm hear of that technique first? Or should Luelle harbour it, so they could not find a way to stop her from using it to her own advantage? She had only just received permission to leave her room to study with Graman. Admitting her new skill with the Power could lead to the princess labelling her a spy and finding a way to stop her using it.

Luelle kept her mouth shut.

Princess Vivyenne pursed her lips, oblivious to the internal debate Luelle was experiencing. "Precision is a good skill to develop. It is a common misconception that the monarch could only ever use the Power as a weapon. It is so much more than that. In our training, I will start by teaching defensive and offensive techniques, but over time, I will expand the lessons. I encourage you to continue practising what I teach outside of our sessions and to continue exploring your skills. I wish to hear of any new techniques you discover or create."

"How many soldiers will I train with?"

"There are around thirty of you in this wave. Although, not all are natural fighters. Mei and her brother will train with you. And I believe you know of the Veseile civillian King Malcolm brought to the capital—Arthyr?"

Luelle nodded, brow furrowing at the realisation that Art must now be living in the capital, too. Was he aware Luelle had been the intended victim of the recent public execution? Surely not, if Malcolm was permitting them to train together.

"From now on, I do not want you to refer to yourself or any other Veseile who train with you as soldiers. As I said, there is much more to our skillset than that," Vivyenne said. "The first wave took to calling themselves the Gifted."

"Won't that cause rifts between us and people without the Power?"

Princess Vivyenne shrugged. "Perhaps, but they cannot deny the truth of the term. The Power is a gift from the gods. Besides, it is more fitting than the term 'soldier' when not all of you will go on to fill that role. Eventually, some of the Gifted in these training sessions will go on to teach and train other Veseile, in the capital and beyond. Order is vital in our new world if we are to care for the lives of the many. Untrained Veseile are at risk of hurting themselves as much as those around them."

Becoming a tutor was everything Luelle wanted. She tried to hide the hope in her stare. The princess seemed to see it, nonetheless.

"As I said, I will be monitoring you closely. Your fate will depend on your continued loyalty and actions over the next few months. If you prove you are no longer a threat and are committed to my brother's reign, as you now claim, I may be able to consider such a role for you. If you do not…" She left the threat hanging unspoken between them.

Luelle nodded her understanding, clinging to the prospect of a life she'd dreamed about long before she'd known Malcolm.

"Training will commence tomorrow afternoon and will occur most days from then onwards. Guards will escort you to the training facilities each day. Be ready for their arrival as soon as you have eaten at midday."

"Will I need different clothes? These are all I have." She looked down at the plain tunic and leggings she wore, identical to every other set in her wardrobe.

The princess appraised her outfit again. "I will have something more appropriate sent to your rooms. You will need to bind your hair, too. Each training session will last for around two hours. Afterward, you may return to whatever else Malcolm wishes you to do."

Luelle offered a tentative smile to the princess. She didn't return it.

"I have some time before I am due elsewhere. Before Mei escorts you back to your room, show me some of what you can do."

Luelle took a deep breath and reached for the Power in her chest.

24

PRESSURE crushed Malcolm's windpipe, stealing his breath. He flexed, trying to claw at the foot on his throat, but his arms were held in place.

The last thing he would see before he died was Zeke's smug, sinister smile, staring down at him.

He jerked awake, panting. His hand rose to touch his throat, but there was nothing restricting his breathing. He was safe in his own home, alone in his bedroom. Sweat soaked his mattress. His bedsheets were tangled between his legs. Wiping his arm across his forehead, Malcolm smeared away the hair slick against his clammy skin.

The nightmare was familiar. When he wasn't reliving his near-death at Zeke's hand—or foot—he watched Vesanya slaughtering his people. Night after night, his family and friends had their lives sucked away and Malcolm was helpless to save them.

Abandoning his bed, he strode to the windows, drawing back the heavy curtains. Warm, orange sunlight was brightening the horizon, chasing away the last few stars and planets glittering high above. Time remained before Malcolm needed to be awake but he had no hope of getting back to sleep now.

Today brought the next step in his publicity campaign. He was visiting a nearby hospital to demonstrate his concern for the sick and to heal a few minor wounds with the Power. The hospital was one of many in the city; Ginny had selected this one in particular for its proximity to the castle. Although every monarch had donated funds to Cerulya's hospitals, Malcolm could not remember his father or grandmother visiting one. He did not stop to wonder, yet again, if he was making a poor decision. Instead, he focused on the help he might be able to provide there. In a few years, after the initial awkward transition, other Veseile would be capable of using the Power to reduce the number of people suffering from simple injuries in the city's hospitals.

Malcolm crossed his room and ducked his head around his door, asking the guards in the hallway to send for his footmen. The morning passed in a blur from the time they arrived. They dressed him in a dark tunic that was easy to move in and only moderately embroidered to avoid distinguishing him too much from the civilians he was about to visit. He stood still and quiet as they worked to create the ideal image of a king. One footman oiled every curl of Malcolm's hair, positioning it to lay perfectly. Another spritzed him with something that smelled of the orange trees Leena's parents grew in the glass houses within their manor's gardens.

Today, Malcolm would wear no weapons, though the Power remained in his grasp at all times.

Before long, he was alone in a carriage, travelling over the city's cobbled streets, surrounded by guards Theo had hand-picked.

Malcolm stared through a small gap in his curtains to watch the city pass as the carriage trundled on. People stared at the vehicle, peering from windows and pointing from clusters at the edges of the street, trying to see who was inside. No markings on the carriage would identify him, but the presence of so many guards indicated the vehicle contained someone of importance, and the hospital staff knew he was coming in advance, so it wouldn't be unusual for the news to leak.

Children ran alongside the carriage from afar, laughing with one another. It didn't feel long ago that Malcolm, Theo, and Leena had been that young and carefree, adventuring through every inch of the castle and its grounds. How different would their lives be if they'd been normal children, like those weaving around the carriage? Would they have been happier?

Malcolm closed the curtain fully, settling back into the cushioned bench and trying to prepare himself for the injuries and sickness he might be about to witness.

The hospital was a blocky, stone building with small, high windows in splintering frames. Waiting outside, a doctor stood, wringing her hands together until the carriage door opened. Theo and another soldier, a human woman named Leigh, trailed Malcolm whilst the others guarded the carriage and hospital entrances to prevent any other members of the public getting too close now the king was exposed.

The doctor was a short human. A constellation of moles decorated her face. Ambiguous stains and frayed edges marred her dark tunic. Her grey-shot, mousy hair was drawn back into a bun and secured with a leather strap. She bowed deeply as Malcolm stepped towards her.

"Welcome, Your Majesty. We're honoured to receive

your visit. I am Nell." She smiled at Malcolm as she straightened.

"Please Nell, the honour is mine." He returned her smile. Pink flushed her cheeks as she met his gaze and averted her eyes almost immediately, her smile deepening.

"Our patients are excited to meet you," she said. "I'm afraid I cannot offer much in the way of luxuries or refreshments, though." Her fingers twitched over themselves.

"There is no need to provide anything. I brought some gifts from the castle for your staff and patients." Malcolm glanced at Theo, who gestured for two guards to begin unloading the carriage. They retrieved the baskets filled with baked breads, cakes, and biscuits. "It is not much, but I hope it will bring a smile to your faces whilst you are working and your patients are healing."

Nell's eyes lit with delight at the sight of the wrapped treats. "You are too kind, Your Majesty! Please, let us move inside, out of the cold. I'll give you a brief tour and then you may speak with any of the patients or staff that you wish."

Malcolm nodded and walked at Nell's side, Theo and Leigh trailing behind them both.

Warm, stuffy air filled the hospital, thick with the scent of bodies and sickness. Herbs burned throughout the room, but they did not extinguish the underlying odour they attempted to disguise. Curtains sectioned off small areas of the large room for each patient, turning it from an open, looming space to an ever-shifting maze that sought to offer the people within as much privacy as possible. Most of the curtains were drawn back to reveal narrow wooden pallet beds occupied by Eile and humans of every age, shape and size. They looked up as Malcolm and Nell entered, eyes wide at the sight of their king. Although the nurses and doctors continued their work, moving quickly between beds and kneeling to speak with their patients, their eyes darted frequently in Malcolm's direction. He stood tall, attempting to feign nonchalance under so much attention.

"Do you specialise in any care here?" Malcolm asked Nell, lowering his voice to avoid disturbing any people behind the curtains that had not been drawn back. They waited at the entrance until Malcolm's soldiers were finished bringing in and distributing the food parcels.

"Some of our doctors and nurses specialise in certain areas, setting broken bones or stitching up wounds, but we accept anyone who is willing to help." Nell gazed around the room. "The majority of our injured are labour workers from the city and the docks, though we do have a few beds and a team dedicated to midwifery and some travelling nurses who offer help to sailors in the harbour who cannot make the journey here."

"And you rely solely on donations?"

Nell nodded. "Your family have been most generous over the years."

Malcolm smiled. "I assure you, the donations my father arranged will continue throughout my reign, and I would always encourage you to reach out to me if there is any further help I can provide."

Nell mirrored his smile, cheeks flushing again. "You have our thanks, Your Majesty." She led him down a makeshift corridor of empty space between the row of beds immediately in front of them. Theo and Leigh continued to shadow them, though Malcolm did not expect to receive any trouble or harassment from the patients in these beds.

To his right, a healer bandaged a woman's leg, covering a long incision held together with dark stitches. She winced with every wrap of the fabric. Opposite her was a man sitting upright in his narrow bed, red rashes colouring both of his arms.

Malcolm their gazes, offering a smile and nod whilst still trying to pay full attention to Nell's tour.

"We have around fifty patients at the moment, though that's only a third of our full capacity of beds," she said as they walked. "Most of our bunks are in storage. We only bring them out when it's necessary. It gives us more space to work and a larger element of privacy, when possible. It always gets busier in the winter, so I imagine we'll be bringing plenty back in soon."

Malcolm nodded, clasping his hands behind his back to prevent himself from fidgeting. Somewhere deeper in the room, a hacking cough began.

Being around injured people was nothing new, but the suppressed pain and lingering scent of death made Malcolm's skin crawl. None of the visible injuries here were as gruesome as some he'd witnessed at tourneys, nor during small skirmishes to prove his worth to his father and the soldiers who would one day follow him—some of the most horrendous injuries that haunted him from those occasions were ones dealt by his own hand. More than anything, the sight and smell of sickness here brought him back to the night of his father's death, weeks ago. Vividly, he remembered holding his father's hand, watching his last breath. Life had never been the same.

Malcolm swallowed, a dry shifting movement. He

spoke to distract himself from the memories.

"How long have you worked here?"

Nell began talking about the days when she'd started working but, as hard as he tried, Malcolm could not concentrate on her voice. His thoughts strayed to Vesanya.

How many people would end up in hospitals like this if Malcolm failed to get rid of the god? Was she already slaughtering his people in some hidden corner of the realm?

At the end of their tour, Nell introduced him to various members of staff and patients who had been in their care for the longest periods. Most had long term illnesses, but the third patient Malcolm met was a young blonde boy with faded sunburn on his cheeks and nose, sparkling grey eyes, and a heavily bandaged leg, forced straight by a splint. He held his gangly limbs awkwardly against himself, as if he was not quite used to their length. He stayed quiet as Malcolm approached, eyes wide and face pale.

"This is Kieron." Nell gestured to the boy. "He's one of our newer patients, came in just a couple of days ago."

"It is a pleasure to meet you, Kieron."

Kieron beamed at Malcolm, revealing a prominent gap between his front two teeth.

"What happened to your leg?" Malcolm asked, unable to stop a smile spreading on his own face in response to the boy's infectious grin.

"Fell off my ship's mast, Your Majesty." Kieron's expression grew sombre. "One of the other cabin boys said he could climb to the crow's nest faster than me, but when it was my turn he kept shouting to distract me and I lost my footing on the rigging. It wasn't my fault. He only did it 'cause I was winning."

Malcolm suppressed a smile at the boy's indignant tone. "You are lucky to come away with so few injuries."

Nell made a stern, wordless noise of agreement. "A broken leg, bruised ribs, and a nasty knock to his head. Could've lost his life, the silly boy." She crossed her arms. "As it stands, he'll walk with a bad limp for the rest of his life and will likely need to find a new ship to work on, since his current captain has already informed us he cannot delay in port here until the boy heals."

Kieron cringed away from her scolding, face flushing pink.

Malcolm knelt beside his bed.

"May I?" He gestured to the boy's bandaged leg.

Kieron nodded hesitantly, pale brows knitting in confusion.

Malcolm rested his palm on the bandages, reaching out with the Power to get a sense of the injury. Human and Eile anatomy had been a significant aspect of his studies growing up, and remained important. It was vital knowledge if he was to use the Power to heal himself or others. He could not simply blast an injury with force; in most cases, it was an intricate, complicated affair that only sped up and enhanced the natural healing process.

As gently as he could, he probed with his Power to gain a mental picture of the injury. Kieron's leg was fractured in two places—the bone shattered below his knee and a clean, angled break in his thigh. Malcolm was once again struck by the boy's luck. It was a nasty injury, but none of the shards protruded through skin.

"Does it hurt?" Malcolm asked.

Kieron nodded. "Miss Nell is giving me something for the pain, though. I—" he lowered his eyes, "I fainted on the way here. They had to carry me."

Malcolm offered him a small smile. "There is no shame in that." He lowered his voice, conspiratorially. "The first time I ever broke a bone, I did the same, but it was only my finger."

Kieron's expression lit up. "Really?"

Malcolm nodded. "I fell off a horse." Somewhere behind him, Theo breathed a quiet laugh, likely remembering the incident. Malcolm ignored his friend and turned his attention back to Kieron's leg. "This might feel a little strange, Kieron. Keep taking deep breaths."

He reached out with the Power again, working as fast as he could to isolate the fragments of bone in the boy's lower leg and the misaligned pieces in his thigh, willing them all back to their normal positions. Kieron gasped at the feeling. His fingers tightened into fists in his bedsheets and his face paled further, but he did not cry out or lose consciousness. Clotted blood already surrounded the breaks. Holding every segment of bone in place with a minuscule tendril of Power, Malcolm willed Kieron's body to heal, lending his own strength to speed up the process.

Kieron sucked a hissing breath through his teeth, blinking hard to stave off tears.

"Do you need me to stop?" Malcolm asked, continuing to work as he awaited the boy's answer.

Kieron shook his head, face scrunched with steely determination. "I'm alright. It's itchy."

"Not much longer."

Malcolm poured more of his Power into the break,

sensing the growth and connection of new cells in a way he would never be able to describe with words. He'd witnessed his father heal many people, and had done it once to himself in the cavern after Zeke's attack, though his injuries had been much less severe and complex. Doing it to another person felt completely different. He likely used more of the Power than necessary, but did not withdraw, keen to avoid making any mistakes.

When satisfied with the newly reconnected bone fragments, Malcolm removed his hand from Kieron's leg and sat back on his haunches. Sweat beaded on his temples.

"How does that feel?"

Somehow, Kieron's eyes widened further, the whites appearing entirely around his irises.

"It doesn't ache any more." One of his hands drifted down towards his leg.

Malcolm smiled. "You must continue to rest it. It might be a few days before you can put any weight on it, so try to avoid climbing any more masts and undoing my hard work."

Kieron nodded, a wide, toothy grin lighting up his face as he glanced between Malcolm and Nell.

"Thank you. Your Majesty," he added, hastily.

Malcolm straightened and turned back to Nell, whose hands were clasped at her chest. Her eyes glistened. Over her shoulder, Malcolm spied several other workers who had stopped to watch, whispering to one another.

"You really are gods-blessed," Nell murmured.

"I cannot help with sickness, but if there are any other patients with physical wounds, I may be able to speed up their recovery."

Nell introduced Malcolm to the rest of the patients and he offered help where he could. Some of the injuries were far too complex for him to heal fully, and the process grew harder with each new person as he was more drained of energy. Despite his fatigue, pride flushed through him by the time they'd completed their second circle of the hospital. Blinking away a momentary dizziness, Malcolm turned to Nell.

"Thank you for hosting me today."

She dropped into a curtsy. "Thank you for all of your help. You've made a real difference here. You have a healer's heart, Your Majesty. Collatus runs through your veins as much as Vesanya."

Malcolm swallowed. Hopefully, Nell would mistake his discomfort at the mention of the gods for exhaustion from using so much of the Power. He had explained to her as they toured that he intended to train other Veseile healers and spread them through the hospitals in his realm to carry out the same work he had today, but that would be a time-consuming process.

Theo left the building first, signalling to the awaiting soldiers that their king would soon be stepping outside and getting into the carriage. Crowds had gathered while Malcolm was inside the hospital, held at bay by his soldiers.

Nell followed him out, walking behind Leigh. Malcolm strode to his carriage, smiling and nodding to acknowledge the people who had come to catch a glimpse of their king.

As he took another step closer to his carriage, a blur of movement and noise to the right caught his eye. Soldiers and civilians shouted as an individual with a shaved head pushed through, ducking under the arms of Malcolm's guards and stumbling into the cleared space several paces away from the king. Wide eyes met Malcolm's. Ragged clothing hung from the stranger's slender body, as unkempt as his dark facial hair. The gleam of shock in his gaze turned darker as he recognised the king.

Pressure pushed against Malcolm's chest from the stranger's direction.

Instinct guided his actions. Malcolm threw up a defensive shield of the Power as the stranger drew back his hands and flung them forward, palms out.

Drained as he was from healing, Malcolm's instinctive shield was only large enough to cover himself and anyone standing immediately behind him. The wave of force that erupted from the stranger whipped around the edges, colliding with soldiers, members of the crowd, and the hospital. Any force that should have hit Malcolm rebounded towards the stranger and the unsuspecting crowd behind him.

Horror dredged through Malcolm as he watched his people get thrown from their feet on all sides of him. The blast flung his carriage onto its side, the wood clattering against the stone floor.

Theo missed the brunt of the attack, standing several steps to Malcolm's side, but had still fallen to the cobblestones. He leapt up, sword drawn. A silent snarl dressed his face but he had no enemy to fight. The attacker was sprawled on the floor, knocked unconscious by the force of his own attack. A pulse thrummed in his throat. Other soldiers scrambled to their feet, eyes unfocused as they rushed to protect Malcolm and assist Theo in restraining the attacker.

Malcolm's ears rang, his vision briefly blurring as he came to the brink of draining himself with the Power. He stumbled and shook his head, shoving away nausea and clutching at consciousness. Panic thickened his throat. He couldn't breathe.

He spun to Nell, closing the space between them in two unsteady strides. Thank the gods she and the hospital workers had been behind him.

"Are you alright?" he demanded of her, clutching her by the shoulders, fighting through the haze obscuring the edges of his vision.

She nodded, eyes wide, face pale.

Malcolm glanced up at the hospital. The blast had shattered some of the windows but the building stood as sturdy as before.

"Get back inside in case he was not alone. Do not answer the door to anyone except my soldiers," Malcolm ordered her and the staff in the doorway. "We will bring in any injured civilians."

Nell nodded, trembling, and retreated inside, ushering her staff in before her.

Soldiers formed a tight ring around Malcolm as the hospital workers fled into the building. Two more of his soldiers hauled the attacker away. Theo shouted commands to ensure any injured civilians got the help they needed and ordered several guards to get Malcolm's carriage upright so they could whisk him away to the safety of the castle.

Malcolm scanned the crowd. Cries of fear and pain echoed from all directions. He pressed a hand against his chest, trying to slow his racing heart. No more pulses of the Power pressed at him. Most civilians had fled the scene but plenty still lay or sat on the cobblestones, dazed. A young child was cradled in a woman's arms, crying. Blood beaded on her temple from a small cut.

Malcolm lurched forward to help them, but his soldiers did not part to let him through, an impenetrable wall of armour. Theo was one of them.

"We need to retreat. We can send assistance from the castle, but you cannot stay out here."

"I can help them now," Malcolm snapped.

"You have already used a lot of your Power today, Nell does not need to care for you, too. I've ordered some soldiers to remain behind and help. Your presence will only be a distraction and will attract more danger to these people if there are others around who wish you harm."

Malcolm yearned to object, to help however he could until he had no energy left, but Theo was correct. He gave a curt nod and allowed his guards to bustle him into the now upright carriage.

Theo entered the vehicle behind him for the return to the castle, leaving two other guards to control the horses and watch for threats. Glass shards and splintered wood littered the carriage floor and seats. Malcolm used the Power to sweep the seats free of debris and immediately regretted it, grabbing at the window frame to stop himself from stumbling to his knees. Theo guided him to sit. The carriage rolled to a lurching start, the ride not as smooth as it had been on the journey into the city. The curtains flapped without the glass to block the wind.

As they retreated from the chaos, Malcolm rested his head in his hands. Had his visit had done more damage than good? Perhaps his reputation would suffer the same fate; he'd brought destruction and fled before he could help anyone.

How could he win over his people if he brought death and violence wherever he went?

25

LUELLE had been desperate to get a good night's rest in anticipation of her first training session. Unfortunately, her nerves had chased sleep away. After lying awake in bed for hours, she gave up and meditated instead, trying to hone her ability to manifest the Power so she could impress Princess Vivyenne and prove Malcolm had been right to allow her to live.

She spent her morning with Graman fidgeting, thrumming her fingers on the table and chewing at the soft skin on her lip, unable to consume any of the words she tried to read. Anxiety tied her stomach in knots so tight she was unable to eat more than a few mouthfuls of her lunch.

The knock on her door startled her, although she'd been listening out for it. She did not recognise the soldiers awaiting her in the hall. Ignoring her lingering feelings of paranoia, she followed them with blind faith, trusting they were leading her to the training and not to a more sinister destination. As always, she walked with her head down, avoiding the gaze of any servants, guards, or noble strangers who passed. Luelle's guards escorted her down a long, spiralling flight of stairs in a different wing of the castle to her room. At the bottom was another short hallway stacked with storage barrels. A single doorway awaited them at its end. The soldiers indicated for her to continue through it alone.

Luelle's fingers trembled as she reached for the handle. She stepped into a large room with stone floors and a vaulted ceiling that stretched higher than she'd expected so low underground. Plain stone columns regularly interrupted the floor space, dividing it into areas around the size of Luelle's current bedroom.

On the far side of the room, five figures stood in a small cluster. Their conversation died as Luelle closed the door behind her. Her footsteps echoed as she walked closer to the group.

Princess Vivyenne wore the same linen breeches and loose overshirt as Luelle and the others in the room. Despite the identical clothing, the princess managed to retain a regal air that set her apart from them. Mei stood to her left, beside Tao, who Luelle had still not spoken to despite travelling with him to and from the Caeleste Peaks. On the other side of the princess stood one of Malcolm's guards, the blonde human with kind eyes who had escorted her to the observatory once. Beside him stood a familiar Veseile with a shock of orange hair interrupted by a streak of white.

Luelle swallowed at the sight of Art. Her heart hammered. Surely Malcolm would not have told a barkeeper from Tolhurst that Luelle had lived in the castle for over five years under a false identity, stolen the Power from King Alaric, and released it to all Veseile. After their brief meeting in Tolhurst, Art had only seen the destruction in the cavern for a short time before being escorted away. Luelle had not seen him at all on the journey back to the capital. How was she expected to handle this situation? Was Princess Vivyenne aware of the complications that might arise from training them together?

She kept quiet as she approached the group. Would Art even remember her? She'd introduced herself to him with a false name—Anne—though had revealed her true name to him when he, Leena, and Malcolm's blonde friend had caught up with them in the cavern after Vesanya had awoken.

Art frowned at her. Nausea washed over Luelle, thick in her throat.

"Luelle?" Art confirmed that he remembered her name. "What are you doing here? You're training here too?"

A glance at Princess Vivyenne's hard stare suggested Luelle wasn't permitted to tell anyone much about the work she was doing or the room she was confined to.

She gave a stilted nod, struggling to meet Art's curious stare. "At my king's command." Perhaps if she kept her replies short, he would not feel inclined to ask her many more questions.

Art glanced around at the others. Tension lay heavy between the small group. Instead of reading further into it, he breathed a laugh.

"Well, I suppose it's a relief to see another familiar face." He shrugged. "I'm excited to start!"

Luelle couldn't stop herself from frowning. Had he not tried to use it yet?

"I will take that as my cue to leave," the blonde guard said, eyes flickering between Art and Princess Vivyenne.

"Enjoy training."

"Thanks for walking me here." Art smiled, eyes following the guard as he marched across the large space towards the door.

"Luelle, you remember my brother, Tao," Mei said, gesturing to the man beside her.

He nodded a greeting at Luelle, but his stern expression didn't lighten.

Luelle wrapped her arms around herself and stayed quiet, letting herself fade into the background as the conversation continued without her.

Other soldiers arrived in a steady trickle. Luelle stayed beside Art, Mei, and Tao as the newcomers poured into the room, listening to Art ramble about his experience in Cerulya so far, which sounded considerably more productive than Luelle's. Despite her caution about reuniting with the barkeep, Art's company was proving advantageous; his conversational nature kept the room's attention solidly away from her.

He'd secured a position working in the castle kitchens, and Theo—Malcolm's blonde guard—had been his personal guide to life in the capital. Luelle chewed at her lip, pondering whether Malcolm had ordered his guard close to Art to ensure the former barkeeper said nothing about Malcolm's time away from the castle after Alaric's death. Was that ease of monitoring the real reason Art was now living in the capital? Surely, killing him would have been easier; Malcolm hadn't had a problem killing someone else in her name, why not do it again now?

Luelle paid attention to most of what Art said, eyeing every new arrival to ensure no one else would recognise her, especially not from her time working in the castle.

Fortunately, none were familiar to her. Tension bled out of her posture as time passed. Despite any physical differences, every member of the small group had the mark of Vesanya, the single streak of white hair at their brow. She was the only one who appeared not to, since hers was currently smothered with dye.

Conversation died when Princess Vivyenne eventually moved to the front of the space. The soldiers straightened where they stood, immediately turning their attention to her.

"Welcome, everyone," her soft tone filled the room. Pressure pulsed from her as she used the Power to amplify her words, brushing against Luelle with the sense of humidity and tension moments before a storm.

"Thank you all for joining me here," Vivyenne continued. "As you know, you are here because we all share a trait. We are blessed by the gods themselves. Once, my ancestors were solely responsible for holding this Power and using it to protect Arazia, but my brother's ascension to the throne has allowed us to share this blessing with others. We are Gifted."

Excitement moved through the small crowd, present in murmuring voices, small smiles, and shifting feet.

"As the king's announcement explained, all Veseile will eventually learn how to wield the Power. You are the third wave of Gifted we are training. Not all of you will go on to be soldiers. Eventually, some of you may become teachers or healers. However, until control over the Power is widespread, your duties are to serve King Malcolm and his current needs, no matter what they may be. You must perfect your own abilities and learn to work together as a unit. You must develop a new level of loyalty to your king and your comrades. Training together provides an opportunity to learn more about the Power and how to utilise it as a tool. We will learn from one another as we work, strengthening the realm and keeping Arazia's civilians safe from any who might choose to use the Power for evil."

Luelle didn't miss the way the princess's eyes flickered in her direction.

"Today, we will start with the basics. I know some of you have been testing your abilities in private, already. However, you must remember that the Power has immense destructive potential without control. Using it without adequate caution and knowledge risks your own life and that of others. First, you must learn how to foster your connection with the Power and how to ration your use based on the task you wish to complete. Mei, please join me."

Mei stepped away from Luelle's side and joined the princess in front of the crowd. The princess gave Mei a sharp nod. When Mei returned the gesture, the steady pulse of pressure coming from the princess increased. Mei's feet hovered above the ground as Princess Vivyenne lifted her guard into their air.

"You will learn to move and manipulate physical objects, including people and creatures," the princess spoke, keeping her eyes on Mei the entire time. She lowered Mei to the ground and turned back to the crowd, holding her palms out, facing up.

Flames grew to life slightly above the princess's skin. Warmth bathed Luelle's face, even from several feet away.

"You can produce and manipulate certain elements." Pressure from the princess grew as she drew the flames away from her palms, forging them into miniature, fiery foxes and birds, chasing each other above the crowd.

Luelle stared with the same wonder as the others. It was no surprise the princess was so skilled with the Power; she'd been taught by Alaric, just as Malcolm had. Sudden emotion caught in Luelle's throat to witness the expertise in person. She was the one who had made all of this possible—she was the one who had returned the Power to its natural owners.

Princess Vivyenne closed her hands into fists, extinguishing the flames.

"I do not know how your strengths will differ or whether the Power will manifest the same way in each of you. However, that is one of the many things I will help you learn during these training sessions. Before I teach you how to harness your abilities to their fullest potential, I must know your current level of control." She pointed to a brunette woman at the furthest edge of the crowd. "Come up here."

The soldier approached, replacing Mei at the front.

Princess Vivyenne gestured to a wooden crate behind her, which Luelle had thought was a forgotten remnant of the stored goods that might have once existed down here.

"I want you to attempt lifting this. Each of you will have a turn, without my guidance."

As the first Veseile made her strained attempt, a whisper tickled Luelle's ear.

"Who are you, really?" Art asked. "I asked Theo, but he refuses to talk about why the king was following you halfway across the realm. Turns out the rest of the world believes he was here, but I saw him in that cavern at your side with my own eyes, even if I barely spoke to him."

Luelle glanced at him, teeth gritted. "If the king wishes

you to believe he was here, you'd be wise not to question it," she whispered.

Art frowned. "Are you living in the castle?"

She hesitated but gave a short nod. Why did he want to know? Was he hoping to use this information against her? Malcolm wouldn't keep him around if he was a threat, would he? And, surely he wouldn't have placed Art and Luelle in a training session together if he did not expect them to interact?

At the front of the crowd, the soldier was still attempting to lift the crate. Beside her, the princess gave no indication of hearing Luelle's whispered conversation.

She did not know what to do about Art. He had covered for her before, in the small inn at Tolhurst, but that didn't mean she could trust him. She would need to speak with Malcolm about it.

To her relief, Art stopped asking about her past. "Have you practised?" He nodded towards the demonstration. The soldier beside Princess Vivyenne lifted the crate an inch off the ground. Pressure pulsed in a strong burst before the crate fell to the ground with a thud. Sweating, the soldier stumbled back into the crowd. Princess Vivyenne motioned for the next Veseile to step forward.

Luelle nodded. "A little. Have you?"

Art shook his head. "I've been too busy with other things, but we can talk about that another time, now I know you're here."

Defences shot high in Luelle's mind. She did not reply to Art. Was it better to freeze him out altogether or to act civil and friendly? She might draw more attention if she was outwardly cruel or dismissive of him. Staring ahead, she pretended to be invested in the demonstrations at the front of the room, putting off the decision by neglecting to respond at all.

Each Veseile worked through the task Princess Vivyenne had set for them with a variation of ease and ability. Some were unable to lift the crate at all, while others managed after a great deal of strain, and some lifted it high into the air without a sign of effort. Two exerted so much of their Power in the process that the crate smashed into the ceiling, showering down in chunks of splintered wood. Each of those soldiers lost consciousness from their attempts. Both times, the princess waved two other soldiers forward to carry the unconscious Veseile aside and used her own Power to clear away the wood and pull a new crate forward.

Every successful use of the Power brought with it a unique wave of sensations, distinguishing one user from the next. Luelle tried to match the sensations to the face of the Veseile they came from, so she might be able to recognise them without relying on her sight.

When it was his turn, Art did not manage to lift the crate. He shrugged off the failure with a laugh.

Luelle felt no desire to laugh when her turn arrived. Instead, her heart hammered with determination to show her worth. She lifted the crate with ease, rotating it in the air as an extra flourish. Behind her, Mei snorted. Princess Vivyenne, in contrast, gave no indication of admiration or surprise. She simply nodded for the next attempt as soon as the crate was back on the ground, immediately dismissing Luelle.

Regret flushed through Luelle, burning hot in her cheeks. She was supposed to be lying low, not drawing more attention to herself. She already knew she was talented with the Power, why did she have such a desire to show off to the other soldiers?

When the show of skill was over, the princess spread them all throughout the large room, placing one of them in each space divided by the columns. Sitting in the middle of one such space, Luelle did not come close to touching the nearest Veseile even with her arms outstretched.

Princess Vivyenne returned to the front of the room to guide them through their first meditation session, explaining the need of it, much as Malcolm had to Luelle on the mountainside in the Caeleste Peaks.

Closing her eyes, Luelle listened for the distinct breathing patterns of the nearest soldiers—how one might breathe faster than the rest or how another person's nose let out a slight whistle with each exhale. Musty dust dominated the scent of the room. Beneath it was the smell of moulding wood from the crates stacked against one of the walls. Floral, citrussy, and woody scents melded together from the perfumes, hair oils, and soap residue that clung to each individual. Coldness seeped into Luelle's breeches from the stone floor.

Throughout it all, her connection to the Power glowed hot and strong in her chest.

26

As soon as Malcolm and his entourage of guards had arrived back at the castle on the day of the attack at the hospital, he had sent soldiers, medics, and supplies to aid the people who had been hurt. Days had passed since then.

By now, most people in the castle and the city had heard of the event, though Malcolm's advisers were working to carefully shape the narrative in his favour. Public word praised Malcolm's actions and painted the attacker as a lone soul intent on violence against Arazia's innocent, vulnerable citizens. Nobles had sought Malcolm out in his home ever since, fawning over him and forcing him to relive the attack a hundred times over just to let them hear his version of the events. He did not want to see any of them, but turning them away risked starting a rumour of injury, so he suffered through their false affections.

Despite objections from Theo, Leena, and several other advisers, Malcolm had returned to the hospital, accompanied by even more guards, including several

Power-users. Although Nell had been outwardly polite upon greeting him, her eyes continually darted to the street beyond and her fingers had fidgeted endlessly, betraying her concerns of a second attack.

Kieron had shadowed Nell and Malcolm, as full of energy as a boy his age should be, testing the limits of his newly healed leg. Seeing him up and about, ready to be discharged, eased Malcolm's conscience, despite everything else he witnessed in the hospital. More of the beds were occupied on his second visit, though few of the new patients had severe injuries. Malcolm helped where he could and left promptly, to ease Nell's mind.

He ordered an increase in donations to medical centres across the city, but it hadn't erased his guilt. Luck was the main reason Malcolm had successfully defended himself during the attack and escaped unharmed; he had drained himself in the hospital—a foolish mistake that had left him vulnerable. He had practically invited the attempt on his life.

Memories of the attack distracted him from his endless meetings and responsibilities throughout the week. He poured over alternative actions he could have taken. What would his father have done in that situation? Could Malcolm have prevented it altogether?

The attacker remained in a dungeon, kept in a hazy state with shadowbell essence. He had not used the Power since the attack. Questioning him under shadowbell's influence proved a difficult task. Malcolm's soldiers reported that the man appeared to be working alone and had not shown any sort of recognition to mentions of Zeke's name. The Veseile's confessions suggested he'd attacked out of anger when the opportunity had presented itself. Fighting through the haze of shadowbell, he managed to spit the words: "Even a fully human king was better than a half-breed mutt."

Malcolm had not hung around to listen to the rest of the insults the man screamed at him.

On top of it all, Malcolm was getting little sleep, once again. His last full night of rest had been after speaking with Luelle on her return from the cavern. During meals and in meetings, Malcolm repeatedly jerked awake after dozing into a light sleep. He ignored the frowns and looks of concern his friends and family sent in his direction.

Today, in an attempt to leave his troubles behind and wear himself out, he was bringing Zasha and Edwyn to their first training session. Plenty of other tasks required his attention, but they were all tedious—sitting in study rooms and discussing petty disagreements over lands and taxes. Putting it off for one more day would not hurt.

His two youngest siblings had been working privately with Viv, not officially joining the third wave of trainees until Viv was certain the soldiers had enough control to prevent any accidental injuries to the youngest prince and princess.

Edwyn had still not managed to manipulate the Power. Malcolm hoped being around so many others who could might help his younger brother.

He led Zasha and Edwyn to the undercroft Viv had selected as a training location beneath the west wing. Something akin to nerves fluttered in his stomach as they reached the door. Luelle would be inside. He had not seen her since that brief morning in his observatory, had not had a chance to see how she was getting on with the training or the research. Even today, he would have to judge her progress from afar whilst he stayed with Edwyn and Zasha. He was here for them above all else.

Viv's voice sounded from inside the room, muffled by the closed door. Malcolm opened it, ushering his siblings in before him and closing the door quietly behind him.

Viv stood at the furthest end of the undercroft, addressing a small crowd of Veseile and half-blooded Veseile. All of them wore the same style of clothing, their attention rapt on Viv. She was in the middle of a demonstration with one of her personal guards.

"If you end up fighting Veseile extremists, you will likely be fighting people with little real battle experience, so you will already be at an advantage. To strengthen that advantage further, you must know how to knock your opponent off-balance—that is the only thing I want you to concentrate on today, particularly until everyone has a better control over their Power. Mei and I will use the Power alone to try and push each other out of the chalk outline I have drawn. Staying still might make it easier for you to concentrate on using the Power, especially as you continue to learn about it, but it also makes you an easier target. This exercise will help you learn to anticipate your opponent's moves by forcing you to read their body language and feel for the pressure before they use the Power. It will also help you learn to multitask, to do all of that whilst wielding the Power to shape your own will."

She straightened, looking out over the crowd to ensure everyone understood. Through the gaps between the crowd, her eyes locked with Malcolm's. A smile twitched at the corners of her mouth on seeing her siblings, but Malcolm, Zasha, and Edwyn stayed back, waiting for Viv to finish her demonstration before distracting the rest of the observers.

"Mei, let us begin." Viv lowered herself into a crouch and began circling. Mei mirrored her movements.

"Who do you think will win?" Malcolm whispered to Zasha and Edwyn at his side.

"Viv, of course." Edwyn frowned.

Even from across the large room, Malcolm felt the pressure of their Power as Viv and Mei tested one another's limits. Occasionally, the people standing closest to their large chalk circle would stumble backwards, pushed off-balance by a stray burst of the Power that had missed its mark.

Both women stayed on their feet, darting backwards and forwards, ever-moving around each other and using every inch of the space within their training ring. Mei landed a hit on Viv's shoulder. His sister retained her footing, spinning with the momentum of the shove. As Viv rounded on Mei, she fired a stronger blast low at Mei's core. Malcolm felt the strength of the blow in the heavy pulse of pressure that reached him.

Mei stumbled backwards, landing heavily with her heel halfway over the chalk boundary of their circle. She cursed, looking down, but grinned.

"I told you," Edwyn whispered. Malcolm nudged his younger brother with a smile.

Both women were breathing heavily as Viv turned back to the crowd.

"This exercise is not just about using as much force as possible; do that and you will exhaust yourself, leaving yourself vulnerable to harm. Learn to conserve your Power and use it strategically. Pair up and move to one of the circles throughout the room." She left the Veseile to pair up and begin the drill, crossing the space to her siblings who awaited her by the doorway.

Malcolm's eyes strayed to Luelle as Viv greeted Zasha and Edwyn. The barkeeper from Tolhurst had moved to pair with her immediately. Together, they walked to a chalk ring. Malcolm suppressed the urge to roll his eyes at their pairing. Arthyr would be no match for Luelle.

"Malcolm."

He looked back to Viv.

"Pardon?"

Viv rolled her eyes. "I said I was surprised to see you here, I thought you had meetings."

"It was nothing important." He shrugged. "How are they all getting on?" He gestured to the soldiers training with a nod. Pressure began to pulse from all angles as the soldiers attempted the task Viv had set for them. Altogether, the feeling was almost overwhelming—a tangled knot of presences. If he tried, Malcolm could untangle and distinguish each individual Power-user, but it took concentration. Instead, he blocked out the feeling and kept his attention on his siblings.

Viv pursed her lips, looking back at the Veseile as they practised. "Some are picking it up faster than others."

"Are there any candidates who might be suitable to practise with Zasha and Edwyn?"

"There are a few I would be happy to set them up with. Alternatively, you and I can assist them on their first session. How long do you have to spare?"

"I can remain here for the rest of the afternoon," Malcolm said, watching as Luelle sent Arthyr stumbling out of their circle, as he'd predicted. He suppressed a smile.

"She is good," Viv said, following his gaze, reluctance

heavy in her tone.

"Well, I was the one who taught her, what else do you expect?"

"You only taught her the basics."

"She seems to be doing well enough with them."

Luelle held out a hand to haul the barkeep back to his feet and they returned to sparring. Mentally, Malcolm gave Arthyr thirty seconds before he would be back on the floor.

"You take Edwyn. There are a few spare circles where you can train. Zasha and I will find another," Viv said.

Malcolm nodded, putting his arm around Edwyn's shoulders and finding the nearest circle, three away from where Luelle trained.

He already knew how her Power felt, so was easily able to find her in the tangle of tendrils surrounding him. He sought her instinctively, drawn to her presence like a moth to the courtyard's flaming torches. The hairs on his arms rose as her Power brushed against him—she felt as peaceful as gazing at the full moon on a cloudless night, a cool but gentle breeze against his skin. It came stronger as she poured more of her strength into her will.

Behind him, Arthyr grunted. Malcolm did not need to turn to know the barkeeper was back on the ground.

Warm satisfaction flushed through him.

"How do you feel?" He knelt on one knee in front of Edwyn.

His brother shrugged, dark eyes shifting around the room.

"Can you feel a change in your chest?" Malcolm touched his fingertips against Edwyn's chest in an approximation of the place he could currently feel pressure from all directions.

Edwyn swallowed and shook his head. "No."

Malcolm's heart sank.

"How is she able to use it?"

He followed Edwyn's gaze to Luelle.

"What do you mean?"

Edwyn's hand reached up to touch his hair. "She does not have the mark, either."

Luelle's gaze met Malcolm's, briefly. He looked away.

"Edwyn... she does have the mark. She covers it with dye." His voice was as glum as Edwyn's expression.

"Why?"

"It's complicated."

"I..." Edwyn swallowed again, blinking fast. His lower lip trembled. "I want to return to my chambers. I don't want to try again today."

"Alright, I understand. We can wait until you are ready. I will walk you back to your room."

"No, I can go by myself. The soldiers can escort me."

Before Malcolm could say another word, Edwyn fled.

Viv frowned, catching his eye across the room. Malcolm stood and shook his head, hoping to convey that now was not the right time to chase after their brother.

"It's a surprise to see you here."

Malcolm turned, coming face to face with Luelle. Pink flushed her cheeks from the practice. Her eyes were bright, despite the silent question they held.

"After hearing what happened in the city. I thought you might be busy upstairs. It's good to see you're unharmed," she continued.

"It was not as bad as reports made it sound," Malcolm said. "Though it reinforces the need for our research and this training."

Luelle nodded. "I didn't want to interrupt. I only hoped to speak with you before you go, and I saw the prince leave."

Malcolm sighed again. "I thought it might help him to come here but I fear it has had the opposite effect."

Luelle cocked her head in question.

"He cannot access the Power. I am starting to think our theory about Vesanya's mark giving a person the ability is correct."

"Oh," Luelle's face dropped. "I'm sorry."

"He will be fine. He has plenty of talents beyond this. It will simply take time. He might yet find an ability." Malcolm ran a hand through his hair. "What did you wish to ask?"

Luelle shifted where she stood, fingers twitching. "A small thing, really. I was wondering if some of the Gifted," Malcolm suppressed another sigh at his sister's name for their newly-trained Veseile, "might be permitted to visit my rooms occasionally."

Malcolm's brows raised.

"I don't mean like that," she corrected, hastily, cheeks flushing further. "I only mean to eat dinner together, so I'm not always alone. We can eat within my rooms to reduce the risk of anyone else seeing me. The Gifted know me from this training, so I thought it would be safe enough, and the princess keeps saying it's important we all forge strong bonds."

He nodded. "I cannot see why not. As long as it does not disrupt your research and training," he lowered his voice, "and as long as you do not stray from my narrative about the changes to the Power."

She nodded. "Of course."

"I will inform your guards. Let them know on the day you wish to eat with someone and they will bring another portion."

"Thank you."

Malcolm nodded and took a deep breath, looking out over the other pairs of Veseile training together. Now Edwyn was gone, there was no real need for him to stay, but the thought of returning upstairs, where anyone could accost him in the halls, was dreadful. He turned back to Luelle.

"Spar with me."

She frowned.

"With you?"

"Yes. Your partner has found someone else and it looked like you could use a slightly more skilled opponent, regardless."

A smile toyed with the corners of her mouth. "Won't your people lose respect for you when they see me beat you?"

Malcolm couldn't help grinning in return. "You will not beat me."

Her eyes sparkled with the challenge. "The last time you thought that, you came away with a bloody nose."

He stifled a laugh, lowered into a crouch within the chalk circle surrounding them and took a step to the side. Luelle followed, keeping toward the far side of the circle, several feet of space between them. Although the Power pulsed from all directions as the Veseile trained, he always knew when it came from Luelle; it was closer, more significant. He shut out everyone else, concentrating only on her.

Light pressure pushed at his shoulders and torso as she felt out his balance. He sent out tendrils of his own Power, testing her steadiness in return.

He aimed to strike first, fast and hard, but she caught his glance at her core and darted to the side, evading the Power that stabbed at her. He drew it back in, the corners of his mouth curling into a smile at the thrill of the battle.

Luelle's hard stare flicked to Malcolm's shoulder immediately preceding a pulse of the Power from her direction. Malcolm sidestepped the blast, sending a returning shove of force as he moved.

She scowled as it caught her hip and stumbled backwards, though not far enough to breach the boundaries of their battleground.

They each fired several more shots at one another. Sweat coated Malcolm's temples, sticking his shirt to his back. He learned Luelle's tells as they fought, how she would take a slightly deeper inhale a second before she used the Power each time and how her fingers twitched into a fist whenever she intended to target him with a larger blast.

He could use that.

He waited for the next twitch of her fingers. When the blast came, Malcolm threw up a shield of hard air, as he had outside the hospital. The force of her own attack rebounded towards Luelle, catching her by surprise and throwing her off-balance. Malcolm dropped the shield and countered, sending a firm punch of the Power at her stomach.

Luelle grunted at the impact. It knocked her from her feet. She landed part way over the chalk line.

Malcolm grinned. He walked forwards to help her up, but Luelle was already on her feet and closing the space between them. Fury lined every inch of her expression.

"You cheat! The princess never said we could shield ourselves, only dodge," she accused him, jabbing her finger in his face.

Malcolm's grin widened. He shrugged. "I was using my initiative. Enemies in real combat will not be predictable."

"Let's go again." She brushed herself off and straightened. "Anything goes."

"Absolutely not!" Viv spoke from behind Malcolm, startling him. He blinked, remembering they were not alone.

"If you train here, you obey my rules. Both of you." Viv glared pointedly at Malcolm. "You may be the king, but the safety of my students outranks even you in this room. If you choose to train here, you accept your role as a student and follow the parameters I lay out."

"Sorry, Viv." He turned back to Luelle, chastened, once his sister retreated to continue her practice with Zasha. "Perhaps we should stop before one of us causes any real damage." He noted the stares from some of the surrounding soldiers, thinking back to the destruction Luelle had caused in Tolhurst.

"Afraid you can't beat me without cheating?" she asked.

He rolled his eyes, sending a nudge of the Power in her direction. She swayed but kept her balance and dropped into another crouch, countering his attack with one of her own.

Malcolm spun away, taking the hit on his shoulder with

a grunt. They attacked one another anew, firing harder and faster than their first round. Sweat dripped into Malcolm's eyes as he dodged and attacked, always staring at Luelle to anticipate her movements. Malcolm had studied the Power for almost his entire lifetime, but Luelle's natural instincts and abilities made her a strong opponent. More than once, she fired a well-placed blast that had him stumbling dangerously close to the edge of the chalk circle. Each time he faltered, she increased her efforts, spurred on by the opportunity to win.

Circling one another, firing and dodging was getting him nowhere. She was too agile for his more powerful strikes to land as he intended, despite the fact both of them were tiring. He would not win like this.

Malcolm changed tactics. Rather than dancing around Luelle to keep the distance between them, he darted forward, using the Power to pull at her shirt.

Her eyes widened at the unexpected move. She stumbled into Malcolm, brushing against his chest as he stepped aside and changed the direction of his Power to push her out of the circle, spurred on by her own momentum. She managed to stay upright as she crossed the line this time.

Malcolm's smile was smug.

"What is your excuse this time?"

She turned, suppressing her own smile. "You're the king. If I didn't let you win, it would undermine your position."

27

Luelle paced back and forth in her room for so long she was surprised not to find a groove in the floor when she looked down.

Several days had passed since she'd received Malcolm's permission to eat with her fellow Gifted. Today was the first time Art's working schedule allowed it.

She had deliberated over how she should treat Art since her first training session with him, overthinking each of their interactions. Despite her continued caution, she tried to be friendly, encouraging him to talk so she did not have to reveal anything about herself. It got harder with every new training session, as he sought to learn more about her and establish a friendship.

Inviting him to her rooms for a private conversation felt like the easiest way to deal with the situation without the risk of being overheard. If she could set things straight with him, he might stop asking so many difficult questions when other soldiers were around. Malcolm had seemed happy enough to allow it, too, when he had joined a training session with them last week.

Following her invitation, Art had gone to wash and redress after their training, giving Luelle time to do the same before he would arrive to eat with her. The guards had not given much response when she'd asked them for an extra portion. However, they hadn't outright refused her. In the worst case, Art worked in the kitchens, so would probably be able to scrounge some extra food.

At training, Luelle had promised Malcolm she would not stray from the storyline he was spreading. It was safest to stick to his narrative, and she felt increasingly little desire to betray him by disobeying. However, the truth was a burden on her shoulders. Despite her new freedoms, it followed her around the castle like a shadow, not just lurking in wait inside her bedroom when she sought sleep. She'd been mistaken to believe distraction might eliminate her troubles altogether.

For what felt like the hundredth time, she ran over the advantages and risks of sharing her history with Art.

Although she did not completely trust him, her confidence in him was growing. At training, he asked questions but never pushed her to answer, and still had not revealed Malcolm's true actions after King Alaric's death to anyone. That, at least, proved he was capable of keeping his mouth shut when it mattered. She did not believe he would tell anyone else the secrets she yearned to share, particularly if she emphasised the necessity of continuing to keep them quiet.

Loneliness ate at Luelle, strengthening her desire to open up to Art. It would be a relief to speak with someone about everything that had happened to her. Living a lie, as if the past could be rewritten into something more suitable, was no easy feat. It drained her like using the Power. The more she tried to ignore thoughts of Zeke, Vesanya, and her old life, the more the memories called for attention. Speaking to Malcolm helped but those opportunities were rare, and inappropriate when Luelle was supposed to be convincing the king she was strong and reliable. Sharing the burden with Art might help her to work through the pain of recent months, to leave it behind so she could focus on the new life she was working to forge.

Art was not working in a position of power or authority within the castle. He might appear close to one of Malcolm's guards and friends, but he couldn't really offer any help to Luelle, either to aid her current goals to leave behind her past. Friendship was the only benefit she could gain from their interactions. Choosing to accept Art's friendship should have been an uncomplicated decision. For anyone else, it would have been. Luelle, on the other hand, had toiled over it before finally extending the invitation to eat with her today.

She had once believed friendship meant sharing every part of herself with someone. However, she had come to learn it also risked exposing herself to a vulnerability she no longer felt so comfortable with. Freya and Imbryl had shattered her trust; Art could do the same.

A knock sounded on her door. Mouth dry, Luelle called permission to enter, no closer to a decision.

Art entered, followed by a guard carrying two trays of food. When the guard left them alone, Art turned to her, grinning. He let out a low whistle, examining her chambers. Fortunately, Malcolm had also instructed a guard to replace the door to her bathroom in anticipation of other Gifted entering, allowing her a shred more privacy.

"This is much nicer than my room," he said, brows

raised.

Luelle scoffed. Art wouldn't like the room so much if he was shut away in it for hours, as she so often was. "Where are you staying?"

"In the castle, in a dorm with some of the other kitchen workers." He crossed the room, grabbing a tray of food and sitting in one of Luelle's armchairs beside the window, foregoing the wooden table in favour of the more comfortable seats.

She picked up the second tray and followed him.

"Is the capital everything you hoped it would be?" she asked, hoping to buy herself some time to continue her internal debate over how this conversation must go.

"There's certainly more happening than in Tolhurst. Although, it was an easier workday under Fee's leadership."

Luelle smirked at the memory of the near-empty inn she'd met Art in.

His smile faltered, likely remembering the rest of that day.

Before he could open his mouth to ask the inevitable questions, Luelle spoke again, the words tumbling from her lips without giving herself more time to overthink her best course of action.

"My history is complicated, Art. I'll answer your questions as well as I can, but I can't promise you'll feel satisfied that you know everything when you leave. I don't know a lot of the answers, myself."

He nodded, slowly. "I suppose that's fair. Although, I think some answers will be better than nothing. Theo refuses to acknowledge my questions, despite the fact that I saw the king in that cavern. I know he wasn't locked away in the castle as everyone says." His mouth tightened in a frown.

Luelle picked up her cutlery. "If that is what the king says happened, you should believe him and stop questioning it." If Art continued questioning Malcolm's whereabouts, he risked learning too much of the truth, and that would only put Luelle's life in danger. He would not hear any more about Malcolm's role on that journey from her, nor her real reasons for being on it.

He took a deep breath, jaw tight, but nodded. "Fine." He frowned. "Can you at least tell me why Princess Vivyenne glares at you so much during training?"

Luelle grimaced. Why had she thought this conversation would be a sensible idea? How much could she explain without revealing the truth about her theft? "She doesn't trust me."

"That much is clear."

She glared at him. "I...I used to live among a group of Veseile extremists. When I passed through Tolhurst, I was returning to them." She hoped that small amount of honesty would be enough to stop Art from asking more questions about why Tolhurst's soldiers had tried to apprehend her.

"Were you undercover?" Art's tone was shocked.

"No."

Wariness washed over his expression. He stayed quiet, processing Luelle's words. His voice was uncertain when he spoke again. "But you didn't return to them. You came back here."

She nodded, sighing. "Their beliefs had evolved into something too violent for my liking. Besides, they found out that one of my parents was human and did not want me to return, regardless of whether I wished to."

Art wrinkled his nose, though he still eyed her with something akin to fear. "Sounds like it was for the best that you left them."

"It was, but I'm still trying to prove myself here. The princess seems to think I'm lying in wait to betray them."

Art picked up his fork, pushing some of the roasted vegetables around on his plate. A frown continued to crease his brow.

"But the king trusts you."

"I believe he's starting to."

"You certainly seem close." He glanced at her from underneath his blonde lashes.

It became Luelle's turn to frown. "What do you mean?"

"Only, you seem familiar with him." Art kept his expression carefully blank.

Luelle tried to do the same but felt heat flushing her cheeks. "We aren't that close."

Art's eyes narrowed. "Are you forgetting you sparred with him in front of all of the Gifted? Do you truly think he would do that with anyone else? I doubt anyone else would have even approached him as you did."

Luelle shrugged, discomfort flooding her. "I was being improper. He probably would've fought anyone else if they'd asked. Our success at training is in his interests, after all."

Art raised an eyebrow, disbelief written plainly across his expression. He shrugged. "I'm certain Princess Vivyenne will come around if King Malcolm trusts you."

"I hope so."

They ate for a couple of minutes in silence before Art's next question burst forth.

"What was it like living with extremists? My family and I heard rumours about attacks against humans and threats against the monarchy when King Alaric reigned. Were you involved in anything like that?"

"No," Luelle lied, suddenly losing her appetite. "It wasn't a nice environment to grow up in. The people I lived with had a lot of hatred for humans and the king. It blinded them to the real problems in the realm."

"Have you been in many fights?"

She shook her head. "I've never been a fighter, really." She swallowed. "Others who I lived with got into fights with humans or soldiers occasionally, but I was never involved."

Art's eyes were wide. He listened intently, despite the scant details Luelle shared.

"It's no wonder the king wants to train you, you must be a good asset to him, knowing the inner workings of his enemies."

Luelle forced a half-hearted smile and nodded, busying herself with the food on her plate.

"Do you think you'll find it hard to fight against extremists, now you're working for King Malcolm?"

She frowned. "We might not have to fight anyone. Princess Vivyenne said scholars and healers will be as necessary as soldiers."

"True, but we're only the third wave of Gifted. If any violence erupts, we'll likely be among the first sent out to suppress it. That might be hard for you if you're fighting against old companions."

Her voice hardened. "I have no loyalty to them. As I said, my views no longer align with theirs. I wouldn't be here if they did."

Art scanned her face and nodded at whatever he found there. "If the king trusts you, I do too."

She resisted the urge to roll her eyes at him.

"Besides, you'll be a good fighter. You're better at wielding the Power than most of the other soldiers we train with." He laughed, oblivious to Luelle's irritation.

Their training sessions revealed her skill was greater than all of them, aside from the princess. Did Art truly think there were others who could match her? Perhaps she needed to try harder to demonstrate her greater ability. It would only benefit her, anyway, to push her limits in building her skill. The stronger she grew, the more chance she stood of becoming an asset to Malcolm and of keeping herself safe if he did need to use her as a soldier.

In truth, she did not fear having to fight other Veseile. Vesanya was the bigger threat—one who was able to suck the life straight out of a person seemingly without a second thought. Luelle could spend years training under Princess Vivyenne and still die at the hands of the god.

If Malcolm was correct, it was only a matter of time until that fate arrived.

28

Weeks passed in a blur after the hospital attack. Some other minor violence occurred throughout the capital, but Malcolm's soldiers patrolled the city, always close enough to apprehend the criminals. So far, no civilians had suffered more than minor injuries. Correspondence from his Thanes described similar happenings throughout the realm. Alongside it all, Malcolm's publicity campaign trudged on in an attempt to strengthen his image and rule.

Although it was all necessary, Malcolm resented his current lifestyle. He had no time to see his friends or family outside of serious discussions about the realm, the Power, or his safety. All of his time was spent with the nobility and his soldiers. Regularly, he sought excuses to visit his friends and family—even a visit to Luelle would have been a welcome break, although she was rarely the best company—but his desires were always brushed aside by more urgent tasks.

The single upside of his hectic schedule was the lack of time to grieve. Memories of his father regularly pained him, but he was not able to give them attention in the constant presence of other people. Today had been particularly bad. Waking up to the realisation he could no longer remember the exact tone of his father's voice had sent Malcolm into a spiralling depression he could not break out of. The arrival of his footmen at dawn had dragged him back to reality, forcing him out of bed. Fortunately, they pretended not to notice his swollen, red eyes or the dark circles beneath them.

He spent his morning overseeing some of his non-Veseile guards' training to boost their morale, shooting arrows at targets, practising manoeuvres with linen-wrapped swords, and praising their work during repetitive drills.

Sweating and aching when practice was done, he returned to his suite. He'd thought his afternoon was free of responsibilities, for the first time in a while, only to discover his mother and Roan in his chambers, announcing he must dress for tea, imminently. Roan's most recent attempts to force the king to consider marriage prospects were less blatant but no less persistent.

Malcolm had the grace not to curse them both until they'd left his rooms. However, he did as they asked and soon lingered in the hallway outside yet another obligation he did not wish to entertain, making idle small talk with the guards outside the room in an attempt to put it off.

When he could no longer delay, he entered the dining room his mother had chosen. Lazy afternoon sunlight poured through the wide windows, bathing the room in gold. Nobles from across the realm and beyond already filled the majority of the seats around the round tables, having travelled to the capital for the upcoming ball that his mother had arranged. Their arrival felt intrusive. Malcolm hoped they would all leave shortly after the dance, next week.

Murmurs of conversation reached him as his guests praised the selection of food laid out at their tables. All of them rose as he entered, dipping into short bows or curtsies.

Behind him, the door closed, sealing his fate. Malcolm suppressed a sigh and plastered a false smile onto his face.

His mother sat at the far side of the room. He moved towards her table, at which there was a spare seat awaiting him, only rethinking the decision when he saw Roan and Talia—who had become the priest's favourite marriage prospect—seated at the other side of the empty chair. Some other vaguely familiar noblewomen sat in the other four seats.

Malcolm's footing stumbled, but they'd all seen his approach; he could not turn around now.

As he took his space beside his mother, the room's inhabitants reseated, falling back into the same buzz of conversation he'd walked in on. After greeting everyone at his table, Malcolm piled his plate high with food, ignoring the frown from his mother and leaning aside so a servant could pour him a cup of imported tea more easily. Floral notes tinted the steam rising from the drink.

"Have you had a busy morning, Your Majesty?" Talia asked, a small smile pulling at the corners of her mouth as she lowered her teacup.

"Quite. I was overseeing some training."

"Oh! The Veseile?" she asked, eyes widening with sudden, surprising enthusiasm.

"Not this time, just castle guards." Malcolm said, feeling a little guilty at how the correction made her expression drop. "Have you attempted to use the Power yet, Miss Barlowe?" On either side of him and Talia, Malcolm's mother and Roan were quiet, listening intently to their interaction.

She shook her head, toying with the pale lace fabric at her wrist. "Please, Your Majesty, call me Talia. No, sadly not. I would not know where to start."

"My earliest lessons consisted of meditation. Lessons for civilians will be starting soon, if all goes to plan. I will put your name forward to be one of the first, if you wish."

Though Talia nodded, something about her smile exuded disappointment. Awkward realisation triggered for Malcolm, recalling her request weeks earlier for private tuition with him. He desired it no more now than he had then. Regardless, his face heated with embarrassment at the social blunder. Ducking his head, he turned his attention to his meal, only for his mother to interrupt, attempting to salvage her son's mistake.

"I do not believe everybody is suited to group sessions, as the soldiers are having. If Miss Barlowe does not find it suitable for learning, perhaps you can give her some private tuition, Malcolm."

He frowned at his mother, the warmth in his cheeks deepening into a burning heat.

"I do not believe I will have the time for private—"

"Nonsense, you will be able to make time." His mother waved away the objection.

Malcolm bit back his retort. He would not be bullied or manipulated into courting, but this was not the place to repeat that argument with his mother. Turning his attention back to his food, he let conversation continue around him, chiming in with short answers when anyone directed a question his way.

It came as a relief, almost an hour later, when a guard slipped into the room. She walked the perimeter to reach Malcolm's table and stepped closer after a nod of acknowledgment from him. Leaning close, she whispered to inform him that Leena awaited her king in the corridor.

Malcolm immediately stood, thanking the guard and allowing her to retreat. His mother's hand caught his arm as he rose.

"Where are you going?" she asked, frowning.

"Leena is here. I must see what she needs."

"I am certain it will be nothing serious, it can wait."

"She would not have interrupted my schedule for something frivolous. This tea party can withstand my absence for a minute while I speak with her." Malcolm shook his mother off, pausing only when he realised the room had fallen silent to observe his actions and conversation. He cleared his throat. "Excuse me." He offered a short bow to the nobility watching his every move and stepped away from his mother before she could find another reason to make him stay. As Malcolm left the room to find Leena, he prayed her news would give him an excuse to leave the tedious luncheon.

She awaited him with crossed arms, leaning against the wall opposite the doors to the dining room. Her plain leather armour was a stark contrast to the nobles he dined with, in their bright silks and laces. She straightened at the sight of him. Silently, they walked several steps down the hall, finding a nearby empty room in which to speak.

"Reports of Zeke have returned. He is causing trouble. We may need to deal with him sooner than we anticipated," she said as soon as they had suitable privacy, foregoing any sort of greeting and leaping straight to the reason for her interruption.

Malcolm's stomach sank. He needed to be more careful what he wished for.

"What did the reports say?"

Leena handed him a folded letter.

"This arrived from an informant stationed in Vidamere. They claim Zeke is contradicting your narrative about widespread Power use stemming from your Veseile heritage. Instead, he is spreading the story that he was truly the one to bestow the Power to all Veseile. He claims you seek to cover up the truth because you do not belong on the throne." Disdain twisted her face. "He has been calling himself Liberator of the Eile."

Malcolm sighed, scanning the tall, angular handwriting.

"How widespread are the rumours?"

"Not very, from what I can gather. My source suggests most Veseile are dismissing it as nonsense and him as a lunatic, but a minority are giving it credence."

"Are there any patterns among those who believe it?"

Leena pursed her lips. "It is hard to say. The informant believes it might be a more common belief among Veseile who desire more authority over humans and other Eile. Zeke is suggesting they can achieve that by joining him."

"Do we know his precise location, yet?" Malcolm frowned.

She shook her head. "This informant did not mention it, but I can find out. I will plant another among Zeke's numbers to feedback information to us. However, word travels faster than people. Vidamere seems to be his current focus, but he could be stationed anywhere and simply sending people to do his work for him."

"Luelle believes he may be in the Razors."

"We can send scouts there, if you wish, but it would be near-impossible to find him if he truly is there. I doubt anyone could live there long-term, in all honesty. Those mountains are as inhospitable as the Northern Wastes," Leena scoffed.

Malcolm smiled at the slight over-exaggeration, though he agreed it was unlikely Zeke would stay in the Razors for long. He ran a hand through his hair.

"Is there anything else we can do at this point?"

Leena shrugged. "You could call a council meeting to discuss it, but I would not recommend acknowledging it publicly. That would only give Zeke more credibility among any Veseile who do not yet believe his claims. You would look as if you consider him a threat."

"I suppose." Malcolm refolded the letter and slipped it into a pocket at his breast. Exhaustion washed over him, intensifying at the thought of sitting through the rest of the afternoon at tea, making small talk.

"I will need to make Edyth aware. Vidamere is in her lands. It may be at higher risk of attacks if Zeke is concentrating his rumours there."

"Perhaps you will need to consider sending more soldiers there."

Malcolm nodded. "Omar is nearby, anyway, in case there is an emergency."

"I will inform Theo and Princess Vivyenne now, but I wanted you to be the first to know. I apologise for interrupting your afternoon." Her eyes sparkled with mirth. She knew just how little Malcolm enjoyed activities like the one she had interrupted.

"I will tell Viv myself. It gives me an excuse to get away." Malcolm grimaced.

"I cannot imagine your mother will be pleased."

"The kingdom must come before tea and cake." Malcolm shrugged. "Even she cannot deny that."

Leena laughed and they parted ways.

Malcolm could sense his mother's displeasure when he entered the dining room once more. Her frown deepened when she read his intentions to leave the party altogether, clear in his body language. He pulled her to one side, away from the table at which she had been seated in an attempt to have some privacy.

"Mother, I apologise but I cannot stay for the rest of the afternoon," he spoke in a low tone, hoping to avoid being overheard.

Her expression tightened with irritation, eyes turning steely. "Why?"

"I cannot explain it all here, but something urgent has come up. I believe we will need to cancel the ball next week."

She gasped, hand rising to cover her mouth. "What has happened?"

He glanced around the room. A few nobles eyed them with curiosity. They looked away the moment they locked eyes with their king. Malcolm lowered his voice further. "Our enemies are demonstrating an influence in Vidamere. The ball is public knowledge. I worry we would be putting the attendees at risk of an attack like the one I experienced at the hospital."

His mother winced, briefly. "Will you need to go to

Vidamere?"

"No, not yet, at least. But it may be a possibility if the situation develops."

Her frown returned as her resolve strengthened. "In that case, we cannot cancel the ball, Malcolm. The people need this. We cannot live our lives in fear of extremists, especially when they are not a pressing problem. The kingdom needs an heir and you will not meet a suitable wife spending all your time with soldiers and in council meetings. The ball will go ahead."

"Mother—"

"No, Malcolm. I will not change my mind about this. I have worked too hard planning it to let something as trivial as this interfere. People have already started travelling to be here. We cannot send them away. It makes us look fearful."

Malcolm sighed. He knew a lost cause when he heard one; he would need a new reason to leave. His mind whirred with ideas but his mother spoke before he could settle on one.

"Now, come back to the table."

He grasped for any excuse. "I must go and—"

"You can do that later. I am certain Leena is already dealing with everything. Miss Barlowe was just telling me about her interest in astronomy, I told her you might wish to show her your observatory."

Malcolm suppressed his groan, wondering what it might take before his mother took his reign and the threats facing them seriously.

29

TRAINING with the Gifted quickly became the best part of Luelle's day. She enjoyed researching with Graman, but most of the documents they poured over were not new to her and failed to satisfy her desire to learn. Their time together was primarily spent organising information, forcing it to fit into the mould of their latest theory, only to later expose all of the flaws in their thinking and have to start afresh. Luelle left the observatory library each morning with a growing list of questions and mounting hopelessness.

Training caused no such frustrations. She excelled at it.

Luelle had never had a knack at wielding physical weapons. Learning to fight with Imbryl and Freya had always tended to involve them hitting her with wrapped weapons for hours until she snapped and quit. The Power was different. She instinctively knew how to manipulate it as an extension of herself, a skill that counterbalanced her lack of talent with a blade. Few other Gifted could match Luelle in their training drills, so she found herself cycled around the room when they had to work in pairs or small groups, never drilling with one person for long.

Occasionally, the youngest princess and prince would attend training sessions. Luelle was never permitted to spar with them, instead seeing them paired with Mei or Tao on the furthest side of the undercroft from her. From the little Luelle observed of them, Prince Edwyn had no success with the Power. Over time, Princess Zasha began to attend alone, without her youngest brother for company.

Regardless of who she was allowed to train with, Luelle was aware of her own supremacy with the Power. That knowledge, and the confidence accompanying it, only soured when Princess Vivyenne announced they would be learning something a little different at one of their training sessions.

"We have focused on using the Power as a weapon until now. However, there is much more to it than that. Healing is the next skill I will teach you. This knowledge will benefit all of you following battles, giving you the opportunity to save fellow Gifted from wounds that might otherwise incapacitate or kill them. When training becomes widespread, the king also hopes to station Veseile in hospitals across the realm, to aid civilians."

Anticipation and excitement rolled through the room.

Luelle glanced at Mei, Art, and Tao, who she gravitated towards the most frequently in training. Learning to heal using the Power would have endless benefits, especially if she found herself fighting Zeke or Vesanya again. Being able to heal the people she wished to call friends would take away some of her anxiety at the thought of losing them.

"Healing with the Power is not magic," Princess

Vivyenne said. Like always, she stood at the front of their group, projecting her voice with her Power. "It requires an immense amount of precision and an intricate knowledge of medical practice techniques and the body's natural healing processes. You cannot banish sickness and some wounds may be so severe you cannot heal them in time to save a person's life."

Doubt crept into Luelle's mind. Growing up, she'd learned some basic medical aid, but knew very little about the underlying mechanics. Healing had never been a keen interest of hers. At best, she followed instructions and memorised procedures so she was able to repeat them when Freya and Imbryl inevitably hurt themselves fighting or hunting. Would that disinterest hinder her now?

"The Power allows us to see the world in a way others cannot," the princess continued. She unsheathed a short knife clipped to her belt. "We cannot alter the body's natural healing processes, but we can isolate them and offer our own energy to speed them up. For example, if I cut my hand," she sliced a small knick into the meatiest flesh at the side of her palm, wincing as the blade bit her skin, "this cut would usually take several weeks to fully heal."

Blood bloomed on the princess's hand, bright red drops. Pressure radiated from her, washing Luelle with the now familiar sense of an oncoming storm that always accompanied Princess Vivyenne's Power. Blood stopped flowing as quickly as it started. The princess's skin began fusing and repairing before Luelle's eyes. She blinked, frowning. Princess Vivyenne wiped the blood from her palm, leaving behind the smallest line of fresh, pink skin.

Several gasps sounded.

"Using the Power, I can speed up the process into mere seconds." The princess voiced what they had all witnessed. "Smaller wounds are easier and faster to heal. The larger and more complex an injury is, the more effort and time it will take to heal. The more complex a wound is, the more vital a good knowledge of healing becomes. If you do not know which processes to isolate and encourage, you could end up harming yourself or another person further. For instance, you could speed up blood loss or allow an infection to flourish."

Luelle swallowed. Fighting with the Power was natural to her. This was a much more daunting task.

"I will not ask you to try anything that complex today, nor will I ask you to put your trust into one another." Viv smirked at the Gifted. "Today, you will do as I have done, healing a small cut on yourselves. Please keep the incisions shallow, I do not wish to work too hard if I am required to save anyone from bleeding out."

She allowed the Gifted to come forward and select a small blade from the stack at the front of the room, though she eyed Luelle when it was her turn to grab one. Luelle retreated to sit beside Mei and Tao, Art following close behind. They sat, cross-legged, on the ground, enough space between one another that they had room to work.

The knife blade gleamed in the torchlight. Luelle swallowed, examining the sharp edge.

"Do you know how it would heal, naturally?" Luelle asked, quietly.

Mei glanced up from beside her, placing her bloodied knife on the floor. She nodded. "All soldiers and guards are taught a basic level of medicine during our training to ensure we can help one another if the need arises. Tao and I extended our education further when we got the chance to read in the castle library outside of our shifts." A bead of blood dripped from her hand onto the ground. She turned her attention away from Luelle and back to the task Princess Vivyenne had set.

Luelle looked down at her own palm. The knife shook slightly as she pressed it against the fleshiest part of her hand, at the base of her thumb. Unfamiliar with the action, she pushed the blade through her skin with more force than necessary. It slid deeper than she'd intended. Burning pain flared from the cut. Blood immediately swelled along the wound. She barely held in a hiss, gritting her teeth hard together and dropping the knife. It clattered on the stone floor. Tears welled in her eyes. She blinked them away, scowling at the knife and cradling her injured hand.

Pressure pulled at her from all directions, signalling that other Gifted had begun attempting to heal themselves. Luelle shut it all out, taking a deep breath to focus her senses on her own Power. Gripping her cut hand firmer to stop its trembling, she closed her eyes and reached out with the Power. To her surprise, she could feel a difference between her palms. Heat glowed from the cut, throbbing in time with the pain she felt.

What was she supposed to do next?

A gasp from Mei pulled her out of her observations. Opening her eyes, she saw Mei and Tao grinning at one another. Mei held up her palm, exposing the thin pink line of a freshly healed wound.

Although Luelle was eager to share in Mei's joy, frustration grew inside her at her own inability to achieve this task as easily as she normally could. Embarrassment seared her face.

"Well done." She smiled at Mei, swallowing her envy.

"It appears I am finally better than you at something." Mei grinned, speaking Luelle's thoughts aloud.

She forced a stilted laugh. She clenched her fist, but the pain of her cut reared its head anew, throbbing to her wrist and fingertips.

"I don't know what to focus on," she admitted.

Mei pursed her lips. "Maybe you need to learn more about the process before you can try. Don't forget what Princess Vivyenne said about the dangers of attempting this if you get anything wrong."

Luelle opened her fist. Blood smeared across her entire palm, sticky and warm. Nausea rose in her gut at the sight. She closed her eyes, ignoring the memories of fighting in the cavern that the bright red bloom of blood elicited. She focused on the wound again, shutting out the celebratory sound of further successful attempts from Mei and Tao. They happily sliced into their hands again to continue their practice, seemingly unaffected by the pain, perhaps due to their experience with minor injuries as soldiers.

At least Art was having as much difficulty as Luelle.

Mounting frustration made it harder to grip the Power in her chest, turning it into something chaotic and slippery. Eventually, Luelle gave up trying, though she knew people could feel her lack of attempts. She focused on meditation, struggling to observe much beyond the discomfort of her hand and the warm slick of blood on her skin.

Towards the end of their training time, the door opened. Luelle turned to peer at the newcomer.

Malcolm stood at the door. It had been several days since she'd last seen him. Luelle's heartbeat sped up as the king met her gaze. He looked away as Princess Vivyenne stood to approach him. From the corner of her eye, Luelle watched as the two spoke quietly, frequently glancing in her direction. Unease spread through her, flaring when the princess left Malcolm standing beside the door and approached where she was sitting.

"Your presence is requested." Princess Vivyenne's gaze flitted to Luelle's hand, now covered in blood, dryer than it had been earlier in some places, but not due to any success at the task of healing. The cut continued to weep, beads of blood slowly running down her arm and fingers to fall to the floor.

Princess Vivyenne scoffed at the sight and walked away. Luelle clenched her hand into another painful fist, keeping her eyes averted as she stood and left her fellow Gifted to meet the king. She tucked her injured hand behind her back so Malcolm would not witness her humiliating failure.

"I apologise, I thought you would be finished by now," he said, quietly, when she reached him. "Do you wish to stay? I can come back."

"No, it's fine."

Malcolm nodded, opening the door for her and following her into the hall. They ascended the stairs outside and Luelle allowed him to lead her through the castle halls towards her room. Several people tried to claim Malcolm's attention as they walked. He dismissed each one abruptly, striding past and leaving Luelle scampering to catch up.

Luelle, like everyone in the castle, was aware of the

upcoming ball. With it came an influx of visitors who turned every journey through the castle halls into a battle. The worst of it would occur just before the event, so, for now, she had another few days of comparative quiet.

Malcolm appeared to find it equally irritating, if his tense shoulders and quick pace were any indication. He strode the path back to her room. Outside Luelle's room, the two usual soldiers stood guard. The guards who had been trailing Malcolm behind Luelle moved to stand at their side.

At some point over the past few weeks, the locks on the outside of the door had been removed, though Luelle had not yet tested whether she would be allowed to leave and walk freely around the castle. At least her guards brought meals into the room now, instead of sliding a plate across the floor through the small hatch at the bottom of the door.

Malcolm did not turn around to face Luelle until they were safely shut inside her room. They stood, staring at one another.

"How was training?"

Luelle almost laughed at the abrupt question, taken aback by the conversational tone the king took.

"Awful," she said, before thinking through the sense of such honesty.

Malcolm frowned. His eyes darted over her, coming to rest on the bloody, clenched fist she no longer bothered trying to hide. The crease between his brows deepened.

She opened her fist and held it up to show him the small but deep cut.

"We were learning to heal. Apparently my knowledge is lacking."

Malcolm stepped closer and took her hand in his, gently turning it to examine the injury beneath the dried blood. The Power pulsed from him. She inhaled, relishing the familiar scent of rain, wood, and earth. For a moment, it was like being back in the Godswood. Her palm itched, but she paid no attention to it. Instead, her eyes were fixed on the king's face. This close, the gold and green flecks in his eyes were visible. She admired their intensity as he focused on her wound. His mouth was pulled into a sharp line, brows furrowed with concentration. Grown longer, the curls in his hair were more prominent.

"There," he said.

She tore her eyes away as he met her stare, looking down at her palm, still held in his. His skin was warm, the calloused pads of his fingers rough against the back of her hand. She took a deep breath, savouring the lack of pain.

"Thank you."

She looked up to meet his gaze again. Their stares locked. Bruise-like shadows lay underneath his eyes. His cheekbones were more prominent than the last time she'd seen him. Luelle frowned at his evident exhaustion. Was no one looking out for him?

"You should wash the blood away." Malcolm dropped her hand abruptly, perhaps suddenly remembering who he was touching. He turned away from her.

Luelle nodded, clenching her fist. She disappeared into her bathing room to wash the blood from her hand, revealing fresh, unmarred skin. Twisting it to catch the light of a nearby moonstone lamp, she could find a thread-thin line of white scar tissue, but no other evidence of the wound. He had poured more energy into it than necessary to heal it so absolutely.

Malcolm was sitting in one of the armchairs beside the window when she came back out. She joined him there.

The gardens below her room were quiet. A gentle wind ruffled the leaves of the shrubbery. Gardeners had cut most of the plants back in preparation for the oncoming colder months. The sun was low in the sky, hidden behind the part of the castle on the far side of the courtyard.

"I will bring you some books on anatomy," Malcolm said, as Luelle sat opposite him. "Learning more about it is the only way you will succeed at this part of your training. You need a basic knowledge of healing and an intricate knowledge of the body."

Luelle nodded, uncomfortable that he could so easily see her inadequacy but eager to obtain the knowledge she needed to improve.

"I asked your guards to bring an extra portion of food so we may eat together. I hope you don't mind."

She blinked. "You want to eat here? With me?"

Malcolm offered her a wry smile. "Is that alright?"

"Don't you have other people to eat with? People more of your station?"

He winced, traces of the smile dying. "Not that I want to spend more time with. Besides, I need to talk to you and I find my schedule getting busier each day. I must make time where I can."

"I can hardly stop you from eating here if you wish. You are the king," she reminded him, apprehension squeezing her chest at the knowledge he was here for a specific reason.

"True, I suppose." His shoulders shifted with a silent

sigh.

"What do you need to talk to me about?"

He glanced at her. "Zeke is stirring."

Dread coiled in Luelle's gut.

"Nothing has happened yet, really," Malcolm continued, "but he's spreading his own version of events, trying to undermine the story I have told to the people. He claims to be the one who orchestrated the release of the Power to all Veseile and is trying to recruit Veseile to follow him and extend their influence over the other races. He is calling himself Liberator of the Eile."

Luelle opened her mouth but did not know what to say. Technically, Zeke's claims held some truth; he had orchestrated the release of the Power, even if it had been a shot in the dark and primarily due to Luelle's hard work. Part of her was unsurprised to hear he was exerting his influence, though another part of her marvelled at how power-hungry he had grown. Had he always been that way? Had she simply been oblivious to it, growing up in his care?

"Have you come to question me about it?"

Malcolm, who had been staring out the window, glanced at her again. "No. I only wanted you to be aware. I know you were close to him, at one point in your life."

She pursed her lips. "I appreciate that. What will you do about it?"

"Nothing yet. Leena believes acknowledging the rumours would give them more credence. For now, few Veseile seem to believe it. However, if that changes, I will need to take action against Zeke."

"I understand."

Anger still burned inside Luelle at Zeke's rejection of

her, after everything she had done for him. Seeing the consequences of his increasingly chaotic actions catch up with him would bring her some satisfaction, but beneath that, she still had little desire to see him hurt or killed. For all of his negative traits and poor decisions, Zeke had been family to her for most of her life.

It was plain that grief continued to eat away at Malcolm from the loss of his father. Would she feel the same losing Zeke? Could she survive it? Hating Zeke was easy while he was alive and continuing to cause problems for her. If he died, her anger towards him might burn out, leaving behind feelings she did not know how to face.

And if Malcolm involved Luelle in an eventual battle against Zeke, she was not sure she would have the courage to kill him.

Conversation between her and Malcolm faded, leaving each of them to silently ponder the situation.

Shortly after sunset, the guards entered, bringing food much more lavish than Luelle's usual meals. An entire roasted bird sat atop a platter. Various sides accompanied it; steamed green cabbage, herby potatoes, carrots cooked in butter and honey, and a carafe of rich, red wine. Luelle savoured the meal, overindulging until her stomach ached. They ate in the casual seats beside the window, abandoning the table and the firm dining chairs on either side of it. As they ate, conversation returned, each of them recapping the more menial parts of their daily routines, avoiding the harder topics of Zeke and Vesanya. Malcolm complained about the attempts by some to force marriage upon him—the thought of such a lack of freedom made Luelle's stomach drop—about the upcoming ball, and the seemingly endless tasks he'd been carrying out as part of a publicity campaign to strengthen his rule. She spoke about her training, the progress she'd made with Graman in their research, and the growing friendships developing between her and some of the other Gifted, informing him of the limited truths she'd shared with Art about her history.

Malcolm did not leave after they'd eaten, when the skies grew dark, dusted by stars. They sat and gazed at the constellations together, as they had in the Caeleste Peaks. Quiet noise emanated from the rest of the castle —footsteps, conversation, squawking birds, the occasional barking dog—Luelle isolated the noises out of habit, finding comfort in the growing warmth of the Power in her chest.

Closer, the sound of Malcolm's breathing was deep and even. She looked at him, finding his eyes closed, head tilted against the cushioned back of his chair, exposing the column of his throat beneath his sharp jaw. She glanced at the door. It would surely cause problems if he was found asleep in her room. However, she made no move to wake him. The shadows under his eyes suggested he had to take sleep whenever he could get it, as she often did. Using the Power, she lifted the softest blanket from her bed, pulling it towards them by the window and draping it across Malcolm's lap.

At some point, she also fell asleep.

The click of her door closing woke her with a start. Her hand rose to massage the ache in the side of her neck.

Outside, the sun had risen, bathing the courtyard in pale, early light. She'd slept peacefully through the entire night for the first time since returning to the capital. Across from her, Malcolm's chair was empty. The blanket she'd given him rested over her own lap.

30

Whenever Malcolm's mind strayed to the previous night, to falling asleep in Luelle's company again, embarrassment made him want to hide from the world. Unfortunately, he had too many obligations with the ever-busy preparations for the upcoming ball.

Visitors poured into the castle, filling the previously empty guest rooms with people Malcolm barely knew. He relied heavily on Philip, who followed him around like an additional guard to discreetly inform him who was approaching him at all of the social events Malcolm was expected to attend, as if the ball itself were not enough.

Malcolm had only extended one personal invitation. His mother and various other council members had handled the rest. His final guests arrived when the ball was only two days away.

Ink stained his hand as he scrawled a reply to correspondence from his Thanes in his private drawing room. Late afternoon sunlight bathed the floor beside his windows in deep orange light. A knock on the door interrupted his work—a servant informing him of his guests' arrival.

His eyes ached from staring at letters for so long. He set the work aside with a deep breath, grateful to delay the chore for a while.

Before seeking out his guests, he stopped by his dressing room. Unruly curls and bloodshot eyes stared back at him from the nearest mirror. Malcolm groaned. He ran his fingers through his hair in an attempt to untangle the curls and straightened his shirt, smoothing the creases that had formed from hunching over his desk for the past hour. There was little he could do to mask the shadows beneath his eyes; they were quickly becoming a permanent feature.

His crown sat on a nearby surface. He dismissed it with a glance. It would be necessary during the ball. Until then, he would continue to avoid its uncomfortable weight.

Satisfied that he looked regal enough, Malcolm left his rooms. Three guards shadowed him from a distance, ever present in his peripheral vision.

His guests were staying in a small suite near to his own. Within, they had bedrooms with private bathing facilities and a small, communal living area, where other guests in the castle could not bother them.

Walking through the castle was a dangerous task, these days. Lurking in every shadow was someone ready to steal Malcolm's time for the rest of the day. He usually managed to avoid his more annoying visitors and advisers, such as Roan who was still tirelessly attempting to place eligible young women in Malcolm's inner circle, but people were always waiting, ready to pounce when he least expected it, as if catching the king off-guard would make him more amenable to their thinly-veiled schemes and intentions.

Malcolm arrived at the guest suite after only two interruptions, which he had quickly dismissed. He turned to his guards.

"Please remain outside these doors. This is a private meeting. If anyone seeks me out, send them away unless it is an urgent matter."

They nodded, shuffling into position either side of the doors. Malcolm knocked and waited until his guests called permission to enter.

Inside, Anwyn, Pansy, and Trent were lingering in the suite's living space, eyes wide and stances awkward, as if they weren't quite sure where to place themselves. Their bright features, so reminiscent of the natural world, were as eye-catching here as they had been when Malcolm had first met them. He winced at the difference in the lodgings he provided compared with their home in the Godswood. Instead of warm, earthy tones, the decor here was light and creamy. Furniture in the castle prioritised opulence and intricacy over practicality.

Despite the attempt at grandeur, the room paled in comparison to its new inhabitants.

Their eyes widened further as Malcolm entered, though Anwyn's narrowed the instant she recognised his face. Malcolm closed the door and squared his shoulders to face his guests, heart racing.

"Mac?" Pansy frowned at him. Her deep brown eyes roamed his fine clothing, so unfamiliar from the plain garb he'd worn in the Godswood. The fine fabrics he now wore were a beacon displaying his noble heritage.

"Malcolm, actually." He offered a sheepish smile.

"You're the king," Anwyn breathed. She instantly dipped into a curtsey, bowing her head and tugging Pansy down with her. Trent shortly followed them with a low bow.

"Please rise." Discomfort flooded Malcolm to witness their immediate formality. "I apologise for lying to you all about who I am." He gazed around the room. Like all guest suites, the living area contained a dining area, bookshelves, a writing desk, and cushioned seats around a large, low table. Large windows in the far wall displayed a view of the sprawling city below. Malcolm gestured to the sofas. "I think it might be best to have this conversation seated. Can I bring you anything to eat or drink? I know you've had a long journey."

All three of them shook their heads. They moved to the seats as Malcolm suggested, glancing over their shoulders at him. They sat on the largest seat, huddling together to find some comfort in familiarity surrounded by so much strangeness.

Malcolm sat opposite them. He took a deep breath, ready to delay his confession with some more small talk, but Trent was the first to speak.

"I wondered what the three of us had done to deserve an invitation to a royal ball, but this explains it. We hosted the crown prince without even realising." He grinned.

Malcolm breathed an awkward laugh. "Yes, I wanted to take the opportunity to thank you for everything you did, but also to ask for your discretion about my presence in your home. Very few people knew I was outside of the capital, and it is vital for that truth to remain private."

The three Meteile stared at him in stunned silence.

"Of course, anything you wish, Your Majesty." Anwyn spoke for them all.

He already missed being an ordinary person to them.

"Is Anne…" Anwyn trailed off, frowning.

"Anne's real name is Luelle," Malcolm admitted. "She is here, in the castle. She does not yet know I invited you here. I was planning to take you to see her after this, if you wish. Though, we can delay that, if you need more time to settle in."

They exchanged glances.

"We need no more time, we would be happy to see her again." Anwyn smiled.

"Will she be at the ball, too?" Trent asked.

A strange, sour feeling arose in Malcolm as he remembered the glee on Luelle's face when she'd danced with Trent in the Godswood. It was the happiest he had ever seen her. The ball would be nothing like that. Instead of joyous, upbeat instrumentals and euphoric, carefree dancing, pairs would practice carefully rehearsed steps against melodious pieces performed by a small ensemble of musicians. It was the last place he could imagine Luelle, though he would relish her commentary of the event.

"Unfortunately, her work requires her presence elsewhere."

"Ah, that's a shame." Disappointment downturned the corner of Trent's mouth.

"May I ask why you were in the Godswood?" Anwyn asked.

Malcolm nodded. He'd dwelled on the inevitable question since deciding to invite Anwyn, Pansy, and Trent to his home. Viv and Graman had questioned whether he could trust them, and Malcolm still wasn't certain he could. However, securing a story with them would tie up the loose end that was his visit to their home. He would build on the narrative the rest of the world knew.

"As you may be aware, there was a slight… complication with my ascension to the throne involving the Power. My Veseile heritage has influenced it in ways we did not anticipate and we believe anyone with Veseile heritage now has the potential to use the Power. I was travelling to investigate the cause of the change and to learn how I can better protect my people if anyone attempts to use the Power for violent purposes."

"We received a missive detailing those changes." Anwyn nodded. "Lord Wren instructed that we increase production of shadowbell across the Godswood."

"Yes, shadowbell offers a temporary solution to neutralise a threat if one arises. The entire realm knows about the changes to the Power, but very few know that I was aware before I officially inherited the throne. If it were to come out now, it may look deceptive, which would destabilise my reign. I am certain you understand why I cannot allow my whereabouts at that time to spread."

As they murmured their agreements, Malcolm took a deep breath, hoping they would not notice how his exhale trembled.

"Of course, I do not wish to taint your visit with this conversation." He attempted a relaxed, welcoming smile. "I am eager to show you my home and the city. I remember you saying, Pansy, how you wished to visit."

Her cheeks darkened with colour. She offered a shy

smile, averting her large eyes to the floor. "It's quite an experience being outside of the Godswood."

"It makes me wish we'd put more effort into our own hosting," Anwyn said. "I assure you, if you honour us with another visit, I would not make you carry water to our camp."

Malcolm laughed at the memory. "It was no trouble. In fact, it was refreshing to speak to you all without the pressures of my station looming over the conversation. You were excellent hosts. The rest of our travels were considerably more comfortable thanks to the supplies you provided us."

Anwyn beamed. "I'm glad to hear it."

"I have a clear schedule for the next hour or so. It would be an honour to give you a tour of the castle. When we are done, I can bring you to Luelle's rooms, so you may catch up with her."

Pansy clapped her hands together. "We would love a tour!"

Malcolm stood and offered her his arm, letting Anwyn and Trent follow close behind as he showed them the highlights of his home. He plucked a yellow flower for Pansy in the palace gardens, listening to his guests's curiosity at the carefully curated nature so different from their home; they lingered in the library, Wren trailing his fingertips across the book spines; they climbed the many stairs to reach the castle roof, marvelling at the view of the city, comparing it with Above in their camp in the Godswood.

Almost an hour later, they approached Luelle's room. Malcolm dismissed the guards standing either side of her door. They moved further down the corridor, remaining close enough that they could quickly return if their king needed them. Nerves churned in Malcolm's stomach at the thought of seeing Luelle again after falling asleep so close to her. Had she felt uncomfortable that he'd done so? She'd placed a blanket on him at some point in the night, but that did not mean she welcomed his presence.

What would she say if she knew he'd considered returning every night since, if only to sleep well again?

"This is where Luelle is staying," he said to his guests, pushing aside the confusing thoughts.

He rapped on the door.

After a moment of quiet, Luelle appeared, a frown creasing her brow.

Her eyes widened to see who stood behind Malcolm. Several times, her mouth opened and closed.

"Luelle, I thought you might like to greet the castle's most recent guests," Malcolm prompted her.

Unfrozen by his words, Luelle stepped into the hallway. She quickly caught on to his use of her true name and turned, beaming, to greet Anwyn, Trent, and Pansy. Anwyn was the first to step forward and give her a brief hug.

Allowing them to meet again was a risk since Luelle could tell them the truth about their journey, but, for some reason, Malcolm trusted that she would not betray him.

31

TRAINING was cancelled on the day of the ball. The break in routine came as a relief to Luelle. Though few of her training sessions involved intense physical exercise, her body ached each morning.

Over the past few days, training had moved on from basic healing to the use of shields. Luelle could now form a barrier of solid air and was quickly familiarising herself with its limitations; she could not use the Power through a shield but an enemy could still target the defence to knock her off-balance, not to mention they could break or pierce her shield if they used a stronger burst of the Power than her own. It added a layer of complexity to their drills that forced her to concentrate fully on training and diminished the opportunity for casual conversation with the other Gifted.

Like the night before it, Luelle spent the previous evening with Anwyn, Trent, and Pansy, enjoying their company without the guilt of deceiving them. They had brushed off the topic early on, allowing her to be her true self and instead using her to learn more about life in the capital.

She would not see them today. After her morning's research, she would return to her room and have the day to herself. The rest of the castle's inhabitants would be busy preparing for the evening's event, including the Gifted, though most of them would be acting in their usual role as guards.

Books and papers surrounded Luelle in messy stacks as she sat in the small library within Malcolm's observatory. Malcolm had stopped by briefly to deliver a selection of papers and books that Anwyn had brought with her, at his request. Most of them solely described Meto, the God of Harvest and Fertility. Luelle scoured the new resources for any mention of the Veseile or the Power that might shed new light on their research.

Overwhelmingly, the texts depicted Meto as a loving God to any who respected the natural world, only ever descending to violence or anger when someone did not honour those ideals. None of them referenced Meto working in collaboration with or against Vesanya beyond the creation of the Eile races.

Luelle sighed and pushed away the current book she was reading, rubbing her eyes.

"I don't know how you aren't sick of reading, yet. I think my eyes have stopped working," she complained.

Graman had spent much longer sorting through the documents, making endless notes and cross-comparisons in his free time when Luelle was training or in the evenings when she was sitting alone in her room. Every morning, he arrived with fresh ideas and theories, only to abandon them when Luelle highlighted their flaws and contradictions.

"I will admit, it feels hard to concentrate this morning, particularly with so many guests in the castle." He pushed his spectacles up his nose.

Luelle made a wordless noise of agreement.

She knew the ball was no place for her, so tried not to pay attention to the preparations, but the strangers throughout the castle were hard to ignore. Their chatter and gossip in the hallways presented Luelle with any information she could have desired about the upcoming party, no matter how much she tried to ignore the conversations. More often than not, she found herself drawn into the loud whispers. Would Lady Eliza of Axton get as drunk as she did at the king's coronation? And, who would have predicted Sir Fion of Benbrook was having an illicit affair with a married noblewoman from the north, who was also to attend?

Beyond the drama they brought, the presence of so many strangers made it harder for Luelle to move inconspicuously through the castle. Her hair was freshly dyed and, as always, guards escorted her on each journey, but that only seemed to make her more appealing to the nobles who had travelled to the capital from further away, as if she was someone important they should know.

She would be glad when it was all over.

"Are you looking forward to the celebrations?" she asked Graman. Despite denying it to herself, part of her wished to attend the ball, to dance and enjoy herself as everyone else in the castle would be later tonight. Instead, she would have to listen to their celebrations from afar, as she had the night Malcolm had become king.

"Gods, no." A rare chuckle left Graman's lips. Wood groaned as he leaned back in his chair. "Unfortunately, I have to make an appearance, but I doubt I will stay for long. I would rather be here searching for the answers we need. However, at my request, Malcolm has invited some connections who could assist our research, so I must seek them out."

"Do you ever take a break from all the work? You could kick back and have some fun tonight."

"My work is fun," Graman said, genuine shock on his face at the suggestion this research might be boring.

Luelle bit back her retort, stifling a smile. She changed the subject. "Do you have any new theories about why Vesanya might be in our world when none of the other gods are?"

He pursed his lips around his tusks. "No, but I wonder if we are approaching that dilemma from the wrong angle."

"How so?"

"Instead of focusing on why the other gods are not in our world, perhaps we should start examining why and how Vesanya is here. She is the true anomaly. All texts we have on the gods accept the existence of six deities, and they all imply the five gods who remained alongside their Eile races joined Mortus in the Underworld after several centuries of living alongside us. If we assume the other gods are indeed in the Underworld, if it exists, we must ask why Vesanya chose to remain in our realm. Or, perhaps we need to wonder whether our concept of multiple gods is the flawed theory."

"I wouldn't say Vesanya necessarily made a decision to remain here." Luelle frowned, instantly dismissing the thought that the other gods might not exist. How could that be possible when there was so much information about them? "Vesanya was angry when she awoke in the cavern—furious. She went on a rampage, slaughtering anyone stupid enough to fight back. Why would she be so angry if she was here by choice? And who would seal themselves in rock, as she was? I think the fact that she was only freed when I returned the Power to the sphere in the cavern suggests someone else trapped her there and the Power acted as some sort of trigger to her freedom."

Graman mused over her words, nodding slowly. "If that is true, then our question should be…"

"What has the Power to trap a god?"

"And is it more of a threat to us than Vesanya?"

Luelle pulled a face. "I hadn't thought of that."

"Since returning the Power to the sphere freed Vesanya, perhaps removing it was what trapped her. We should look into the first documented monarch who used the Power to get an idea of our timeframe. We may be able to locate any myths written of or around that period."

"Maybe." Luelle frowned. "But, Malcolm and I both tried to remove the Power from the crystal sphere after we returned to the cavern. Neither of us were able to."

They stewed in concerned silence until Graman spoke up again.

"For now, we should deduce from what we know. Vesanya exists, so it would be reasonable to believe the other gods must, too."

"Surely a god is the only other being powerful enough to trap another god," Luelle suggested, twirling a quill between her fingers as she contemplated.

"Exactly. So, perhaps we should be searching for evidence of tension between the gods."

"Some of Zeke's sources mentioned things like that, I'm certain. Although, I would need to find them again." She eyed the piles of unsorted texts.

"I know of several myths that might help us too. I can bring over some sources from the castle's main library."

"My training is cancelled this afternoon, so I can stay as long as you're able to."

"Brilliant." Graman smiled. "I also want to narrow down the relevance of the map in the cavern. We have not touched on that enough."

"If there is any." Luelle shrugged. "Maybe the people who carved it were simply astronomers."

Graman rubbed at his brow. "I am certain there is more to it. You and Malcolm both testified to seeing Vesanya show an interest in the archway, and the depictions of the planets align to create a perfectly straight line between the archway and the sphere where you deposited the Power. We must be missing something, I just cannot see what."

"Do any star maps here match the sketches you took in the cavern?" Luelle asked. Graman's sketches of the cavern floor were stacked on a nearby table, untouched to avoid any smudging of the charcoal markings.

"Possibly. You can search for some whilst I am retrieving more resources from the main library. I will show you where they are. It is probably time we took a break from reading." Graman stood and straightened his tunic.

He led Luelle to a large chest tucked away at the back of the main observatory room. Inside were hundreds of large sheets of parchment, stored vertically. Graman pulled one out at random, revealing an intricate, annotated map of constellations, complete with the date and time of the observation.

"This should keep you busy until I return."

"Is this all of them?"

"There are two other chests, but you can start with that one," Graman said as he left the room, heading out to the wider castle.

Luelle huffed a sigh and retrieved Graman's sketches, ready to start the comparisons.

32

CELEBRATION filled the Great Hall. Over the past two days, servants had worked tirelessly to clean and polish every inch of the room until the entire thing gleamed for the realm's nobility.

A sea of people stood between Malcolm and the exit—not that he could excuse himself so early from a party he was supposed to be hosting. Music drowned out most of the conversation, turning it into a buzz of indecipherable words against the backdrop of upbeat, lilting melodies from the string ensemble.

Malcolm drained the last of his wine in a single gulp and exchanged his empty glass for a fresh, full one from the nearest servant, hoping it would lift his spirits enough to get through the rest of the evening. A small crowd of noble lords and ladies trapped him at their centre. He nodded along to the conversation around him, chiming in with some small response when people paused for his input. In truth, he was paying little real attention. A nearby lord with thinning hair and a crooked nose made a crude joke, fuelled by the wine he drank. Laughter boomed. Malcolm attempted to smile, though he had missed the punchline.

A hand touched his arm. He turned to see his mother.

"May we speak?" she murmured.

He nodded and excused himself from the small circle. His mother slipped her arm into his and pulled him away, walking him to another part of the room where the crowds were less dense.

"At least try to look as if you are having a nice time." Her chiding tone was a stark contrast to the warm smile upon to her face.

Aside from Malcolm's coronation, the ball was their first celebration since his father's death. It felt too soon for the castle to experience such joy again. It left a sour taste in Malcolm's mouth that no amount of wine seemed to wash away.

Seeing his mother here, dressed in her dark widower's gown without his father at her side, caused a sharp stab of sadness in his gut. Malcolm struggled to find his breath. Whenever his grief struck, it was as strong as it had felt on the night of his father's death. These days, it crept up on him when he least expected it, prompted by something small that held a forgotten memory, a reminder that his father was truly gone and things were never going to be the same. Each time, the pain was as harsh as a physical wound. How could the world keep turning after such a loss? How could people expect Malcolm to carry on as if everything was normal? It seemed a cruel joke.

He blinked away the sudden tears pricking his eyes and plastered a similar, false smile across his own face. Concern flashed in his mother's eyes. Malcolm ignored it and sipped his drink.

"Do you wish to dance? Miss Barlowe would relish the opportunity to do so with you. If not her, there are plenty of others here who would appreciate your time for the space of a song. This is all for your publicity, after all. It presents an ideal opportunity to connect with some of the nobility who cannot visit our home as frequently as those who live in the city."

"I have danced enough."

Three dances with women who only wanted to demonstrate their suitability as a love match or strategic alliance for him had been enough to make Malcolm flee the dance floor. Pairs still twirled and spun gracefully across the room, completing the intricate steps that had been a non-negotiable part of Malcolm's tutelage since well before he was a teenager.

In the midst of the crowd, Malcolm watched his Meteile guests mingling. How did they view the festivities? The dancing was nowhere near as energetic or passionate as the celebrations he'd witnessed at their home in the Godswood.

Memories of Luelle and Trent dancing together replayed in Malcolm's mind. The images were tinged with the hatred he'd felt towards her for stealing from his father as he died. However, Malcolm found himself wishing she was here, dancing with the same energy, the same delight on her face. If nothing else, she was certain to make the evening more interesting with her blunt turn of phrase and unusual outlook on life. He could imagine her standing at the sidelines, laughing at his stiff attempts to move with some grace.

The temptation to invite her to the ball had been overwhelming when he'd been in her room a few days ago, informing her about Zeke, but the words had died on his tongue knowing she couldn't really attend. Any servants who recognised her would endanger her. Restricting her movements was the best for both of their safety, even if he knew she must be able to hear the celebrations from her room and how isolated it must make her feel; he'd felt the same way throughout his childhood when noble humans and Eile children had ostracised him for his dual heritage, despite his high rank.

"If you refuse to find someone else to talk to or dance with soon, I will choose for you," his mother warned, pulling him back to the present.

"I am no longer a child, there is no need to threaten me." Malcolm resisted the urge to roll his eyes, reinforcing the false smile on his face. Scanning the crowd, he knew he would not find Leena anywhere to rescue him; she was off-duty tonight, spending the time with her sweetheart from the kitchens, far from the hassle of the ball. Theo was working. Malcolm spied him across the hall, stealing glances at Arthyr, who looked very out of place trapped in a conversation with an old duke.

Malcolm drained his glass, ignoring his mother's grumbled disapproval, and set off further into the room, leaving her behind to make polite conversation with some other noble. Though the wine made him a little unsteady on his feet, he was able to move through the room with more ease than most as the crowd parted for him, dipping into shallow bows and curtsies as he passed, each individual waiting to see who their king would approach.

He made his way to the spot where Anwyn and Pansy were standing, at the edge of the dance floor, swaying to the music and talking quietly to one another. Trent was already on the dance floor, spinning a young Veseile woman around more enthusiastically than any of the other dancers. Both he and his partner ignored the alarmed, judgmental glances directed their way.

Anwyn and Pansy curtsied when Malcolm reached them. Like their features, their clothing honoured the natural world, rich in colour with intricate, delicate details. Embroidered leaves decorated Pansy's layered skirts, and bright, beaded flowers climbed Anwyn's bodice.

"Are you both enjoying the evening?"

"Of course." Anwyn smiled at him. "Thank you, again, for inviting us."

"Your home is beautiful." Pansy nodded.

"Ours must have seemed quite cramped in comparison." Anwyn fingered the silver acorn pendant hanging between her collarbones.

"On the contrary." Malcolm smiled, ignoring the people nearby who made no attempt to hide their eavesdropping. "Your home is beautiful and your enthusiasm for dancing is definitely more fun."

They laughed with him, all three of them turning to watch Trent and his partner, both smiling wider than any other dancers around them.

Across the dance floor, Malcolm's eyes locked with Roan's. The human priest was standing beside Talia. Roan waved at Malcolm, grabbing Talia's hand and murmuring something to her without looking away.

Malcolm cursed underneath his breath, gritting his teeth.

"Pardon?" Anwyn raised an eyebrow.

He cleared his throat. "Pansy, dance with me? We never had the chance during my stay in the Godswood. If you do not mind, of course, Anwyn."

Anwyn smiled. "I was just about to go and get myself another drink. I would appreciate you keeping Pansy company in my absence."

Pansy smiled up at Malcolm from beneath her long, dark lashes, colour rising anew in her cheeks. She placed her dainty hand in Malcolm's outstretched palm. He led her to the centre of the floor, glancing at the couples around him to try and pick up the correct footwork for this stage of the song. As they danced, he guided Pansy as far from Roan as possible.

Roan narrowed his eyes but retreated.

"This is quite an honour." Pansy smiled up at Malcolm, quickly picking up the steps for the dance. "I imagine none of my friends will believe me when I tell them I danced with the king."

He breathed a laugh. "You will not say that when I step on your toes." With each spin, he wished he had drank less.

"Relax a little. Feel the music inside you." She moved her hand from his shoulder to tap his chest.

All Malcolm could feel was the wine sloshing in his stomach.

"I doubt I will ever achieve the same grace as you and Trent." He held their adjoined hands aloft for her to spin beneath, relishing the break in movement for a second. "Is the capital living up to your expectations?"

Pansy nodded, beaming. "It's so different from home. The buildings are amazing, as tall as our trees, some of them! It's incredible that people can make such structures."

Malcolm smiled. "I suppose I had never thought about what an achievement it is. I felt much the same admiration seeing your home amongst the treetops."

The song they were dancing to drew to a close. They stepped apart, applauding the musicians.

"Thank you for the honour of dancing with me." Pansy curtsied, glancing at the changing partners around them as the musicians set up their next song.

Across the floor, Roan and Talia were making determined progress towards them.

"Dance with me again?" Malcolm asked Pansy. "We started halfway through the song, it hardly counts."

Her brows drew together. "Wouldn't you rather dance with someone else? I'm sure there are plenty of people here hoping for your company." Her eyes flitted around the room.

"Not at all." Malcolm breathed, grabbing her hand again before she could move away. "You are my honoured guest and much better company than most of the others here," he said in a lowered, conspiratorial tone. "Besides, I need to learn how to move with some grace, and you are the best person here to teach me."

Pansy laughed, placing her other hand back on his shoulder. "I suppose I can't decline if my king commands it."

Malcolm grinned back at her, stifling the yearning inside him to be anywhere else.

33

As much as she tried to ignore the music and distant swell of voices leaking into her room, Luelle was unable to sleep on the night of the ball. She tossed and turned in her bed until her sheets were a tangled mess. Missing training earlier in the day had disrupted the pattern her body had adapted to, leaving her yearning for something to tire herself out.

She'd stayed researching with Graman until late in the afternoon, when he'd finally been called away to prepare for the festivities. Back in her room, she practised using the Power. No matter what she tried, using it alone was less physically exhausting than sparring with a partner, and she still itched with energy when she lay in bed trying to slumber.

Perhaps fresh air would help. Clambering out of bed, Luelle strode to the window, throwing it open with a clunk; it only allowed noise from deeper within the castle to flood in louder.

She leaned against the windowpane, sighing. Stars watched her from above, twinkling in time with the crescendo of the current song. Indulging for a moment, Luelle let herself imagine she'd attended the ball, dancing with Art or Trent. Of course, Malcolm would never be allowed to dance with her, but she fleetingly let herself imagine a world in which they might be friends without judgement. Her stomach clenched with disappointment knowing it was an impossibility.

The Great Hall wasn't far from her room—across the garden, in through one of the doors to the ground floor rooms on the far side of the courtyard, and a few minutes of walking through the maze of castle hallways. If she entered through the same floor her room was on, she could lurk in the balcony within the Great Hall, watching the dancing from above, hidden in the shadows. She knew the castle well enough to manage it without being seen, especially whilst most other inhabitants were already occupied at the festivities. Her clothing wouldn't blend with the nobility but it might camouflage her against the servants, who would be so busy they likely wouldn't keep track of who else was around.

None of that changed the fact that guards remained stationed outside of her room to prevent her from leaving. She closed her eyes and reached out with the Power, sensing them standing there, even now. Beyond that, her bedroom was too high to access the garden and find her way back inside when she was done.

She would have to stay listening from afar.

Luelle gazed at the familiar gardens, trees half-undressed of leaves that had been swept into neat piles around their trunks. Earlier in the day, gardeners had been hard at work to tidy the courtyard, cutting away ivy that ventured too high and weeding the flower beds. They'd shaped the shrubs, trimming them to be orderly and symmetrical. A smattering of plants pushed out a final bloom before winter arrived to snatch it away until spring. Luelle spent so much time staring at this garden from her window, she was certain she could sketch out the exact placement of every plant.

Her eye caught on something new in the furthest corner.

She leaned forward, hanging half outside the window, squinting at the strange new item. It leaned against the castle wall behind a tree, tall and slender, almost hidden in the shadows.

A ladder.

She gasped. A gardener must have left it behind after trimming plants that climbed the castle walls that morning. In the darkness of the cloudy night, it was impossible to examine the ladder's quality from afar. Ignoring the splinters pricking her palms, she gripped the windowsill tighter and leaned forward, scouring every inch of the gardens for people. Finding no one, she reached out with the Power towards the ladder before she had a chance to think through her actions.

It was unexpectedly heavy. The solid wood clacked against the wall beside her window as she manipulated it, panting from the exertion of the task.

Satisfied it was sturdy enough to hold her weight and had not been left behind due to damage, Luelle willed it to rest against the wall beneath her window. She held her breath and peered down to see if it reached her.

The top rung of the ladder was a couple of feet below her windowsill.

Glancing over her shoulder to her bedroom door, she reached out again with the Power. The guards had not moved.

She swung her leg over the windowsill.

The ladder wobbled beneath her when both feet stood on the first rung. Flashbacks of descending the castle walls on a rope haunted her, anxiety a tight fist around her heart. She reached out with the Power to hold the ladder steady, counting her breaths and staring only at the ladder rungs as she descended. She didn't look around again until her feet touched solid ground. Grass blades tickled the small strips of exposed skin at her ankles.

It had been a long time since she'd set foot in this garden. When she'd worked here, undercover as a servant, she'd crossed it once or twice to reach guest rooms, though most of her time had been spent in the wing housing Alaric's rooms, where the Queen Mother still lived. It usually teemed with servants and nobles.

Now, it was empty. Everyone in the castle was distracted, as they had been when she'd escaped with Alaric's Power, months ago.

If she wanted, Luelle could slip away, just as she had then, and start a new life. Leena and Malcolm knew that Freya and Imbryl now dwelled in the Caeleste Peaks, so she couldn't join them, but she could find a home in a faraway city.

The thought of escaping lacked the appeal it might've had several weeks ago. Though she knew, deep down, she remained a captive here, she was happier than she'd been in a while—since travelling with Malcolm. Researching the truth about the gods with Graman gave her a purpose, a way to help people in Arazia, even if none of them knew about it. And, for the past several weeks, she'd risen every morning looking forward to the afternoon's training, to honing her skills with the Power, unlocking her true potential, and making friends whilst doing it. She was one of the Gifted, training among equals.

Once, she'd thought Zeke and his collection of companions were her equals in the same way. Now she knew their world views had never been as aligned as she'd thought. Despite knowing him properly for less than a year, Malcolm seemed to understand her better than Zeke ever had. He shared the same mixed heritage —not that she'd ever known her parents—and he was the only other person here who understood the threat Vesanya posed. He knew why Luelle was torn between guilt over unleashing the god into the world and pride at restoring the Power to those it belonged to, even if he still likely wished she had not achieved it.

She didn't want to escape. She wanted to be part of something bigger; to help Malcolm improve life for everyone in Arazia, for people like her who hadn't yet discovered their true potential.

However, understanding that change in desire didn't mean she had to stay in her room, meekly waiting for Malcolm to lengthen her leash. As far as everyone in the castle knew, the traitor who had escaped from Alaric's room months ago was dead. Luelle knew well enough how to keep from sight; there was no harm in her going to the Great Hall and watching the nobles celebrate for a while.

She pulled the ladder away from the wall by hand, struggling under its weight as she tilted it on its side and tucked it behind the shrubbery against the wall. She would need it to get back inside her room and it was near-impossible to see in the shadows, unless someone knew what to look for. Moving it would have been easier with the Power, but paranoia held her back from using it. She was no longer in her room. Any Veseile in the castle would feel her using it and be able to locate her if they tried. Every Veseile's Power had its own signature; the Gifted she trained with would be able to identify her if they were near enough. If Princess Vivyenne felt her nearby, Luelle was certain she would assume the worst.

With the ladder safely hidden, Luelle dashed across the gardens, slipping inside the doors on the far side. Keeping her head down, she strode through the castle. Before every corner, she paused, listening for voices that might betray people waiting up ahead. It took her longer to reach the Great Hall but reduced her chances of being caught.

The few times she passed a stranger, none gave her a second glance, dismissing her plain clothing.

Music and chatter remained muffled but grew louder with every step she took. Luelle ascended a quiet staircase to the upper floors and continued until she reached one of the many doorways to the wraparound balcony within the Great Hall. She peered inside to ensure no Gifted awaited her on the other side and slipped in.

A few pairs of nobles leaned over the bannister to watch the festivities below but the majority of the crowd were enjoying the celebrations downstairs.

Noise drowned out any thoughts Luelle might have. She wandered the balcony until she found a sheltered, shadowy spot with a clear view of the floor below.

Intricate chandeliers of moonstone hung regularly from the high, painted ceilings, accented by warmer candlelight from sconces on the walls.

Luelle scanned the crowds for people she knew.

Art lingered at the edge of the room, laughing and chatting with Mei and Tao, his expression bright despite the white-knuckled grip on his wine glass stem. Mei and Tao must both have the night off. They wore fine, navy silks accented with silver threading, looking far from the hardened soldiers Luelle knew. Mei's gown hung from her muscular form like flowing water. Delicate jewellery glinted at her wrists and throat, matching the threading on Tao's intricately embroidered tunic.

Further into the crowds, Anwyn picked a small piece of food from a round, silver tray, held by a servant. Trent and Pansy stood nearby, cheeks flushed with energy and joy. Luelle's heart lurched with longing to return to their camp in the Godswood, when she and Trent had danced for hours before she'd gone to sit with Malcolm Above, watching him gaze at the stars and musing over the strange situation she'd found herself in.

The entire crowd below revolved around the king. Surprise sparked in Luelle to find him on the dancefloor.

Malcolm was the night sky incarnate, dressed in a black tunic adorned with silver embroidery and sparkling white gemstones that swirled like constellations. He stood a head taller than the Veseile in his arms—a beautiful noblewoman with sparkling eyes, upturned full lips, and jewels braided into her upbound hair. Her posture was immaculate, elegance radiating from every inch of her. Together, Malcolm and the unfamiliar woman were beautiful. Other pairs on the dance floor kept several steps away to give them space, stealing glances as they swept past.

Sour envy curdled in Luelle's stomach as she watched them. Malcolm hadn't joined her in dancing at the

Meteile camp in the Godswood. Perhaps he was more comfortable with this style, synchronised as part of a whole. He still stood out from the rest. What she wouldn't give for the freedom to dance again, uncaring of the eyes on her—welcoming the stares.

Luelle watched the king and his partner for the rest of the song, unable to tear her eyes away. They stayed together for another song, until someone new interrupted and allowed their chaperone to introduce them to the king. He danced with the new partner for two songs and broke away, beelining for a servant with a tray full of clear, sparkling wine in crystal glasses.

The change in pattern broke Luelle from her mesmerised state. She shouldn't be here. The balcony had grown busier while she'd been distracted. Guests seeking a break from the dancing or a new vantage point to watch over the event now crowded around, leaving scant space along the bannister for newcomers to slot in.

Below, Art and Mei had taken to the dance floor together. Tao was no longer visible, and it was enough to fill Luelle with nerves. He would certainly recognise her if her ran into her in the hallway.

It was time for her to go, before someone mistook her for a servant and tried to engage with her, or worse.

Keeping to the wall, Luelle crept back to the doorway she'd entered through. Safely back in the hallways, she upped her pace as she weaved the same roundabout route to the gardens outside her room. She lost her way once, heart thundering as the risk of being seen or recognised seemed to increase the longer she stayed out.

Sweat coated her palms when she finally emerged into the gardens, dashing to the bushes where she'd stowed the ladder. Taking several deep breaths to centre herself, she used the Power to move it into place and hold it firm as she climbed, throat dry and limbs trembling.

Her window remained wide open, the room still dimly lit by her moonstone lamps. Climbing back into the room was harder than getting out. She heaved herself up and swung one leg over the sill, in a hurry to get inside and replace the ladder where she'd found it.

"Luelle?"

She froze, halfway through the window and looked up, locking eyes with Malcolm.

34

Luelle was leaving him.

Hurt and confusion bloomed in Malcolm's chest, amplified a thousand times by the amount of wine he'd consumed.

The one person in the world who knew the true extent of the problems he faced and, still, she was leaving him.

He couldn't provide a real life for her here, where she was in danger if anyone recognised her true identity, but that wouldn't last forever and he was doing all he could to find other ways to bring her happiness here. Aside from upheaving every servant who knew her face and replacing them with new staff, what did she expect him to do?

Although, if that was what it took to get her to stay…

He opened his mouth to offer it but Luelle spoke first, one leg still hanging out the window.

"It's not what it looks like," she said.

Malcolm closed his mouth and stared at her, unsure how to untangle the emotions in his chest to form a response. In the absence of a reply, she returned into the room and continued.

"I was coming back." She gestured to the window. "Someone left a ladder in the gardens. I just wanted to come and see the ball, watch the dancing for a few minutes, but I swear no one saw me."

Malcolm continued staring, relief flooding him hard enough that it took considerable effort to keep upright— or was that the wine? He crossed the room, placing a hand on the wall beside the window to steady himself and looked down to find the ladder she'd been climbing. What was it with her and clambering out of windows?

She was grinning when he glanced back up at her. He couldn't help returning the smile, feeling lighter than he had all evening.

A steady pulse of pressure radiated from Luelle as she sent the ladder drifting across the garden, hiding it behind some trees in the distant gloom. The undeniable sense of her Power washed over him, instantly soothing his nerves.

"I thought you were running away," he admitted.

Her smile faded. She shook her head.

"Why are you here?" she asked after a moment of awkward silence in which Malcolm continued staring at her, like an idiot. "Shouldn't you still be hosting the ball?"

He grimaced. "I've been waiting to get away since it started. I made an appearance, I hope that's enough. The entire event was my mother's idea. It's only to appease the nobles, it's not as fun as it looks," his words slurred, slipping from his mouth uncontrolled, like a mudslide.

"Won't people come looking for you?"

He shrugged. "I doubt it." He straightened his tunic,

remembering why he'd sought her out. "Come with me, I have something for you."

He ignored her frown and turned, walking back to the door in what he hoped was a straight line. Behind him, he heard Luelle close the door, but her footsteps did not follow him. He turned back.

She stood, hesitating in the empty hall, fingers still resting on her door handle.

"Where are my guards?" She looked around as if they might appear from thin air.

"I sent them away." He gestured broadly with one hand and closed the distance between them. "You are safe, though. I promise. I'll keep you safe. Come on." He grabbed her wrist and tugged her after him down the hallway, the short walk to his own rooms.

He closed the door to his suite behind Luelle, not missing the way she eyed the guards at his door. She hesitated again inside, frowning at him. Malcolm skirted around her.

"This way," he said, leading her away from the reception area and towards his personal chambers. Once inside, he spoke again. "Go and sit, I will return in a moment." He pointed past his bed to the lounging sofas, either side of a long low table hosting a carafe of wine and two glasses. "Help yourself to a drink," he offered, leaving her in his room while he went to his dressing room.

He wriggled out of his stifling tunic and undershirt, donning a looser linen shirt and rolling up the sleeves. The documents he intended to give her lay on a side table in the dressing room. He grabbed them before returning to her.

She was sipping at her wine, seated stiffly upright on the sofa. A second glass was filled, awaiting Malcolm on the table, but he did not think he could stomach another drop. He swayed over to her, as unsteady as he was when travelling by sea. Their knees brushed as he sat; neither of them moved away. He held out the papers.

She took them, setting her glass beside his on the table.

"Is it news about Vesanya?" she asked, running her fingers along the edge of the parchment, not looking at the words written on the sheets.

Malcolm shoved unwanted thoughts of the god away. "No. Gods, no. It is about your parents."

Luelle froze where she sat. Malcolm couldn't bear to look at her but, somehow, couldn't tear his eyes away from her face. Had he gone too far? The topic was so personal, perhaps she wouldn't want to discuss them with him. He'd only ever intended to bring her some peace, some answers.

No, he reassured himself, this was a good idea.

He was the king. Kings didn't have bad ideas.

He grabbed his wine glass, twirling the stem to distract himself and offer something to look at whilst he explained.

"I remembered you telling me Zeke found you in Vidamere. My Thanes keep records of all citizens born in their jurisdictions, so I sent for a copy of the Southlands' records and searched through the names that might match your age and situation. Finding you allowed me to find your parents name and once I had them, I asked my Thane to send me more information about them. It might not be everything available, since the librarians there had quite a short timeframe to scour the data, but it offers a starting point." His words tripped over each other in their rush to get out. It would be a miracle if she had understood any of them.

Luelle's fingers tightened on the papers, crinkling their edges. Her throat bobbed as she swallowed, eyes wide and fixed on Malcolm's face. Heat burned in his cheeks.

Oh gods, he'd gone too far. She must think he was insane. Maybe it *was* a bad idea.

"Why?" she breathed. "Why would you do that for me?"

He sipped his wine to calm himself and grimaced. "Because I cannot imagine not knowing my family. I know how hard it is to feel like you do not belong and Zeke revealed your true heritage so abruptly." He frowned, anger burning through him anew as he remembered the shock and hurt that had flushed Luelle's expression during that confrontation in the cavern. "You deserve to know more about them."

Finally, her gaze averted from his face to the papers in her lap. A muscle flexed in her jaw.

Malcolm's heart raced and his head swam. Was it wrong of him to use the resources at his disposal to find some answers for her? He should have asked, first. Wine sloshed close to the rim of his glass as he twirled it.

She placed a hand on his arm, stilling the fidgeting. Warmth radiated from her palm.

"Thank you."

Her eyes were glistening when he glanced up.

He nodded, swallowing. "I do not expect you to read through it all now. That's a copy. You can keep it. And it is only a starting point. If you want to know more, tell me and I will find all I can for you."

His heart lurched at her smile—the only stable thing in a room that was starting to spin.

"For now, you should know their names at least." He leaned closer to her and narrowed his eyes to peer at the words on the paper. They blurred. Closing one eye helped. "Their names…" He scoured the paper, but she interrupted him.

"Thank you," she repeated. "I know how busy you are. It means a lot to me that you made time for this."

"I get little sleep these days, I have plenty of time." He huffed a dry laugh, missing the warmth of her hand as she moved it away.

"Cutting back on the wine might help." She glanced at the glass in his hands, liquid tilting precariously close to the rim again.

"Drinking is the only thing that helps," he said, tilting his head back on the cushions behind him and closing his eyes. "I dream of her—of Vesanya—otherwise." In truth, he had already tried to cut back on drinking but it was still the easiest way to achieve a dreamless sleep. The only other time he felt safe enough to get some real rest was in Luelle's company.

"Talking about it might help," Luelle suggested.

Malcolm shook his head, keeping his eyes closed. "No one understands. No one believes me when I explain how dangerous she is."

"I understand."

He opened his eyes, rolling his head to look at her. The papers he'd gifted her remained clutched in her hands, crinkling under the strength of her grip. He opened his mouth but no sound emerged. The words were trapped in his throat; he didn't know where to begin.

"I see her, too, in my dreams," Luelle said quietly, speaking so he didn't have to try. "I think about her every day, wondering if I made a mistake by returning the Power. And sometimes, I wonder if we're overreacting. She just disappeared. Maybe Graman and the others are right to doubt how dangerous she is. If you hadn't been there to witness it all alongside me, I think I'd start to believe I dreamt the entire thing."

As much as he wanted to open up, Malcolm didn't want to think about Vesanya. But, he also didn't want Luelle to leave. With her, he felt calm.

"Tell me something about you," he murmured.

Gently, she took his wine glass, placing it on the table. She turned towards him, tucking her legs on the sofa cushions between them, keeping the papers with her parents' names on her lap. The nearby moonstone lamps glowed in her eyes.

"What do you want to know?"

"Anything. Everything." He thought back over their time together. Had he really only known her for a few months? It felt so much longer. "Where did you learn to fish?"

She laughed, surprise flitting over her face. "Well, I didn't learn properly until I joined Zeke, but I was catching things long before then. As you know, Vidamere is situated on a large lake, it's a big fishing community. When I lived in the orphanage, I remember spending time in the water with the other children. I can't remember not knowing how to swim." She toyed with a stray lock of hair as she spoke, eyes becoming far-off, lost in memories.

Malcolm watched carefully as she recounted her

childhood, noting how expressive she was—how her eyebrows twitched as she spoke and she smiled radiantly at the memories as if she was reliving them. He felt himself mimicking her expressions, smiling when she recalled a funny moment and frowning when she explained problems she'd experienced.

"There were all sorts of creatures living in the shallows. Some would bury themselves in the mud, and there were others that would hide in the reeds and nibble at our toes. If we caught any on a quiet day, sometimes the fishermen would cook one up for us. Imbryl was the one who taught me how to fashion tools to catch the faster fish, when I was older."

She continued, speaking at length about what she could remember of her childhood. Listening to her talk, the rest of the world melted away.

Malcolm didn't realise he'd been falling asleep until Luelle was pulling him up from the sofa, hooking his arm around her shoulders. He let her lead him, stumbling beside her so his weight didn't crush her until they reached his bed. She pulled the covers back and helped him in, probably as she'd helped his father, months ago, before he'd left their realm forever.

His breath choked in his throat.

Malcolm's fingers closed around Luelle's wrist before she could move away, fighting to keep his eyes open.

"Will you stay?" he asked, heartbeat racing at the thought of being alone again.

She glanced at the door.

"What if—"

"Please."

He didn't know what she saw when she met his gaze,

but she nodded. Malcolm's fingers loosened on her wrist, relief washing over him. She walked back to the sofas to grab her papers and returned to his bed, sitting atop the covers beside him. Malcolm watched her face as she unfolded the documents and began reading the scant information he'd managed to collect, knees tucked up against her chest.

Sleep claimed him, quickly.

35

LUELLE got little sleep the night she stayed in Malcolm's room. She read and re-read about her parents in the low light until her eyes ached, committing every detail to memory. Lucia, her mother, had been a human who worked as a seamstress. Abel, her father, had been a Veseile fisherman.

Tears spilled over her cheeks as she mourned the family she'd never known, their absence a re-opened wound that had never truly healed. She had always believed her family hadn't wanted her, had thrown her away. Now she knew that might not have been the case. However, although the information about them was a balm for her heartache, it didn't change the fact she was still alone. Anger battled with her grief; fury burned in her at the injustice of having no memories of these people, of losing them when so many others still had their parents. Why had Mortus needed to claim hers?

She yearned to know their faces. Could Malcolm find their portraits for her? Would portraits of them even exist? She glanced at him, lying still beside her, every exhale warm on her bare arm. Shadows nestled under his eyes. She couldn't wake him to ask; there would be plenty of opportunities to request more from him, though he'd already given her so much more than she could ever have asked for.

For now, she created mental images of her parents. The papers Malcolm had gifted her offered some details—their hair and eye colour: *brunette, brown eyed,* both like her. Had their eyes and hair been the exact shade of hers? Or had she inherited the specific hue from only one of them? The papers even included the name of some other family members—grandparents in other parts of the realm, and birth cities of her parents, where other distant relatives might still live.

Twice through the night, she fell into a doze. Each time she jolted awake, paranoid she would open her eyes to find someone ready to haul her away in chains for daring to be in the king's private chambers.

Malcolm had more lavish taste than his father. Thick woven rugs softened the floor. Velvet cushions and knitted blankets were scattered over the bed and every chair. Landscape paintings adorned the wall space between bookshelves that were full to overflowing, with uneven stacks of books spreading to the floor in front. Even his bedding was opulent, silky and warm. His scent clung to the sheets, filling every breath Luelle took.

Sunlight bled through the window, bright since neither of them had pulled the curtain closed last night. Despite that, and for all Malcolm claimed he was unable to sleep, he hadn't stirred once through the night. Luelle turned on her side and watched his chest swell with each deep breath. Morning light limned the lines of his face with gold. A stray white curl fell across his brow, the tip brushing against his long eyelashes. Slowly, so as not to wake him, she pushed it back, nestling the unpigmented hair against his darker curls.

She couldn't stay here forever, even if he continued to sleep through the day. Training was scheduled to resume this afternoon, after another research session with Graman.

As she began to consider waking Malcolm or fleeing to her own room without an escort, a soft knock sounded at the door. Luelle sat upright, snatching up her paperwork, heart thundering. Malcolm's blonde human guard, Theo, poked his head into the room.

He frowned seeing Luelle in Malcolm's bed. The expression only softened when his gaze drifted to Malcolm's still-slumbering form. Staying silent, he gestured for her to follow him into the reception room.

Luelle got the hint. She climbed from the bed, smoothing her hair so the guard didn't get the wrong idea as she followed him out.

"Graman has been asking for you," Theo said as soon as the door to Malcolm's bedroom was closed. "My soldiers informed me King Malcolm had retreated to his rooms with a red-haired companion last night. I assumed it would be you."

"It—that wasn't what it looked like," Luelle said, unable to read his expression. Her gaze dropped to the floor. Was she in trouble? Did anyone other than Malcolm even have the jurisdiction to punish her? Theo knew the truth about her identity, but nothing had happened between her and Malcolm. He had only wished to gift her the papers she still clutched.

Theo sighed, resting his hand on the hilt of the sword

sheathed at his hip.

"As head of his guard, the king's *safety*," he emphasised the word, "is my sole concern. Who he chooses for company in private is none of my business, even if I do disagree with the decision."

She gritted her teeth, cheeks burning. "Nothing happened."

His expression remained unreadable. "Do you wish to return to your rooms before heading to the observatory library?"

She nodded, letting Theo escort her back to her room to change into fresh clothes before attending her usual research with Graman.

In the following days, Luelle did not see Malcolm again, giving her plenty of time to overthink his reaction to waking up alone. Did he regret asking her to stay with him? Had she overstepped a boundary—beyond the obvious ones regarding the difference in their stations and the fact she'd committed treason against his family months earlier? Would he face any repercussions if people thought he had bedded her, no matter that nothing had happened?

She and Graman made no progress finding evidence that Vesanya had been trapped by another god, but the stilted frustration of their research was offset by her progression during training sessions with the Gifted.

By now, almost all of them were more confident fighting with the Power, even against multiple opponents, so the princess had introduced a new weapon to them— small projectile spheres containing powdered shadowbell to knock an enemy unconscious following the weapon's detonation. Practising with them was much more dangerous in the close quarters of their training hall, so they had not used the actual weapons properly more than twice. Instead, they drilled with hollow brass balls the same size and weight as the glass spheres, projecting them at mannequins formed of straw-filled sacks.

Sessions on healing with the Power continued alongside the fighting. Luelle's extracurricular reading helped her a little, but she had no natural talent for it. Art and Mei excelled, and Luelle was happy for them. She funnelled her efforts into perfecting her skill as a warrior, comforted that her fellow Gifted would be around to patch up any wounds she took. Physically cleaning and bandaging cuts might be all she was ever good for.

Tired and aching from her afternoon's training, Luelle returned to her room. Guards stood outside, as always, but had not followed her through every inch of the castle since the night of the ball.

She rested her muscles, stewing in a long, luxurious bath to pass some time. White strands were beginning to show through the dye in her hair. She would need to reapply it tonight or tomorrow to continue hiding her Veseile streak.

She only left her bath when her stomach was growling. By now, her dinner should await her in her room. She wrapped a towel around herself and exited the bathroom, jolting to a standstill when she found Malcolm perched on the end of her bed.

His head snapped up as the door opened, eyes widening when he saw what she wore. He sprang up from his spot. Heat flushed her face.

"Apologies, I did not mean to startle you." He averted his eyes, looking anywhere but her. "I—uh, I meant to call on you sooner, but my schedule has been so busy waiting for the castle to quiet once again after the ball."

"It's fine." Luelle shrugged, though her stomach did not stop its somersaulting at the sight of him. "Do you need me?"

He nodded, glancing at her and away. "We need to talk."

"I'll get dressed." She edged past him, careful not to brush his fine clothes with her damp arm. Snatching clothes from her wardrobe, she retreated into her bathing room. Malcolm was stood beside the window, looking into the gardens when she returned to him.

"Will you have dinner with me again?" he asked, still unable to meet her gaze.

She nodded, nerves intensifying. There was no food on her table, yet. What else was there to discuss other than the regret he felt over asking her to stay with him on the night of the ball? Should she reassure him she knew it meant nothing? When he said they understood one another, she knew it was only because they shared the same trauma from witnessing a massacre.

Malcolm led her from her room. Instead of turning toward his private suite, as she'd expected, they walked the route she took every morning towards the observatory.

Night transformed the room. Beyond the large mechanical model of the solar system, city lights shone bright through the windows. The stars reflected in the sea shone brighter, a shimmering mirror reflecting the clear, moonless sky above. A few moonstone lights glowed within the observatory, highlighting the doorways, but none were luminous enough to distract from the view or dim the stars.

Malcolm closed the door behind them as they entered, sealing off the rest of the castle. He strode towards the tower that housed the telescope and other rooms Luelle had never needed to see during her daytime visits.

They stepped into a small cartography room with rounded walls. Rolled maps, tied together with yarn and stacked on shelves, filled most of the space. In the centre of the room was a large, square table, covered in partially-complete, hand-drawn maps and some of Graman's sketches from the cavern.

Luelle approached the table, brushing her fingertips over the inked constellations on the charts.

"I wanted to apologise. For the night of the ball."

She turned, surprised. Malcolm stood by the door, weight shifting from one foot to the other. His eyes flitted to rest on everything else in the room but her.

"Apologise?" Luelle mirrored his frown. She should be the one apologising—she was the one who had overstepped a boundary by staying in his rooms. Not to mention she'd disobeyed his instructions to remain hidden, risking being seen by servants just to watch the celebrations.

"I should not have forced you to stay with me. And I should not have given you those papers whilst I was so intoxicated. I know how personal that information is."

Luelle offered him a smile. "I don't care about you coming to me drunk. I apologise for staying as long as I did, and for leaving my room in the first place."

Malcolm shrugged. "Nobody saw you besides my guards and they are sworn to secrecy in my private dealings on pain of death. You cannot stay locked in your room forever. You are aware of the risks for both of us if someone recognises you. I trust you to be careful. And you shouldn't apologise for staying. I was the one who requested it and I am grateful you did. I slept better than I have in weeks." He breathed a dry laugh. His hand rose to rub the back of his neck, still unable to meet her eyes. "I did not—Theo should not have made you leave that morning. I spoke with him about it."

"As much as I would've liked to spend the day in bed, as I'm sure kings are allowed to do, I had to research with Graman."

He finally met her gaze, eyes glinting with humour. "I didn't spend the day in bed. Although I did oversleep and miss several arranged meetings with visiting guests."

Luelle grinned and turned back to the maps, hoping to hide her relief that he hadn't been angry at her for staying despite the differences in their stations. "You've been trying to match the star maps to the chart from the cavern, too?"

She felt him step to her side. Charts and maps shifted on the table as Malcolm moved them using the Power so all were visible beside one another with Graman's sketches lined up above.

"Yes. Graman showed me the matching one you found in the library before the ball. I knew we had earlier records stored here. I believe I have found a pattern." He pointed to the chart on the furthest left, panning his hand to the right. "These are in order of the earliest recorded, but it is a repeating event depicting the date when the planets in our solar system align. Records claim you can see the planets with the naked eye if you travel away from the cities. These records are dated every fifty years. I think if we look back further, we would see the pattern repeating again."

"Do you have earlier records?"

Malcolm nodded. "In storage."

Luelle examined the most recent chart, dated long before she and her former friends discovered the cavern. "So the next time this happens is…"

"Less than half a year away." Malcolm finished her sentence.

She looked up, meeting his wary gaze.

"Do you know what it might mean?"

He shook his head, brows knitting in frustration. "It must be important, though. It cannot be a coincidence Vesanya was trapped in a cavern with this specific celestial event carved into the floor."

Luelle crossed her arms, glaring at the charts as if she might intimidate them into revealing their secrets.

"There is more," Malcolm said, lips downturned. "But, we should eat, first. I had food brought upstairs for us." He gestured towards a spiralling iron staircase on the far side of the room. Luelle ascended with Malcolm close behind, distracted as she wondered if the map could be a misdirection. Were they trying to find answers there for no reason? Or did it hold the key to trapping Vesanya again? Could it connect to Zeke's belief that it was possible to steal a god's Power?

They trekked up the stairs until they reached the top of the stout tower. The ceiling was a dome of glass revealing endless stars. A large, rotating telescope sat in the centre of the room, lens pointed towards the ceiling. Only two wall sconces were lit, the two closest to a small table that hosted two plates, piled with food.

Luelle accepted the seat Malcolm pulled out for her.

Hunger gnawed at her stomach. Seeing and smelling the feast of roasted, herb-rolled meat and buttery vegetables brought Luelle's attention to her appetite. Ravenous, she tucked in without waiting for Malcolm, which was just as well, since he only picked at the food.

She slowed, remembering he had more to tell her.

"What's wrong?"

He glanced up, pulled from silent thoughts. "You should finish eating, first."

She frowned. "No. Tell me."

He looked away, taking a deep, shaking breath. "I received a report today from Omar, my Field Master General. He is training some of my soldiers on the border to the Southlands. A few days ago, some of them were exploring the surrounding area on their rest days and they found a farmhouse, which they believed to be abandoned."

Luelle put her cutlery down. Anxiety rose like a sickness inside her. Had they stumbled across Zeke?

"It did not take them long to find the owners. There were two adults and one child, all three bodies desiccated, as if they had died years before. The food in their kitchen was unusually fresh, but there were no signs of others living there. The vegetables were soft. They had not even had time to mould before my soldiers found the place."

Memories of Vesanya's rampage in the cavern replayed in Luelle's mind. Her meal became a heavy weight in her stomach.

"She's back," she whispered.

Malcolm's eyes reflected the dread she was certain was in her own. Luelle wiped her clammy palms on her thighs, clenching her fingers into fists to hide their trembling.

"I only received the report this afternoon. I wanted to tell you before anyone else." He ran a hand through his hair, pulling his curls back from around his face. "I plan to travel out there this week to investigate. I may be able to find a trace of where she went after the attack."

Luelle's throat dried.

"I'm coming with you."

Malcolm said nothing, expression undecipherable. Eventually, he nodded, knowing he would not win if he tried to argue.

"We will leave as soon as possible. Ideally tomorrow, but more likely the day after, since I need to inform the council and prepare for the journey. We will travel with a small group of soldiers, a mix of the Gifted and regular fighters."

"What if we see her?"

Luelle knew with grim certainty she would die at Vesanya's hand if she tried to fight the god.

"We retreat." Malcolm's voice was firm. "Despite the work you and Graman have done, we do not know how to stop her and I refuse to allow anyone to be needlessly killed. We will collect evidence. I want to confirm whether it really is her or if we face a different threat. My soldiers are currently guarding the area to prevent anyone from entering or changing the scene. They are also searching for survivors who might be able to provide eyewitness accounts. I need to learn her intentions. If she is moving towards densely populated areas, I may need to evacuate the civilians."

Luelle nodded. Numbness spread through her body. All emotion was dull beyond the nauseating anxiety in her gut. The thought of returning to her room, alone with nothing but rising fear, filled her with dizzying dread. She stared at the remnants of food on her plate, her appetite vanished.

Malcolm's voice interrupted her spiralling thoughts.

"Can I show you some of my favourite constellations?"

Though the question was innocent, understanding shone in his eyes. He shared the need for a distraction from the news, if only for the time they spent here.

She nodded.

He blew out the candles around their table, plunging the room into darkness beyond the pinpricks of light offered by the stars above.

His hand found hers, pulling her to her feet and towards the telescope several steps away, not letting go even as he adjusted the direction in which the lens pointed.

With each new constellation he showed her, Malcolm told Luelle some small story about the memories attached to it. She listened with fascination, gazing at the sky with new eyes as Malcolm unveiled the beauty of the stars to her. In contrast to the vast, incomprehensible universe around them, Vesanya seemed a small problem.

At some point, they abandoned the telescope and ended up lying on the floor, arms touching from shoulder to wrist, hands still clasped as they stared through the glass ceiling at the sky.

When Luelle fell asleep on the hard observatory floor, she did not dream.

36

As expected, several members of the council put up a fight when Malcolm announced the report from the farmhouse and why he intended to investigate it in person. None of them were happy at his insistence to endanger himself instead of sending soldiers and remaining safely tucked inside his castle walls. Malcolm stood his ground, though he left the council chambers feeling little satisfaction about winning the argument.

Travel arrangements were quick to finalise. Two days after he'd received Omar's report, Malcolm and a large group of soldiers, including Theo and Leena in his personal guard, left the capital.

He didn't speak with Luelle again since the observatory until seeing her in the courtyard as they prepared to leave the capital. She stood near Arthyr and Tao. They wore the same plain leggings and shirt with only a simple leather jerkin to offer protection from the wind as they rode. Grey clouds ahead promised rain through their journey. She wouldn't be comfortable.

Malcolm was moving towards her before he could

think twice about the action.

Tao straightened at his approach. Arthyr and Luelle glanced at him with frowns before realising their king was walking to them. Arthyr imitated Tao's stance. Luelle simply raised her brows at him, lips pursing to conceal a smirk.

"May I speak with you?" Malcolm asked her, ignoring the Gifted around them and hoping no one noticed the heat that flushed his skin when Luelle met his gaze.

She nodded and followed him a few steps away from her companions. The courtyard was large but full enough that they could find no privacy; soldiers lingered around Malcolm at every step to ensure his safety, the Gifted loitered in a group, humming with nerves and excitement for their first journey out of the castle walls as a new type of soldier, nobles gathered at the fringes of the space and looked down upon them from balconies and windows, and servants skirted through every gap to tend to anyone in need. Malcolm led Luelle to the side of his carriage, speaking in a low tone to try and prevent any curious ears from overhearing.

"It will rain on our journey," he said.

She glanced up, a line appearing between her brows. "That's what you wanted to talk to me about?"

His face warmed further. "No—I mean, yes. I wanted to offer you to ride with me. In my carriage. Your jerkin will be uncomfortable in the rain."

She met his gaze again. "Isn't that improper?"

"Why would it be?"

She opened her mouth, cheeks blushing pink, eyes flitting to his lips and away. "Oh, because I'm a Gifted and you're the king. I think it would be better for me to ride with them. Art says I already don't treat you like the others do. I should probably try and remedy that."

"No," Malcolm said, frowning. She cocked her head in question. "You treat me like a person. Don't change that," he tried to explain.

She held his stare, nodding after a moment. "I won't," she said, softly. "But I should ride with them. A little rain never hurt me before."

Disappointment flooded Malcolm, but he did not stop Luelle as she returned to Arthyr and Tao. He could not grow dependent on her, even if her presence was the only thing allowing him to feel any peace.

The journey gave Malcolm the opportunity to catch up with Theo and Leena. Despite the rain, which started the moment they left the city walls, he requested that the three of them ride instead of travelling inside the carriage. He glanced over his shoulder ever few minutes, eyes straying to Luelle, ears pricking up when the wind carried the sound of her voice or laugh. Having her nearby, if not beside him, kept his dread at bay. If she was brave enough to join him on this journey, knowing they might encounter Vesanya at any point, he could face his fears too. It was a silent, mutual agreement passing between them whenever she met his gaze on the road.

After a few days of fast-paced travelling, Omar's camp appeared in the distance. Lines of fabric tents and training areas filled with soldiers interrupted the greenery. Above it all flew Malcolm's royal crest on their flagpole— a tree with blue leaves to symbolise his demonstration with the Power at his coronation.

Soldiers greeted them on their approach to the camp and escorted them in, taking their weary horses and providing everyone with food and drink rations. Malcolm gestured for Theo and Leena to follow him, but before they went to Omar's tent, he strode towards Luelle.

Mei nudged her with an elbow as Malcolm approached. Luelle turned and shot him a small, nervous smile.

"I want you to accompany us in speaking to Omar." He ignored his own nerves, hoping they weren't plain on his face. "We will receive a report from him before travelling to the farmhouse."

She swallowed and passed her drink to Tao, who stood tall and silent beside her.

Malcolm knew little about Tao but sought to remedy that when he returned home. He bit down on his irritation at the Gifted who Luelle had chosen to spend her time with over him. Nerves were making him restless. Turning away, he let the others follow behind him so he did not have to see the expressions on Theo and Leena's faces; he could already feel their eyes burning into his back.

Passing soldiers dipped into short bows as he passed through their camp. Malcolm acknowledged each one with a nod, unsure how they could remain so cheerful and animated when each of his steps were growing heavier. His heart was beating so hard against his chest, it felt like someone was throwing punches at him. He swallowed—a dry, rasping movement.

Omar's tent was spacious and bright, sunlight permeating the pale linen walls in the main living quarters.

Omar looked up from where he stood, gazing at documents strewn across a large table. Shadows had settled underneath his eyes since leaving Cerulya. His expression relaxed upon seeing Malcolm.

"You made good time, Your Majesty." Omar stepped closer and dipped into a short bow. As he straightened, his dark eyes flickered to Malcolm's three companions. He gestured further into the tent, to three cushioned benches. In their centre, on the coir flooring, sat a tray with a tower of wooden cups and a small iron kettle. Steam poured from the spout.

"Please sit, I had drinks brought here when the scouts reported your approach. I should have greeted you, I apologise."

Malcolm shook his head, clapping his hand on Omar's shoulder. "Nonsense. We came as quickly as we were able. We would have arrived sooner, but you know how the council can be."

Omar snorted and led them to the benches, stepping around cluttered stacks of weapons and armour with an apologetic glance. He poured a mug of tea for each of them. Malcolm took the cup, wrapping both hands around to soak up the warmth. His fingertips turned pink at the sudden change in temperature.

"How far is the farmhouse from here?" He jumped straight to the point, unwilling to let it linger over him any more.

Any remaining light vacated Omar's expression. "Slightly under an hour's ride. We can go today, if you wish. I did not know if you would want more time to prepare yourself."

Malcolm recognised the trepidation in Omar's face.

"How bad is it?" he asked, softly.

Omar's eyes dropped to the floor, his jaw tightening. "I have never seen anything like it." He wrapped his own fingers around his cup but Malcolm didn't miss their tremble. "I thought someone must have moved the bodies there when we investigated and found fresh food. All of their animals are still alive. But, there was no trace of another person. We have not found any survivors."

"Have you moved the bodies?"

Omar shook his head. "I ordered everything left where we found it until you arrived, in case you noticed something I missed. Soldiers are guarding the farmhouse now, looking after the animals and making sure nobody enters."

Malcolm's gut clenched. He sipped his tea, scalding his tongue. Glancing sideways, he found Luelle staring at her fists in her lap, face pale. Muscles in her jaw pulsed as she clenched and unclenched her teeth.

"Have you found any similar incidents elsewhere?" Malcolm asked.

"No. I sent soldiers to all of the nearest settlements when we found this one, but there have been no others."

It was a drop of relief in the sea of dread.

Malcolm looked to Theo and Leena. "We will take half an hour for everyone to rest, then I want to head out."

They nodded. Theo left to spread the message to the soldiers; Leena and Luelle disappeared to find food before they travelled to the farmhouse. Omar departed to prepare a select few troops of his own to accompany them. Malcolm remained in the tent, simmering with anxiety. His stomach tied itself in knots, each one tightening as the time to leave approached.

Borrowing fresh horses from Omar's camp, they reached the farmhouse quickly. As he'd said, soldiers waited outside the building, guarding its entrances and strolling the perimeter.

The atmosphere was strikingly different from the camp.

The earlier rain had departed, leaving a clear, crisp autumn sky stretching above the house. Rolling green hills formed the backdrop. Bleats, snuffling snorts, and scratching feet floated on the wind from a large pen containing sheep, goats, a cow, and too many chickens to count. Most of the soldiers lingered around the animals, staying as far from the house as they could. They spoke in low tones, frequently glancing at the horizon. The tension in their shoulders did not melt away as Malcolm, Omar, and their small group of troops approached.

Malcolm's horse had barely stopped before he was dismounted and striding towards the house, his heart in his throat. He did not wait for anyone to join him.

Inside, the air was thick with silence.

The overly-sweet smell of rancid food hit him before anything else. Covering his nose and mouth with his hand, he walked inside, steps slow and quiet so he could hear any movement. Omar's soldiers had checked the house several times for any other signs of life, but Malcolm could not lower his guard even if he had wanted to.

The first body was outside of the kitchen.

Lying at the bottom of a wooden staircase, what must have once been an adult man was now a withered, dehydrated corpse, mouth wrenched open in a silent scream. Malcolm fought the urge to retch. Both of the corpse's arms were angled upwards, hands reaching for their neck. Beside the body lay a knife—the blade clean.

Malcolm averted his eyes, stepping around the corpse and ascending the stairs. Omar had reported three bodies.

Footsteps sounded behind him. Malcolm spun to find Leena at his back. She tore her eyes from the body, offering him a stiff nod; she would watch over him. Tremors wracked his limbs as he walked, despite the slow, deep breaths he took in an attempt to calm himself.

The second and third bodies were in the farmhouse's only bedroom. Smashed pottery and scattered clothing littered the doorway. Another adult-sized corpse lay at the foot of the bed in a similar position to the first—hands grabbing at the space around its throat, skin the same dry, leathery texture.

The third corpse was considerably smaller than the other two—barely bigger than Edwyn—curled up in the small space between the bed and the wall, arms lifted protectively over their head.

Malcolm's breath came fast but he was unable to find any air.

He'd brought this fate on this family, on his people. If he couldn't find a way to stop Vesanya, devastation like this would continue.

Tears pricked his eyes, but he could not tear his gaze from the small body in the corner of the room.

37

Luelle's body was numb. She walked through the farmhouse in a daze, envisioning the fear this family must have felt in their last moments, as two parents defended their child to the end.

She'd followed Theo and Leena inside, all three of them trailing Malcolm as he discovered the bodies one by one. They'd found him motionless in the farmhouse's bedroom, staring at the corner of the room where the dead child was curled up. He had only jolted out of that frozen state when Theo had placed his hand on Malcolm's shoulder, pulling him away from the room.

Neither Luelle nor Leena had lingered there for long.

Malcolm ordered a couple of soldiers to wrap the bodies in the largest sheets they could find inside the house, in an attempt to give the family some dignity in their death. Whilst the soldiers worked, Luelle searched through the rest of the house with Leena and Mei, desperate to find clues to indicate why Vesanya targeted these people and if the god planned to continue her savagery elsewhere.

The kitchen contained nothing unexpected: shelves filled with utensils, scratched and worn from years of use; a small pantry with wilting vegetables; a counter presenting a dough rolled flat, a crust of age formed on its surface. Half of the dough had been shaped into small raw biscuits, fingerprints present atop each one. The task had been abandoned halfway through.

Luelle searched every inch of the room for the clues she sought but found nothing. She left the soldiers to remove the spoiled food and turned to the living area, where Leena was sorting through the few documents they'd found downstairs—ledgers, sketches, a journal, and some scribbled schedules.

Leena looked up as Luelle approached. Pink tinged the white of her eyes. She sniffed, returning her gaze to the paperwork.

Luelle sat nearby, wrapping her arms around herself in an attempt to fend off the chill seeping into her bones.

"Have you found anything?" Her voice was quiet.

Leena shook her head. "They were an ordinary family, Veseile. Looks like they traded goods at a village nearby for most of their income." She shoved the paperwork away and waved a hand to gesture at the rest of the house. "Their positioning was entirely defensive, too. I do not understand what they might have done to provoke an attack."

"Mei might find something upstairs."

"There was nothing in the kitchen?"

"No. As you said, it's a completely normal home."

They sat in silence. Murmuring voices and shuffling bodies were the only noise as other soldiers moved around. Leena was the first to break the quiet.

"I did not believe you and Malcolm before. Not really. I saw the bodies in the cavern but I suppose some part of me thought you were both mistaken about how long they had been there." She met Luelle's eyes. "I am sorry for that. Seeing it here—" she inhaled a deep, shaky breath. Luelle replied before she could continue.

"I understand. I wouldn't have believed it either if I hadn't watched it happen."

An unfamiliar sense of peace settled between them.

"Are you certain it was Vesanya?" Leena asked, frowning. "I cannot understand why a god would do this."

"I don't know who else it could've been. She is the God of Chaos. How are we supposed to understand her motives?"

"This wasn't chaos, it was murder." Leena's voice was bitter. "It is more befitting of Mortus than Vesanya."

Luelle stayed quiet, unsure what she could say. She looked around the living space. Knitted blankets made from dyed wool lay over the handmade wooden chairs. Dust lightly coated most of the surfaces. Someone had lit the fireplace while she'd been in the kitchen. The smoky scent disguised the stench of rotten food but the air still felt stale. Death clung to the house, suffocating.

"I need some air." Luelle stood, abruptly leaving Leena in the lounge and striding away so she could breathe again. Leena's words echoed through her mind—*this wasn't chaos, it was murder.* Could that mean Vesanya was not responsible for the deaths they'd witnessed here, despite killing in the exact same way at the cavern? Did a bigger threat lurk in wait for them? Perhaps whatever had trapped Vesanya in stone? She would have to speak with Graman about it.

Deep in thought, she made her way out of the building. She had not realised how long they'd spent in the house until she left it. In the distance, most of the other soldiers were gathered together, as if numbers might guarantee their safety. Art and Tao stood among the rest, all engaged in sombre-looking conversations.

Averting her eyes from the final glare of the setting sun, Luelle walked in the other direction, circling around the farmhouse. She had no desire to talk to anyone after what she'd just seen. How could she explain why she wasn't reacting with the same sorrow and horror they felt? She'd seen it all before. Now, it just left her hollow.

Rounding the corner, she tripped over something on the floor, toppling to the ground.

Vile curses spewed from beside her.

Heart racing, she scrambled to her feet, finding Malcolm sitting in the shadows of the house.

"What are you doing hiding down there?" she demanded, shocked at the torrent of swear words he'd spoken, unlike anything she'd heard from him before. Accusation rang clear in her tone to shift the blame from herself.

He glared at her, rubbing his leg. "I needed a break from that house," he mumbled.

She straightened, her annoyance dissipating as quickly as it had arrived.

"Want company?" Though she'd felt eager to remove herself from the other Gifted and soldiers, the thought of sitting here with him offered a shred of comfort.

He hesitated, but eventually nodded. Luelle stepped around him and sat, leaning against the house to mirror his position. Cold air made the hairs on her arms rise. The only warmth emanated from Malcolm, close beside her. She didn't need to turn her head to know he would be looking up, searching for the first few stars now the sun had set.

"How are you feeling?" Luelle asked, tentatively—a stupid question, considering what they'd witnessed today.

He glanced her way, saying as much with the brief look.

"Sorry." She shifted, pulling her knees up to her chest and wrapping her arms around them.

Malcolm rubbed a hand over his face, up through his knotted curls. "No, I am. I do not mean to take this out on you or anyone else. It is hard witnessing my failure to protect my people, and having so many other people see it, too."

Luelle frowned. "This isn't a failure of yours."

Malcolm didn't respond.

Her frown deepened. She rocked where she sat, nudging his shoulder with her own. "I mean it. Nothing could've stopped Vesanya when she set her mind to doing this again." Although, Leena's comments returned to her mind. What had Vesanya gained from this? What was the purpose of a God of Chaos?

"That is the problem," he insisted. "I should know more by now. I must learn how to stop her from doing this again. I am the king, my job is to protect people and I have failed at it. I am a poor king."

"You aren't a poor king." Luelle resisted the urge to roll her eyes. "I doubt anyone expects your responsibilities to include defeating the gods themselves."

He glanced at her again, amusement battling with the self-deprecation in his eyes.

"Besides," she continued, "I'm the one who released her, aren't I? If anyone is to blame, it's me." The admission was bitter on her tongue.

"I do not blame you for this." Malcolm shook his head. "I think we are prioritising the wrong thing during our research. At this point, it does not matter why Vesanya was trapped in the cavern, or who did it, just how we can achieve it again."

Luelle chewed at her lip. "But we can't learn that without knowing who did it and why. It's all linked. We have to start somewhere."

He exhaled a heavy breath.

"Leena said what happened here wasn't chaos." Luelle voiced the thoughts that had been circulating in her mind since leaving the farmhouse. "Do you think there's a chance we could be wrong about who did this?"

Malcolm shook his head. "It was her. Who else could it have been? Perhaps we are simply mistaken about what chaos means."

"Graman will have an opinion, I'm sure."

He breathed a laugh through his nose. "He will. We are all missing something, I know it."

"We'll find it."

He shifted, tilting his head to look at her properly. "You sound so sure."

"I am." She shrugged. "You made short work of finding me when I stole from you and were stubborn enough to follow me halfway across the realm, despite the dangers to yourself. You defended us both against a large group of enemies in that cavern. You were the second deadliest person there, after Vesanya herself. And your skill with the Power makes the rest of the Gifted pale in comparison. If Zeke managed to learn what he did about the gods and the Power, I have no doubt you will manage it in a fraction of the time."

He averted his gaze, the blush on his cheeks evident even in the dim light. "Well, I have been taught how to use the Power and fight physically for almost three decades, so if I was worse than the rest of you or incapable of holding my own, there would be a serious problem." He attempted to lessen the easiest of the compliments she'd thrown his way.

"Oh? And how do you excuse the rest?" She raised a brow at him, pleased to be the one who had banished the despair and fatigue from his expression.

The apples of his cheeks rounded as he fought a smile. "I imagine you are the only person who would consider stubbornness to be a redeemable trait."

She fought a failing battle with her own smile, grinning at the horizon. Tension bled from her posture.

"Thank you," he murmured.

Luelle was surprised to find him looking at her again.

"For admiring your stubbornness?"

Amusement returned to his eyes. "For the kind words."

"You're welcome."

The dark marks underneath his eyes drew Luelle's thoughts back to the night of the ball.

"Have you been sleeping?" she asked.

"Not really. Your presence seems to be the only thing that staves off my nightmares." He breathed a humourless laugh. "I imagine seeing all of this will make the problem worse again, for a while."

Luelle knew the same would be true for her. Already today, the anxiety and paranoia she'd felt those first few weeks after the cavern crawled over her skin as strong as before. She was speaking before she could evaluate the sense of her suggestion.

"I could stay with you again."

Malcolm's head snapped up.

Heat burned in her cheeks. "I mean, only if it might help. If it might allow you to get some sleep, not because I would try anything else. I don't mean to make you feel uncomfortable. I could sleep on one of the sofas in your chambers. It will be like the old days, in the Godswood." She stumbled over her words, silently cursing herself for the strange offer. Theo's reaction to finding her in Malcolm's room after the ball demonstrated exactly what a bad idea it was. She'd refused to ride in his carriage; sleeping in his chambers would be significantly worse for his reputation if anyone were to see, even if it meant nothing.

"You would do that for me?"

She glanced over at him and nodded, despite her concerns.

He exhaled a low, long breath, shoulders relaxing slightly. "I would like that. As long as you would not feel uncomfortable. Thank you. Although, maybe we should wait until we return home, as it will be hard for me to sneak you unseen into my tent."

She chewed at the inside of her lip. It made sense. Of course, Malcolm already knew how improper it would look and that she only offered it as a way to help him rest; her intentions were not carnal. However, Theo had clearly believed something had happened between her and the king, and once that thought returned to her mind, she could not shake it.

Shadows clung to the contours of his face, softening his stare and drawing Luelle's eyes to places she might not usually examine during their conversations—to the sharp line of his jaw, offset by the curve of his lips, the delicate curls falling over his brow and around his ears, the small triangle of his chest revealed by the cut of his shirt.

She swallowed and looked away, ignoring the feeling of his gaze still on her, ignoring the twitch of her fingers that yearned to brush against his cheek and see how he might react. It was entirely inappropriate; they'd both just witnessed the aftermath of a horrific attack and he was her king.

Malcolm cleared his throat, startling her. In her peripheral vision, she saw him shake his head. His face was still darkened with a blush from her compliments earlier in their conversation.

Her next words broke the tension that had formed between them.

"What's going to happen to them?"

He met her stare, the unspoken question in his eyes.

"To the family," she amended.

Malcolm turned back to the horizon. "Graman would want them returned to Cerulya for the coroner to examine but I doubt their bodies will reveal anything new. He has already evaluated the corpses from the cavern and could not tell me anything I needed to know."

"What would you want to happen to them?" She lowered her voice, though it still felt loud in the darkness.

He lay his head back against the building, exposing the full length of his throat in silhouette.

Luelle looked away, cheeks heating anew, frowning at her inability to pay attention. The stress of the day was getting to her.

"I would want to keep them here. Let them rest on their land. Though, we will most likely end up selling it to another farmer for the wellbeing of the villages this family sold their goods in."

"So, let's do that."

He frowned at her.

"You're the king," she pressed. "If you want to bury those people here, a potential future owner can't stop you. There are tools inside for tilling and digging. I can fetch them and get some soldiers to help me."

"No," he spoke hastily, amending himself when he saw the flash of rejection cross her face. "I mean, leave the soldiers. I want to do it myself. These people deserve that much from me."

Luelle nodded, relief spreading in her chest. "Wait here. You'll only get pulled into another task or conversation if you go back in."

She got to her feet and slipped inside the farmhouse, collecting a hoe and two shovels. Most of the soldiers who had been inside earlier had left to join the others gathered in the distance, so she was in and out quickly, unnoticed.

When she returned to the back of the house, Malcolm was on his feet, rolling his sleeves to the elbow. He said nothing at the sight of a second shovel, only nodding a silent acknowledgment and thanks.

Together, they dug until their clothes were damp with sweat and their muscles screamed—until they'd driven some of the guilt from their souls.

38

THE arrow Malcolm fired was off its mark by several centimetres, but he nudged it back on track with his Power before it struck the target. It buried into the bullseye, nestled against the last two arrows he'd shot. Whoops and cheers sounded as the soldiers around him applauded, clapping him on the back, grins spread wide on each of their faces.

His shoulders screamed in protest at the friendly hits and the continued exertion, still aching from last night's digging. Memories of that moment felt distant. Luelle had stayed with him the entire time, digging the graves, using the Power together to gently lift the bodies and lower them into the ground, nestling the child between their parents. Using the Power together like that, intertwined in their task, was an intimacy he'd never experienced with another person. His mind had reeled with the feeling of her for hours after.

They'd refilled the graves by hand, with the shovels, eager to feel the burn in their muscles. It had been a strange sort of penance for unleashing Vesanya into the world.

Malcolm tried not to dwell on the way Luelle's shirt had clung to her back as they'd dug, of how the moonlight gave her skin an ethereal glow, or how, for a moment when they were sitting together beside the house, he'd thought she might lean in closer—how he had *wanted* her to.

As agreed, she did not come back to his tent, but through the entire sleepless night, Malcolm looked forward to having her beside him in his castle chambers. She remained with the other Gifted today, somewhere deeper in Omar's camp while Malcolm carried out this new part of his publicity campaign.

Theo had been the one to suggest it—training practice with the troops stationed here. The soldiers were due to remain in this area for several more weeks, potentially longer if the threat of Vesanya continued. A morale boost would be beneficial, doubly so if it strengthened the soldiers' admiration and loyalties to their king.

Malcolm handed his bow to the nearest person, excusing himself to have a drink. Theo and Leena waited for him beside a small table covered in cups of water. Theo held one out as Malcolm approached.

"Thank you," he murmured, taking a sip and pushing his hair back from his damp forehead. "What next?"

"Archery for another ten minutes or so. Then Omar mentioned you would show them some of your swordsmanship," Leena said, resting her hip against the table. "If you are up for it, that is." She eyed Malcolm rolling his shoulders.

"Of course." He didn't let his doubt leak into his tone, sipping his water.

Theo and Leena had found him and Luelle last night, as they were pushing the last few clumps of dirt over their newly dug grave. Neither of his friends had said anything but Malcolm hadn't missed the concerned glance they'd exchanged.

Another one flashed between them, now. Malcolm scowled.

"Just say it," he snapped.

"Say what?" Leena raised an eyebrow.

"Whatever it is you are both thinking."

Another glance. Theo cleared his throat, eyes roaming the soldiers, the horizon—landing everywhere but Malcolm. Leena plucked up the courage to speak for them.

"We are concerned about you."

"What is there to be concerned about?"

"You are spending a lot of time with Luelle."

"And?" Malcolm scoffed. "She is instrumental in helping me learn more about the threat Vesanya poses. After yesterday, I thought you would understand the importance of that."

Theo narrowed his eyes, finally meeting Malcolm's glare. "We all know that is not the limit of your interactions, though. Or are you forgetting I was the one who found her in your bed?"

Leena's lack of surprise confirmed his friends had spoken about it already.

Malcolm's cheeks heated. "Nothing happened. Not that it is any of your business if it did. She is a friend." Shock sparked through him at the truth of the words. When had he stopped considering Luelle a prisoner and started considering her a friend? Leena and Theo glanced at one another once more, reigniting his fury.

"Your safety is our business," Leena interjected. "She stole from your family. She is a traitor. She could have other plans to disrupt your reign."

He put his cup back on the table with a little more force than necessary. "Leena, do you truly still believe that after all of your interactions with her?"

She frowned. "Well, no, not really. But if there is any doubt, I must consider it. We are only looking out for you."

"I trust her. That should be enough for you."

They exchanged another glance.

"Stop doing that!" Malcolm snapped.

Leena took a deep breath. "You must also be wary about giving her false hope, Malcolm. She cannot develop feelings for you. You are the king. She is not a suitable match. Interacting with her so much might encourage an attachment to form, which would make things awkward for you when you must reject her."

Malcolm averted his eyes, looking at the soldiers who were continuing their drills around them. Of course, he already knew that, but the discomfort in his chest was confirmation that Luelle was not the only one in danger of forming an attachment. His thoughts strayed to her with an alarming frequency and his eyes sought her out whenever he thought she might be near. His heart raced when he caught sight of her hair, glinting copper in the sunlight.

"We are only trying to help," Theo said.

"I know." Malcolm sighed. "I did not mean to bite your heads off. I have not been sleeping well. But I am telling the truth when I say nothing like that is happening between Luelle and me. We are working together to eliminate the threat we face, that is all."

They accepted his answer with only minor uncertainty. It was good enough.

Malcolm moved away from the table, strolling over to where his soldiers were setting up a training area to practise their sword fighting drills, abandoning the rest of the scheduled archery. Someone handed him a wrapped blade. He accepted it with a nod of thanks, watching the soldiers for a moment before stepping in to spar with them.

Pain radiated through his shoulders with every strike, every blocked blow. Sweat quickly coated his temples and stuck the fabric of his shirt to his torso.

It was only when Malcolm spotted Luelle watching from the sidelines and threw himself back into the sparring with renewed ambition to win that he realised he might be in trouble.

39

Luelle launched back into her routines after they returned to Cerulya. Mornings of researching with Graman bled into training with the Gifted in the afternoon and eating dinner with Art, Mei, or Tao in her room whenever any of them were available. She was stronger than she could ever recall being, both physically and mentally.

And each evening, when the rest of the castle's inhabitants were preparing for bed, Malcolm would arrive at her door, inviting her to his chambers so they could each get some real rest. At first, she tried to insist on sleeping on one of his sofas, but he only brought his pillow and blanket to the second settee to be closer to her. After another brief argument, they agreed it simply made more sense for them to share his bed. It was excessively large enough that they need not touch one another through the night; there would be no mistaking that this was a platonic endeavour by two friends trying to help one another. Malcolm had even placed a pillow between them after they awoke from their first night, tangled together, having somehow found one another during their sleep. Each morning, she snuck out before his servants arrived, slinking back to her rooms so rumours would not spread that the king had taken a lowborn lover.

Despite the hardships of training and research, the regular sleep meant Luelle woke each day with renewed eagerness to progress.

Upon their return to the capital, she had shared every detail of the trip to the farmhouse with Graman, including the unsettling words Leena had spoken. There was no denying Vesanya had been at there—or someone with the ability to kill exactly as she had.

Luelle stared at the words in the book on the table until they blurred on the page. She rubbed her eyes and sat back. Graman was examining the star charts once again, standing at a desk across the room with his hands clasped behind his back.

"I've been thinking about our theories."

He dragged his eyes from the sketch in front of him. "Which theories?"

"That another god trapped Vesanya."

Graman nodded for her to continue.

"We've analysed mythology about the gods who created every other Eile race and found no evidence that any might have a vendetta against Vesanya. I know we moved on from the theory, but I realised last night, we hadn't actually been considering all of the gods."

Understanding sparked in Graman's eyes. "Mortus."

She nodded. So far, they had ignored the God of Death in their research. But, waiting for sleep to claim her last night, Luelle wondered if they had been wrong to disregard Mortus. Leena had already pointed out that the scene they'd witnessed in the farmhouse was death rather than chaos. Could Mortus be involved there, too?

"We have assumed the other gods must exist, since Vesanya does, but we've ignored Mortus this entire time."

"Legend consistently states Mortus dwells in the Underworld, so it makes no sense that he could have trapped Vesanya in this realm, nor that he could have killed the victims you saw in the farmhouse, as you suggested a few days ago." Despite shooting down her suggestion, Graman's voice was kind, approaching the debate from a neutral, scholarly position.

"There's no evidence to suggest he can't access this world, though. In fact, I would claim the opposite. Vesanya came here and we've assumed the other gods might be able to come here too, despite the fact we haven't seen them. If we're sticking to the claims of legend, we have to remember that legend states our souls travel to the Underworld from this realm. Why do we assume Mortus cannot make that journey? Surely he could travel here using the same route."

Graman frowned. "I suppose we have never considered it because no Eile race descends from Mortus in this world. According to legend, the Moreile live alongside the God of Death in the Underworld, helping him guard the souls of the dead."

"True. However, legend also states that every god abandoned this realm millennia ago and we know that isn't the truth because Vesanya is here now. Myth suggests the Underworld is just a portion of the gods' own realm. So we shouldn't ignore Mortus as a possibility."

Graman took a deep breath, rubbing at the frown lines in his forehead.

"Unfortunately, all of our theories are conjecture, and I am not sure that will change without finding older sources or speaking with Vesanya herself." He laughed at the suggestion, oblivious to the icy shiver that overtook Luelle at the thought.

"Let's run with it, though," she said. "Since we can't prove the other gods had a vendetta against Vesanya, let's consider whether Mortus did. We could search through mythology surrounding him, see if he might have had a motive to trap her in the cavern. Or if there's a way he could be influencing her actions now."

"Regardless of his motive, we still do not know how he was able to trap her. If any another god trapped Vesanya, we may not be able to replicate the process."

"It has to be relevant to the plinth and crystal sphere."

Graman raised an eyebrow.

"Vesanya didn't change in all the years I lived in that cavern. We thought she was a genuine statue until I put the Power in the sphere." Luelle took a sip of water, trying to banish the dryness in her mouth that always surfaced when she remembered that afternoon in the cavern. "You've suggested it before and I dismissed it because neither Malcolm nor I were able to remove the Power from the crystal again. However, Mortus is a god. He might have been strong enough to."

Graman tapped a large finger against his jaw. "Perhaps. It is a creative theory but we still have no real evidence to support it. And, if it is true, we would be unable to stop her without involving another god. How are we to do that?"

"Maybe that's where the star map comes in." Luelle changed course, frustration growing. "Maybe we can contact the gods on that date, when the planets align. Or maybe we can remove the Power from the sphere if we attempt it on that date."

Graman's frown returned. "It is a very specific celestial event to mark out on the floor. I had thought it a strange coincidence to find it in that cavern."

Luelle nodded, spurred on by his agreement. "Maybe we need to lure Vesanya back into the cavern and remove the Power from the sphere on the plinth whilst she's inside to trap her again. Maybe it acts as a trigger, or a key, of sorts."

Graman sipped his tea. "It is as strong a theory as anything else we have," he said, as diplomatic as ever. Luelle knew the theory was weak but they had little else to contend with it. Graman continued. "However, if true, it could pose problems, since it may involve removing the Power from the Veseile race all over again. We would need to confer with Malcolm."

Luelle nodded, sighing. The last thing she wanted was to lose access to the Power. There had to be another way to solve the issue.

"Some of the texts Malcolm dropped off around the time of the ball described people's interactions with Meto —requesting his help to protect their land. Maybe we need to search for the same thing with Vesanya. If there's any suggestion of interaction with her or her trying to help and protect people, perhaps there's a chance we can use that as a final resort. If we can't trap her again, maybe we can find a way to communicate with her and strike a bargain."

Surprise lit Graman's face. "That would definitely be worth investigating. On top of research about Mortus, let's search for tales of people requesting favours or bargaining with Vesanya. We know she cannot be omnibenevolent after the action you witnessed in the cavern and the recent trip to the farmhouse, but any patterns we can identify might help us."

Luelle nodded, taking a deep breath and trying to mentally prepare for the work ahead of her today.

Hours wiled away as she read, finding endless stories about interactions with the gods: a human trading eternal obedience to Vesanya in the Underworld in exchange for an Eile lifespan; several tales of hopeless romantics showering Dilectya with earthly gifts in exchange for the love of another; a Colleile who made an exchange with Collatus, receiving a solution that would heal any stranger's wound but inflicted pain identical to that suffered on the bargainer with every use; even a tale about a Veseile striking a bargain with Mortus, giving up their Veseile heritage to spend one day with their deceased human lover on earth, and transitioning to become Moreile when the sun set.

As Luelle devoured the stories, noting down any she thought Graman might wish to read, a nagging voice questioned whether she would find anything more than myth. Zeke had always been the expert at finding evidence and now he was Luelle's enemy. He would likely be hoarding anything vital he possessed to prevent her, and anyone else, from learning the truth, particularly if Freya and Imbryl were correct and Zeke thought he stood to gain something from Vesanya's presence.

Luelle and Graman had made little real progress, despite studying their sources for months, now. How long did they have until Zeke became an equal threat to Vesanya, or bigger, if he found a way to steal her Power?

40

Malcolm hesitated outside Luelle's door. Almost two weeks had passed since their return from the farmhouse and he was feeling better than he had in months, having had several hours of uninterrupted sleep every night since.

Leena had arranged tonight's plans shortly after their return, deciding they all needed to blow off some steam. Malcolm still hadn't worked up the courage to invite Luelle, despite waking up alongside her each morning.

He hadn't told Leena or Theo that he planned on bringing Luelle, although there was no doubt they'd bring their own plus ones. Kit, Leena's sweetheart, was essential for supplying the wine. He smuggled it from the castle kitchens—it wasn't entirely necessary since Malcolm could simply request the drinks from Philip, but the illusion of sneaking around made the experience more fun. Theo would likely bring along Arthyr, who always seemed to shadow him in their time off. Luelle's presence was vital so Malcolm had someone to talk to when his friends became distracted. These private social gatherings were among the few times Malcolm got to truly relax and he did not plan on spending it sitting in silence whilst his friends were preoccupied with their puppy loves. He planned to have fun, to talk about whatever stupid topics sprung to mind and drink enough that he stopped thinking about how much he wished to draw Luelle into his arms every time she got into his bed. He'd been forced to place a pillow between them after their first night together to hide that evident desire from her.

He took a deep breath and knocked on her door.

Luelle sat up from where she was lying on her bed. On seeing him, her head tilted in an inquisitive fashion, eyebrows arched.

"This is earlier than normal," she said. "I haven't even eaten, yet."

Malcolm blamed stress for the way his heartbeat increased and nerves fluttered in his stomach upon seeing her. His mind went blank, the carefully planned request that she joined him dying on his tongue. He stood in the doorway, mouth gaping. No words emerged.

She must think him an idiot.

She filled the silence. "I know we've avoided talking about it, but I want to tell you about some of my theories regarding Vesanya—"

"Tomorrow." Malcolm cut her off, relishing the flash of annoyance that crossed her expression. Most other people would accept his rudeness with immediate forgiveness and apologies. Tonight would involve no talk of Vesanya; they both needed a break from the worry. "No business talk tonight. We have plans."

The agitation in her glare softened into guarded curiosity.

"Come on." He held the door open.

"Where are we going?" She shuffled off her bed and followed him.

"A private social gathering." He shrugged and closed her door behind them. "I figured we both needed it."

He grew uncomfortable with her gaze roaming his face, seeing too much for his liking.

"You still blame yourself for the farmhouse," she murmured.

Malcolm turned from her penetrating stare. He thought of the victims who had died in that farmhouse every day, saw their bodies whenever he was lax enough to let his thoughts stray.

"Let's not talk about that tonight." He started walking. Behind him, her footsteps followed, soft but sure.

Their destination wasn't far. Malcolm's suite contained a small, spiralling staircase that led to the castle roof, one of several available if people knew where to look—though very few did.

Brisk night air whipped at their clothing when they emerged onto the roof, closing the door tight behind them.

Luelle wrapped her arms around her torso, gazing out at the city. Torches and moonstone lights glimmered across the sprawling metropolis below, snaking down to the harbour, where the lights were replaced by a shimmering reflection of the bright moon and a billion stars.

Malcolm glanced up rather than out, instinctively locating his favourite constellation. Luelle followed his gaze.

"The Time Turner," she said.

He nodded, surprised she'd been paying attention when he'd pointed it out to her that night in the observatory.

"You never told me why it's your favourite."

"It is a symbol of our mortality. Eile or human, Mortus will come to collect us all, one day. The thought is as terrifying as it is refreshing."

"How very morbid of you."

A smile tugged at his lips. "It reminds me that life continues. I am the same as anyone else in the grander scheme of things, no matter how much the people in my court try to inflate my ego." He looked around, spotting movement in the shadows across the roof where he, Theo, and Leena would usually set up camp for their drinking. "Come on." He held out his hand. Luelle accepted it, letting him guide her.

Laughter and the pop of a corked bottle opening echoed towards them as they approached. As predicted, Arthyr sat beside Theo, their elbows touching. A blush already flushed the Veseile's freckled cheeks despite the wine only just being opened. Kit lounged beside Leena, his arm wrapped tightly around her. His thumb stroked a pattern on her hip. They all looked up as Malcolm and Luelle approached. Arthyr and Kit's smiles stretched, a sharp contrast to the ones that died on Theo and Leena's faces, seeing Malcolm holding Luelle's hand. A warning look from him ensured they wouldn't voice their disapproval here and now. If they must, they could berate him in private.

"Good evening, everyone. Luelle, have you met Kit?" Malcolm asked, guiding her to sit on the floor beside him, Arthyr on her other side.

"Nice to meet you." Kit smiled at Luelle, handing her a

drink and pouring another for Malcolm.

Luelle murmured a thanks, casting glances between Leena and Kit as she tried to make sense of the connection between the two. Malcolm ducked his head to hide his smile. Few people got this glimpse into Leena's personal life and every one of them had the same reaction. With her role in Malcolm's court, most expected Leena to end up with a warrior of equal skill to her own. Instead, her entire heart belonged to Kit, a short, plump human with kind eyes, perpetually rosy cheeks, and rusty brown hair that no comb could tame. Even Malcolm had been sceptical when the man first caught Leena's eye, but Kit had a quick wit and a knack for seeing the best in everyone that Malcolm admired endlessly. Leena was fiercely protective of him, as she was with everyone she loved.

Luelle sipped her wine. Though it seemed casual, Malcolm could tell she was consciously averting her stare from Leena and Theo to focus instead on Arthyr, who was prattling on about something they'd practised in training that afternoon. Malcolm accepted his wine from Kit, taking a long, much-needed drink.

"—Tao said my problem is my balance," Arthyr was saying, waving his hand around as he spoke, "but I managed to get a good hit on him, so it can't be *that* bad."

"One good hit and he thinks he is a soldier." Theo grinned.

Leena snorted.

Colour deepened in Arthyr's cheeks but he mirrored Theo's grin. "I'll be at the top of that class soon. Although I'll definitely need more practice before I can best you, Lu. You make it look more natural than any of the rest of us."

She hid her smile in a sip of wine, eyes sparkling with amusement. "I have a flair for the dramatics, that's all." She shrugged.

"It sounds like cooking," Kit said. "Once you've perfected the basics, you can get more creative and work some magic."

"Is your creativity what we should blame for the charred biscuits you tried to bring here tonight?" Leena turned on him, smirking.

His cheeks flushed almost as pink as Arthyr's. "I may have left those in the ovens a little long but I didn't want them to go to waste."

"Malcolm hasn't tried one yet." Theo pointed out.

Leena sat upright, almost quivering with glee. "Nor Luelle. Come on, my love, stop hiding them." She reached behind Kit, fetching a small wicker basket, its contents hidden with a white cloth.

"Oh, no, really, I don't think anyone else needs to—" Kit spluttered, grabbing for the basket. Leena held it out of his reach, snatching away the cloth and thrusting it towards Malcolm and Luelle.

"These were biscuits?" Malcolm tried to disguise his horror upon seeing the small blackened circles inside the basket.

"They *are* biscuits," Leena corrected him. She shook the basket. One of the biscuits crumbled. "Go ahead, try one. Kit worked really hard on them." She threw her empty hand over Kit's mouth when he continued to object.

Luelle reached for one first, holding it tentatively between her thumb and forefinger. Malcolm followed her lead, meeting her reluctant, concerned stare with one of his own.

Endlessly brave, she was the first to lift the biscuit to her mouth, taking a bite that sounded close to breaking a tooth. She crunched, wincing as she chewed.

"It's good," she said, around the biscuit.

Malcolm did not believe her.

"Your turn," Theo urged, gesturing to the biscuit in Malcolm's hand.

He stared at it. Closing his eyes, he braved a bite, imagining his favourite foods instead—sweet strawberries drizzled with honey, tart lemon biscuits, freshly baked bread slathered with butter.

The biscuit was hard and crumbling all at once. Any flavour was lost under the overwhelming taste of soot. Malcolm took a breath to lie to Kit about their quality, only to inhale some rogue crumbs. He choked, spluttering and coughing. Cackling laughter drowned out his suffering.

Draining his wine, Malcolm managed to get his breathing under control, blinking tears from the corners of his eyes.

"Yes, really great, Kit," he managed to choke the words out.

"Does that count as an attempt on the king's life?" Leena asked, further tormenting Kit, who hid behind his hands.

"We should move this party to the dungeons," Theo declared.

Malcolm grabbed the nearest wine bottle to refill his glass. He should feel embarrassed but his minor battle for air had been worth it to hear Luelle's laugher joining in with his friends'. It made him feel drunk in a way the wine never could—a high he might never come down from.

The evening passed in a blur of clinking glasses and exaggerated stories. Leena slumped further into Kit's lap and Theo's hand found its way into Arthyr's. Malcolm's heart swelled for his friends' happiness, even if a small part of it still yearned to be allowed a connection as genuine as theirs. The more he drank, the stronger his feelings burned.

Eventually, he was lying beside Luelle, staring up at the night sky. Leena and Kit had disappeared for some privacy and showed no sign of returning, whilst Theo and Arthyr had left on a mission to raid the kitchens for something more filling than charred biscuits.

Above them, stars glittered. Awe swelled within Malcolm, turning into something warmer and more chaotic when he felt Luelle shift, brushing her fingers against his. He took her hand, interlocking their fingers, and turned his head to meet her gaze, ignoring how the world spun around them.

Stars shone in her eyes, the entire universe staring back at him. Malcolm thought she was beautiful when he woke up beside her each morning—golden sunlight kissing every bare patch of skin, highlighting the freckles on her cheeks, and calling forth the copper sheen to her hair that could not be stifled by the dye she still applied—but seeing her in moonlight transformed her; she came alive in moonlight.

Emboldened by the wine, he reached his free hand to brush a tendril of her hair away from her face, marvelling at the softness of her skin on his fingertips.

Any doubt of who he wished to look at him with the same adoration his friends looked at their plus ones tonight vanished. His fingertips travelled along Luelle's cheekbone, trailing down to her jaw. He slid his hand around the back of her neck, tangling his fingers in the warmth of her hair as he closed the gap between them.

He brushed his lips against hers, hesitant that she would turn him away. He retreated, opening his eyes to give her that option, but found her smiling. Relief flooded him. His cheeks ached with his own smile. Nerves fluttered in his stomach as he prepared to lose himself in her eyes again, but Luelle didn't let him move back any further before she kissed him, less tentative than he had been. He felt the shape of her smile against his, tasted the lingering wine on her lips. The night's chill no longer bothered him.

By her side, he was the happiest he would ever be.

41

A punch knocked the air from Luelle's lungs, sending her flying through the air. She landed on her back with a grunt, pain throbbing through the rest of her body in the same tempo as the ache in her temples.

Ignoring Mei's guffawing laugh, she dragged herself to her feet.

The headache and the conflicting emotions churning a storm in Luelle's mind left her preoccupied—a state that saw her knocked down repeatedly during training. Her scowl deepened every time she hit the ground, growing increasingly irate with herself.

Memories of last night lingered at the edges of her mind, beckoning her to relive the evening. Although she'd been apprehensive when she and Malcolm had arrived at the rooftop with his friends, her cheeks had ached as much as her head this morning from the hours of laughter. Experiencing such happiness again was terrifying—not to mention the danger of her feelings about what had happened after Malcolm's friends had left.

She couldn't think about *that* without a smile tugging at her lips, giddiness overtaking her.

They'd stayed under the stars for a long time, exploratory hands and kisses eventually giving way to a simple embrace as they fell asleep together. Orange sunlight stained the sky when Malcolm had gently nudged her awake, a smile still curving his lips. He'd taken her hand as they'd retraced their steps across the roof to his private staircase, not letting go until they reached the entrance to his suite, where he'd lifted her hand to brush a final parting kiss on her knuckles—

Pain erupted in Luelle's stomach. Groaning, she stumbled to her feet, the distraction of last night leaving her vulnerable to Mei's attack once again.

Mei helped her upright, a quizzical frown creasing her brows.

"What is wrong with you today? That should have been easy for you to block."

Luelle released a long breath, rubbing at the ache in her abdomen from the hit.

"Did you sleep badly?" Mei persisted, rolling her shoulders. Sweat glistened on her forehead from the toll of using the Power as much as the physical exertion of their training.

"Something like that," Luelle muttered.

"Shall we meditate instead? Knocking you down is starting to lose its satisfaction."

Luelle glared at Mei, but felt the amusement in her own expression. "That's probably for the best, before I get a concussion." *Or vomit*, she added silently. Clearing her mind was exactly what she needed.

Mei snorted.

They sat beside one another, legs crossed, arms relaxed, hands flat on the floor. Vibrations pulsed faintly into her palms and fingertips as other Gifted moved around the room, their steps drumming against the ground. Luelle closed her eyes.

Meditating as and when needed was something Princess Vivyenne encouraged them all to do, particularly if their lack of attention was hindering them in their fights. She'd claimed meditation at will was natural, expected for anyone at the earliest stages of training with the Power, but having to stop for it only inflated Luelle's frustration.

Around her, grunts and muffled thuds sounded from every angle, preceded by tugging pressure as each Gifted used the Power. Luelle focused on distinguishing individual fighters with her eyes closed, untangling the unique threads of the Power connected with her own. Inhaling deeply, she breathed in the blend of sweat and leather, far stronger than the dust and must lingering in the undercroft. Voices interspersed the fighting—quips, playful taunts, quiet curses, and praise for clever or successful manoeuvres. Luelle sunk into her senses, strengthening her connection with the Power and the world around her, but it wasn't enough to prevent her thoughts from slinking back to the topics she sought to avoid.

She regretted nothing about last night, but the feelings that had stirred within her flooded Luelle with anxiety and fear. She was more attached to the king than she wanted to admit to herself, and that path would only lead to hurt. Their stations in life were too different and the risks he took being seen with her were too great. Even if no other servants or court regulars recognised her true identity, her fate was not tied with Malcolm's—it could never be. He was destined to be with someone of noble heritage who was able to rule Arazia alongside him. Working together to stop Vesanya and Zeke from causing further harm was one thing, but it wasn't fair for either of them to forge an emotional connection.

Both of them had consumed a foolish amount of wine last night—that was what was to blame for their actions. It was the sole reason. Malcolm would not want things to go further than the heated kisses they'd shared.

Shoving the king from her mind, Luelle focused on the other problems plaguing her. Progression in her research with Graman remained sluggish; there seemed no way forward without seeking her old mentor. Zeke's new theories and ambitions proved that he must be hiding information about Vesanya. On top of the value of his resources, Zeke remained a threat. Malcolm had already informed Luelle that Zeke was spreading rumours, trying to rally the Veseile behind him and donning the title Liberator of the Eile. She suppressed a scoff at the name. Zeke had never been one to let go of grudges. Being bested by Luelle and Malcolm in the cavern was not something he would forget. Finding and eliminating Zeke would allow Malcolm to focus on Vesanya and would put some much-needed space between Luelle and the king.

Plans formed in her mind as she pretended to meditate. When Princess Vivyenne called an end to their training session, Mei helped Luelle to her feet.

"Feeling any better?" She quirked her unscarred eyebrow.

Luelle shrugged. "Not particularly." There was no easy solution to her problems. No part of her wanted to leave Malcolm and the capital behind but it would be best for him and his reign, as well as saving her own heart from breaking as it had when Zeke and her old friends had rejected her. She couldn't bear hearing those words from Malcolm, too, when the time inevitably came.

Discomfort grew within her when she turned around and locked eyes with the king, awaiting her at the back of the training hall.

Her throat dried at the sight of him leaning against the wall. He smiled. Her heartbeat quickened and the pain in her head thudded with it.

Luelle left Mei to gather with the rest of her friends, heart sinking at how little time it had taken her to consider them such. Attachment seemed inevitable, no matter how much she tried to avoid it, knowing the pain it might bring her.

"Walk with me?" Malcolm asked, when she was close enough to hear him murmur.

She nodded, unable to refuse a request from the king, and willed her face to show none of the anxiety she felt. She had no desire for this conversation—to hear him explain last night had meant nothing.

Instead of going to her room, his suite, or the observatory, where they usually tucked themselves away, Malcolm wove a path through the halls leading to the main palace gardens, far from the ones Luelle could see from her bedroom window. As they walked, nobles and servants alike stopped to bow to their king, peeking from beneath their lashes at who he was with. Tension tightened Luelle's posture.

Outside, cold air bit at her cheeks, bringing with it the salty scent of the nearby ocean. Brown leaves rustled on the trees around them. Their footsteps crunched on the stony paths as they strolled beside one another, walking the winding paths until they were alone, only Malcolm's usual guards trailing far behind them.

Luelle didn't miss how Malcolm walked with his hands clasped behind his back, preventing their fingers from brushing in public.

Her heartbeat stumbled when Malcolm took a breath and opened his mouth. She spoke before he had the chance to hurt her.

"I need to find Zeke," she blurted.

His head snapped towards her, steps faltering.

"Our research into Vesanya is slowing, and we know Zeke took documents with him before he fled the cavern. I know it might be nothing, but I'm unwilling to keep ignoring the warning Freya and Imbryl gave me about Zeke's newest theories. If he knows how to steal a god's Power, he'll know how to stop one. We need that knowledge now Vesanya is active again."

Malcolm blinked. "That makes sense."

She charged on, encouraged. Reaching out beside her, she let her fingertips brush against the taller flowers they strolled past.

"I spoke to Graman about it a little, but haven't had the chance to tell you. I think we've depleted the information our current sources can provide. Zeke always had a way of finding the most obscure things and I know he would've taken the more important ones with him when he fled. I have theories from our reading, but nothing substantial, no evidence to support them." Frustration leaked into her tone, even as verbalising her tangled thoughts released some of the coiled anxiety in her chest.

"What theories?" Malcolm asked, brow furrowed. Luelle had assumed Graman was keeping him updated, but perhaps Malcolm's schedule during the day was too busy for that.

"Only another god could have the sheer Power necessary to trap Vesanya. Since we can't find evidence of tensions between her and another god in any of the mythology we've studied, I think we should focus on Mortus, though Zeke might have evidence that weakens that theory. I've also been wondering if we couldn't remove the Power from the crystal sphere in the cavern because we were trying at the wrong time. That might be how the star map plays in. Maybe we have to trap Vesanya in the cavern on the date the planets align," she rambled, frowning as the theories tumbled out sounding weaker now than they had in the observatory library.

"Even if that is true, we still have no understanding of *how* to trap her, only when," Malcolm pointed out. "If we require another god to do it, I think we are out of luck. One is bad enough to deal with, I cannot fathom having two in the realm."

"That's why I need to find Zeke. If he believes he can attain a god's Power, we will be able to trap Vesanya ourselves."

"I do not think anybody should have such a level of Power."

"Not even you?"

Their eyes met in a sideways glance. Luelle looked away as fast as she'd looked over, heart skipping a beat. She raced to explain herself.

"Had I never interfered, you'd be the only person with the Power, as has been the case in your family for millennia." She swallowed. "My actions might have changed that initially, but you obtaining more Power would be no different to that, really. It would strengthen your rule, which is what you wanted."

Malcolm pulled a face. "Perhaps. Though I have started to think things are better this way. Power can corrupt. Having the Power did not solve the problems my ancestors experienced, it only gave them a way to suppress the chaos by force. You only need to look at the tensions between human and Veseile to see that. Besides, Viv has been studying you all as you fight and train. She believes there is a natural variation of Power levels among the Gifted."

"What do you mean?" Luelle frowned.

"Surely you have noticed during training." Malcolm turned his head to watch her expression as they strolled. "At some point, we must consider that it isn't a lack of understanding or learning, and simply a case of the Power differing in each individual. You consistently best the majority of the Gifted you train with and push the others to their limits even when they do win a fight. Few have the same ability. Tao is doing well in combat, apparently, but many of the others are only able to actively fight using the Power for minutes before exhausting themselves. Some are better suited for healing or defensive manoeuvres. Concentrate in your next training session, when you can feel someone draw on the Power. You can feel the strength of a person's force. Whenever I attend, I can feel you more than the others; they fade in contrast to your presence." He shrugged.

Luelle's frown deepened. How strong was Zeke? He lacked the cohesive training she was receiving, but he was well-versed in the history of the Power. Even if she was able to perfect her combat skill, could she beat Zeke if there was a chance he was stronger than her or able to battle for longer? Besting the other Gifted she currently trained with did not mean she would be superior to any enemies she faced.

Malcolm cleared his throat. "I do agree with you though, we cannot keep ignoring Zeke. I received more reports about him today. More Veseile have been joining his ranks. There has been an uptick in violence in the Southlands." He took a deep breath, chest swelling. "Let me speak with my advisers. I will arrange a time for us to pursue him. I can excuse it as some sort of publicity tour and visit some cities as we travel."

Luelle slowed to a stop, nerves churning in her stomach. He turned to face her after several steps walking alone.

"You can't come with me."

He scoffed. "I will not allow you to go alone."

"It's too dangerous."

"Exactly."

Luelle squirmed where she stood, unable to meet Malcolm's intense stare.

"He almost killed you last time," her voice emerged quieter than she'd expected. "He wouldn't hesitate to try again, and we have no idea how strong he is."

"That would not happen again, I am prepared now. And you are just as vulnerable to harm from him. He went out of his way to hurt you last time, even if not physically."

She did not respond.

"Say I did allow you to go after him, where would you even start? Do you know where he might be, beyond the vague clue of the Razors from your old companions?" Malcolm closed the distance between them, annoyance plain in his clenched jaw and the furrow of his brow.

"No, but I'll seek him out again. I'll start there and track him." Luelle shrugged, trying to make the suggestion sound easier than it would actually be.

"You would chase him blind and run to your own death. That is exactly why I will not let you go without me. I do not suggest we travel alone again, but we both know the threat Zeke poses. Preparation will be paramount for our success. We will travel with a large guard of traditional soldiers and the best of the Gifted. I would send scouts ahead for the clues you hope to find yourself—people who have been trained to track for considerably longer than you."

Irritation flared at the challenge in Malcolm's tone.

"Besides, I am counting on him to try and kill me again," he said.

She finally met his stare, incredulous. Before she could sputter out a response, Malcolm continued.

"That is why I must be there. My presence will draw him out of whatever hiding place he is choosing to lurk, particularly if he thinks I do not consider him a threat. I doubt he could resist the temptation, trying to assassinate me in the midst of a tour designed to show my strength and stability."

Luelle closed her mouth. She couldn't deny his logic— Zeke had always loved to embrace theatrics.

"Anyway," Malcolm shook his head, putting the entire subject to one side, "that is not what I wanted to speak about."

"We don't need to talk about last night." Luelle

stepped back, panic choking her, a sudden ringing in her ears drowning out the distant birdsong. "I know it didn't mean anything to you. I mean, I know we could never— you don't need to…" she trailed off, uncomfortable, unable to face the frown on his face, the hurt in his eyes. "I should sleep in my own room tonight."

As she turned away to flee the conversation, Malcolm's hand closed around her wrist. He tugged her to a stop, pulling her to meet his gaze before she left him alone in the gardens.

"Do you regret it?" His stare was vulnerable, tension in every inch of his stance.

The truth slipped out unintentionally, a whisper.

"No."

Luelle tugged her arm free and strode away, steeling her heart against the glimmer of relief and satisfaction that flashed over Malcolm's expression at that one word.

42

Omar and his soldiers had found more bodies.

Malcolm stared, unseeing, at the report laying on the table in front of him. He'd read it multiple times, as if the words might blur and transform into something different. He'd called a small, unofficial meeting, but couldn't bring himself to read aloud the contents of the letter when Viv, Graman, Theo, and Leena arrived. Instead, he let them pass the report around, watching each of their faces pale as they read, until the sheet was back in front of him.

Viv called for drinks whilst they sat in tense silence. Malcolm barely noticed the servants enter and deposit a selection of refreshments on the table. Fatigue ate away at him again, sleeplessness returning in full force for the last few nights that Luelle had been staying in her own room. As much as he'd tried not to, he'd grown reliant on her presence.

Their conversation in the gardens replayed in his mind every night. Malcolm still couldn't make sense of it. She claimed their intimacy had meant nothing, yet did not regret it. Surely it had meant something if she no longer wished to sleep beside him. Had he hurt her, somehow? Upset her?

Leena was the first to speak, bringing Malcolm out of his miserable thoughts. Red liquid sloshed against the rim of his goblet as he lifted it to his lips; his second cup of wine that morning.

"Are we going to visit this one, too? Omar says there was a survivor. They might have information that confirms whether Vesanya was the aggressor."

Malcolm nodded, though there was no doubt in his mind that Vesanya had done this.

"The survivor is young. A teenage human. I will respond to the letter this afternoon, asking Omar to remain there with troops to protect and prepare the witness for us."

"When will we leave?" Theo asked.

"This week. It will be a longer trip than last time."

"Omar said this one is only an hour or so from the first house they found." Viv frowned.

"I know, but our research here has slowed." Malcolm turned to Graman. "Luelle told me about your most recent theories. You are coming to an end of the resources in our libraries, correct?"

Graman nodded, sending an uncomfortable glance around the table. "Sandport's libraries are the largest in the realm. They may contain some of the answers we seek." Sandport was the furthest city in the realm from Cerulya, nestled on the coast in the south-east corner of the island.

"On top of that," Malcolm continued, "I am sure you have all seen the most recent reports regarding Zeke's influence in the Southlands. Luelle believes he took his most valuable research from the cavern when he fled. Finding and apprehending him, we could solve both problems, eliminating the threat and taking the research for our own study."

"I thought the reports gave no location." Viv's frown deepened.

"Correct, but all of his activity is in the Southlands, so he is likely living there. Leena, have you managed to post any informants in Zeke's numbers?"

Leena nodded. "Yes, but I cannot guarantee when I will next hear from them. We have arranged a silent postman."

Blank stares met her gaze. She cleared her throat and explained.

"A location for them to receive my commands and send information back to me so I can send a letter requesting anything you wish to know, but I do not know when they will be able to safely get to the location. If they do not get a chance to go, I cannot communicate, and if it is discovered, they must destroy it and eliminate any witnesses to protect their cover."

The scant information they currently had about Zeke's motives and movements described a cult-like dedication from his followers. Several had been observed with the red sigil of the Liberator of the Eile—a stylised 'L'—painted on their foreheads when they'd been out tormenting humans.

Malcolm nodded. "Fine. Even so, I do not need to know his exact location. I will be able to find him."

"How?" Suspicion laced Leena's tone.

"We will send scouts to the foothills of the Razors as we pass through the Southlands on the way to Sandport.

Even if they find nothing, I believe Zeke would be unable to resist trying to apprehend us when he learns I am within striking distance."

Viv slammed her glass on the table. "I knew it. I just *knew* this impromptu meeting was a way for you to suggest another stupid and reckless idea," she spat the words.

Malcolm's tone rose to meet his sister's. "There is nothing stupid about this, Viv. Our people are being *slaughtered*. I must find a way to stop it."

"By constantly putting yourself in danger? We had the exact same argument before you chased your traitor halfway across the realm."

"Yes, but I achieved exactly what I needed to and returned here with the Power."

"Whilst almost getting yourself killed in the process and releasing the Power to the world," Viv seethed. "You cannot pretend that mission went exactly as intended."

He ignored her second statement. "But I did not get myself killed. I am more than capable of defending myself, and this is not something we can delay. If there is even a chance this could provide a way for us to trap or eliminate Vesanya, I must take it," he snapped.

Viv closed her eyes and rubbed at her brow with a finger and thumb, despairing.

Malcolm glanced around the rest of the table, tensed and ready to defend himself against whichever of his friends would attack next. Leena surprised him.

"I think it's a good idea."

He gaped at her, trying and failing to hide his visible surprise. She glared at his reaction.

"Have some faith, Malcolm." She rolled her eyes. "I

saw the bodies at the last farmhouse. If you think this is the best way to stop it from happening again, I support you. I—" she took a deep breath, "I trust Luelle."

Hearing Viv scoff, Leena clarified her statement.

"I trust her to an extent, I mean. She has shown increasing...*dedication*," Malcolm's face heated at her implication, "to the crown over the past several months. Time will tell if it is an act, but I cannot see us progressing if we continue to treat her like a threat, especially when faced with a more immediate one." Leena gestured to the letter, then turned to Viv. "Theo and I would accompany the king, as we did before, but this time we would be able to take an additional body of soldiers with us. Malcolm would not make this trip unguarded."

"We would frame it as a publicity tour, so I would travel with a large company of soldiers and Gifted. The larger the party, the better, the more likely it is to draw Zeke out," Malcolm agreed.

Viv's nostrils flared as she inhaled a long, deep breath. She rubbed at her temples. "With all of the gallivanting you do, I am starting to feel I have spent longer ruling the realm since Father passed." Despite the harsh words, her voice lacked the bite it had contained a moment earlier.

"Is that your way of accepting my suggestion?" Malcolm asked.

She drained her glass of wine, the redness slightly staining her lip. "Map out the route you would take. I will correct the most reckless places you suggest visiting and then give you my answer. We will need to make the trip appear legitimate if you are hoping to lure this friend of Luelle's out, so you will be continuing the publicity stunts you so despise."

Though he suppressed a groan, Malcom nodded. He tilted his head back, draining his wine while Theo fetched a map for them to study. His attention wandered as they discussed a potential route, returning to Luelle as it had been all too frequently for the past few days.

43

DISCONTENT shrouded Luelle following her confrontation with Malcolm. Restful sleep abandoned her. Nightmares of Vesanya and Zeke returned in its stead. She longed to flee back to Malcolm's side but persevered in her isolation; the decision was for the best, even if she wished it could've been another way.

She fell back into her old routine of researching, training, and returning to her room to toss and turn in bed until the sun rose, all without encountering the king, even from afar. Disappointment filled her during the first few evenings when he did not call at her door, despite being the one who requested they sleep alone again. However, after a week away from him, she forced herself to come to terms with her new life; any pain she felt now was nothing compared to what she would've felt if they'd continued and he'd eventually pushed her aside to choose someone more appropriate. Her heart raced whenever she saw a dark head of hair from the corner of her eye in the castle hallways, but it was never Malcolm. Perhaps he was avoiding her altogether. Annoyance and sadness festered within her at the thought as she strode to her afternoon's training.

Inside the undercroft, Princess Vivyenne immediately cornered her, pulling Luelle from her brooding thoughts.

"You are to help me lead today's session," the princess said, quiet enough that none of the other Gifted, who were steadily streaming into the room, could hear.

Luelle gaped.

"Has the king failed to update you?" The princess eyed her. "You are leaving in two days with the majority of the Gifted to carry out this ridiculous scheme you both devised. To draw out your old friends whilst he pretends to be on a publicity tour through the south."

Luelle nodded, trying to hide the shock from her face. She hadn't seen Malcolm since fleeing him in the gardens, but hadn't wanted to dwell on how she felt about it or when the next stage of her plan might take place.

"And that means you want me to lead today's session? I don't know anything about the king's plans, not really." Luelle sounded defensive, even to her own ears.

"Your friends are the ones we hope to draw out. You are best-placed to prepare the rest of the Gifted to fight them."

"They are no longer my friends—Zeke and the others." Luelle's cheeks burned under Princess Vivyenne's cool stare.

"Regardless." She shrugged. "I want you to teach everyone what to expect. Why you think Zeke might fall for Malcolm's trap, what actions he is likely to take, how you are most likely to beat him, and so on."

"I've been away from them a long time, I don't know —"

"You know better than anyone else."

Princess Vivyenne's stare hardened, silencing Luelle's objections. It wasn't quite the distraction she wanted but it was good enough.

The princess turned and strode several steps, before spinning back with a frown.

"Follow me, then," she snapped, exasperated, as if she had expected Luelle to anticipate the command.

"Oh." Luelle rushed to catch up, pressing the backs of her hands against her cheeks in a vain attempt to cool her flaming face.

At the front of the room, Luelle stood in silence beside the princess, watching the rest of the Gifted enter the undercroft. Few noticed Luelle standing at the front of the room until Art and Tao entered, laughing together about something. Tao frowned and Art did a blatant double take.

Luelle tilted her head towards the princess, keeping her voice low enough that it was hidden beneath the general clamour of the Gifted.

"How should I begin? How much do you want me to reveal?"

Princess Vivyenne glanced towards her. "I will introduce you. You may choose how much of your history with Zeke to disclose, but you may not reveal that you stole the Power from my father on his deathbed and are responsible for everyone here having access to it. A select, trusted few know that information, and it will stay that way."

"Like Mei?"

The princess gave a short, sharp nod. She didn't look over again, but Luelle felt a small, steady pressure emanate from Princess Vivyenne as she abruptly ended their conversation to amplify her voice through the hall. The faint crackle of a storm accompanied the princess's Power.

"Today's training session will differ slightly from the norm."

The crowd snapped to attention the moment the princess began speaking, abandoning their own conversations and facing the front of the room.

Luelle's cheeks heated under the sudden curious stares of so many. Discomfort made a home within her. Her gaze dropped to the floor. Soon enough, she would be able to sink into the background again.

"As most of you know, you will be leaving Cerulya this week to accompany the king on a publicity tour," Princess Vivyenne continued, her voice clear and steady, face expressionless. "However, most of you do not yet know the true reason for this trip."

Luelle didn't miss the small shaking breath Princess Vivyenne took, her only sign of emotion during the speech.

"We recently received another missive from the Field Master General reporting a second home found with corpses inside, in the same state as the bodies you witnessed during your trip east with the king a couple of weeks ago." She met every gaze staring back at her.

Most of the Gifted in the undercroft had accompanied the king to the farmhouse. Those who had not made the trip had heard reports from others. They all knew well enough the horrors they might encounter. Luelle's stomach churned at the thought.

Viv continued. "Our world is changing, and we all

stand here as proof. The king suspects these changes are more significant than we initially thought. He will stop to pay his respects to the dead before continuing to Vidamere and Sandport. There, the king will retrieve research that may help us find some answers about our new form of Power. However, the secondary motive for this trip is to draw out a known extremist cell. We currently believe they are sheltering in the Razors, although we do not have an exact location. We believe they may be linked to these deaths and intend to show them the full strength of the king's Gifted. They must learn that actions like this will never be tolerated and will not go unpunished. We cannot yet anticipate if we will succeed at drawing them out. However, if we do, you will all be responsible for the life of the king in battle." She turned slightly towards Luelle. "Luelle spent some time living amongst these extremists. She knows them better than anyone else here and will share vital information with the rest of you today, to provide the Gifted with an advantage."

Luelle shifted with discomfort as every pair of eyes in the room swivelled towards her. She became all too aware of how she slouched where she stood, weight shifted onto one hip, ink staining her hands from the morning's research. Princess Vivyenne was her polar opposite, standing with a straight back, hands delicately clasped, not a single hair daring to stray from the intricate braid weaved atop her head like a crown.

"Uh, hello," Luelle croaked, offering a small wave to her audience. Heat flooded her face seeing Mei, grinning gleefully at the awkward introduction.

She cleared her throat and tried again, straightening. "The group we're looking to draw out are predominantly

Veseile, but all have extremist beliefs about eliminating humans and anyone with human heritage, which is why we believe they may attempt an attack on Mal—on the king." She gripped her shaking fingers into fists, looking at distant points on the far walls to avoid meeting the many pairs of eyes pinning her to the front. "Their leader is a Veseile named Zeke who has a particular interest in the gods and in the Power. I imagine he will have wrangled some form of control over it by now, if he's able to access it as we are."

Princess Vivyenne nodded beside her and spoke up again. "At this point, we must assume all other Veseile are capable of using the Power and have gained some control over it. Testing has supported our theory that it is limited to those with Veseile heritage, not to any other Eile. Individuals who do not bear Vesanya's mark," she gestured to her white lock of hair, "do not appear to have the ability, but if our enemies are aware of that, they may hide their marks to gain an element of surprise, as Luelle has been able to demonstrate for us." She gestured to Luelle's hair, freshly dyed this week. "Therefore, you must accept no surrender from any extremists you encounter. Even after laying down physical weapons, any one of them has the potential to harm the king. Leave none alive."

Luelle swallowed the lump in her throat, nauseated at the idea of such a massacre, whether it was necessary or not. It was easy to ignore the severity of the situation they would walk into when she was safely hidden within the castle walls. Out there, using the Power would no longer be a training exercise. She pressed on.

"Zeke is calculating, so it is very likely he would encourage subterfuge if he realises the significance of the

Veseile mark." Luelle grasped for secrets to share without revealing her own murky history. "He's unlikely to attack in the open, nor to enter into a fight he doesn't believe he can win. I believe his chosen tactic will be to draw us into a location he has already scoped, where he can plan his positioning to give his people an advantage, especially if he can take us by surprise on top of that."

"How many troops does he command?" Tao spoke up, expression as solemn and pensive as ever.

Luelle pulled a face. "I don't know exact numbers. His followers have never been organised soldiers, but I believe he's been trying to recruit again." She glanced at the princess, who nodded. "They're likely to be self-taught fighters, so won't hesitate to resort to trickery or dirty tactics. Don't assume anything is off the table when it comes to their methods. Like their physical fighting skills, I believe they will primarily be learning how to control the Power through trial and error, experimenting with its limits in any ways they can think to. I don't think they will favour training in formation, as we have been. They're more likely to use chaotic tactics or try to break apart any formations we use to isolate fighters and pick them off when they're most vulnerable."

Princess Vivyenne nodded, sharply. "That is something we can prepare for. We have favoured formations and group tactics recently. Today, we will focus on how each of you can defend yourselves if you are isolated and fighting against multiple enemies."

Luelle glanced sideways, trying to determine whether she was the unlucky chosen one who had to attempt that defensive strategy first, but the princess had other plans for her.

"Tao, up here with us," she instructed, stepping back

and straightening her shirt. As she spoke, she wandered to one of the weapon racks lining the back wall, selecting a short, curved sword with its blade wrapped to blunt the edge. "We will start in groups of three—one person versus two attackers. Rotate the positions, so everybody gets the opportunity to defend themselves, but also to experience how the enemy might be thinking, the types of moves they will look to take advantage of."

Tao stepped beside Luelle, nudging against her gently in greeting before standing to attention for the princess.

"I will go first, against Tao and Luelle. Following our demonstration, I will divide the rest of you into groups to practise. As the afternoon progresses, we will increase the size of the groups and the number of attackers each person must face at any one time."

"Are we using only weapons, or the Power, too?" Tao asked.

"Both. Use anything in your arsenal. You must continue this practice when you are travelling, too, learning to use unfamiliar terrain to your advantage."

Tao nodded, wandering to the weapons rack. He showed none of the nerves Luelle felt.

She couldn't fight Princess Vivyenne. Fighting Malcolm was one thing; they had—or used to have, before she ruined it—a friendship. Luelle trusted him. The princess hated her.

"And how do we win?" Tao asked, returning and handing a short, wrapped blade to Luelle.

"If you land what would be a killing blow or push me beyond the borders of our training ring." The princess nodded to the large chalk circles that had been drawn anew on the floor throughout the room. She turned to the crowd, briefly. "In these attempts, use the Power to push your opponent off-balance or out of the training circle, as we've been practising for the past couple of months. You will notice I have widened the circles in anticipation of today's practice. In an actual fight, you will be able to use the Power slightly differently—as a weapon of its own, rather than just a defensive tool. You can use fire to burn or blind an enemy, for example, though you must be wary of the energy that would cost you."

"Will we have the projectile weapons?" Mei asked. They had practised using the shadowbell bombs during several more sessions, but it remained difficult without half of the Gifted inhaling the powder and spending the rest of the day unconscious.

"We will not include them in practice today. You will take them with you on the tour with the king, but the decision to use them if you encounter the extremists will entirely depend on whether it will give you an advantage. On a wide, open battlefield, the shadowbell projectiles are a good way to stop an enemy before they reach you, but it will be harder to control them if you are fighting in closer quarters."

Princess Vivyenne turned back to Tao and Luelle. Tao had his own wrapped blade at the ready, but Luelle remained frozen with conflict.

"You need not go easy on me." The princess crouched, her lips curving into a smirk.

Tao immediately began circling her.

A sharp shove landed on Luelle's shoulder, preceded by the slightest pressure from the direction of the princess. She stumbled back, quickly regaining her wits and shaking off the nerves holding her back. This was only practice—she wouldn't hurt the princess.

Fanning out in the opposite direction to Tao, she attempted to cut off Princess Vivyenne and end the harmless circling.

The princess sprung into action. Darting into the middle of the circle, a blur, she shoved Tao hard with the Power, up and away. Simultaneously, she pushed Luelle's face with the Power in the opposite direction. Pain burned in Luelle's cheek as if she'd been slapped. She turned, subconsciously following the direction of her head, leaving her back exposed to the princess.

Fresh pain erupted across Luelle's back and shoulder as the princess's blade struck her with a Power-enhanced blow. Silently, she thanked the gods the weapons were wrapped. However, the hard blow had done its intended damage and numbed her arm. Luelle's fingers spasmed; she dropped her blade.

A hard kick to the back of her knees sent Luelle sprawling on the ground in a heap.

Muted thuds filled the air as Tao engaged the princess, their wrapped weapons clashing.

In a real fight, the blow to her back would have incapacitated Luelle, crippling her arm at the very least. In their training, she knew she should consider herself dead and watch the remaining fight. However, Zeke and his followers would fight to the bitter end. Twisting, Luelle stayed on the ground. Hoping to trick the princess, she willed a hard push of air to sweep Princess Vivyenne's feet from underneath her, but the princess anticipated the move, feeling the pressure of Luelle's oncoming blow.

Before Luelle struck, the princess crouched her legs

and leapt, propelling herself with the Power to flip backwards through the air. She landed in a cat-like crouch near the edge of the ring. Tao followed her, eyes locked on his target—and ran directly into the path of Luelle's attack before she could reel in her strike. He fell, sprawling as Luelle had moments earlier. Air left his lungs in a breathy grunt.

Princess Vivyenne sprang forward again, calmly dragging the tip of her blade along Tao's chest before turning and resting it on Luelle's throat. The princess had acted so quickly, her actions a single fluid movement. Luelle could do little more than stare up at her, astonished.

After a moment's pause, laughter and cheers erupted from the crowd, loudest from Mei and Art.

Luelle's brow furrowed. Glancing at the rest of the Gifted, heat rose in her face. She yearned to escape the laughter, but had no opportunity to get to her feet. The princess still held her wrapped blade against Luelle's throat, the blunted tip poking into her skin with more pressure than necessary. When her eyes returned to meet Princess Vivyenne's stare, a bead of fear trickled down Luelle's spine at the cold hatred she observed there.

Princess Vivyenne took a deep, slow breath and broke their contact to turn back to the crowd. "When one fight ends, switch roles. Practise in groups of three until I call a stop. I will give you an hour or so before we increase the group sizes. Conserve your energy." She stalked away from Luelle without looking back, moving to the weapon rack to put her sword away.

Tao was on his feet. He grabbed Luelle's arm with one large hand and hauled her upright, eyes shining with amusement at their failure—his amusement a sharp contrast to the icy panic Luelle had felt.

"Chin up. You might win the next round." He grinned.

44

WEAPONS clashed, the force of the hit pulsing through Malcolm's shoulder. He parried, managing to push Theo slightly away and retreat for a second before diving back in with a fresh, vicious attack.

Their wrapped blades connected over and over until Malcolm's muscles screamed with effort. He grunted with each strike, each block. Sweat rolled down his forehead and temples, blinding him, sticking the loose material of his shirt to his chest and back. His breath burned in his throat.

Around them, other soldiers drilled, practising on a large patch of open grass, away from the bulk of people accompanying Malcolm on his publicity tour.

Fatigue slowed his movements, but not enough to give Theo a significant advantage. Bruises would bloom over his torso and arms tomorrow.

This journey was a stark contrast to Malcolm's last. Instead of only the Gifted for company, he was surrounded by so many people that their tents looked like a small town each evening; soldiers, the Gifted, a selection of nobles, and enough servants to attend them all, maintaining the pretense that this was a royal tour.

Sleeping on the floor, as he had when chasing Luelle across the realm months ago, was a distant memory, replaced by a bed in a spacious, private tent, laden with throws and cushions. He even had a small hosting area with a table and chairs, offering space to build on his relations with the nobility who were accompanying him. Every morning, servants heated Malcolm a shallow bath, sparing him from the exertion of using his Power to heat the water they and his soldiers washed with. Theo was the only one who objected to such treatment, and strolled in to use Malcolm's private bathing facilities each day, refusing to experience the icy baths the others took.

Malcolm would trade it all for a simpler, quieter journey, where he would be free to be himself and speak openly with his friends about his concerns and true motives. Restlessness followed Malcolm like a shadow. Sleeping alone, he woke frequently through the night, drenched in sweat, gasping for breath, and blinking away haunting images from the night terrors that plagued him. By now, his mind had an endless cycle of ghosts and enemies to torment him with: Vesanya, Zeke, his father, Willa. He relived his worst memories every night, almost dying under Zeke's foot, the explosion at the hospital, Vesanya's massacre, his own act of murder at Luelle's false trial.

Malcolm stumbled, caught in those memories, barged aside by Theo's shoulder.

"Break!" Theo called.

They stepped away from one another and lowered their weapons, chests heaving as they caught their breath. Malcolm wiped the sweat from his forehead and eyes with his arm.

A small crowd of the nobles travelling with him had gathered at the edge of the makeshift training area, murmuring appreciation and critiques to one another as they watched Malcolm and his soldiers train. A few of the Gifted drilled together, off to one side, though their practice was restricted by the number of people around at risk of injury from a misplaced blast of the Power. They would train properly later, away from the nobles and tents.

Stockpiles of shadowbell essence were steadily growing. They had an entire carriage full of the powder, stored in tightly sealed, waxed wooden containers to prevent anyone from accidentally inhaling it. Malcolm doubted the powder bombs would be practical to use in a fight against Zeke, when the process required so much energy and put their own soldiers at risk of losing consciousness.

He followed Theo away from the sparring soldiers towards a table set up by the servants at the edge of the space. Theo plucked two skins of water from the table, passing one to Malcolm.

"You seem distracted this morning," he remarked, casting his eye across the field to monitor how the other soldiers were faring.

"I slept poorly." Malcolm rolled his shoulders.

Theo looked over, one eyebrow cocked. A small smirk curved his lips. "Oh? I thought it was because you and a certain traitor were quarrelling."

"She's not a traitor," Malcolm mumbled. "And we aren't quarrelling." He glared at Theo.

"It certainly looks as if you are. You spend most of the

day distracted, staring at her like a lost pup while we ride. You haven't even heard the jokes I have been telling to keep us all entertained."

"Have you ever considered that I do not laugh at your jokes because they simply aren't funny?" Malcolm snapped, irritated that he'd been so obvious in watching Luelle. If Theo had noticed, there was no way she hadn't —how embarrassing.

"My jokes are funny." Theo frowned at him. "If it's any consolation, you are not the only one making others suffer because of whatever fight you had. Art says Luelle has been equally ill-tempered."

It wasn't a consolation. Even if it was true, Luelle was not sulking for the same reasons as Malcolm. She had been the one to call an end to their... whatever had been happening between them. Malcolm's stomach dropped whenever he remembered their confrontation in the castle gardens, when she'd set him straight and called off their strange agreement.

He should never have kissed her—that was what started all of the complications. For a moment, during that night together under the stars, he'd believed she returned his sentiments, but the wine had clearly influenced her decision to return his affection. He wouldn't begrudge her for turning him down. He would give her space, even if he spent every second yearning to talk with her or claim some of the peace her presence offered.

It was harder to bear the distance from her at night, alone in his bed, or when he felt the cool caress of her Power against him, pure moonlight embodied.

"Your Majesty," a soft voice sounded from behind

Malcolm.

He and Theo turned to face Talia, who Roan had insisted be part of the king's entourage during the tour. They each bent into a small bow, which she returned with a curtsy.

"Good afternoon, Lady Barlowe. How may I assist you?" Malcolm asked, suppressing his renewed annoyance toward his meddling chaplain.

Theo murmured some excuse about checking on the drilling soldiers, abandoning Malcolm to what was certain to be a polite, if awkward, conversation. Roan clearly favoured Talia for the future role of Queen. Malcolm's interest in that topic hadn't grown since his last argument with the court chaplain but he wouldn't be rude towards Talia. It wasn't her fault Malcolm had no desire to court her. Was this how Luelle had felt when she'd rejected him?

"Please, call me Talia, Your Majesty," she requested, as she did every time they spoke. "I only hoped to receive an update on our progress. A few of the other ladies and I overheard someone stating that we will arrive at the army training camp tomorrow, is that correct?" She smiled up at him, cheeks and lips darkened with rouge as the noble women seemed to like.

"I believe so." Malcolm nodded. "We will rest here tonight and leave at dawn tomorrow. As long as we continue to make good time, we should reach camp by the early evening."

"Wonderful." Talia beamed, eyes sparkling in the afternoon sunlight. "Your fighting skill is very impressive, Your Majesty." She inclined her head towards the general area in which Malcolm and Theo had been sparring.

"You are too kind, my lady." He glanced around, hoping to find an easy excuse to leave the conversation, but Theo was now preoccupied correcting the stances of a nearby pair.

"I hope this is not too presumptuous, but I was wondering if you might like to dine with me tonight," Talia said. "Not alone, of course—that would be quite inappropriate." She laughed, resting her fingertips on Malcolm's forearm. "But, with myself and a few other lords and ladies accompanying us. We are all most interested to learn more about your intended research at Sandport, and you have been quite busy since the ball."

Malcolm breathed an uncomfortable laugh. "My advisers have kept me very occupied," he agreed, settling on a lie to tell her. "I must finalise some strategic points before we arrive at camp, in preparation for meeting my Field Master General. If I finish those with time to spare, I would be delighted to join you all, though I cannot make any promises." He had no intention of dining with her and the other nobles but refusing outright would be improper. When his mother heard of it, she would give him an earful.

"The realm must come first," Talia agreed, disappointment shining through her poised smile.

"If you will excuse me, I must return to training. Enjoy the rest of your afternoon, Lady Barlowe."

She dipped into another curtsy. "Of course, Your Majesty. I hope to speak with you again soon."

Malcolm turned away from her. As always, his eyes sought out the reddish-brown of Luelle's dyed hair. He found her in an instant, heart stumbling as their eyes locked for a second. She'd already been watching him with a scowl before he had turned to face her. She whirled to Arthyr and Mei, who were standing beside her, leaving Malcolm staring at stiff shoulders.

He couldn't remain staring at her all day, not if he wished to escape Lady Barlowe and the other nobles. He looked around for Theo on the training field, finding his friend already staring at him, as Luelle had been, a sly grin on his lips.

Malcolm rolled his eyes and grabbed the nearest wrapped sword, nodding to a free space where he and his friend could continue battling one another and distract him from his troubles.

45

LUELLE's body ached. Every moment she did not spend riding, she was training with the Gifted, both physically and with the Power. Her nights were spent on a thin bedroll that softened none of the lumps on the ground. Mei shared her tent, offering some solace from the fear that gripped Luelle in the dark, but she never slept deeply. Every slight noise startled her awake. Exhaustion wore her temper thin.

She and Art rode beside each other in silence all morning, acclimating to the early start as well as they could. Travelling with the Gifted allowed Luelle to get to know her peers better than training together once a day ever had. She learnt which of them needed time to warm up to the day, as she did, and which woke full of energy, eager to chat from the moment they emerged from their tents. She learnt which were the most resilient to the unique challenges their travels posed—the lack of comfort and privacy—and which faced it all with constant complaint, dreaming of life back in the capital. She also got to meet plenty of Gifted soldiers who had been training in different groups, at other times from those who fought alongside Luelle.

"Can I ask you something?"

Luelle looked away from the spot on the horizon she'd zoned out staring at, turning her head towards Art, who glanced at her with hesitation in his eyes.

"Of course." She straightened in her saddle. Malcolm's carriage was up ahead but he was riding alongside Theo and Leena, several rows of horses ahead of Luelle. Glimpses of his immaculate posture were her constant reminder to correct her own hunched state.

Art angled his horse slightly closer and lowered his voice, glancing around to ensure no other Gifted were near enough to hear.

"Are you nervous to see your old companions again?"

Luelle took a deep breath, nodding.

"You wouldn't...I mean, I can trust you, right?"

Her lack of sleep made it hard not to snap at Art. The question was fair.

"You can trust me. I have no desire to return to that way of life." She gazed out at the horizon again. "My past isn't simple, Art. I never knew my parents. The leader of this group took me in at a young age and taught me everything I know. I believed in his way of life because it was all I knew. To be honest, I still believe a lot of it, but my ideals are not the same as theirs. I no longer agree with the methods they're using to achieve their goals."

"Violence against humans?"

She nodded, a beat of silence falling between them, though it was never quiet on the road. Hooves and footsteps crunched, conversation was a constant hum.

"I still dream of the bodies in that cavern where we

caught up with you and the king."

Luelle turned her head to stare at Art. He hadn't mentioned that journey since their initial, short conversation about it in Luelle's bedroom at the castle. She permitted the conversation for now. She would not need to stop it unless Art continued to discuss Malcolm's presence there.

"You do?" She'd never wondered how the brief visit to the cavern had affected him. She'd mainly dwelled on the impact for her and Malcolm, having been the ones who witnessed the slaughter firsthand.

Art nodded. "It was the first time I ever saw a dead body," he admitted. "Were they your friends?"

She shook her head. "I barely knew any of them by then. I had only been close to a handful of the people who remained and they escaped safely, but even then, our relationship was very different."

"Do you think you'll be capable of fighting them?"

Luelle glanced at him, throat drying at the question she'd managed to avoid thinking of until now.

"I mean, I trust that you won't betray us. But I imagine it'll be hard to hurt your old friends, even if they attack us, like everyone expects them to."

Luelle chewed at her lip. She had no hesitation when it came to fighting strangers, even those among Zeke's companions who she did not know well enough to consider old friends, but Zeke himself? She wanted to believe she could fight him, to protect herself and her new friends from his violence, but she'd frozen in his presence at the cavern. Zeke knew exactly how to manipulate her—to make her feel like nothing. How could she overcome that?

"I won't pretend to understand your past. Maybe one day, you'll be able to share more of it with me, but the king forgave you and so did Theo. That's good enough for me," Art said. "I'll be there to support you if that time does come, to fight them. So will Mei and Tao, and the rest of the Gifted."

Luelle swallowed the lump in her throat. Art's sincere acceptance of her, regardless of her past, was a stark contrast to Zeke's rejection. She blinked away the sudden tears pricking her eyes.

Hooves sounded louder than the general din as Leena reared away from Malcolm's side up ahead, circling round to ride alongside Luelle. Art excused himself to join Mei and Tao in front, leaving the women with as much privacy as possible when riding in such large numbers.

"Everything alright?" Leena asked, raising a brow at the emotion on Luelle's face. The slow pace of travel had forced Leena to alter her appearance. At the castle, the floral, swirling patterns that decorated her shortly shaved hair were sharpened every few days, reinforcing their refined lines. Instead of taking the time to maintain that style during their travels, Leena had shaved her entire head to the skin when the fuzz of regrowth had initially disrupted the botanical art on her scalp.

Luelle nodded, shoving away her concerns as she had for days, preparing to deal with them some other time.

"Why are you ignoring Malcolm?"

She startled at Leena's abrupt question. Heat rose in her cheeks.

"I'm not ignoring him."

"That is not how it looks to me."

"It's hardly appropriate for me to approach him in this

environment, where the nobles and other soldiers can see. I'm no one of importance." Luelle shrugged, irritated to be interrogated.

"When has propriety ever stopped you before?"

She scowled at Leena, straightening her spine after what must be her hundredth glance towards Malcolm. Anger boiled in her chest.

"Why must I be the one who approaches him? He is perfectly able to come and speak to me, too," she snapped.

"Do you think I haven't told him that?" Leena levelled her with a stare. "Theo and I are sick of his moping but we cannot pull him out of it. Whatever happened between you, perhaps you should both just drop it and forgive one another."

"It's more complicated than that."

"Is it?"

Luelle set her jaw. How much did Leena know about their situation? She wouldn't be this forthright if she knew how Luelle really felt about Malcolm.

Although, perhaps the harsh words Leena would provide were exactly what Luelle needed to put the feelings behind her and move on with a platonic friendship with the king.

"Our lives are too different for us to carry on as we were. I know it isn't my place to get in the way of his responsibilities as king. Distancing myself now is going to save me a lot of pain in the long run."

Leena's chest heaved with a quiet sigh. She nodded. "Malcolm is one of my oldest friends and my king. He is always going to be my first priority. But I also like you, Luelle."

Luelle blinked with surprise.

"I understand what you are saying and, honestly, I agree with you, but I still think you should speak with him. It will be better for both of you to leave things on a happy note if that is what you feel you must do, and it is the least he deserves."

When Luelle said nothing, Leena simply shrugged.

"Think about it."

Luelle looked away. Why was everyone determined to make her think about things she was perfectly happy ignoring?

46

THE sun was still high in the sky the following day when Omar's camp appeared on the horizon. Their arrival gave Malcolm the opportunity to abandon his noble travelling companions in search of his Field Master General.

Leena nudged her horse forward to join him whilst Theo organised the soldiers and the Gifted into the new camp, setting up their tents beside the main site, where the servants would also stay. The nobility had their own camp up-wind of the main site.

Omar was waiting for them outside his large tent, in conversation with a couple of his officers. Each of them dipped into a deep bow as Malcolm dismounted, handing the reins to a lower-ranked soldier who approached to tend to his mount.

"Your Majesty. How was the journey?" Omar's tone was light but tension lined his stance. Like their last visit, shadows had deepened underneath his eyes.

"Fine. We made good time. I would say I am pleased to see you again so soon but I do not feel it is appropriate, given the circumstances of our visit."

Omar made a wordless noise of agreement. His officers departed, leaving them with some privacy.

"Where is the witness?" Malcolm lowered his voice, trying to recall the scant detail in Omar's letter.

"In my tent." He nodded towards the pale canvas structure behind him. "She is shaken up, as you might expect, but her confidence is growing since we brought her back here."

"Has she spoken about what she saw?"

Omar shook his head, frowning. "One of my officers managed to get a few details out of her when they first brought her back but we decided not to press the topic, knowing you might want to question her in person."

"What did your officer discover?"

"The girl is named Allie. She is a human, but was taken in by a family of Veseile as a child. A tall woman who matched descriptions of Vesanya approached their house whilst they were out tending their animals. When Allie's father approached, the woman seemed strange. Apparently she showed no initial signs of violence. Allie's mother instructed her to go inside with her siblings and stayed outside to help. There were two other children, but neither have been found."

"The bodies you found, were they like those in the first farmhouse?" Dread clogged every pore in Malcolm's body. He gritted his teeth against the nausea rising in his throat. What could've happened to the other two children?

Omar nodded, paling at the memories.

Malcolm turned to Leena, who had listened in silence beside him. "Fetch Theo and Luelle. I want you all to be there when I speak to the girl."

She nodded, striding away to find them.

Omar gave a general report as they waited for Leena's return, updating Malcolm about training progression and sightings of extremist Veseile. When Leena returned with Luelle and Theo in tow, Malcolm did not look at them, instead nodding for Omar to take them inside his tent.

Clutter decorated the tent, the floor strewn with piles of paperwork under random pieces of armour acting as paperweights. Hunched over the table was a petite human with tawny hair and sun-browned skin. She jerked as the tent door opened, eyes wide and flitting between the new guests. She tucked her trembling hands under the table.

Around her were items that must've come from her home—blankets, books, a small hand-sewn doll, fraying at the seams. Beside her, atop some of Omar's paperwork, was a plate of food, cold and untouched.

Omar halted several feet away from the teenage human, forcing Malcolm and the others to come to a stop behind him.

"Allie, I apologise for disturbing you." Omar's voice was softer and quieter than Malcolm had ever heard it. "King Malcolm has arrived to speak with you, as we talked about. Are you happy for him and some of his soldiers to ask you some questions about what happened at your home?"

She nodded, gaze dropping to the tabletop.

"If it makes you more comfortable, Omar can stay," Malcolm offered.

The girl chewed at the inside of her lip and shrugged. Her eyes were glazed, clear of the emotion Malcolm had expected to see there. More than anything else, she looked exhausted—exactly how he felt waking up each morning after another restless night reliving his worst memories.

Malcolm took the seat opposite her. Omar found more makeshift seating for them all, enlisting Theo's help to bring one of the cushioned benches closer, so they all had space to sit around the small table.

Luelle ended up at Malcolm's right. From his peripheral vision, he could see her eyes moving, glancing at him, but kept his own gaze fixed on the girl. Now wasn't the time to let himself get distracted, and he had no desire to make Luelle feel uncomfortable under the weight of his constant staring, as he no doubt already had over the past week of travelling.

Malcolm waited for them all to settle before speaking. Allie stared at his hands on the table.

"Good evening, Allie. My name is Malcolm. This is Leena, Theo, and Luelle. Thank you for agreeing to speak to us."

She gave no indication that she'd heard.

"Omar has told us a little about what happened at your home but I would appreciate hearing your account."

She looked at each of them, eyelids heavy.

"We were attacked." Her voice cracked, as if those three words were the first she'd spoken in a while.

"Perhaps you could tell us about that day, from the start," Leena suggested, her voice as quiet as Allie's.

Malcolm nodded in silent encouragement.

Allie's gaze dropped to the tabletop again, but she complied.

"Every morning we complete our chores. Pa was fixing some of the shutters on the house while me, Ma, Yara, and Oscar fed the animals. Oscar was the first one to see the lady approaching." Her tone was monotonous. "He shouted a greeting to her but she never replied. Pa told us to stay where we were and went to ask who she was, see if she needed help." Allie swallowed. "They spoke for a bit but I couldn't hear them. She kept looking past him at the rest of us. Ma sent me, Yara, and Oscar inside. Told us to wait in the house until she came and got us. I took them in and didn't look back, not even when I heard Ma scream—" she broke off.

Malcolm's heart raced. Panic lingered at the edges of his vision, creeping closer as Allie told her story. She continued before anyone could reassure her of her safety.

"I made Yara and Oscar hide downstairs in the basement. I couldn't lock it from the inside, so I locked them in, told them to cover themselves with something. I went upstairs and hid under Ma and Pa's bed. Ma never came back inside. Maybe if I'd gone and checked sooner, they would've—" she choked out a sob, slamming her lips together to stop any more words tumbling forward. Two silent tears streaked down her cheeks.

Malcolm could see the scene play out in his mind— Vesanya strolling through the massacre as casually as she had in the cavern, sucking the life out of these innocent civilians, out of *children*—

Pressure squeezed his knee. Malcolm looked up to meet Luelle's stare, solemn and understanding. He focused on the feeling of her hand, the insistent squeeze of her fingers, to ground himself in reality. Gulping down deep breaths, he held her gaze until his fists stopped trembling and a fraction of tension left his shoulders. If the others noticed his reaction, they said nothing. Allie had returned to staring, silent and emotionless, at the tabletop.

"Did you hear anything when you were hiding?" Malcolm managed to ask.

Allie shook her head. "I didn't even hear her come into the house. The basement door had been ripped off its hinges when I went down." The monotony returned.

Malcolm lowered his trembling hands underneath the table.

Leena stepped in.

"Can you describe the person who approached your home?"

"Tall. Taller than Pa. She was Veseile, like him. Had the streak in her hair. She was dressed in armour."

"Like Vesanya?" Theo asked.

"Someone dressed like her, I suppose." Allie looked up again, fury simmering in her gaze, lip curling. "But it wasn't her. The gods don't exist. If they did, this wouldn't have happened."

Malcolm's ears were ringing almost too loud to hear the words Allie spat. How was he supposed to protect his people against this threat? He excused himself from the table, mumbling a vague thank you to Allie for her testimony and stumbling towards the tent's entrance. Movement sounded behind him but he didn't look back or wait for whoever followed.

Nearby, a soldier had unsaddled Malcolm's horse and attached it to a lead rope in the ground. His hands were trembling too hard to untie the rope, so Malcolm simply yanked his dagger from his waist and sliced straight through it.

He swung onto the horse and kicked her into a gallop. Wind tore at him, snatching what little breath he could inhale. Soldiers leapt from his path as he weaved between the tents until no more obstacles remained, giving his mare a free charge.

Malcolm clung to composure until he was far enough from the camp that no one saw him dismount and fall to his knees. He fisted his hands in the grass, chest heaving, stomach churning.

He barely sensed Theo's horse pulling up beside his. He didn't see his friend dismount or kneel beside him, but when Theo gently pulled him upright and into a tight hug, Malcolm gripped his friend like a lifeline, half-choking on the tears in his throat.

47

LUELLE sat silent among the Gifted until Leena returned to fetch her, informing her that Malcolm was back in the camp and wished to scope the farmhouse. She followed Leena through the maze of tents. Anxiety and anticipation warred in her chest at the thought of seeing the king again and witnessing Vesanya's newest slaughter.

Somehow, seeing Malcolm's panic whilst speaking to Allie had staved off her own spiralling fear. She ignored most of the girl's testimony, instead focusing on the way Malcolm's breathing sped up, how his face paled and his jaw tightened. When his hands started trembling, she reached for him underneath the table, aware she couldn't do much else with Omar and Allie in the tent, able to see and question her actions. She had longed to follow him when he'd fled the testimony, but Theo had been the first to stand. Instead, Luelle remained with Leena and Omar, asking Allie any other questions that might be useful so they could inform Malcolm of the answers when he returned.

She rode beside Leena as they travelled to the

farmhouse. Several other soldiers and Gifted accompanied them on the journey, but they remained outside the house whilst Malcolm, Luelle, Theo, and Leena scoped it for the first clues.

Omar had stationed more soldiers at the farmhouse to tend the animals and block entry, as he had for the first incident. They patrolled the perimeter of the building and pens in pairs, watching over clucking hens and grazing goats.

Luelle followed the others inside the house.

The bodies had already been moved. They lay on the kitchen table, wrapped in blankets. Omar had already confirmed the bodies were in the same state as those they'd found in the first farmhouse. Luelle didn't bother double-checking.

Not far beyond the bodies, she found the door to the basement, no longer attached to its hinges. Splinters of wood coated the floor between the distorted door and the frame it had once been part of.

Luelle's breathing was shallow. Metal hinges remained in the frame, but they were warped and bent. Beyond the doorway was a slim flight of wooden steps, shrouded in darkness.

She descended them.

Rows of food, stored in containers, barrels, and glassware, filled the shelves that lined the basement. A dim moonstone light descended from a net attached to the ceiling, bathing the room with an eerie blue glow. Luelle had expected more destruction after witnessing the state of the basement door, but nothing down here seemed out of place—no shattered glass, no containers knocked onto their side, no signs of a struggle.

She wandered the room, her footsteps loud in the silence. If Allie's testimony was true, her two younger siblings had been hiding down here.

There was no evidence of their bodies. When Vesanya came, she must have made quick work of their deaths, for once clearing away the remains after killing.

Luelle ascended the stairs, trembling. She didn't bother searching the rest of the house; there was nothing else she needed to see. She strode outside and sat on the ground, lowering her head between her knees and taking slow, deep breaths. When she had stilled her shaking, she straightened to watch the goats curled up beside one another, peering at their shifting shapes through the gloom of the night.

Minutes or hours could have passed before footsteps approached.

Malcolm's face was pale in the moonlight.

She accepted his outstretched hand, as clammy as her own, and let him pull her upright, taking the second shovel he held.

Theo and Leena helped them bury the bodies this time. They worked in silence, none of them resting until the last handful of dirt covered the people who had once lived there.

They remained silent on the ride back to camp. Soldiers were waiting to take their horses away when they arrived.

Leena and Theo strode towards the tents erected for the soldiers, where Luelle was also meant to return, but she hesitated.

Leena glanced over her shoulder, finding Luelle's stare lingering on Malcolm's retreating figure as he moved towards the part of the camp restricted for nobility and the higher ranking soldiers. She gave Luelle a curt nod of encouragement.

Swallowing her nerves, Luelle followed the king.

"Malcolm," she called his name, softly, jogging to close the distance between them.

He glanced over his shoulder and slowed so she could catch up with him.

"What is wrong? Are you alright?" he asked, eyes scouring her face.

"I…" She glanced around. No one else was in sight. Only rows of tents surrounded them, tall moonstone lamps casting a pale glow at every junction. "I wanted to make sure you were alright."

A frown flickered across Malcolm's expression but he quickly smoothed it back to neutrality. "I am fine." He turned away from her.

Luelle grabbed his arm to stop him from leaving.

"I know you aren't. You're not sleeping again, are you?"

A muscle in his jaw clenched but he didn't shake himself free of her grip. "It does not matter."

"Yes it does." She frowned at him. "Zeke is dangerous. We all need to be alert when we leave here and travel closer to the Razors. He might make another attempt on your life. You need to be ready to protect yourself."

"Luelle, must we have this argument now?"

The exhaustion in his voice was almost enough to make her retreat, but not quite.

"Yes. Why are you avoiding me?" Her heart hammered. She knew she had no future with him, but if she could help him now, she would. Her feelings didn't have to complicate their friendship.

"I am giving you space." He shrugged, unable to meet her eyes. "That is what you wanted."

"No it isn't." Her frown deepened.

Malcolm's gaze roamed the tents nearby. He shifted his weight, the colour in his cheeks evident despite the low lighting.

"I understand you want nothing more than friendship and I do not want to make you feel uncomfortable. You made it clear you do not wish for things to progress further between us and wish to leave behind what happened on the roof. I apologise for the hurt and embarrassment my actions caused, though I cannot bring myself to say I regret that night."

"What?" Luelle huffed a laugh. This was why he was sulking? "I never said that, Malcolm."

He finally met her gaze, his own stare unconvinced.

"Yes you did. You said we could never be together."

Luelle swallowed and shifted, preparing for her own confession.

"I suggested we don't continue because you're the king and I'm…" she scouted the sky as if it might contain the words she sought, "well, I'm no one, really. You're meant to be with someone noble, like the people who accompanied us here, like that Veseile Lady you're always speaking to—someone worthy of ruling alongside you. I didn't want to continue pursuing you when I know we can never be together in the way I desire, and I will only end up hurt when you find someone more appropriate." Her cheeks burned at the admission.

Malcolm gave no reply. Just as Luelle was about to admit defeat and look at him again to gauge his reaction, his body collided with hers. One hand tangled in her hair and the other snaked around the side of her neck, thumb pushing her jaw to tilt her head up as his lips crashed against hers.

Luelle's eyes widened. She tried to speak but her words were muffled nonsense against Malcolm's mouth. She tilted her head aside to free her lips but he did not step back to give her more space. Instead, his lips travelled along her jaw, planting insistent kisses on a path down her neck.

"Did you not hear what I just said?" she asked, her hands sliding up to Malcolm's shoulders and eyes fluttering closed, even as her mind called out silent warnings that this was a bad idea—that she was only going to end up disappointed.

"I do not want anyone else," he mumbled against her neck, changing the direction of his kisses to return towards her mouth. "I will never hurt you."

"You say that now," Luelle took a shaking breath, fighting to clear her mind, "but I know your family and advisers would never accept a real relationship between us. They have other people in mind. I've heard the nobles gossiping about it."

Malcolm pulled back enough to meet Luelle's eyes. His grip on her remained firm. To her surprise, annoyance lined every inch of his expression. Her eyes dropped to his lips, swollen with kisses.

"Why is everybody so insistent that I cannot make my own decisions on this matter? I am the king. What good is my crown if I cannot even choose who I want to spend my life with? I do not want anybody else, I want you. I have never been happier than with you at my side. I have sacrificed so much of my life and freedom for the realm —I am choosing myself now, for the first time. I am choosing you," he insisted. "Please, choose me too." The final words were a whisper.

Luelle didn't let herself consider all the ways things could go wrong before she was nodding.

"I choose you," she murmured.

He smiled, exhaling low and slow, resting his forehead against hers.

She pulled him back down towards her for another kiss, gentler, less urgent than the previous ones. When Malcolm broke away a second time, it was to pull her in the direction of his tent.

48

MALCOLM woke to the soft sounds of bare feet padding against a rug and the rustling of fabric. He opened his eyes, blinking to clear the remnants of sleep clinging to him.

Luelle was crossing the tent, gathering items of her clothing that had been strewn across the floor the previous night, putting them on as she went.

"Sneaking away from me already?" Malcolm pushed himself into a slightly more upright position, adjusting his pillows to support his head as he watched her.

She turned her head so he was able to see the roll of her eyes.

"It's for your benefit, not mine," she said, tightening the laces of her trousers.

"Let people see you leave, I am not ashamed of you, if that is what you think." He frowned.

She bent to grab her shirt. He followed every move she made, eyes tracing the soft bare skin he'd taken the time to grow familiar with last night.

"I know you don't but you aren't thinking this

through." She ambled back towards the bed when her shirt was in place, perching beside him.

He opened his mouth to object but Luelle cut him off.

"I'm not saying I regret this or assuming you do. But, if I'm seen leaving your tent every morning, people will talk and I don't want to be the thing that undoes all of your hard work to stabilise your reign."

He grabbed her wrist, tugging her atop him. "Every morning? I like the sound of that." He smiled against her skin, shifting the loose neckline of her shirt aside with his nose to press a kiss against her bare collarbone.

She pulled away, pink cheeks rounding with a smile even as she narrowed her eyes at him. "I don't feel like you're taking this very seriously."

"You're distracting me."

"I'm the one trying to have a conversation about this." She raised her brows.

Malcolm sighed, letting his fingers trail up and down her arms as he spoke. "I can handle my advisers. And I would not let anybody gossip about you."

She scoffed. "Even the king cannot stop gossip. Besides, the gossip isn't truly what concerns me." She mirrored his movements, tracing a gentle pattern on his bare chest, her fingertips cool against his skin. Fine hairs rose on his arms at her touch. "Your reign isn't stable yet and the actions I took to release the Power to all Veseile only made that instability more extreme. It's hard enough for you to maintain peace and order right now. It will only create more havoc if people learn you're sleeping with a commoner."

"Is that all this is?" He couldn't help the stab of hurt, bleeding into his tone.

She met his stare, brushing a curl away from his eyes. "I didn't want to assume anything. We didn't exactly take the time to discuss it last night."

"I want all of you. Anything you'll give me." The confession slipped out before he could reconsider it.

Surprise flashed across Luelle's expression, though she smothered it quickly.

"I don't know what that would look like for us. I don't want to be the one responsible for creating more chaos— more than I already have."

Malcolm tightened his grip on her. "We can take it one step at a time and work through the challenges together. Theo, Leena, and Viv already have their suspicions about my feelings for you, it will not come as a surprise to everyone." Doubt crept in. "Or do you not want more?"

"Of course I do. I think I'm just being more realistic about the reasons why we can't have that." Her expression was guarded. Frustration leaked through in her furrowed brow.

"I can have whatever I wish, I am the king." He pulled her towards him again, this time brushing his lips against hers. He smoothed his thumb over her brow, trying to erase her concerns. "If it makes you feel more comfortable, we can keep it quiet for now, but I have no intention of letting you go—not when this is something we both want."

A small smile slipped past her defensive walls.

"Alright. Though, you need to let me go soon or your servants will see me leaving."

"Or we could stay in this tent all day. I can pretend I am sick."

She laughed. "Sorry, *Your Majesty*," her tone lilted on the title, "but we can't delay your tour. Your schedule dictates that we must leave for Vidamere today."

Malcolm sighed, loosening his grip. They shifted, moving to sit beside one another. He scanned the tent for his own clothes, scattered across the floor and hanging off random pieces of furniture.

"Even if we must keep this between us for now, you do not need to ignore me in front of others. I talk to all of my soldiers," he said.

She smiled. "Fine. I like the sound of that."

He took her hand, lifting it to press her knuckles against his lips. "I do not know how I will resist you outside of this tent." An idea sparked in his mind. He withdrew his hand, slipping his father's amulet over his head and holding it out to her. "Take this, so I know you have a piece of me with you."

Her smile faded. "I can't take that. It's too special."

He looped the chain over her head. "Let's not argue about this, Luelle, I have made up my mind."

Her fingers rose, brushing against the metal pendant. She tucked it inside her shirt, accepting the token.

"I will see you tonight, even if not much through the day."

She stood, pressing a final slow kiss against his lips. "Of course." She smiled over her shoulder as she slipped out of his tent.

Malcolm tidied his clothing away once Luelle left. Outside, the sky was still dark, but servants soon arrived with heated water for him to bathe in. He washed and dressed quickly, feeling refreshed and eager to make good time. The faster they left this area, the faster they might learn some useful information to defeat Vesanya. With that in hand, he could return home and inform his mother about Luelle, stopping her pesky intentions to arrange a marriage between him and some stranger. Of course, she might have some objections about Luelle at first but Malcolm's mother valued her children's happiness above most other things; she would not stand in his way when he revealed the extent of his feelings.

He strode to Omar's tent as servants and soldiers began to dismantle his own. Leena and Theo were already inside, discussing something with the Field Master General. All three of them clutched hot drinks, gathered around a map of the surrounding area spread over Omar's table.

"Good morning." Malcolm smiled, greeting the trio.

"Is it?" Leena asked, exchanging a smirk with Theo. Omar, thankfully, did not appear to understand the loaded remark.

Malcolm shot her a quick glare.

"What are you looking at?" He approached the table.

Omar fetched Malcolm a cup and poured him tea from an iron kettle. "I was telling Leena and Theo about some rumours of trouble the soldiers have heard from nearby civilians. A few farmsteads and smallholdings in the direction of Vidamere have been reporting antisocial behaviour from a group they believe must be dwelling in the area." He handed Malcolm the drink and pointed to the area he was referring to, several miles south of the Eastern Road they'd intended to travel on.

"What sort of things?" he asked.

"Objects moving without being touched, vandalism, people masking their faces and lurking around isolated farms."

"Sounds like it could be Veseile who have figured out how to use the Power," Leena said. "Are you planning to investigate it further?"

Omar looked at Malcolm. "I wanted to run the situation past you before taking any action."

Malcolm pursed his lips, considering. Could these Veseile be linked to Zeke?

"Perhaps we can take a detour and handle it for you. It is in the right direction and offers an opportunity to provide the Gifted with some real battle experience against other Power users. So far, they have only fought one another."

"How would you explain that to our other soldiers? And the nobles?" Theo asked. "We cannot risk bringing all of the nobility and servants into a battle."

"We can send them on the original planned route. Our regular soldiers can guard the nobles along the Eastern Road and we will travel off the beaten track to deal with this threat. We will meet with them again in Vidamere."

"How will you explain splitting the party up?" Leena pressed. "They are only here for you."

"Must I explain? I am the king after all." He shrugged. A spark of excitement flared inside him as he realised travelling with fewer eyes on him would provide more opportunities to spend time with Luelle—the nobility were the ones she was so concerned with and they would be miles away.

"I suppose not, but I imagine they will have questions." Leena frowned.

"We can tell them the truth, mostly. We will explain that I am leading the Veseile soldiers on a detour for a training exercise or an operation that is too dangerous for them to accompany, so our more experienced soldiers will escort them on the planned route and we will rejoin them before we all reach Vidamere," Malcolm said.

Leena sighed. "That will have to be good enough."

Malcolm straightened, pleased with the plan. "Omar, what else can you tell us about these rumours of trouble?"

49

JOURNEYING without the nobles and the majority of Malcolm's soldiers was quieter. Luelle found herself riding with relaxed shoulders and a smile on her face, laughing and joking with her friends in a way she hadn't felt free to on the first leg of their trip.

When her eyes sought Malcolm in their ranks, she didn't tear them away, scolding herself for being so obvious. If anxiety over facing Zeke once again became too much, she burnt energy sparring with the Gifted, no longer having to restrain herself out of fear of accidentally hitting a noble who was observing the training. She threw herself into the drills, victorious in her fights almost constantly by now. A small portion of the Gifted continued to practise using the Power for healing, but Luelle did not join them, staying in the realms of fighting where she was more assured of her success. She had attempted to heal again when training in Cerulya, but the frustration she felt after failing caused her to give it up. It was pointless anyway; so many other soldiers were capable of using the Power to heal, Luelle could just seek one of them if she received an injury when fighting.

Malcolm, Theo, and Leena led the patrol at a fast pace on the first day. They made camp before the sun set and it became too dark to see their tent pitches. Their campsite was much more humble than it had been when travelling with the nobility—even Malcolm's tent was smaller, with no space for hosting. A large campfire formed the heart of the camp, the tents spiralling out from that point, with Malcolm's closest to the centre. Several smaller fire pits sprung up at other parts of the camp, with clusters of Gifted seated around them.

Luelle sat with her closest friends among some other Gifted at the edge of the camp's main fire after their training had finished. She ate her allotted ration of bread and dried meat and sipped from a small cup of wine Art had managed to find for them to share with Mei and Tao.

Malcolm sat a few people away from her, the curve of the seating arrangement giving them a full view of one another. She relished the fluttering in her stomach as he boldly returned her gaze.

She kept her promise to join him in his tent when the other soldiers were asleep, moving quietly and quickly to ensure the Gifted who were guarding the camp at night did not spot her weaving through the tents. Malcolm swept her into his arms the moment she slid inside the canvas door, lips touching every inch of her skin until it felt that his smile was branded on her.

Time passed too quickly whenever they were alone together.

Over the following few days, Leena, Theo, and Malcolm led the small party with maps borrowed from the Field Master General's camp.

Eventually, after calling them to another stop, Malcolm split their party into smaller groups as the Gifted unloaded their horses. Luelle didn't miss how he claimed her for his own scouting party, alongside each of their friends. When the groups were allotted, Malcolm stood in front of them all, amplifying his voice so even those at the furthest edges of the small crowd could hear could hear him easily over the gusty wind.

"This is the last known location of the people we're searching for. As of yet, there are no proven criminal charges and we do not know for certain if these people are even able to use the Power. However, they are causing panic and fear among the local residents."

The wind toyed with his hair as he spoke. Luelle's gaze followed the fluttering curls, trying to keep her mind on his words and not the memories of her hands carding through those strands last night.

"We do not seek these people to harm them. Our aim is to locate anyone who is breaking the law and protect innocent civilians. You may question people you encounter, but do not restrain them unless they give you reason to believe they are using the Power for unsavoury means. If you uncover any other crimes, we will simply report them to the local guards. If you encounter Veseile who attempt to use the Power against you, your aim is to render them unconscious, either by force or using shadowbell essence, so that we may detain them. If that occurs, we will transport the captives to Vidamere, where Thane Edyth can enact justice."

Nerves churned within Luelle at the potential of upcoming fights. Was she prepared? Could she ever be prepared enough? What if one of her friends got hurt?

What if she was hurt—taken out of action before she had a chance to confront Zeke again?

She battled to keep fear from her expression.

"Some soldiers will remain here to establish our camp and guard against suspicious activity in the immediate surroundings," Malcolm continued. "The rest of us will search until dusk and return here before nightfall. I do not want anyone to risk staying out later, when we would be more vulnerable to attacks from people who know this land and its layout considerably better than us. If we find nothing, we will press on with our journey and inform the Field Master General when we reach Vidamere. Your priority is to keep one another safe. Do not forget the training my sister has taught you over the past months. Trust your instincts. Trust the Power."

A shiver ran down Luelle's spine, though she couldn't say whether it was from the king's words or from the chill wind.

At the end of his speech, Malcolm went to each group individually, highlighting the areas on copied maps that they were to search. Luelle, with Art close at her side, approached Theo, Leena, Mei, and Tao, the other members of their scouting party. Malcolm would join them when the other groups were ready to depart.

Conversation about nothing important flowed until Malcolm returned, ready to leave.

"We are heading south," he informed them, rolling the map.

They rode slow enough to talk to one another as they scanned the horizon for any lurking presences.

"You look nervous." Mei pulled her horse alongside Luelle's.

Malcolm glanced over his shoulder at them but didn't fall back to join their conversation.

"Aren't you?" Luelle asked, wiping a clammy hand on her leg and adjusting her position in her saddle.

"Only excited." Mei flashed a fierce grin. "You may be more adept at using the Power than me, but I know my way in a fight. The open battlefield is where my real talents lie."

"We might not find any criminals," Luelle reminded her.

Mei shook her head. "A fight is coming. I can feel it."

Art drew up to Luelle's other side.

"Mei, you're utterly bloodthirsty. You should join me in using the Power for something more virtuous." Sanctimony laced his tone.

Luelle snorted at the glower Mei shot to Art.

"I know how to heal well enough, thank you. Besides, I will be the one tearing people apart on the battlefield, there will be no need to sew them back up."

"I don't need that image in my mind." Luelle grimaced. "The people we're fighting today hardly sound like fierce foes. I imagine they're little more than a group of rogue bandits. And we aren't fighting to kill."

"I know, but you must be at least a little excited." Mei frowned. "This is what we have trained for! You must understand a little, Luelle. Surely you felt the exhilaration of a fight when you defended Leena and me from those bandits in the Caeleste Peaks."

Art's gaze swung to her. Discomfort oozed through Luelle at the memory, the screams that had echoed as her victims had descended into the valley.

"I mainly remember feeling scared," she said, grip

tightening on the reins.

"I suppose you passed out too quickly afterwards to know what I refer to." Mei shrugged.

Though she couldn't bring herself to admit it aloud, Luelle could understand some of what Mei spoke of. Fear swelled inside her chest at the thought of another fight, but this would be nothing like the slaughter in the cavern. Although it had been horrific at the time, defending herself, Mei, and Leena in the Caeleste Peaks had proven Luelle's instinctive fighting ability with the Power; her training since then had only strengthened it. Hidden somewhere amongst her anxiety, eagerness fluttered. This was another opportunity to prove her worth, to make amends for her mistakes.

Mulling over her conflicted feelings, she almost rode straight into the back of Malcolm's stationary horse.

"What's going on?" she murmured to Art, shifting in her saddle to try and see why they had stopped. Peering around Malcolm, she found the reason. Down the hill, not far ahead, the road they followed wound through a large copse of trees. One had fallen, obstructing the route.

They pulled their horses closer around Malcolm to analyse the problem from afar.

"We can go around the copse altogether but it might be worth moving the tree the help the locals," Theo suggested, stretching his neck to either side.

"Do we have any rope?" Leena asked.

Tao patted a bag attached to his saddle. "Enough to make this work."

"Wait." Malcolm shook his head, a short line furrowing between his brows. "Something is not right."

Luelle followed his stare to the tree trunk, holding up her hand to shield the glare of the sun directly above them.

"Look at the base," he continued, "the lines are clean. The tree was cut, it did not fall."

"You think someone felled it on purpose?" Leena squinted to better see the tree.

"I've seen bandits use this tactic before," Luelle said. "It slows people down so they're easier to attack, vulnerable and off-guard as they focus on the obstruction."

"Those trees would be a good place to hide," Leena agreed. "But, that does not guarantee that we will find enemies. What do you instruct, Your Majesty?"

He didn't answer immediately, analysing the options they faced. Luelle nudged her horse forward, in line with his.

"Why don't we just check if people are waiting up ahead?" During a previous training session, she had told Princess Vivyenne and the other Gifted briefly about the technique she had developed for scoping a route ahead of her, though she did not yet know if the information had been shared with Malcolm.

Breathing slowly, she closed her eyes to see more clearly with the strange vision the Power granted. She reached out with a long thread of the Power, sweeping it from left to right to get a sense of what lay ahead of them. Searching for individuals here was harder than it had been in her room at the palace, since the entire world around her thrummed with life's energy. Pulses reverberated to her from the plants, the trees, birds flying overhead and animals hiding in the undergrowth—

anything living that her Power touched. She took a deep breath, untangling the threads from the natural world to isolate the telltale signs of human or Eile life that she'd come to recognise from her practice in the castle. They were brighter than the rest.

"Incredible," Malcolm murmured.

Luelle shushed him, frowning at the distraction.

In a few moments, she located what she searched for—thrumming pulses like heartbeats, as distinct from one another as the people might be in personality.

"There are eight—no...ten people in the trees. Five on either side of the path, some further back into the groves. There might be more beyond those." She opened her eyes, reeling the Power back in and wiping the sheen of sweat from her brow. Her breath came heavily.

Malcolm frowned at her. "Who taught you to do that?"

She shrugged. "I experimented with the Power in my room. Those first few weeks in the castle were quite productive."

"Teach me."

"I'm not sure now is the best time." She looked, pointedly, towards the trees ahead.

Malcolm's frown deepened. "Later, then. Tonight."

"Are you certain those numbers are accurate?" Leena asked.

"No. There may be others further ahead or deeper in the trees, it would exhaust me to sweep through the entire copse, especially from this distance," Luelle said. "But, I definitely felt ten figures crouched close to the road, by the felled tree, like they witnessed our approach and are waiting for us to pass."

"At least they no longer have the element of surprise."

Leena glared at the trees.

"We cannot guarantee they are Veseile or using the Power until we encounter them properly," Malcolm said.

"Does it matter?" Tao asked. "It sounds like they plan to ambush us, either way."

"We can't just leave bandits here where they might hurt people." Art frowned.

"I agree." Luelle joined in on the discussion. "Who knows how many times they've already succeeded at using this tactic. If we can stop them, we should, whether they're Veseile or not."

"Yes, but we cannot—"

An arrow whizzed from the trees, cutting off Malcolm's sentence as Leena cried a warning. Mei used her Power to throw a shield in front of them in time for the arrow to clatter harmlessly to the ground.

Figures emerged from the trees.

50

MALCOLM straightened in his saddle at the sight of ten bandits. Their mismatched clothing hung askew, ill-fitting on their bodies. Most held weapons—a worn bow, daggers, a curved sword. Only a few stood tense and empty-handed. All bore the streak of white hair that marked them Veseile, though none had painted the stylised 'L' on their head that reports suggested Zeke's followers used. They emerged on foot. As long as no others remained in the trees, Luelle's prediction of their numbers was accurate.

From the corner of his eye, Malcolm saw Luelle startle as the strangers emerging from the trees halted and cried out in unison—a dissonant, challenging shout. Silence descended when their cry faded.

"Very intimidating," Leena remarked, her tone thick with amusement at the theatrics.

Behind Malcolm, someone snorted a laugh.

The small host of bandits ventured no further than the edge of the trees, impatient to have waited so long for their prey to stumble into their well-laid trap. Malcolm assessed the distance between them. A fight in the grove would be harder than one on the road, particularly for them on horseback. Were the bandits astute enough to recognise that, or would they be over-eager to charge into conflict?

One of them raised a bow, stringing up a second arrow.

Luelle scowled. A pulse of her Power tugged at Malcolm's core as she whipped the bandit's weapon out of his hand, pulling it through the air towards them and breaking it into pieces as it soared.

A couple of the bandits stumbled back, eyes wide.

Nerves and exhilaration coiled in Malcolm's stomach, adrenaline making his fingers tremble. He clutched his reins tighter to disguise the shaking.

Though a group of bandits this small should pose no problem for his trained soldiers, he'd never fought against a group of enemies who could all use the Power. A battle like this was untested. He felt the same nauseating determination and fear that he had when first charging into a fight as a teenager. They still knew so little about how the Power affected the general population of Veseile, despite their observations at the capital.

One of the bandits, a tall man with an unkempt beard, drew his arm back. Pressure tugged at Malcolm's chest, the faint sense of a frosty morning raising the fine hairs on his skin.

Guided by instinct, Malcolm threw a shield of air around his companions, protecting them as the bandit swept his arm forwards and used the Power to hurl rocks in their direction. The rocks rebounded from Malcolm's shield, thudding to the ground several feet in front of their horses. He stroked his mare's neck, murmuring quiet reassurances to soothe her as she shuffled and huffed. The rocks ranged in size from small pebbles to stones as large as his clenched fist. Was this to be how they fought? Their saddle bags contained a small number of the shadowbell spheres, if that was the case. Heady confidence oozed through him.

"I suppose that answers our question about whether they know how to use the Power," Leena muttered.

Malcolm peered at the Veseile's reactions as their stones had no impact. Annoyance bloomed on the faces of several and surprise lit up some others. One's eyes flicked between the tall bandit and Malcolm.

A silent snarl twisted on the face of the man who had thrown the stones. He glanced at the ground, lifting both of his hands, palms facing the sky. As his hands rose, more stones followed their movement, hovering in the air around him. Another steady pulse tugged at Malcolm as the man worked, once again flinging the projectile weapons as if he was throwing them with his own arms.

Malcolm kept his shield in place. Identical to the first attack, the stones rebounded, scattering to the road.

Sweat glistened on the stone-thrower's forehead, apparent even from as far as they were. The pressure of his Power had felt weak to Malcolm but, even so, the exertion was clearly taking a toll. With a curt gesture, the stranger and his companions retreated into the trees.

Malcolm sighed. "I had hoped they might choose to make it easier for us."

"We're going in after them?" Arthyr asked, uncertainty in his voice.

Malcolm nodded. "Pair up. I want at least one person with healing expertise in each pair. Watch each others' backs. This will be over soon enough. Avoid killing any of them unless you must."

"We should dismount," Theo said.

Malcolm gave a wordless noise of agreement. "I want two volunteers to stay behind and watch the horses. I do not want any bandits sneaking past us and using our own mounts to escape."

"Leena and I can," Theo suggested. "We would be at a disadvantage in the trees since we cannot sense the Power as you can."

"I'll stay, too." Arthyr's voice trembled.

Malcolm eyed the nervous Veseile. It wasn't worth the time it would take to remind Arthyr that a fight was just as likely beside the horses. As long as he could warn and shield Theo and Leena, they stood a chance of making it through a conflict.

"Fine, we have uneven numbers, anyway. Tao and Mei, you can take the forest on one side of the road. Luelle and I will take the other." He swung himself off his horse and handed the reins to Theo. Before departing for their hunt, Malcolm untied the small bag from his saddle that contained several spheres filled with shadowbell and attached them to his belt, noticing Luelle do the same.

Apprehension tightened Malcolm's chest, a familiar companion, as he turned to stride towards battle with her at his side.

"Malcolm," Leena interrupted before he could walk far. She had dismounted and jogged closer to him to speak quietly. "This is not a good plan. We should call for support."

He frowned. Did she not have faith in him? Leena did not have the Power; she could not feel how pathetic their enemy was in the same way he could.

"We have more skill and strength than them, Leena," he attempted to reassure her. "I could feel it when their ringleader used the Power, and he is likely the strongest of them. Our reserves are larger. We can easily eliminate the threat they pose, and we risk letting them escape if we retreat to get support. This offers a good opportunity to test the shadowbell projectiles in real combat."

Her mouth was pressed into a harsh line. She frowned, clearly unhappy with the situation but gave a stilted nod and let Malcolm walk away. Perhaps she was simply disappointed to be left out of this fight.

Luelle made no comment about the brief interaction as they walked towards the trees.

The last time Malcolm and Luelle had fought alongside one another, they'd been unaware of the oncoming conflict. Now, things were different. They were instigating this fight, and both of them were confident in their ability to use the Power. This would go more smoothly than their last battle.

Though, that fact did little to ease the tendrils of fear tightening around his heart.

It was the same before any conflict—fear for his friends, for the people fighting alongside him and in his name, and now a new, fresh fear for Luelle. She was a natural talent with the Power, teaching herself to wield it in ways he had never considered, but the same could be true of their opponents—both here and when they eventually found Zeke and his cronies.

He abandoned the thoughts as they reached the tree line, clearing his mind and listening for sounds that might indicate nearby enemies. With a gesture, Malcolm sent

Mei and Tao to the left side of the road. Luelle followed him to the right.

Scanning the surrounding area, they crept through the copse, close enough to reach one another with an outstretched arm. Leaves and twigs crunched beneath every slow, careful footstep. When the road was obscured behind them, Malcolm gestured, drawing Luelle to a stop. They stood side by side, turned slightly away from one another to guard against unseen attacks. If their enemies used the Power, they would feel it, but a physical attack was just as likely.

"Can you search for them again?" he asked, his whisper barely louder than the breeze rustling the leaves above.

Luelle nodded, preparing herself with several slow, deep breaths. Pressure tugged faintly against him, immersing him in the feeling of a cool, clear night sky, gazing at the moon and stars. Instinct made him want to throw a shield around them in their moment of vulnerability but that would only cut off Luelle's ability to explore with the Power. Instead, he settled for eyeing the surrounding trees, listening for footsteps, opening himself to feel the pulse of Power from any direction beyond Luelle.

The pressure stopped and the world around Malcolm grew still once again. Luelle met his questioning gaze, pointing to the left and raising two fingers, repeating the gestures slightly to the right.

Four enemies.

"Can you tell which are closer?" Malcolm murmured.

Luelle pointed again to the left.

Together, they moved in that direction, stepping on moss and plants wherever they could to soften their steps.

Malcolm felt the attack before he saw the bandits.

Pressure tugged at the centre of his chest from both sides. He threw a shield around himself and Luelle, angling his back against hers. Debris scattered against it, clouding the air with dust. He kept the barrier up as he peered through the hazy air, searching for their opponents. His sword remained sheathed, a last resort in the crowded trees. These bandits were happy to fight from the shadows, strengthening Malcolm's confidence in their poor fighting abilities. Victory should be swift and easy.

Instead of his sword, he slid one of the small, fragile glass spheres from the leather pouch on his belt. A tiny thread of his Power anchored their shield in place as the dust settled.

Malcolm focused his senses, tuning in on every sound to isolate the location of their lurking enemies: Luelle's steady breathing, faster than normal from adrenaline; rustling leaves, jostled by the wind through the branches; birdsong fluting above, unbothered by the tension in the air—

A crunching step.

He dropped his shield and darted toward the noise. A flash of movement betrayed the figure hidden behind a wide tree trunk. Malcolm stopped short of going behind the tree, unwilling to chase the stranger and get separated from Luelle. The woman behind the tree peered around the trunk and froze, gasping at Malcolm's proximity to her. Her eyes were as wild as her hair.

He drew his arm back and threw the glass sphere.

The woman ducked away, but it made little difference.

As the sphere neared her, Malcolm willed the glass to burst and held his breath, for good measure. Shadowbell powder exploded, a cloud of silvery particles engulfing the bandit. She scrambled from her sheltered position, gasping for a breath of fresh air.

Malcolm willed a gust of air to follow her. Its movement pushed most of the dust, less draining than trying to manipulate individual particles.

Noise sounded behind, pulses of the Power tugging at him. He didn't turn to watch Luelle's progress lest it break his own concentration. He trusted her. Instead, he threw a shield behind his back so she did not need to worry about his fate whilst she was distracted with their second enemy.

The Veseile woman in front of him fell to her knees. Each scrabbling movement was slower than the last. When she stilled, Malcolm watched for a moment longer, heartbeat pounding, until he was certain the shadowbell had worked. Only her chest shifted, evidence that she lived. Sweat coated Malcolm's brow from the effort of manipulating the dust. He would not be able to use that technique frequently in a larger battle.

Malcolm turned. Luelle was out of sight but the sensation of her Power was strong. She stepped out from behind a tree, into his line of sight, shielding herself with the Power against an onslaught of rocks.

Her fingers flicked towards her shield, though Malcolm felt no additional pressure to indicate she was using the Power with the movement. He frowned at the strange twitch, until a sharp tug of her Power shoved him in the direction she'd subtly pointed towards.

Cursing himself for his own slowness, Malcolm darted

forward to assist, willing a shield in place once again.

Luelle's opponent did not let up their attack, preventing her from dropping her shield to throw her projectile weapon. A large man ran towards her in a random path, weaving behind the cover of trees whenever he threw a fresh wave of debris. His Power felt like plunging into warm water.

Malcolm stayed back, slinking wide around the man. Trees and low branches blocked his path, preventing a clean throw. Whilst the man was distracted by Luelle, who occasionally threw her own barrage of pebbles and dirt, Malcolm tossed another glass sphere into the air. Holding it steady above himself with his Power, he eased it forward slowly, guiding it around tree trunks towards the bandit.

It nudged the Veseile's head. He turned.

Before Malcolm had a chance, a pulse of Luelle's Power flickered against him and the glass exploded in the bandit's face, engulfing him in a cloud of powder that followed his jerking movements to escape. He sprinted directly into a tree trunk and fell flat on his back.

Malcolm stayed alert in case the man stood again, but the stranger stilled as the shadowbell powder settled around him.

Luelle approached the body.

"Two down," she murmured.

Malcolm strode to her side. Sliding a finger under her chin, he tilted her head to look at him. Small grazes sliced into her cheek, only an inch away from her eye, where they might've caused some real damage.

His stomach dropped.

"You're injured."

She shook her head, loosening herself from his grip with a frown. "It's nothing. Just a scratch."

"Why didn't you shield yourself?"

"I was too busy to think of that. Really, I'm fine. Are you alright?"

He nodded, eyes lingering on the redness marring her skin.

"You're certain? You didn't suffer a head injury?"

His brow furrowed.

She shrugged, the corners of her mouth twitching as she fought a smile. "You took so long to decipher my instruction to circle the man, I assume someone knocked your brain loose."

Malcolm snorted. "Your instruction was as clear as a rough diamond. What was I supposed to think this meant?" He repeated her gesture, hand pressed against his hip, fingers jerking forwards and backwards in an exaggerated manner.

She shoved him, scowling. "Are we leaving the bodies here?"

He nodded. "That dose should keep them out for several hours. We will deal with the other two on our side of the woods first, then make sure everybody else is alright before we bring the bodies back to the horses and —"

A sharp tug yanked at Malcolm's chest.

He threw a shield around them, flinching away from a burst of fire that enveloped the shield, angling his body to cover Luelle's in case the shield failed. Heat warmed him through the invisible barrier.

Heavy breathing filled the silence when the flames died. Sweat stuck Malcolm's shirt to his back. Several leaves and branches surrounding them had caught fire in the blast. A frantic glance revealed that Luelle seemed unharmed, beyond the scrapes over her cheek. He followed her glare to the two bandits behind him.

They had snuck up from behind, taking advantage of their momentary lapse in attention. One of them sagged against the other from the exertion of channelling so much of their Power.

Being attacked with stones no longer seemed so bad.

Malcolm fished his final glass sphere from his pouch—Luelle would have to use her own for the remaining bandit.

"As soon as I drop my shield, run to your left," he instructed.

She gave a sharp nod, lips thinning.

He released his shield and darted away from her toward the nearest tree, praying the bandits would target him before Luelle. He threw his sphere forward, driving it towards his enemies.

Another pulse of the Power and a second wave of fire swept forth, shattering the glass sphere long before it reached them and burning up the powder within in a cloud of flames.

Malcolm shielded himself, feeling Luelle's Power from afar as she did the same, but the fire did not reach them before the bandit who conjured it passed out from exhaustion, having failed to ration their energy. When Malcolm glanced around the tree trunk, the final bandit had disappeared.

"Let's spread out again. I doubt they'll abandon their friend," Luelle said.

He tried to grab her, to check her for new injuries and

heal her face, but she darted away.

The desire to follow her was overpowering. Malcolm choked it down, instead obeying her instruction, heart pounding. Throwing up a shield to protect against any further attacks, he crept in the other direction, sheltering behind a large tree near the unconscious bandit.

A crack sounded.

Above him, a branch was torn from the tree. Malcolm cursed and ducked away, his shield dropping. The thick branch thudded against the ground where he had been standing.

Masculine shouts erupted nearby. Malcolm's heart stumbled. *Luelle.* He needed to protect her.

He sprinted toward the voice.

When he reached the bandit, the man was fighting against a cloud of shadowbell powder. On the other side of him, Luelle watched the stranger, leaning casually against a thick tree trunk, far enough back that the powder did not affect her. She grinned at Malcolm.

His chest heaved from fighting and the use of the Power. When the bandit stopped twitching, Malcolm passed him to stand at Luelle's side. Shadowbell powder stirred around his ankles as he walked through the settling cloud.

"To the other side of the copse or back to the horses, first?" she asked.

He bit back the insistence to heal her before anything else, knowing his friends may need him. "Horses first. Arthyr was nervous about the fight and Theo and Leena do not have the Power. The three of them are the most vulnerable."

They kept quiet, speeding through the trees in the

direction they'd come from. Emerging from the copse, they saw Theo and Leena in the distance, dodging attacks from two bandits who were flinging stones and logs towards them and the horses. Two bodies lay between them. Dark metal blurred in an arc through the air as Leena hurled one of her small, curved throwing knives.

One of the bandits dropped to the ground, the blade lodging in their eye.

Malcolm broke into a sprint, Luelle at his side. He shoved at the bandits from behind with a wave of the Power, pushing the final Veseile off-balance enough to halt their attack.

"I have no more shadowbell," he shouted as he and Luelle spread apart, splitting their enemy's attention.

She reached into the small pouch at her waist, tossing her final two glass bombs into the air and shoving them towards the Veseile. Powder exploded when Luelle willed the glass to shatter but the bandit threw up a shield and ran.

He sprinted towards Malcolm, every inch of his face lined with desperation.

Malcolm braced. The bandit kept himself shielded as he leapt for Malcolm. Malcolm spun away, narrowly avoiding being knocked down without even coming into contact with the stranger.

The pressure against Malcolm's chest died as the Veseile dropped his shield. He grabbed the bandit's arm as he passed, twisting it up behind the man's back. Kicking at his knees, Malcolm drove the bandit to the ground.

The Veseile struggled. Malcolm grappled for his free arm and held them together behind his back, shoving the man's face into the dirt.

"Luelle!" he shouted. Pressure began to build as the bandit clawed at the final scraps of his Power, shoving it against Malcolm in an attempt to free himself.

Malcolm swayed, tightening his grip and tugging the man's arms upwards in the hopes that the pain might halt his attack.

Powder swirled into the corner of Malcolm's vision. He held his breath, leaning as far back as he could while still restraining the man. Luelle's Power pulsed against him as she manipulated the powder.

When the bandit's struggles slowed to twitches, Malcolm leapt to his feet and staggered away, chest heaving for fresh, clean air.

Luelle appeared at his side, her hands on each of his cheeks as she met his gaze and checked for injury.

"I am fine. Thank you." He nodded, still breathing heavily.

The concern in her eyes faded. She smiled, patting his cheek lightly. "Those last two both count as mine." She winked and turned to run towards Theo and Leena, who were now crouched beside the two bodies that had already been on the ground when Malcolm and Luelle had arrived.

Malcolm opened his mouth to ask if she'd been keeping a tally of their defeated enemies this entire time, but she was too far to hear him. Frowning, he jogged to catch up.

Arthyr had been one of the bodies on the ground, lying alongside another bandit. Theo was helping him sit up.

"Are you all alright? What happened?" Malcolm asked.

"We are fine. Glad for the help. Art got this one but managed to inhale half a mouthful of the powder he'd thrown at the bandit." Theo scowled at the red-haired Veseile, voice clipped with frustration and worry.

"Why didn't you shield yourself?" Luelle asked.

"I was shielding Theo," Arthyr slurred, cradling his left wrist.

"Idiot," Theo scoffed, though his tone softened considerably.

"I would have been grateful for the shield," Leena grumbled to Luelle, who hid her laugh in a cough.

"We can patch you up at camp," Malcolm said to Arthyr. "Luelle needs healing, too. Can you ride?"

Arthyr nodded, though the haziness of his stare suggested he might need some time to work off the shadowbell's influence.

As Malcolm stood, preparing to search for the others, Mei and Tao emerged from the copse. Tao carried a body over his shoulder. Mei dragged another by the ankle, uncaring of the way the woman's head bounced on the ground.

Malcolm jogged towards them.

"Are you both alright?"

They nodded.

"This one snuck up on us. I bashed him over the head before we could use the powder." Tao jiggled the body on his shoulder. "I do not know how long he will remain unconscious."

Malcolm nodded. "We can make sure they inhale some before the journey back to camp."

"There are a couple more bodies in the forest," Mei said.

Malcolm beckoned Luelle over to help him retrieve the Veseile bandits they'd left among the trees.

51

TRANSPORTING prisoners made their travels less comfortable. When Luelle and the others reunited with the rest of the Gifted, the Veseile bandits were bound and gagged. Malcolm chose to keep them unconscious with regular shadowbell inhalation and shoved them inside one of the two carriages the Gifted had taken before departing from the nobility days earlier.

Despite the sedation, the Gifted remained wary of their prisoners. At all times, two Gifted worked together to hold a shield around the vehicle, containing any potential damage from the Veseile trapped within. They only let up the barrier briefly to rotate shifts, to administer more powder, or to probe inside the carriage with the Power, feeling for any movement.

Malcolm and Leena had spoken to the prisoners once when the first bout of shadowbell powder had worn off. Luelle and the other Gifted stayed back, close enough to help if they were needed but far enough that they could protect the horses and supplies from any fallout. It had been a dull, tense hour. When Malcolm and Leena returned, having conveyed appropriate threats to the bandits lest they attempt to escape and offered them food and water, the shield was securely back in place.

Malcolm assigned short shifts to the Gifted, so none spent too much of their energy shielding the carriage. As they neared Vidamere, an attack from Zeke grew more likely. None of them could afford to leave themselves vulnerable.

Luelle took her shift early on, working alongside two other Gifted to ensure no inch of the carriage was uncovered. She worked until they reached their chosen destination for the evening's camp. Another Gifted arrived to replace her, relieving her to find wherever Mei had set up their tent.

Although her reserves were far from depleted, using the Power consistently over the course of several hours had drained her—not in the same way she'd experienced at Tolhurst, where a single, overwhelming burst of the Power had sucked every ounce of her energy, knocking her unconscious minutes later, but the way she used to feel after a long shift working in the castle. All of her muscles ached, despite doing little more than riding her horse alongside the carriage. Fatigue dulled her mind, clouding her thoughts.

Beyond their camp, Lake Vida stretched wide over the horizon. One of the many small villages on the lake's shore stood nearby, its buildings clustered at the water's edge.

Tomorrow, they would reach Vidamere, Luelle's birthplace, not that she could remember much of it.

Luelle found Mei and their tent close to the heart of the camp. Slipping inside, she changed into fresh clothes whilst Mei prepared hot drinks for each of them. When she emerged, Mei had disappeared elsewhere, leaving Luelle's drink on a log. Luelle picked up the steaming up and weaved through the nearby tents to reach the camp's central fire pit. There, she found Mei and her friends, standing together in a small crowd. She approached, sipping her drink and relishing the warmth of it trickling down her torso.

"How do you feel?" Luelle asked Art.

He probed the bruises and scrapes on one side of his face. "Sore," he admitted with a wince.

Mei had healed Art the moment they'd returned to camp and secured the bandits. Malcolm hadn't allowed anyone else to touch Luelle. He'd taken her aside and healed her himself, pouring more of his strength into the act than necessary to ensure every inch of her skin was unmarred, despite her objections that the scrapes would heal naturally with time.

Art continued. "Mei said I've sprained my wrist. I'm not looking forward to our next battle."

Her stomach tightened with nerves, as it always did when she thought of the upcoming fight against Zeke. None of the others noticed her reaction. Art continued speaking with Tao and Mei, discussing how to improve his battle strategy going into a fight against more coordinated opponents since a small group of wild bandits had proven such a challenge. Their words were a distant buzz.

Something nudged Luelle's arm, pulling her out of her thoughts.

She turned to find Malcolm at her side.

"Will you come and eat with me?" he murmured, quiet

enough not to disturb the other conversation.

She nodded, concentrating on her breathing as she walked at Malcolm's side, blindly following his lead. As soon as they emerged past the last line of tents, Malcolm intertwined their fingers, tugging her along with renewed enthusiasm. Luelle shoved away thoughts of Zeke, focusing on the man at her side, the warmth of his skin against her palm and the weight of his amulet against her chest, hidden beneath her shirt.

Awaiting them underneath a tree overlooking the lake was a small blanket, two parcels of food, and a bottle of wine.

"What's this?" Luelle asked, a smile tugging at the corners of her lips. Imagining Malcolm sneaking away from his soldiers to lay out this scene eased the knot in her chest.

His cheeks darkened in colour. "It is not much but I wanted to have some privacy before we arrive at Vidamere."

Luelle could no longer hide her smile. She sat cross-legged on the blanket, gazing over the view as Malcolm lowered himself beside her.

"How are you feeling?" he asked, fingers automatically seeking her out again, coming to rest on her leg. His gaze lingered on her cheek, where she'd been cut during their fight.

She shrugged. "Tired."

"I do not only mean after guarding the carriage. It must be strange being here." He gestured to the lake.

Luelle sighed. "I know. Apprehensive, I suppose. I'd managed to forget why we were really here for a while."

"It will go better than last time." He grabbed her hand

again, tracing the contours on her palm with the pad of his thumb.

She nodded. He was right. They were better prepared, this time. Zeke's forces could not be organised or well-trained in the time he'd gathered them—not compared to the Gifted.

"Before you know it, Zeke will be imprisoned in a carriage like our other bandits. We will transport him to the capital and you can forget about him forever."

Though it was a chilling thought, Luelle found herself breathing a laugh at the absurdity of it.

"Will his prison cell be as comfortable as mine?"

Malcolm frowned, a discontented grumble escaping the back of his throat. "Even I can admit your room was never the prison my advisers wanted it to be."

"I'd never have stayed if you tried to put me in a real cell." She smirked.

He snorted.

"I know. Perhaps that is why I could never bring myself to put you in one." He reached for the wine with his free hand, tugging the cork from its neck with his teeth and spitting it over his shoulder away from her. "I did not bring cups. I will return to the camp for one if you wish."

She shook her head, accepting the drink and sipping straight from the bottle as Malcolm unwrapped their food. The small parcels contained the same rations they ate each night, supplemented by the few greens the Gifted had scavenged as they'd travelled.

"I'm glad I stayed. At the castle, I mean."

Malcolm glanced at Luelle, a playful smile ghosting his lips. "We both know the reason for that."

She rolled her eyes, snatching a slice of stale bread and

hard cheese from in front of him. "You say that as if I initiated this but you're the one who kept seeking me out."

His smile deepened. "Perhaps we are tied by fate, destined to seek one another out no matter how far we roam." He shifted closer so their thighs were flush.

"You believe in fate?"

Malcolm chewed his own slice of bread and cheese as he thought. "No, but I did not believe the gods could walk the earth, nor that the Power belonged to the Veseile, and look how wrong I was. I have questioned a lot of my beliefs since meeting you."

Luelle took another swig of wine. Chills skittered down her spine at the reminder of Vesanya. Zeke occupied so many of her thoughts on this journey that she'd forgotten the bigger threat they would face when he was locked away.

"Where do you think she is now?" she asked.

Malcolm instantly knew who she referred to. "Wreaking chaos somewhere nearby, I am sure. Though, I do not believe she could travel close to civilisations as large as Vidamere or even these small fishing villages without our hearing of it."

The words were little comfort. Their small, open camp felt less safe than it had over the past few days. She and Malcolm ate in silence, occasionally passing the wine bottle between them. As the sky darkened, specks of brightness flared to life in the nearby village—lit torches and unshuttered moonstone lamps. The lights shimmered on the water's surface, where they were reflected.

Malcolm spoke again when they were near the end of their bottle.

"How do you feel about returning to Vidamere?" After eating, they'd sprawled closer together, limbs entangled, his torso flush against her side to share body heat. Luelle lay flat on her back, her head beside Malcolm's elbow. He had propped his head up with his hand to gaze down at her. His fingers traced a light pattern over her outer thigh as she considered her answer.

"I don't know. I don't remember much of my time there. Zeke had never planned to stay there for long and finding me didn't change that. Even if I could remember more than vague streets, I doubt the city is the same as it was when I left."

Malcolm opened his mouth to speak thrice, losing the courage each time.

"What is it," Luelle pushed, concern rising within her about whatever words he was holding back.

"If you could see where your parents lived, would you want to?" His hand stilled on her leg.

Hollow sorrow constricted Luelle's chest, despite never having known her parents. She pursed her lips. "I don't remember it, so I wouldn't know where to start. I doubt it's still there."

"It is."

Her eyes flicked up to meet his.

"When I asked Edyth, my Thane, to look into your family records, I gave you everything she'd found. However, since then, her librarians uncovered more information. She sent it in a letter that arrived the day before we left, since she knew I would be visiting. She does not know what it is for, only that I was interested," he rambled, filling the silence as Luelle continued trying to swallow the lump in her throat. "I meant to tell you before we left but, honestly, I was avoiding you and I was so busy. I thought you might think I was meddling or trying to blackmail you back into my bed. I thought it would be easier to show you when we arrived but I know it is personal and you might not want—"

Luelle silenced him by leaning up and pressing her lips against his, muffling the excuses. She felt him relax against her.

"I want to see it," she said, when she broke away from him. "But not before…everything. Can we—would we have time on the way back to Cerulya? After Sandport."

He brushed a lock of hair away from her face, tucking it behind her ear. "Of course." He smiled. "Whatever you want."

She hesitated but asked the question on the tip of her tongue regardless of her discomfort. "What will happen when we return to the capital?"

Malcolm's brow creased. "We will continue searching for a way to defeat or contain Vesanya, I suppose."

"No, I mean between us."

"I do not follow."

"Come on, Malcolm. We won't be free to act so informally in the palace." She looked pointedly at their bodies pressed against one another. "Will we continue hiding? Will I continue sneaking into your bed until your advisers arrange your marriage?"

"Must we decide tonight?"

She nodded, plucking every scrap of courage she could find. "I think so. The outcome won't be the same for us. I'd like to prepare myself if this journey is the only time we truly have together."

His grip on her tightened. "I will not let this end when

we return to the capital just because you believe I must end up marrying someone with a title."

"You can't—"

"I can, Luelle." He held her gaze, frustration and stubbornness ringing through his voice. "I told you, every decision I have made in life has been for others—for my family, my kingdom. Why must I rule alongside someone I do not love or care for, simply because they have the right name? Am I not allowed a say, even in this? I choose you now and I will keep choosing you, no matter how often you try to push me away. Until the day you truly do not want to be with me, I will choose you."

"Your family—"

"I will speak to them." He cut her off again, bringing her hand to his lips and pressing a kiss against her fingers. "As soon as we return, I swear it. I am not letting you go so easily. I—" he cut himself off abruptly and swallowed, taking a deep, trembling breath. "You make me happy. I am happier than I have felt in a long time. I will not throw that away because of silly traditions. Everything in this kingdom is changing. Being with someone I care for should be the least of my adviser's worries."

Luelle buried her head into the crook of his neck so she didn't have to hold that intense stare, unsure how to respond. Zeke's rejection of her had raised doubts in Luelle's mind of finding love or friendship again. She'd had no desire to pursue trust in others in case it resulted in the same painful abandonment. Such unabashed, complete acceptance from Malcolm—someone who knew the truth about her past and heritage, who had seen her worst traits and accepted them—was overwhelming.

"So long as you want that too, of course," he

murmured after a few minutes of silence. "You are correct that there may be some," he hesitated over the words, "...resistance from my advisers. I would not begrudge you for not wanting to experience that but I swear I will stand at your side through all of it."

She tilted her face to smile at him, pulling him down for a slower kiss in answer.

52

THOUGH Malcolm had visited Vidamere several times throughout his life, this was the first time as the king, in the role that had always been his father's. A stab of grief reared its head, sharp and sudden. He weathered it, staring at the curls on the back of Theo's head until the memories receded.

Another small group of soldiers met them at the city gates, sent by Edyth to offer a safe escort through the city. Malcolm ordered them to focus primarily on the nobility, whom they had rejoined this morning, allowing his own trusted soldiers and Gifted to provide his protection.

Civilians crowded the streets as Malcolm and his procession arrived. Vidamere was similar to Cerulya, with winding streets and cobbled roads, though it lacked the crisp sea air of Malcolm's home city, and the buildings lining every road were constructed from darker stones and wood.

Malcolm nodded and smiled at the city's people. Following Leena's advice, he held a shield around himself and his horse for the entire walk to protect against an attack like the one in Cerulya. None came.

Edyth awaited them in the reception room at Kestrel House, Malcolm's estate in the city. Soldiers stood guard at the property gates and front doors. Theo parted from their company almost immediately to ensure the perimeter was adequately monitored against intrusion.

Edyth dipped into a low bow as Malcolm entered. He nodded a greeting to her, watching from the corner of his eye as Luelle followed Graman further into the house, likely seeking the building's small library to start their research.

"Welcome, Your Majesty. I trust that your journey was uneventful?"

"On the contrary, I am afraid." Malcolm lowered his voice. "We captured and contained some Veseile who have been causing trouble in several villages to the west of here."

Edyth's brows rose a notch. "I see. Where are they being kept?"

"They are currently in a carriage guarded by the Gifted, who await further instruction from you on the best place to transport them."

"The Gifted?"

"The Veseile soldiers in the capital have adopted the name for themselves."

"Rather exclusionary, is it not?" Her brows rose once again.

Malcolm shrugged. "I have bigger concerns for now. I can spare a few Gifted to assist with guarding the Veseile prisoners if necessary. Some of them will remain here when I leave for Sandport to offer further training to your own Veseile soldiers."

Edyth dipped her head. "I am grateful, Your Majesty. Speaking of troublesome Veseile, I received some intelligence regarding those that you wrote me about." She scanned the reception hall, eyeing the guards standing to attention and the servants surreptitiously bustling around.

"Perhaps we should retire to a more private location," Malcolm suggested.

Edyth nodded, gesturing for him to follow her and leading him to the nearest drawing room. Inside, she had already taken the time to spread a map across the desk. Malcolm stepped closer, examining the sketch of the city they were in and its surrounding lands, stretching from the Razors to the coast.

Edyth circled the desk and pulled a roll of paper from a pocket inside her embroidered jacket. She passed it to Malcolm and spoke as he unfurled the parchment.

"I received reports from two separate towns north of here, each describing bandits using the Power. They may belong to the same group of thugs you apprehended."

Malcolm's throat dried. "When did this occur?"

"One report arrived yesterday and one the day before. I imagine the actual attacks occurred a day or so before I received each letter.

"Do they describe the attacks in detail? How many were hurt?"

"Thirty-three people hurt, though none dead, thankfully." Edyth's lips were downturned into a tight frown.

Only now did Malcolm notice the bruise-like smudges of colour underneath his Thane's eyes.

"These letters describe the attacks. There are several accounts from each town. You may make more sense of it than I was able to but the chaotic descriptions make me question their accuracy. I sent some trusted soldiers to the villages to bring me an accurate account of the damage and corroborate the information I currently have. The first of those returned just before you arrived. I wanted to bring you up to speed before hearing their full report. You are welcome to join me in that meeting. The second party is due to return tomorrow."

Malcolm took the letters from Edyth and scanned the descriptions of toppled buildings, scorching fires, and innocent civilians being flung through the air by invisible hands. For a second, his heart froze with fear that Vesanya had caused the devastation, but each account described a group of people, their foreheads marked with a red 'L'.

Putting the letters aside, Malcolm scanned the map, locating both towns along a river feeding Lake Vida. Upstream, just over a week's journey away, were the Razors, where Luelle's old friends had claimed Zeke was now living—albeit, months ago.

"There is something else."

He glanced up, reading the tight apprehension in Edyth's expression.

"The soldiers who returned just before you arrived had a prisoner in their charge. A Veseile man who refuses to speak to anyone but you."

Malcolm's heart stuttered. Could it be Zeke?

"Where is he being held?"

"I had some cells under the barracks modified to hold Veseile prisoners once you informed us about the Power.

They took him there while I came to greet you."

"Take me to him." Malcolm folded the reports and tucked them into the inner breast pocket of his jacket.

Edyth nodded, her unchanging expression suggesting she had expected the request.

Before leaving, Malcolm briefly updated Leena and Theo. Theo left to find Luelle and returned with her shortly. In under a quarter of an hour, they were all piled into Edyth's private carriage, speeding towards the barracks.

Malcolm's stomach was a heavy weight. He squared his shoulders as they arrived. Edyth led them all through the plain, clean building, weaving around soldiers to reach the cells that held the prisoner, far beneath ground level.

Few torches lit the corridor. Doors lined each side, short enough that Malcolm would have to duck to walk through one.

"He is bound, Your Majesty, though I do not think it wise for you to go into the cell alone," Edyth said when they came to a stop in a particularly dim part of the hallway. Silence emanated from beyond the door beside them.

"What measures are in place to stop him from using the Power?" Leena asked, eyes flashing with concern.

"His hands are bound and he is on a dose of shadowbell. Not enough to put him to sleep. Only enough to keep him from thinking clearly. My soldiers have been topping up the dose regularly to keep him in such a state."

Malcolm nodded. "Having his hands bound will do nothing to stop him from using the Power but the shadowbell should be enough."

Despite the reassurances, Malcolm raised a shield between himself and the prisoner as he entered the cell, the others close behind him.

A petite man was tied to a small wooden chair in the middle of an otherwise empty room. His head lolled, rolling to the side and back and he tried looking at his visitors. Tufts and clumps of hair stood up at all angles on his scalp, a single streak of white among the brown. One of his eyes was swelling from a recent hit. Smeared across his forehead was the remnant of a red mark.

"An audience." The Veseile's voice was slurred, his smile wide and lazy. His pupils were blown wide, black obscuring all but a sliver colour from his irises. No pressure of the Power radiated from the stranger. Malcolm kept his protective barrier in place all the same.

"What is your name?" he demanded of the captive.

Quiet, giggling laughter bubbled from the man's lips. Glee shone in his glazed eyes. Impatience simmered in Malcolm as he waited for a proper response, but none came.

"Care to share what is so funny?" he asked, hoping the stranger mistook the shake of his voice for cold anger rather than the unease it truly was.

"I didn't think you'd come." The Veseile beamed.

Malcolm did not give himself time to second-guess whether it had been the right decision. "You said you would only talk to me. I am here, so speak. What did you wish to say?"

"The Liberator knows you're here," the man garbled, words slipping from his mouth like silk. "He's waiting for you."

"I have no intention of chasing petty, insignificant

thugs. He will be waiting for a long time."

"He said you wouldn't come to him." The man smacked his dry lips, unfocused stare sweeping across the room in a vain attempt to look at the others in his cell. "But he said he'll make you."

"How does he intend to manage that?" Malcolm's heart hammered. He fought to keep his tone even.

"He knows where to find Vesanya. You'll meet him or they'll unleash enough chaos to liberate the Eile and destroy any evidence that your human-tainted family ever ruled us." The man tried to spit, but his lips did not cooperate in his inebriated state. Saliva dribbled slowly down his chin.

Regardless, Malcolm's blood ran cold.

"We are done here." He turned and walked from the cell, leaving his shield in place until his companions were safely in the hall alongside him and the door was closed tight, muffling the peals of laughter that rolled from the prisoner.

"He is a madman," Edyth muttered. "Did any of that make sense to you?"

"Unfortunately." Malcolm locked stares with Luelle, seeing the same apprehension on her face that he could feel flooding his chest.

53

KESTREL House's library was considerably smaller than the one Luelle had grown used to studying in, within the castle's observatory. Graman's hulking form at the opposite end of the table made the space feel even more cramped. Books were stacked like mountains between them.

Luelle cradled her head in her hands as she read. Her eyes stung. The two of them had been studying for hours, pouring over any resources they hadn't already analysed in Cerulya in search of information to further their theories.

Hope was a small spark quickly smothered. Words floated on the page, out of Luelle's grasp, no matter how many times she read them. All she could think about were the slurred words spat by the Veseile prisoner in Edyth's dungeons the day before. Zeke was waiting for them—for Malcolm—and sounded more prepared than she'd anticipated, or at least more bold. If the recent accounts Malcolm had shared with her were true, Zeke had developed a good understanding of how to use the

Power and wasn't hesitating to wield it against innocent people, just like Vesanya did.

Would he find a way to pair up with the god against Malcolm? Was such an alliance even possible? According to Imbryl and Freya, Zeke wanted to kill the god or at least steal her Power, not fight at her side. Had he realised the impossibility of that plan? Or did he simply know more than them? Even if she had time to seek Imbryl and Freya again, it would be useless if they had stayed away from Zeke, as they'd claimed to desire.

Luelle rubbed the heels of her hands into her eyes and read the page in front of her afresh, starting from the top. She had no expectation to find something worthwhile but she had to try.

Five minutes later, she gave up again.

"Have you found anything new?" she asked Graman, who had already poured through a small pile of texts.

He glanced up, nudging his spectacles higher with a knuckle and pursing his lips into a frown.

"Nothing truly different from the information we've already examined. I believe we will have more success when we reach Sandport."

Luelle didn't voice her concern that it might be a case of 'if' rather than 'when'.

Fortunately, she was rescued from further research by Malcolm's arrival. Only a few hours had passed since she'd last seen him, since she'd crept from his room before his servants were due to arrive. They'd spent hours last night discussing what lay ahead of them, both dealing with Zeke and beyond. Nervous excitement fluttered in her stomach as Luelle returned Malcolm's smile, letting herself imagine, briefly, what their life might be like when they returned to the capital. When Malcolm publicised his intent to court her, they would inevitably face backlash, likely from his advisers and other nobility. Despite that, he swore to remain at her side throughout it. Repeatedly, he assured her he would only walk away if she was the one who decided she no longer wanted to be with him.

Yet, lines of tension lay underneath the mask of Malcolm's smile, clear in the rigid set of his mouth and the tightness of his jaw.

He pulled a chair at their table and slumped into it, inhaling a slow, deep breath.

"Anything new?" He waved a hand at the piles of papers on the table.

"No, Your Majesty." Graman repeated his answer to Luelle's earlier question.

Malcolm's mouth twisted into a frown. "Perhaps we will be able to retrieve the research Zeke took from the cavern when we apprehend him."

"Have you received any more news about him?" Luelle balled her fingers into tight fists below the tabletop. She focused on the scent of books around her, the hint of Malcolm's aftershave lotion, the press of her fingernails into her palms—grounding herself to keep in control of the Power writhing inside her.

Malcolm nodded. "Another of Edyth's soldiers returned. She sent more to guard the villages that were attacked and to help people rebuild and recuperate. This morning's messenger confirmed the extent of the damage. Zeke has more control over the Power than I had hoped, and I imagine his people will be more skilled than the bandits we encountered a few days ago. This will be a more challenging fight."

"Were there any more prisoners?"

He shook his head, dark curls brushing against his cheekbones. He shoved his hair back. "No. I visited the first again this morning to see if I could wring any more information out of him." He raised his hands in defence seeing the glare Luelle shot his way. "I know I promised to tell you if I was going to see him again but it was faster simply to go. He said nothing else, regardless. I doubt he actually knows anything about Zeke's plans. Zeke would never have let him be captured alive if so."

Luelle kept her frown in place, though she agreed with the assessment.

"What now? Do you still want to risk going after him if there's a chance he's trying to ally with Vesanya?"

Malcolm shrugged, fingers tracing absentminded patterns over a small slice of bare tabletop. "I doubt the prisoner was telling the truth about that. I imagine Zeke is only trying to spread fear or use the claim to gain more loyalty from his followers."

Graman spoke up. "From our research, I cannot envision a god in alliance with a mortal. In the few myths in which it has occurred, the mortal has always needed to trade for help, and I cannot think of anything Zeke could offer her. Even if Vesanya had reason to, her violent tendencies so far within the realm do not suggest she would be inclined to listen to anyone who wished to work with her."

Malcolm made a wordless noise of agreement. "Either way, I cannot leave the problem of Zeke unsolved. He is like an infected wound, he will only fester and rot if I do not treat him."

Luelle raised her brows at the imagery.

"Sorry, I know he was your—" he cut off with a frown that dissolved into a wry grin. "Honestly, I am still not quite sure what he was to you. Regardless, we will not stay in Vidamere for long. I plan for us to leave tomorrow and detour north. Is there a map in here?"

Graman gestured to a basket of scrolls nearby. Malcolm rooted through until he found one showing the lands he required and spread it over another small table in the room, beckoning Luelle closer so they did not disrupt Graman's research. He pointed to two small towns along the river feeding Lake Vida from the Razors.

"These are the towns Zeke attacked. Tillham," he pointed to the town furthest north, "is along the route we would take. Information Leena managed to gather suggests Zeke might be hiding in cave systems between there and the Razors as the terrain climbs."

Luelle huffed a sigh. More caves. "Do you have anything more specific?" She frowned at the unfurled map, at the expanse of space Malcolm had brushed his fingertips across.

He shook his head, lips pressed tight together.

"We're going into this at a real disadvantage." She wrapped her arms around her middle, fresh nerves unsteadying her.

Malcolm placed a hand on her arm, sweeping his thumb in soothing motions.

"We have overcome worse odds."

Luelle glanced at Graman but he was too preoccupied with reading again to notice the small piece of affection. She offered Malcolm a small smile. "I suppose. When would we leave?"

"Tomorrow morning at dawn. That gives us the rest of

today to ensure everyone is well-rested. Edyth will supply us with fresh horses and some more soldiers to flesh out our numbers."

"What will happen to your nobility?" Luelle's thoughts strayed to their companions who had rejoined them outside Vidamere. Malcolm hadn't shown any enthusiasm at their arrival, spending more time beside her and the Gifted, though that hadn't stopped the nobility from seeking him out and interspersing themselves among the soldiers.

"They will await us here. We will swing back through on our way to Sandport to deposit any prisoners in Edyth's care."

Luelle took a deep breath and nodded. "I'll help Graman look for anything else that might help us before then."

Malcolm caught her wrist, pulling her back as she turned toward the larger table in the room.

"Tomorrow or the next few days, whenever we find Zeke, I know it will be hard for you. Graman will cope here by himself for the rest of the day. He will remain here with the nobility as my representative, so he is in no rush to complete all of this reading today. You should rest your mind. You will need all of your strength for the fight ahead." His hand slid from her wrist to intertwine their fingers together. He lowered his voice. "Spend the afternoon with me. We do not need to go into the city yet, we can save that for our return as you wished, but I would like to show you the grounds of this house. I spent a lot of time here with my family, growing up."

She smiled and nodded, eager to ignore what lay ahead of them for a while longer.

54

MALCOLM sought out Luelle as often as he could on their travels north, relishing every opportunity to brush his fingers against hers as they passed one another, locking eyes with her from afar, and pulling her into his tent every evening. None of it was enough; every morning he wished their time alone together could last longer. He came alive in those small stolen moments, treasuring the opportunity to think about the future that awaited him at her side and forget the obstacles they would have to first overcome in order to reach it.

Their arrival at Tillham ended his daydreams.

People had already started to fix the damage from Zeke's attack. Rubble sat in piles, gathered away from the roads so carriages and horses had a clear path through. Charred walls lined most of the streets. Some buildings suffered more damage, with entire rooms exposed to the elements. Skittish citizens watched their arrival in small clusters at the roadside or from behind twitching curtains.

Malcolm and his soldiers offered what little help the people would accept, consulting several eyewitnesses who recalled the attack with varying levels of dramatics and detail.

In all, Malcolm was glad to leave the village behind. When he was back in Cerulya, he would be in a better position to help, reallocating resources and wealth to rebuild the homes and lives Zeke had destroyed.

They travelled north for another two days, following the river towards the Razors in the direction of the second village, Fairview. Scouts travelled ahead of them, a constant rotation searching for a suggestion of Zeke's whereabouts. Frustration and apprehension coiled like a tightly wound spring inside Malcolm each time a scout returned with no new information. If not for Luelle at his side each night, he would never find enough peace to sleep.

He was meditating alone in his tent when she sought him out on their sixth evening away from Vidamere. Soft footsteps outside indicated her arrival, followed by the brushing of his tent door's fabric against the ground and the faint floral scent of some product in her hair, carried to him by a gentle breeze that disappeared as she refastened the door behind her.

He opened his eyes and offered her a small smile, feeling tension drain from his shoulders at the sight of her.

"Theo let me in," she explained, walking over to sit beside him on the coir flooring. "I didn't see you at dinner."

Malcolm shoved a hand through his hair, pushing it out of his face. It was getting too long—yet another thing he would have to remedy when they returned home.

"I lost track of time." The excuse sounded lame, even

to his ears.

Luelle ran a hand up his spine. Her touch was as electrifying as it was soothing.

"You need to eat."

"I know." He sighed. "I just wanted time away from everyone tonight. I hate this waiting game. The longer we wait, the more anxious everyone becomes. It will not help us in battle."

"Zeke might have the benefit of surprise but we're prepared for him. The Gifted have been meditating and drilling formations every day since we left Cerulya. No matter what level of control Zeke's people have over the Power, he won't have taught them that level of discipline. You and I both saw the chaos of his tactics when he attacked in the cavern. Without superior numbers, he would never have beaten you then."

"We have no idea of his numbers now, though." Malcolm leaned back into her touch. "Although he may have lost some support after the events in the cavern, he has had time to rebuild. Reports from Tillham suggested a lot of Veseile and consistently referred to him as the Liberator. His cult of followers may very well outnumber us."

"True, but everything seems more chaotic during a battle." Luelle shrugged. "You should have more faith in your people, any who have joined Zeke would be a minority."

Malcolm's amulet still rested beneath her shirt, a bump in the fabric. He reached out, untucking it and watching it glint in the candlelight of his tent. He took a deep breath.

"I hope you are right."

"You're a good king, Malcolm. Not every ruler could have maintained the control you have after experiencing such an upheaval."

Malcolm shot a sideways glance at her, finding nothing but fierce sincerity in her expression. He breathed a laugh, thinking of how far they'd come.

"What?" Luelle frowned.

"I never thought I would come to care so much for a traitor whose first real encounter with me consisted of threats, insults, and a punch to the face."

Colour rose in Luelle's cheeks, but her mouth curled into a smile. "I—"

A thunderous boom sounded in the distance away from the tent. Tremors vibrated through the ground. Shouts arose.

Malcolm threw an arm in front of Luelle to push her behind him. He willed a shield around them both as their heads whipped to the door. His heart raced.

Theo's voice shouted orders outside, urgent and commanding, growing louder as he moved closer. He burst into the tent.

"We're under attack."

Malcolm was on his feet, striding across the space. He attached his weapon belt, equipped with a short sword and two serrated daggers. Luelle snatched up a nearby bandolier, equipped with eight small throwing knives.

"Put on armour," Theo snapped at Malcolm.

"There is no time. I can shield myself," Malcolm replied, his tone equally vicious.

"Don't be stupid. You are the king and must be protected." Theo picked up a nearby mail vest and shoved it at Malcolm's chest.

Huffing, he donned the armour and turned to Luelle. He gripped her bicep before they moved to leave the tent, attempting to shut out the sounds of chaos outside.

"Shield yourself. Stay near me. We can watch one another's backs. Do not try anything reckless and do not go after Zeke without me," he ordered.

She nodded, face pale. Determination shone through the fear in her expression.

He would not consider the risk of her getting hurt. He would not let it happen again.

Following Theo into the camp was like stepping through a doorway to another realm. Smoke plumed from tents on the furthest edges of the camp, almost invisible against the night sky but evident in the charred fumes tinting Malcolm's every breath. Shouts and screams of pain peppered the gaps in noise between explosions and clashing weapons.

"What direction are they attacking from?" Malcolm shouted to Theo as they ran, trusting his friend to lead them to the heart of the battle where they could offer the most help. He threw glances over his shoulder to Luelle every three strides to ensure she was keeping pace with them, though it was unnecessary when he could feel the faint pulse of her Power, a warm blanket of calm around himself as she held up her shield.

"To the north, but they have surrounded the camp," Theo shouted back to Malcolm. "Leena—"

A strong pulse of unfamiliar Power tugged Malcolm's chest from their left. He threw a shield in front of himself and Theo, bracing against it as a wave of fire burst towards them. Heat bathed Malcolm through the barrier. The flames died away quickly.

Smoke obscured their attacker.

Malcolm darted forward, feeling Luelle close behind him. A Veseile woman with a scarred cheek and a red 'L' painted on her brow bared her teeth at Malcolm on the other side of the smoke. Pressure tugged at him as she readied to attack again. Malcolm struck first.

In unison, he and Luelle dropped their shields and shoved at the attacker, sending her flying in a high arc away from them, soaring over tents and into darkness. Her cry of surprise ended abruptly.

Theo rejoined them, eyes scanning every person running between the tents to check for enemies. They continued.

Battlefields were always chaotic, but adding a new, unpredictable weapon and so many obstacles created a type of combat that felt entirely new.

Pressure tugged at Malcolm from Veseile using the Power in every direction—a sensation as overwhelming as the roar of noise. Each one brought with it a rush of feeling, marking the unique signature of its user.

Two short figures rounded one side of the tent immediately before them.

Seeing Malcolm, Luelle, and Theo, they charged. Malcolm threw another shield in front of himself and unsheathed his sword, gripping it tight in his right hand and holding one of his daggers in his left. He dashed towards their enemies. Pulses hammered at his makeshift barrier as the Veseile tried to attack him.

Several steps away from his enemy, Malcolm dropped his shield and pushed out with the Power in an attempt to unbalance the Veseile. Theo ran at his side, slicing and slashing with his sword. Blood sprayed the linen walls around them.

A pulse of Power from behind confirmed Luelle was fighting but Malcolm had no time to look. He leapt at the second Veseile. Too close to use the Power, he relied on physical fighting.

The Veseile dodged and retreated from his blows. Malcolm gritted his teeth, forcing the stranger against the unsteady wall of a tent. He swung his sword down, but the Veseile blocked it with the Power holding Malcolm's arm in place above him.

Undeterred, Malcolm hooked his dagger into the Veseile's side with his other hand, slicing skin and clothing alike as he twisted and tore his serrated blade free. The Veseile's eyes widened. He wore no armour; the blade dug into his flesh like cutting into butter.

Malcolm's sword arm fell as the Veseile's Power gave out. The blade continued its original path, cutting deep into the curve of exposed skin where the man's shoulder met his neck. Bone offered resistance, though it was too late to save the man's life.

Malcolm left him to bleed out.

Theo was still fighting the first enemy, but had turned his attacker so their back was towards Malcolm. He darted forward and stabbed his dagger into the side of the Veseile's neck. Ripping it out, he left Theo to finish the fight and spun to check on Luelle.

Her opponent was already on the ground below her. She stood, wrenching two of her small knives out of the attacker's eyes. She nodded at him once, face pale beneath the freckles of gore spattered across her cheekbones.

They continued through the camp. Twice more, they

were forced to stop and fight a path through Veseile bandits.

There was no coordination to their enemies' tactics. They fought with vicious intensity but fear shone in their eyes when Malcolm and the Gifted engaged with them.

Malcolm, Theo, and Luelle suffered no injuries beyond minor cuts and bruising, but they left a path of bodies in their wake.

Despite rationing his Power, Malcolm's chest heaved with the toll of the fight. Sweat prickled his skin, making his grip slippery. Breath tore from his throat. Fatigue slowed his movements as they reached the edge of the camp.

Beyond the final line of tents, Zeke came into sight. He stood back from the main battle, protected by a tight group of armoured Veseile bandits. His hair gleamed silver in the moonlight. A sadistic grin curled his lips as he watched the violence unfurling.

It wasn't the location Malcolm would have chosen for the fight but it was better than it could have been. Bodies littered the ground between him and Zeke, tripping the fighters still hacking at one another with physical weapons. Invisible bursts of force and pressure soared from all directions.

"Shield us," Luelle said as she tossed two of her knives high in the air.

Immediately, Malcolm threw a shield in front of them. Theo stepped behind them, guarding their backs against threats.

Pressure pulsed against Malcolm's chest as Luelle manipulated the Power above his shield, angling her knives high above them. She projected them forwards.

Moonlight glinted off the blades, highlighting them as they sliced through the air.

Zeke noticed them, or perhaps the pulse of Power propelling them, at the last moment. He flinched away, ducking low.

Instead of striking their target, the blades buried themselves deep into the two Veseile bandits who had been standing behind Zeke. Fresh chaos broke out. The pressure against Malcolm's chest died. Luelle hissed her frustration.

Fury blazed in Zeke's expression as he straightened, locking eyes with Malcolm. A thin cut sliced across his cheekbone, blooming with fresh blood. It dripped a path to his jawline.

Malcolm braced for the inevitable retaliation, extending their shield to cover all around them. Zeke's lips moved as he barked orders but Malcolm could not make out the words from this distance.

Instead of retaliating, the Vescile turned.

The Gifted were overpowering Zeke's fighters wherever Malcolm looked, cornering fighters and rendering them immobile. Zeke could see it, too.

"We cannot let him escape," Malcolm snapped. "This ends here."

Zeke's fighters broke away from their individual battles where they could, sprinting to follow their leader's retreat.

"Arrange a reserve of soldiers to watch over the camp and deal with any remaining attackers," Malcolm instructed Theo. "Any Gifted you can spare, order them to mount and follow me."

He gestured with a nod for Luelle to stay with him, calling similar orders to any Gifted they ran past on their way to find horses. By some miracle, or perhaps a sign of Zeke's inexperience in a true battle, none of their horses had been harmed or released.

Malcolm found his mount, forgoing a saddle. He swung up. Around him, Luelle and other Gifted soldiers followed his lead, some rushing through the motions of putting a saddle and reins on their horse, others saving time and riding bareback, like their king.

He kicked his horse into a canter away from the camp, letting her pick the best route among the fallen bodies and still-flaming debris. He'd already lost precious minutes but the slowest of Zeke's retreating numbers quickly became visible on the murky horizon, disappearing along the edges of the river.

Luelle rode at his side.

"They're going underground," she shouted, her voice barely audible over the wind whipping at Malcolm's ears.

Gritting his teeth, Malcolm kicked his horse to sprint faster.

55

Luelle's eyes burned from the wind when they slowed their horses, stopping and dismounting beside the riverbank. She eyed the rising rocky crevices but there was no movement through the darkness. Dropping the shield she'd been holding around herself and her horse, she reached out with the Power, seeking their enemies. When she found none nearby, she pushed the sense lower, through the crevices and hidden tunnels in the rocks. Sweat dripped down her temples and neck. She hadn't used much of her Power during the fight at the camp but the toll of constant shielding was almost as tiring as using larger bursts of the Power. A wave of dizziness unsteadied her as she searched for their enemies.

"They're below. I think the caves open up but the tunnels feel narrow in a lot of places." She frowned, trying to translate the feeling the Power gave of the physical space.

Malcolm's jaw clenched. His Gifted stood between him and the tunnel entrances, ready to protect their king with their lives against any surprise attacks.

Mei, Leena, and Tao pulled up at the edges of the group and dismounted. They weaved between the Gifted to approach Malcolm and Luelle at the centre of the group. Leena's expression darkened as Luelle repeated her suspicions.

"Are you certain they fled underground?"

"As certain as I can be without going down and searching for them," Luelle confirmed.

"We cannot let Zeke escape again," Malcolm interrupted. "We must either kill or capture him today. He cannot remain free to keep stirring up trouble. It puts us at risk of a civil war."

"He could have anything awaiting us down there," Leena snapped. "We are at an enormous strategic disadvantage and we do not know that they will remain down there if we follow. There may be a back entrance, like there was in the last cave system. It must be a trap."

"We will take precautions, but we must go down there." Malcolm's jaw tightened, his eyes blazing with furious determination. Sweat shone on his temples, highlighted by the moonlight.

"We can move slowly, scan each section ahead of us for enemies before we move into it," Luelle suggested, trying to keep the peace and solve their problem quickly so Zeke could not flee.

"Did anyone bring shadowbell?" Malcolm asked.

Luelle shook her head. Around them, other Gifted patted down their saddlebags, coming away empty handed, having left the camp too quickly to follow their king.

"We can send waves of fire through, instead, and shield ourselves as we enter the narrowest points until we can fight openly again," Luelle said.

Malcolm nodded, a muscle flexing in his jaw.

"Fine, but Malcolm, you must remain behind the front lines," Leena said.

"No. Zeke will be waiting for Luelle and me. We must remain at the front to draw him into the fight."

"Absolutely not." Leena stood her ground. "You are the king. I am not suggesting you stay out of the fight altogether but you must remain safe while we clear the tunnels. Use your head," she hissed.

"Fine. This discussion is wasting time. We need to move." He scowled, dismissing the conversation.

Leena and Mei organised the ranks of soldiers and Gifted quickly. Before she had time to consider what horrors she might wander into, Luelle entered the gloom of the cave's tunnels, following close behind two rows of the Gifted. Malcolm strode, tense, at her side.

Rounding every twist in the passage, their party halted so the Gifted on the front line could sweep the area for enemies. Each time, they sent a wave of fire to weed out any Veseile they missed. The Gifted rotated with each wave, moving fresh soldiers to the front to limit the risk of fully draining anyone's Power.

Luelle kept her gaze high, ignoring the few charred bodies in her peripheral vision as they progressed. She took shallow breaths, trying to suppress nausea at the scent of burning flesh.

"The bulk of the forces are up ahead," Mei murmured over her shoulder to the rest of the party as they approached a final curve in the tunnel. Blue moonstone light leaked from up ahead, spilling onto the floor. "The caves open out. People are scattered around the edges, from what I can tell. Another wave of fire will only waste our energy. I imagine the bandits will have shields in place."

"Put up shields and prepare for combat. Watch one another's backs," Malcolm ordered those around him, trusting them to pass his instructions to any Gifted too far to hear. "Do not hesitate over a killing blow. If we can bring back any bandits for questioning, we will, but do not risk your own safety to achieve that."

Luelle swallowed. Zeke lay in wait beyond this tunnel. Her old life ended here, today.

Mei whispered more instructions to the Gifted, informing them of the most populated areas within the cave to target. Luelle was distracted from the words by Malcolm's voice tickling her ear as he leaned close.

"We will fight alongside the others, but we must ensure Zeke does not escape again."

She nodded, gritting her teeth. "Let him try."

Malcolm's lips curled into a smile, sinister in the shadows of the tunnel.

Pressure tugged at Luelle's chest as she felt each of the Gifted form a tight shield around themselves. Using a thread of her Power, she did the same, following the soldiers as they charged into the wider cave with Malcolm close at her side.

Soldiers clashed immediately. Shields dropped as the Gifted and bandits shoved each other with the Power, swinging weapons and lashing out with fire. The cave was smaller than the cavern in which Vesanya had come to life—a bleak, rocky landscape with uneven flooring and long, thin stalactites hanging from the high ceiling.

Standing back from the main fight, Luelle scanned the

area for Zeke. He stood alone at the furthest edge of the cave, expression grim, fists clenched.

Fear briefly flickered through Luelle, remembering the threat made by the prisoner at Vidamere, but Vesanya was nowhere to be seen. Zeke was working alone and his forces were little match for Malcolm's.

"Over there," she called to Malcolm, pointing to Zeke.

Her old mentor locked eyes with her, lips curling into a hateful snarl.

"With me," Malcolm instructed.

Luelle followed him into battle.

Two Veseile closed in on Malcolm as soon as he entered the fray. One swung a chipped blade at him. The second held out her hands, pouring flames towards the king. Both attacks rebounded from his shield.

Luelle darted forward, feeling the intensity of Malcolm's Power increase as he poured more energy into his shield to survive the onslaught. She slid a knife from her bandolier. Five remained.

Dropping her shield, she punched a small burst of the Power into the eyes of the sword-wielding attacker.

His head snapped backwards and he fell limply away from Malcolm, clutching at his face. The sword dropped from his fingers, clattering on the stone. Flames died as the second attacker sought to help her companion but Luelle did not let her reach him.

She leapt close to the Veseile, stabbing her knife deep into the side the woman's neck and using the Power to bind her arms tight against her sides.

The woman opened her mouth, coughing blood into Luelle's face as it filled her airways. Tugging her knife out, Luelle shoved the woman's body away and wiped the gore from her eyes, blinking hard to see clearly as she turned to help Malcolm.

He was gripping a new opponent's wrists tightly with one hand, angling them away to send the flames spewing from the Veseile's hands into the air.

With his other hand, Malcolm sliced his dagger across the man's eyes.

He cried out. Malcolm ended his pain quickly.

Bile pooled in Luelle's mouth but she had no time to waste with bodily reactions. Another Veseile rushed forward, foregoing the Power. A sword in each hand, she approached, raising both arms and leaping, swinging the blades down.

Luelle threw herself in front of Malcolm, willing a shield. Adrenaline caused her to fuel it with more Power than she'd intended.

The Veseile rebounded, flying backwards.

Luelle dropped her shield and pulled another knife free from her bandolier, gasping for breath. She threw it, guiding it with the Power to bury it in her target between the Veseile's eyes. Her body was lost in the ever-moving crowd of fighters.

Side by side, Luelle and Malcolm pushed on. They picked no fights, only defended themselves and each other.

The Gifted made ground, driving Zeke's Veseile backward, overpowering them here as easily as they had at the fringes of their camp.

Seeing their approach, Zeke turned from the battle to flee down a tunnel on the far side of the cave. Luelle grabbed Malcolm's arm, drawing his attention.

"After him," Malcolm instructed, voice barely audible

over the general din. He lurched forward, the familiar pulse of his Power indicating his shield—the fresh scent of rain in a forest. Luelle could distinguish it from every other thread of the Power as easily as she could spot Malcolm in a crowd. She held onto it, following only a step behind her king.

"Mei, follow us when you can," she shouted to her friend, engaged in a battle not far from them. She did not wait for a response before continuing after Malcolm, terrified to let him charge ahead alone. Her heart hammered watching him weave around fights, seemingly blind to any danger beyond losing Zeke again. He didn't stop to sweep the tunnel Zeke had disappeared down, nor to cleanse the route with fire as they'd done so meticulously when entering the tunnel system.

Malcolm slowed as they emerged into a smaller cave, allowing Luelle to catch up. She stopped three paces behind him, chest heaving as she caught her breath. Exhaustion threatened to overwhelm her away from the chaos of the battle. The damp air felt colder against the sweat on her skin. Her entire body ached. Injuries began to cry out for attention—small stinging cuts, a bruise blooming over her jaw, a twinge of pain that shot up her ankle with every step. Fatigue glazed her movements, her limbs feeling heavier than normal, as they often did after training with the Gifted.

Satisfied Zeke was not an immediate threat, Luelle dropped her shield to conserve energy and looked around the empty space, as Malcolm was doing. The lack of his presence suggested he was preserving his Power in the same way.

She had two knives left to battle Zeke.

Moisture dripped from the stalactites hanging from the

ceiling, falling onto large rocks and boulders that partially obscured the distant passages Zeke must have disappeared down.

"We should wait for support before pursuing him. We don't know which direction he went and don't want him to get behind us." Luelle's voice bounced back at them from the rocky walls.

"You are right." Malcolm cursed, a muscle in his jaw jumping as he clenched his teeth. Blood and sweat from the fighting stained his skin and matted his hair. "Let's return to eliminate his followers. The faster the main fight is over, the faster we can pursue him."

He turned to look at her but his gaze slipped past her, eyes widening.

"Watch out!"

His cry startled Luelle. She spun. A pulse of Power, larger than any she'd felt in a single burst from Malcolm before, pulled at her from his direction—familiar rainfall, but accompanied by a gust of cold air and crackling embers. Malcolm sent a blow of his Power towards Luelle's attacker.

The Veseile who had followed them had flung a small ball of fire towards Luelle, but Malcolm's wave of Power pushed it backwards, igniting the bandit and flinging her through the air. Her skull cracked against the cave wall.

Luelle's heart raced.

She turned, trembling, to thank him.

But, something about Malcolm's expression was not right.

His eyes were wide, mouth ajar. Luelle frowned, gaze falling to his hand, which had drifted to his chest—

Impaled in his chest was a stalactite, emerging point

first.

Horror rolled over her, cold and nauseating.

Malcolm fell to his knees.

Behind him, on the far side of the cave, stood Zeke. His eyes were wide with surprise. Triumph replaced it when he met Luelle's stare. A burst of Power erupted from him, striking Luelle in the chest—the sense of embers and cold wind accompanying it. She began to stumble back, only to be pulled forward as Zeke's Power tore the amulet from around her neck, tugging it towards himself. When it landed in his palm, he turned and ran.

Luelle did not chase him. Instead, she closed the short distance between her and Malcolm and dropped to her knees in front of him, ignoring the pain that jarred up each leg. She threw a spherical shield around them both to protect them from any other attacks.

The stalactite tip stopped her from getting too close.

"Malcolm. Malcolm, look at me." She cupped his face in her hands, desperate to capture his increasingly unfocused gaze. "Oh gods. It's going to be alright Malcolm." Panic laced her tone.

He moved his mouth but could not form the words he wished to say.

Luelle moved one hand to his shoulder, struggling to hold him upright as her other hand pressed against the edge of the stalactite piercing his chest, trying to stem the slow but steady flow of blood. Her fingers slipped against his mail vest, slick with crimson. His head lolled, forehead crashing against hers.

She cursed, trying to prop his head up but only smearing more blood over his cheek. "Stay with me, we can fix this." Her voice sounded higher pitched than normal beyond the ringing in her ears.

Reaching for another thread of the Power, Luelle willed the wound to heal as she pressed her hand against it again, but she did not know how to fix an injury this complex; she could barely manage a small cut. She had to get the rocky spike out of his chest, but wouldn't be able to stem the subsequent blood flow alone, let alone rebuild the tissue and heal the damage to Malcolm's organs.

Healing had never been her specialty.

"Mei!" she screamed for her friend.

Malcolm slumped against her, his weight knocking her off balance. Luelle pushed back against him, holding him as upright as she could. Tears thickened her throat, blinding her as they welled in her eyes and streamed down her cheeks.

She screeched for Mei again.

Malcolm fell to the side. Shattered links from his mail vest clinked against the ground like fallen coins. Luelle laid him on the floor as gently as she could manage. The stalactite prevented him from lying on his back, so she rested him on his side, scrambling to cushion his head and suppress the gore leaking from him.

Footsteps sounded at the cave's entrance.

Luelle added more Power into her shield, unable to look away from the man below her, to stop murmuring for Malcolm to hold on, to *look at her*.

"Luelle!" Mei's voice broke through the haze.

"Heal him," Luelle ordered without looking away from Malcolm.

"I—Luelle, you need to let me in."

Luelle glanced up. Mei stood at the edge of her shield,

face pale, hands braced against the invisible barrier.

Luelle dropped it. She continued cushioning Malcolm's head against the hard ground and murmuring comfort as Mei dealt with his chest.

Malcolm's eyes were glazed and unblinking, staring past Luelle to the walls of the cave. She dropped her face closer to his, stroking his curls, begging him to look at her. The words were an incoherent babble.

"Luelle, I can't fix this." Mei's voice was quiet.

"You can!" she shouted, turning her face away from Malcolm so he did not face the brunt of her volume. "He's your king. Save him!"

"What has happened?" Leena's voice sounded as she entered the cave. Her footsteps stalled as she took in the scene.

Luelle rested her forehead against Malcolm's again. "Please don't do this," her voice broke, a sob penetrating the whisper. "Please don't leave me."

Leena appeared in Luelle's vision. She crouched on the other side of Malcolm. Luelle looked up at her, but for the first time, Leena looked as lost as she felt. Her hand trembled as she reached for Malcolm, pressing her fingers against his neck to feel for a pulse.

"We need to get that thing out of him." Luelle's grip on Malcolm tightened. She nodded towards the rock penetrating his chest and back.

"I—" Leena choked. She inhaled a shaky breath, frozen in place.

"Mei, take it out so you can heal him."

"He is already gone, Luelle."

A surreal wailing noise reached Luelle, piercing the roaring in her ears. She pulled Malcolm's head into her lap and crouched over him, only realising the sound must be coming from her as it muffled when she buried her face into his shoulder.

56

Camp was quiet.

Luelle stared at the rising sun, numb to the chill of the morning. Blood no longer coated her hands, gently washed away by Art when they'd returned to the camp. Gore still stained her clothing. She hadn't had the strength to change.

Malcolm's body was wrapped in cloth, laying inside a carriage in the heart of the camp. When watching soldiers place him inside, Luelle had vomited over the floor.

Nausea still rolled in her stomach whenever she looked towards the carriage but she couldn't bring herself to move away from it—away from him.

Sleep evaded her, impossible without Malcolm's chest pressed against her back, his warmth leaking into her own body, his hands tangled in her hair. Every time she closed her eyes, she saw his face, twisted with pain and shock; she saw the stalactite protruding from his chest.

He wasn't dead. He couldn't be dead.

They'd barely had any time together.

She hadn't even said goodbye.

"How are you doing?"

Luelle turned, looking up at Art who had approached on silent footsteps. Steam furled from the cups in his hands. How could he ask that?

He lowered himself to sit on the floor beside her, placing one of the cups in front of her. She did not move to touch it. He took one of her hands, squeezing it in his.

"You're freezing." Art frowned.

Luelle's gaze dropped to their hands. She didn't feel cold. She didn't feel anything.

"Theo sent a letter to Graman, telling him to return to the capital. Leena and Theo, they're—" Art swallowed. "They're not in a good way, either. We're leaving today, to take his body—"

"Don't," Luelle choked the word out, gasping at the sudden pain in her chest. "Please don't."

Art closed his mouth, squeezing her hand again. Tears rolled down his cheeks. They sat in silence until the tea in front of Luelle was cold. Noise further away indicated that their camp was being dismantled but Luelle couldn't tear her gaze from Malcolm's carriage to see.

"It's my fault," she whispered.

Art frowned at her. "Don't say that. It wasn't—"

"It was. If he hadn't tried to protect me, it wouldn't have happened. He could've shielded himself. The only reason he didn't was because I was too careless to keep my own shield in place. I didn't ration my strength. If he'd just let the other Veseile hit me, he would still—" she broke off in a choke, fresh tears stinging her eyes. Her breath came too quickly but none seemed to bring her any air.

"You don't know it would have been any different,"

Art said. "Nobody thinks it was your fault—not Theo, not Leena, not Mei." He removed his hand from hers to wrap his arm around her shoulders, pulling her into a tight hug until her gasping breaths were under control. "He wouldn't have wanted you to blame yourself."

Fury washed over Luelle. Art shouldn't be speaking about Malcolm in the past tense. She squeezed her eyes shut and tried not to think about anything—not about the way Art's arms around her felt so wrong, so different from Malcolm's, not the way she could've saved him if she'd been more careful, not the fact she'd never hear his laugh again or watch his eyes brighten as she made him smile.

She'd spent so long believing Vesanya was their biggest threat but Zeke was the true evil in her life, lurking in the shadows to tear away any shred of happiness she might experience. That had been why Malcolm's Power had felt so different in the cave—it had been entwined with Zeke's. Luelle knew exactly how Malcolm felt. She could've picked him from an entire room of Gifted even if she was blindfolded. Why had she ignored the difference in the cave? She hadn't questioned why the unusually strong burst of Power could feel so familiar in such a new way until she'd turned around.

Zeke had escaped again. Their entire trip had been planned around his capture and he'd slipped through their fingers, despite sacrificing his entire army to achieve his goal of murdering the king.

Vesanya remained in the world, too, though no further sightings had occurred since the last farmhouse.

Leena approached and silently sat on Luelle's other side, drawing her knees against her chest. Art extended his arm to lay his hand on her shoulder.

"Are we almost ready to leave?" he asked.

Leena nodded in Luelle's peripheral.

"I can't come with you," Luelle said, her voice hoarse.

"Why not?" Art frowned.

She could not bear the thought of being back in the capital. Every memory there revolved around Malcolm or his family. How could she cope if she returned to such familiarity? All of Malcolm's things remained where he'd left them but he would never touch them again. Luelle would rather see the entire castle burned to ashes than see it without him in it. Over time, servants would change the decor and furnishings until his influence might not exist at all.

"Princess Vivyenne won't want me there. I have no home in the city." She gave the lame excuse instead of trying to explain.

"She won't blame you for this. You can stay in my quarters," Art insisted. "It's not as fancy as your current room, but it's enough."

"No, Art. I can't—" She swallowed. "I can't go back there."

"You can stay with my family." Leena spoke up, her own voice hoarse with emotion.

Luelle said nothing. Leena knew as well as she did that Malcolm's family did not trust her. Luelle had failed to save her king. It might be enough to earn her own death. There was no point in making plans.

Regardless, Leena continued.

"I am taking a horse today and going back to the capital alone. It will be fastest. I will explain what happened to Princess—" she stuttered, "to...to Queen Vivyenne. She will show you mercy when she hears what truly happened."

Luelle stayed quiet. All she could think about was Malcolm. A headache pulsed in her temples.

"What will happen next?" Art murmured.

Leena stiffened at Luelle's side. Her voice was monotonous. "A funeral. Queen Vivyenne will take the crown. I imagine Theo will remain working in the castle but I will finish Malcolm's task of eliminating Vesanya and I will destroy Zeke and all he holds dear."

Luelle turned. Their eyes met—steely resolve in Leena's.

"I will not pressure you yet, not so soon after—" Leena pressed her lips together. "But you can help me, Luelle. You and Graman had theories I will need to use. I will not let Malcolm's legacy be in vain."

Luelle turned away. Eliminating Vesanya seemed a minor problem compared to the others she now faced. The thought of returning to those musty documents with Graman, to hours of reading and researching conflicting information about the gods, made her stomach drop. She'd been doing it all for Malcolm, but she had failed him.

He was the one Arazia needed, yet his soul had been sent to Mortus at Zeke's hand.

"Luelle, will you help me?"

Leena was giving her a final opportunity to find Zeke. This time, when they were reunited, Luelle would not let him walk away.

"I will."

The gods

Adagna — God of Wisdom and War
   Collatus — God of Hunt and Healing
   Dilectya — God of Love and Invention
   Meto — God of Harvest and Fertility
   Mortus — God of Death
   Vesanya — God of Chaos

wouldn't be where I am now, in the position to express my creativity so freely if it weren't for my wonderful family and their endless support.

Finally, last but not least, thank you to Dan. Thank you for reading through my early manuscripts and endlessly helping me untangle plot lines whenever we're in the car. I couldn't ask for a more supportive partner. It's been a busy year, especially bringing Hera into our little family, and I wouldn't have finished this to the same standard without you there to encourage me. Love you with my whole heart.

The Eile

Adeile — A race descended from Adagna
    Colleile — A race descended from Collatus
    Dileile — A race descended from Dilectya
    Meteile — A race descended from Meto
    Moreile — A race descended from Mortus
    Veseile — A race descended from Vesanya

Acknowledgements

Once again, I've come to the most challenging part of writing a book. I'm not sure I'm truly capable of expressing the depth of gratitude I feel to everyone who has been a part of this process, but I will certainly give it a good try.

Firstly, thank you to anyone who has read this book, and Vesanya's Curse before it! It's so surreal to me that anyone has picked up and finished one of the little stories that have been circling my mind for years, but I'm ever so thankful for each and every person who has. Hearing people's thoughts and reviews has been such an insightful, cool experience, and I'm so excited to learn what people think of The Last of His Name.

I'd like to thank Stu and Felipe, my trusty beta readers. Every suggestion and piece of feedback has been so, so valuable. I'm very grateful to have such good friends in my life.

Thank you to my family, particularly my mum and everyone else who dedicated their time to checking out what I've been working on. I love hearing all of your reactions to my stories, and can't wait to see what you think of this one. I